The Sword of Jedar

The SWORD OF JEDAR

Ross van Zyl

TATE PUBLISHING & Enterprises

Published by Tate Publishing & Enterprises, LLC
127 E. Trade Center Terrace | Mustang, Oklahoma 73064 USA
1.888.361.9473 | www.tatepublishing.com

Tate Publishing is committed to excellence in the publishing industry. The company reflects the philosophy established by the founders, based on Psalms 68:11,
"The Lord gave the word and great was the company of those who published it."

Book design copyright © 2007 by Tate Publishing, LLC. All rights reserved.
Cover design by Chris Webb
Interior design by Janae Glass

Published in the United States of America
ISBN: 978-1-6024725-7-X
1. Fantasy   2.Adventure
07.06.05

Conᴛenᴛs

Prologue

† † † † † † †

Shadows flickered menacingly in the torchlight. The air stank of a treachery rooted in hate. As he moved down the hall, he heard voices above, unaware. Turning the corner, he found the room and slipped inside. Walking carefully, he chose the exact crate he needed. He pulled out the vial of the clear deadly liquid that came from the Shai root. The rare root had taken months to find and nearly as long to extract the precious liquid it contained. For centuries it had been the most effective means of assassination. The chicken, wrapped in a salt-laden cloth, was ready for the evening meal. It would work best. A single drop of the Shai liquid was enough to kill a grown man, but there were no risks to be taken here. He poured the majority of the contents of the vial onto the raw flesh; the rest was poured inside the meat for complete saturation. Carefully, he rewrapped the small package of death. As he lowered the lid of the crate, the wood squeaked. The boots of a guard walking towards the room could be heard. The assassin crouched behind the door. His years of specialized training had taught him exactly how to kill without a trace. He grabbed the guard's neck and twisted it in the familiar, sudden movement that left the guard dead in his hands. The assassin cursed at the extra time this would cost him. He crept back down the hall, carrying the body on his shoulder, careful to make sure no one could hear him. The old wooden door was slightly ajar, as he had left it. The crisp night air greeted him with the first hints of autumn. Above he could hear the cooks beginning to prepare the dinner. *Enjoy your meal, Sire.* The scar on his left cheek quivered as he risked a victorious grin. Now he would begin the long ride back home.

The sun rose as Athon walked down the corridors of the West Wing. Athon had been doing his job faithfully for more than forty years, long enough to be proud of the man he served. He pushed open the door. "Sire, the morning greets you," he said in his old familiar way. "Sire?" His master had always been an easy riser. Athon walked closer to the bed and saw his master's eyes open and still. There was no pulse. Athon stumbled back and began to mumble and then to shout, "Dead! He is dead! The king is dead!"

Beginnings

† † † † † † †

Blood-red paint splashed up against the old barn door. Paul was painting the door to the barn when he turned to see the world around him grow brighter. The sun rose slowly over the coastal town of Egon. Few people were awake and the town was generally quiet. He had been working like this for two months, and he had at least another ten to go. It was tradition for every seventeen-year-old man of the Kingdom to spend a year in service for the coming of age ceremony. Paul had been sent to the town of Egon to live with people he had never met, and he had no idea who these people were and what they were like. The host family was not allowed to know the background of the young man who was sent to serve them. It was strictly on a first-name only basis. There were times Paul wished he could tell them who he was, but that was against tradition and custom. This had been his home for the last few months, and the people whom he served were kind. Their names were Segan and Eston Oldyer. The town around him began to come alive, doors were opening, and people began to open up their small stores in the marketplace. Finishing the repairs, Paul set aside his tools and decided to take some time to enjoy the view. He sat on an old wooden chair and looked out at the rolling green hills that stretched several miles to the cliffs that boarded the ocean. The Oldyers' house was as simple as the others in the city, located along the main dirt road of Egon. Paul sighed. Suddenly there was a high-pitched scream followed by a massive explosion. Paul spun to his right to see a house a few doors down engulfed in flames. All at once a shout came from down the street:

"*Flamethrower!*"

Panic immediately erupted among the nearby townspeople. Paul ran inside his house and found Segan and Eston searching for their armor. Paul froze as he tried to understand why the two elderly people would be trying to find their armor.

"W-what are you doing?" stammered Paul. Immediately his thoughts jumped to how he could protect the old couple.

Segan drew his sword and began walking out the door, only to be met by Paul standing in the doorway.

"We have to go out there and fight, Paul. Please stand aside." Segan's voice carried a strong tone of command. Paul sheepishly backed away.

"Paul, saddle the horses, then put on your armor." Paul stared. He had never heard more than a few words from Segan at one time, and now he was giving commands like a general. Paul ran outside where he was met once again with the screams and cries of the city. More and more houses were burning now, and Paul noticed that many of the villagers were suiting up for battle. He reached the stable and saddled two horses. He quickly led them out in front of the house. The horses were frightened by the acrid smell in the air and the flames frightened them even more. Segan and Eston were on the horses almost as soon as Paul let go of their reins. He dashed inside to put on his armor and buckled his sword onto his hip. He had not much more than chain mail to protect him, but it was better than nothing. Paul dashed outside and mounted his own horse. Segan led the three to the town square, where most of the villagers had gathered. Panicked men talked among themselves, fear evident in every one of their faces. *This is madness. None of these people know how to fight!* thought Paul. *Their captain will surely send*

Segan and Eston home. However, to Paul's surprise, the people all saluted Segan as he rode up.

"Segan, what are we going to do?" asked one of the men. The crowd became silent as Segan prepared to speak.

"My dear townspeople. It has been a long time since any of you were called upon to take arms against the enemy, but now it is time!" Another high-pitched scream came, as two more houses burst into flame. "You all know what we face, and we shall meet our enemy head-on! If any of you wish to leave, leave now." Not a single man moved. "Very well. To battle!" Segan's cry was met with cheering. He turned his horse and sped out of the town. Segan led them to a large, green open field. Paul noticed that there was no longer any fear left in the people. They arranged themselves quickly, archers in the back, cavalry and swordsmen in the front.

On a hill on the other side of the field stood a lone, dark figure clothed in black. In his hand was a pitch-black sphere. It was a dark black—a deep, terrible, empty black. He slowly pulled back his hand. Suddenly he hurled the sphere into the air with ferocious power. An ear-piercing shriek could be heard all around the field. It was the sound of a thousand monstrosities of hate and malice. The ball came down, bursting into flame before touching the ground. A sickly, pale Gray Slime exploded. The fire fed off this Slime, growing and spreading. It burnt the grass and trees all around it.

The figure on the hill was a Flamethrower. Dark, powerful, evil, and extremely dangerous, Flamethrowers could take out an entire city by themselves. However, they were normally accompanied by a hoard of Ashkah. Ashkah, meaning "Worthless" in the dark tongue, were cheap, expendable soldiers. They often survived only one mission, and therefore had no rank. Their strength was in numbers—and ferocity. The Flamethrower threw another orb into the sky. This time, when exploding, the Gray Slime splashed onto a horse. Almost instantly a hole burnt through its armor, flesh, and bone to the other side, sending a burnt flesh smell through the area.

Paul stared in horror and vomited. The horse died seconds later from the flames. The rider too was burnt alive. The air grew cold. The wind seemed to pick up. The horses grew uneasy. Then, not 200 feet away, the grass turned a sickly gray. The trees withered. A low rumbling shook the ground. Paul shot a questioning glance at Segan, who simply nodded. Then everything stilled. Even the Flamethrower stood deathly still on the hill.

"What was that?" cried Paul alarmed. Before Segan could utter a single word, the ground exploded before them. Sand and dirt were thrown everywhere. Out of the newly formed tunnel, a torrent of Ashkah poured out, swords raised. They had mutilated, flat faces. Their eyes were pitch black. They wore no armor, but carried crudely shaped, jagged-edged swords. They charged towards the stunned townspeople. Segan raised his sword and shouted, then came down on the first of the Ashkah, catching it in the neck. Paul was shocked that such an old man could wield a sword of that weight so quickly. Paul caught sight of one of them. Its horrible black eyes seemed empty. They were there for one reason. Destruction. Paul was lost in the maelstrom of the battle, the collision of iron and steel, the screaming sounds of men and Ashkah alike crying their last, the smell of blood and sweat. His eyes couldn't keep up with the speed of it all. He blindly swung his sword, fearing he would kill a comrade. He looked for Segan, fearing the worst, but found him alive and clearing a path through the dark mass. Paul surged towards him. Every few seconds the Flamethrower devastated a large portion of the already small army. Paul had never been in a battle before. A group of Ashkah leapt in front of him. Within seconds they each had arrows through their heart. Paul looked back to see Eston sending huge volleys of arrows at the hordes of Ashkah. She had saved his life. Energized, he raised his sword and started killing.

He caught sight of the Flamethrower. He knew every second that he stood there the army had less hope of surviving. He turned his steed towards the hill, and raced to the Flamethrower. Then he felt it. It was like something had reached inside his head and gripped his mind. Paul felt fingers digging into his consciousness and ripping his mind apart. The pain in his head was excruciating. Voices in his head screamed at him. He felt as if his head would explode. Then he collapsed. Segan saw Paul, lying motionless on the ground. He charged up to Paul. The Flamethrower shrieked, turned, and disappeared over the hill. The remaining Ashkah turned and disappeared down the hole in the earth. Eston raced to where Segan stood over Paul. They picked him up, and lifted his limp body onto Segan's horse and rode back into town.

Paul opened his eyes. The room was musty and dark. Outside the small window the day was cloudy and overcast. A small fire burnt in the corner, creating moving shadows. The heavy door creaked open, and Segan stepped in. He was still in his bloodstained battle gear. He walked across the creaking wooden floorboards and sat in his old chair. Paul could smell the scent of blood and sweat everywhere. Segan sat still, not speaking. Paul tried to move, and pain shot up his arm, forcing him down. He gasped for breath.

"Hold on, Paul. Slow down. You were badly hurt in the battle."

"Is it over? Where is everyone? What happened?"

"You are lucky to be alive, Paul. And so are we all. The battle is over. We lost many good men today."

"So we won?"

"Won? We hardly won, Paul! We lost over half the town fighting the cursed Ashkah. There are hundreds of new Ashkah each day. The loss of Ashkah is nothing, but the loss of men is severe. You should rest."

Paul sat back confused. How had they managed to defeat the horde of Ashkah and the Flamethrower? His head ached, and he turned over and fell into a dark sleep.

. . . . .

The next morning Segan was up early and making breakfast. Normally Paul would have done it, but he was still recovering from the battle. Segan felt old. Where had the years gone? It felt as if it was yesterday that he had been marching to battle with the old king, fighting for his people, but now he was at home, old and frail. Inside he still had the heart of a lion, but outside he was dying. Segan sighed. The day was still dark, and the sun had not risen. Segan heard movement in Paul's room. A few moments later Paul emerged, obviously in pain but looking better.

"Good morning, Paul. How do you feel today?" Paul glanced at him and groaned as he sat.

"A little better, but I had to get out of that bed."

Segan looked at him. "Well then, you better get started on your chores, shouldn't you?" Paul looked up quickly, and then mumbled, "of course."

Segan knew Paul was expecting not to work today with his injury. He also knew Paul couldn't go back to bed now that he had said he needed to get up. He liked Paul. He reminded him a lot of himself, though there were many differences. He had always been willing to serve and help, whereas Paul sometimes served out of obedience, not willingness. Paul slowly stood and walked out the door. When he went outside, dawn was just breaking. He loved seeing the sunrise. It was different here than at home. He would watch the dull colored sky explode into vivid reds and pinks. It made him feel warm. He started on his chores. His arm ached, and his head throbbed. Why hadn't he stayed in bed? He hadn't thought Segan would make him work after yesterday's battle. But he had. Paul continued his work. He was quite amazed at himself. There was a time when he would never have wanted to work. Everything he had to do was a huge task and only made him more and more selfish. But now, after nearly two months of work, he had almost started to enjoy it. The early morning dew soaked his shoes as he walked back to the house. He walked inside to see Eston sitting at the table by Segan.

"Good morning, Paul. Feeling better today I hope?"

"Yes ma'am, thank you."

Paul moved to the dirty breakfast dishes and started scrubbing.

"Oh Segan, you can't really expect him to work after yesterday's battle!"

"Why Eston, of course! He's a strong young man. A little battle-weariness won't do much!" Eston eyed Paul.

"Well, if you are going to be working today, I'd like you to go to the blacksmith and have the horses re-shod."

Paul nodded and went back to work.

That evening Paul was resting after finishing all his chores. He had done everything and even taken the horses to the blacksmith. He was exhausted. Segan came in and noticed a worried look on Paul's face.

"Is something wrong, Paul?"

"Well, I was walking to the blacksmith's with the horses, and all around the town people were walking away from me and avoiding me. The blacksmith wouldn't even look me in the eye!"

"Paul, do you know why you collapsed during the battle?"

"No. I guess I just passed out from all the action."

This boy must have lived a sheltered life indeed to know nothing of the Flamethrowers and their weapons, thought Segan. "No. You were viced. The Flamethrower you were charging saw you. They have a mental weapon we call the mind-vice. They reach inside your brain and shut off your body. Most men are killed instantly, and only the mentally strong or prepared can survive. The people know that a Flamethrower will pursue anyone who survives a mind-vice and will slowly possess their bodies. The townspeople think you might be in the first stages of a possession, and that makes you dangerous." Paul was silent.

. . . . .

He sat thinking, then spoke, "But how could I have survived? I haven't been trained to withstand that."

Segan eyed Paul. "Some people are born with the gift. This gift has saved your life, Paul. We will talk more in the morning. Good night." Segan stood, and again he seemed old, but Paul had a much deeper respect for him. The firelight flickered across his face, and Paul saw a twinkle in the old man's eyes. He walked out of the room and shut the old door. Paul was left alone to think. He had survived. He had survived where very few had before. He felt a sense of destiny; the fact that he had such a rare gift obviously was for a purpose. But to what end? What was he supposed to do with it? He suddenly realized again how tired he was. His muscles ached after a hard day's work. He was still weary from the battle. He closed his eyes and fell asleep.

Paul woke with a start. He had heard some noise outside. The day was still dark, and everyone was fast asleep. He peeked out of his window, trying to see if he could see any movement. Nothing. But he was sure he had heard something. He sat back but couldn't fall asleep. His head still throbbed, and his muscles burned. He stared at the ceiling. Then slowly the soft sound of rain could be heard outside. He looked out and watched. He loved the rain. It meant he didn't have to work. He was going to ask Segan more about the Flamethrowers and the Ashkah, about his personal life, and about the mind-vice. There were so many questions that he hoped Segan was up for talking. He knew he couldn't fall asleep again, not with all the questions swirling around in his head. Morning felt so far away, and he knew he would need the rest. He put his head on his pillow and forced himself to close his eyes. His mind was racing, and he kept tossing and turning. Finally, somehow, he must have fallen asleep because when he opened his eyes, the sun had risen, but the day was still rainy and wet. He knew it was late, but it didn't matter, and Segan hadn't bothered him this morning. He got up and dressed slowly. He opened his window and let the moist, fresh air waft into his room. More than the sound and sight of rain, he loved the smell—the smell of growth, freshness, and healing. Today was a day of healing from the war and from his uneasy mind. He opened the door and found Segan sitting by the fire, reading an old book. Paul took a seat, not saying a word, despite the fact that his mind was ready to burst. Segan noticed Paul's anxiety.

"Ah, Paul! No work today. I trust you are feeling better?"

"Yes, sir. Thank you." Paul's voice hinted at his impatience. But Segan just nodded and went back to his book. Paul did not want to keep bothering him but he had so many questions! Finally Segan peeked over his book and saw Paul on the edge of his seat looking eagerly at him.

"What is on your mind, Paul?"

Paul cleared his throat before speaking, "I was wondering if you could answer some questions about the Flamethrowers for me. Who are they? Where did they come from?"

"Ah, yes, of course. Well," Segan closed his book and shifted so that he could see Paul better, "let me start at the beginning. Firstly, the name Flamethrower is a common name for them. When they were first formed, they were called the Bazrukal. Many fear the name alone, and hence the title of Flamethrower was given to them, for obvious reasons. They were the closest servants of the Dark Lord. There are six of them, though the last time several were seen together was in the final battle of the great Jedarian War. It is said though, in ancient folklore, that one day there will be a terrible war. One like this land has never seen before. And all six of the cursed Bazrukal will be there. They are the darkest, foulest, most evil servants of the Dark Lord."

"But how were they created? Where did they come from?" Paul asked eagerly.

Segan shot a questioning glance at Paul. "Paul, because it is against tradition, I will not ask, but I can only surmise you have lived a sheltered life to be so ignorant about the enemy." Paul flushed and struggled not to react to the old man's comment. Segan continued. "They came from the evil city of Maugrax. They are the fusion of demonic power and mutated life forms. They have no body. They find a mind that has survived their mind-vice and then prey on it, and slowly, after months, take possession."

"Then…can it be killed?"

"Technically, if you were to cut off its head, yes, the body would die, but the spirit would simply find another host body."

"What do you mean technically?"

"There were only a few people who were ever skilled enough to engage them in combat. No ordinary man has ever fought a Flamethrower with a sword and survived. Those things are monsters."

Paul looked at the floor, shocked. How were they to fight an enemy like *that*? "And what about the Ashkah? The ones we fought?"

"Those are the foot soldiers for the dark army. They are fast and can muster a massive army very quickly."

"How?"

"Paul, have you studied geography?"

"Not much, but yes."

"How much do you know about the Jedarac Desert?"

"I know it is said to be growing."

"Correct. That desert was a battleground. Many years ago, a huge battle took place in that land. The dark armies tunneled upward, and the tunnels themselves created the desert. The mere exposure to so much evil caused the plants, trees, and any living thing to die. And never will anything grow there again. The problem is, throughout the land, more and more tunnels are being formed similar to the one you saw at the battle. However that one was small. The largest known tunnel was nearly fifty feet in diameter. It is in the center of the Jedarac Desert."

"So many Ashkah. What are they? Are they like the Flamethrowers?"

"Similar, but not quite. They are bred in huge pits deep in the heart of Maugrax. You see the evil empire was losing on every front while they were on land. So they set up a Kingdom underground. That's why it's so hard to know where they are. They have an elaborate system of tunnels, networked to create fast access routes. Hundreds are created every day and sent out in raiding parties. Our world is turning into a desolate wasteland because of them."

Paul got up and stretched. The rain continued hammering outside. Paul looked at Segan. The fire made his face appear mysterious, as if there were something about Segan he had not known before. Something important. He opened the door and stood there thinking—so much destruction, so little hope. But why then, weren't the cities uniting? Why wasn't everyone trying to fight back this evil? Questions raced in his mind, and he walked back inside and sat by Segan.

"Sir. If there is such a massive army of these Ashkah and this terrible power of Flamethrowers, why haven't the people of the land united? After all, one would think that together we'd be stronger against them."

"That's a perfectly logical question and one I've asked myself and others many times before. But the problem is this: No one seems to notice the importance of it. The only time they would be willing to unite is if there was someone strong leading them. Our king seems reluctant to go to war."

There came a knock at the door. Paul jumped up and opened the door to see a man dressed in royal garments, soaked though they were, standing there.

"Message for Paul," he said.

Paul was taken aback. He had never received a letter, at least not while he was here. Something was wrong, terribly wrong. Paul took the letter and tore it open and read the short note. He looked up at the messenger, his eyes bleary with tears. He turned to Segan and Eston.

"Paul! What is it?" cried Eston. Paul struggled to speak. His throat was constricted and dry. He breathed deeply. Shock enveloped him as he stumbled to a chair and slumped down in it.

Burden

† † † † † † †

"Paul, do you want to tell us what's going on?" Segan asked patiently.

"I...my..." Paul stumbled. He took a deep breath. "My father is dead."

The room fell silent. "Oh, Paul! I'm so sorry!" Eston looked overwhelmed. Segan looked at the messenger, then at Paul.

"Paul, who exactly was your father?"

"My father?" Paul hesitated, and then spoke. "My father is...or was the king."

The room went silent again. Even Segan, who normally was calm and collected, was surprised.

"You mean...you're the prince?"

"Yes, sir."

Segan sat back and sighed. Paul's voice trembled.

"I have to go back to Calarath." Segan nodded. Paul stood and walked dumbfounded to his room. What was happening? He was sure this was a dream, a hellish nightmare that he would soon wake from. Things like this didn't happen to him! He morbidly packed his bags. The rain hammered harder and harder outside. Thoughts and memories of his father flooded his mind. Thunder could be heard in the distance. Suddenly he was struck by a realization—he was the only heir to the throne! He was going to have to take over not only the huge castle, but also the entire city, and beyond that the entire land. He caught his breath. The foreboding sense of responsibility shadowed him like an immense cloud. He finished packing and walked out of his room. He began to thank Segan and Eston, but he could not speak. Segan nodded, and Paul stepped out into the rain. He hardly felt it. He saddled his horse and mounted. The messenger came out moments later, and then they set off. The day was still bleak. Paul saw nothing as they traveled for hours on end.

The messenger respectfully gave Paul his space by riding ahead and leaving Paul to his thoughts. Finally the rain seemed to stop, but the day remained overcast and dark. He wanted to collapse on the ground and not get up. What was he going home to? They continued their tedious trek.

At sunset they pitched camp and lay down for the night. The horses were set free to graze. Paul could not sleep. He had too much on his mind. *Why did his father have to die? Why hadn't he been able to hold on, at least send word to his son?* Now Paul sat, feeling very alone. *What if he never went back? What if he just ignored it all and they pretended that he had been killed? A new heir would arise, and he could live simply.* Then he thought of his mother. The death of her husband must have been an enormous burden, but to load her with news of his own death would certainly destroy her. His mother was strong but cared so deeply about him and his father that he knew she would be taking this harder than he was.

When dawn rose, Paul had not slept. After a meager, cold breakfast, he wearily climbed into his saddle and set off again. The miles rolled by slowly as if forcing him to think of his father and everything he had lost. His father had been a wise man. He had been strong, firm, but also gentle and soft. He was the best king the land had seen for generations. Everyone loved King Mark. His father believed that everyone was valuable. He had changed many things while he had been king. He had put into place The Garden Acres, a vast plot of land, divided into separate portions, each portion for a member of the city. There was no cost, and it was designed to provide food for the people. The people themselves had to plant, grow, and harvest the food, but the land was free to any who asked. Paul had thought it was a brilliant idea and told his father so. His father had replied, "Well son, one day, when you take my place as king, I hope you too will devise something as ingenious as this," and then winked at him. Paul loved his father and his sense of humor. His father was busy but often canceled a meeting or discussion to see what his son was learning, fight a bout with him, help him with something, or just talk with him. Paul had taken it all for granted. There were times when he had been angry with his father, but that seemed so insignificant and childish now.

They continued past a lake where they stopped and filled up their canteens. As he dipped his leather canteen into the cool blue water, he saw his reflection. He looked older and more mature, but also scared and frightened. He looked for some resemblance to his father in his face but found none. That was not comforting. He had hoped he would be able to lead the people as well as his father had, but he had never expected to have the Kingdom thrust upon him at the tender age of seventeen. He remounted his horse and continued to follow the messenger. They had ridden in silence since they left, Paul lost in thought. Finally Paul spoke.

"How long until we get to Calarath?"

The messenger squinted as if seeing the distance with his eyes. "I'd say about three days, Your Majesty." *Your Majesty?* Never had he been called that. He had only been the prince, and while he had been staying with the couple, he hadn't even been called that for a long time. King Paul. The name sounded out of place. The words sounded like they were not supposed to go together. Maybe that was a hint, a sign that he was not supposed to become king. Wearily he tried talking to the messenger again.

"Excuse me…"

"Endos. Endos Longbow at your service, sir."

"Well, Endos, how long have you served my father?"

"Oh, nearly four years, sir." Paul nodded. The king had made many friends and often met people from the city or neighboring towns, employing them in the castle. Silence again enveloped them. It seemed as if they could not strike up a conversation.

"What did you think of my father?"

"Oh, a fine man indeed, sir. He was kind, generous, and always ready to serve. That's what this land needs." Paul had always been annoyed by people calling him "sir" every few sentences. He had told most servants not to, but he had not told Endos.

"Firstly, Endos, you do not need to refer to me as 'sir.' You are, after all, older than I am, and though I am the prince, and soon the king, I would appreciate it if you would humor me in this." Endos chuckled.

"Just like your father, I see. Of course, Paul." Paul was struck by the words. They warmed him a little. Obviously his father had the same contempt for obsessive titles.

"I am very sorry about your loss, Paul. He was a close friend of mine. Though I am a messenger, the king often took me on journeys with him, just for company." Paul could not see why his father would choose this man to come on a journey. There were plenty of other servants who were much more talkative and lively. He kept his thoughts to himself.

Again dusk came, and they pitched camp. Tonight, however, Paul soon fell asleep. When he awoke, his muscles were tired and stiff. His neck hurt when he moved. Breakfast was no more than some warm meat and water. The air had chilled and Paul felt miserable. He had hoped for a relief from the bad weather, hoping it would help his mood, but it had only become worse. He was angry, impatient with the horses, and tired. The day sluggishly dragged on, the scenery tediously rolling by. The land between the Oldyers and Calarath was generally flat grassy plains except for the Kraan River they had to cross and the Orkat Forest they would pass through.

They stopped at the Kraan River to relax and to refill their water. If he had not been in his present circumstance, Paul might have enjoyed it. Paul felt that perhaps Endos had brought a guard along, in case Paul wouldn't go back, and constantly felt as if he was being watched. Sleeping the next night was easier, but Paul woke stiff and miserable. He walked out of his makeshift tent to find Endos looking more excited.

"Paul! We've made good time; we'll be in Calarath by mid-day." Home. He hadn't seen his mother or his house for two months. He longed for home. He longed for his father. What would life be like without him in the palace? The place would seem dead. They had a quick breakfast and set off. Endos told him the funeral was still five days away, but there was much to be done. They rode without speaking. Before reaching the border of Calarath, his beloved town, Paul spoke.

"It feels so good being home, after all this time."

"Indeed. I am in and out almost every fortnight, but I still miss home."

"I haven't seen my mother in two months. I miss her. And my father."

"Aye. I miss my wife and precious daughter of only two years." Paul had never had a sister. He had longed for a brother growing up or even a sister. But now he was to be king. He no longer had time for childish things. He had no more time left to grow up. They passed into the city and rode through. Many people simply pretended they hadn't seen him and busied themselves. Others gave him a pitiful glance. He passed the house of one woman who handed him a flower. Paul looked at the flower and then back at the woman, who smiled back at him.

They made their way to the castle gates. The doorman bowed and signaled the stable boy to come and take Paul's horse. As he swung off his horse and set his feet on the familiar soil, he felt uneasy. Paul looked up at the grand castle and was taken in once again by its magnificence. Paul sensed that there was much sadness as he stepped into the castle. It was as dead as the very stone it was made from. Normally the castle was alive and energetic. Paul walked inside and immediately one of the servants hurried quickly to announce to his mother that her son had arrived. After a few short moments a servant announced the queen's presence. She was aging but nevertheless elegant and graceful. She held herself with a regal poise that Paul had always admired. Even now, alone with her son after the loss of her husband, she retained her dignity. Paul ran to her and hugged her. Now in the warm embrace of his mother's arms, he felt better.

"Oh Paul…" Her eyes flooded with tears. "We would have sent word sooner, but it was so unexpected." Paul looked at his mother, concerned. She had dark smudges under her eyes; she obviously hadn't been sleeping well. She looked pale.

"How are you doing?" Paul asked. His mother tried to appear calm.

"I'll be all right. I'm more concerned about you." Paul couldn't help smiling at his mother's selfless attitude, even in great pain. Finally Paul asked a question that had been burning in his mind.

"How did he die?"

His mother sighed. "It started one night after dinner; he said he wasn't feeling well. In the morning Athon went to wake him as usual…" She choked. "It was so fast, so unexpected…" her voice trailed off.

"What else needs to be done?" asked Paul, changing the subject.

"Nothing the servants can't do." She smiled. "I want you to just relax, Paul. You've been through a lot. Why don't you get some rest? You look tired." Paul nodded. He was exhausted from lack of sleep, but also grief. His father had died. Gone forever. He couldn't even imagine it.

He stepped out into the quiet corridors. He walked across to his room and opened the door. His room seemed enormous compared to what it had been at the Oldyers.' He fell down onto his bed and sighed. He was still shocked and dazed, but he was tired. He closed his eyes and fell into an uneasy sleep. He dreamed of his father. He dreamed he was not dead, but instead had come to Paul for his manhood ceremony.

Paul felt as if he had just fallen asleep when he heard the door creak and opened his eyes. A servant stood at the door. Paul squinted against the bright sun streaming in through his windows. Finally he recognized Jaxon, the cook, who was his very old friend.

"Mornin' to ya, Paul. I am sorry about ya loss, me ol friend—very tragic." He spoke with a deep voice and a thick accent that showed clearly that he was from the Bromken Highlands. Yet he was one of Paul's best friends. Paul had no friends his age. Sure, there were people his own age, but he really only got on well with adults.

"Will ya be joinin' me for breakfast? Or would ya rather take yer breakfast in bed?" Paul tried to smile. Jaxon was always willing to accommodate others, even if he didn't have the time.

"I'll join you in a moment. Thank you." Paul's voice was croaky and sore. He was still tired and felt as if he had not slept. He couldn't believe he had slept this late and not felt it. He slowly got up, his heart heavy.

After he was dressed and ready, he went down to the kitchen. All the energy that used to thrive in that place now had diminished. Only the dogs, ignorant of what had happened, seemed lively and active. Jaxon was preparing Paul's breakfast when he walked in. The smell of real food helped Paul. After all, it had been three months since his last meal at the castle, and the last few days he had had warm meat and water. He sat down to a rather delicious breakfast of eggs and toast. No matter what the ingredients, Jaxon always managed to make his food taste better than any other cook in the land. Paul always ate breakfast in the kitchen. At first his parents had made him eat in the dining hall with them, but he soon grew tired of it, and they allowed him to eat alone. Paul, though he enjoyed the comforts of the castle, often got very frustrated at the formality of the place. His father had done well in keeping the mood relaxed but firm. In spite of that there were times he felt like he wished he didn't have to go through it all. He ate in silence. He picked up his plate and prepared to start washing them but was soon met with a nervous looking servant trying to take the plates from him. Then Paul remembered that he was in the castle and that he need not do everything himself. He nodded to the servant and walked to his mother's room.

He met a servant coming out.

"Excuse me, is my mother in her room?"

"No, sir, she had a meeting with one of the leaders from Yambor." Paul thanked her then rushed downstairs. He was supposed to be at that meeting but had forgotten. He reached the meeting room and opened the door. There sat his mother and a young man about thirty years of age. Paul walked in and sat down. The meeting room was a large hall with a shining marble floor. Around the perimeter stood pillars supporting the elaborate domed ceiling.

"Ah, Paul, may I present Sir Gelaray. He and I were just discussing the plans for the town of Yambor now that the king has passed away." Sir Gelaray eyed Paul suspiciously.

"Good afternoon, sir. I am sorry I am late. I hope I have not missed much?" Paul tried to keep from staring at the man's large crooked nose.

"In fact, Her Majesty and I were just talking about you. How do you feel about being the next heir to the throne Paul?" The question caught him off guard. He sorted his thoughts.

"Although the Kingdom-ship has been forced upon me at such a young age, and I admit that I am a little flustered, I am willing, and I will do my uttermost to do my duty." Paul was amazed at how clearly and confident the words had come out despite his still being emotionally raw about the topic. Sir Gelaray nodded.

"Spoken like a true king!" he said smiling, though Paul sensed he was displeased at his answer.

"Well then, assuming everything goes as planned, the funeral shall take place in a few days. Thank you, Sir Gelaray!" The queen rose and the interview was over. Afterwards Paul felt like he wanted to know more about Sir Gelaray. He found his mother walking towards the library.

"Paul, what's on your mind?"

"Well, I was wondering about the meeting today with Sir Gelaray. What exactly did he want? Who is he?"

"Of course. Sir William Gelaray is one of the governors of Yambor, and he came to discuss a few matters of state concerning the current situation. He presented his case for Yambor to be the new military base and training facility for the Kingdom, evidently relieving Calarath of 'unnecessary burdens' for a young king. He believes that Calarath should be the administrative capital of the Kingdom. He is an ambitious and calculating man, and I would advise you to proceed cautiously. He is willing to cooperate with a new king as long as he gains something from it. The world is not made of kind men like your father, Paul." Paul swallowed. He missed his father so much. *Could Gelaray have been ambitious enough to provoke him to murder? Could I have just been talking to my father's killer?*

"Oh, and Paul, the funeral has been moved to the end of the week." Paul hugged his mother and walked back to his room. He knew that after the funeral was his coronation ceremony. He was to be both an accepted adult and the crowned king. He tried to push it off in his mind. He went down to the lecturing halls and looked for his former swordsmanship teacher, Master Lugaro. He couldn't find him anywhere. Finally he asked one of the servants.

"Oh, Master Lugaro hasn't been seen for nearly a week. No one knows where he is." Paul walked off confused. Where had he gone? Master Lugaro had never taken a leave of absence. Perhaps it was simply the death of the king that had saddened him. He and his father had been very close, and often his father brought Master Lugaro in on matters of state. Master Lugaro was not only the best swordsman in the region but also very wise about a variety of things. He wanted to consult him more about the Flamethrowers and Ashkah but had no time to go looking for him. He went back to the dining hall where dinner was being served. He sat down but did not feel hungry. The long wooden table had been in the castle for centuries. Its thick, heavy top was made of Orun Oak—the wood from the heart of the Great Forest. Use of this wood had been banned because the trees they came from were in danger of being extinct. They were old trees, heavy, solid, and pure. The wood would never warp or bend, and it was strong. It would hardly wear. The king of the time had ordered a large table made from this wood to be built in the hall. It was to seat over seventy-five people. Today, as he sat with the few remaining generals and leaders, it seated only twelve. Paul looked around at the blank faces of all the nobility.

Towards the end of dinner Paul rose and excused himself, nodding as the generals and leaders around the table stood respectfully. He thanked everyone at the table and walked upstairs. He lay on his bed, hoping sleep would come. He needed rest. Sleeping let him get away from thoughts of his father and him being the king. Finally, after several hours, he drifted off into a light sleep.

When morning finally broke, it was dreary. The day was just like any other day, yet it had been spoiled by the mere fact that today was the funeral of Paul's father. The air was crisp, carrying the first hints of autumn. Slowly Paul climbed out of bed and splashed water on his face. His face felt stretched and salty. He guessed he had been crying in the night. Walking over to his wardrobe, he chose a full black outfit for the funeral. He had done well to compose himself, and now he would hold that composure as long as he could.

The kitchen staff was small as Paul ate a light breakfast and then went to the library to take his mind off the funeral which was to begin at noon. The hours seemed to drag by while Paul browsed through a few books on various subjects. Finally, while he was halfway through *Pre-Jedarian Battles*, a servant caught his attention and informed him that the funeral would begin shortly.

Paul followed the servant through the back of the castle and out to the Garden Estates. There thousands upon thousands of people had gathered. A small stage was set up where the queen and her entourage sat, along with all the governors and dignitaries of the nearby cities. Paul took a seat near his mother. Finally, after a few minutes, a large man in ornate black robes known as the Master Cognoscente stood up behind the podium. Everyone stood as, slowly, a full military procession guided the coffin through the crowd. Each of the generals of Calarath in the procession was dressed in full ceremonial military gear. The crowd grew eerily silent. As the coffin stopped at the stage, the generals and nearby soldiers all turned to face the coffin and saluted, holding their salute for a full minute.

The Master Cognoscente spoke, "I stand before you today the representative of a family in grief, of a city in mourning, before a Kingdom in shock. We are all united not only in our desire to pay our respects to our great King Mark but also in our need to do so. For such was his extraordinary leadership that all those who never even met him feel that they too lost someone close to them. Today we mourn the loss of one of the finest men to ever have walked this Kingdom. He will be missed by all. His Majesty exemplified everything for which the Kingdom stands. He went above and beyond what was required of him as a king and did everything he could to make this world a better place."

Paul could hear sobs in the crowd. The Master Cognoscente continued his speech on how great and magnificent Paul's father was. Paul was glad that at least people appreciated his father. "… and so we mourn. We pray now that the great Ara'tel will watch over him." The speech was finished. The people began to disperse. Paul stood and walked to his father's coffin. This was the first time he had seen his father in a long time. At the sight of his father, stone faced and pale, Paul choked. He felt tears welling up inside, and he quickly ran from the gathering. He tried to breathe deeply to calm himself. He had to get away—just to distance himself from his father and his feelings.

Paul ran to the stable and saddled his own black horse. As he clicked his heels, a servant opened the gate and he shot out. He raced through the streets, finally passing the outskirts of the city. He looked up to the Nerek Mountains, a small mountain range at least fifteen miles outside of the city. Paul raced towards the mountains, not knowing why he was going there or what he was doing. All he knew was that he needed to get away. After an hour of riding the sky was turning a bluish purple. It became harder and harder to see, but finally, Paul reached the base of the mountain. He fumbled around and tied his horse to a tree. From previous visits Paul knew of a cave nearby and stumbled through the darkness to find it. After a few minutes he found it and threw himself onto the hard stone floor. He did not care if he lived or died. Dark depression seized him as he curled up on the cold surface and wept.

Dawn broke. Paul saw the sun rise but did not get up. He lay still, unmoving. Here there was no one to make him do anything—no one to tell him what to eat, where to eat, and when to eat; no one to tell him what he could and couldn't do. Most importantly, though, here he didn't have to be responsible for the entire Kingdom. He was alone. He liked the thought. He got up and walked out into the crisp, fresh air. The autumn wind blew across his face, tossing his long brown hair across his face. He felt strong. He was going to face the challenges of being alone. His thoughts were interrupted because he thought he heard movement, but dismissed it. No one lived in these forsaken mountains.

Assassin

† † † † † † †

The night shuddered as Bôren listened to the sound of a horse riding full speed toward the palace. It was three hours past midnight. The rider, clothed entirely in black and covered by a dark hood, glanced around nervously as he took the stairs up to the palace entrance. Bôren turned to King Jonak and announced that the rider had arrived. Moments later the door flung open and the dark man stepped in. The man's appearance gave Bôren chills down his spine—a rare thing for a seasoned general as himself. The man was an assassin.

Standing, King Jonak of Nehgrog walked forward to the assassin and nodded gravely. The man bore a long scar across his left check, stretched now as he grinned in sick delight.

"My liege. The deed is done. The king of Calarath is dead."

"You're sure of this?"

"Absolutely. I witnessed the funeral." The king smiled maliciously. "And there's more. The young prince is not going to be a problem. I didn't even have to take care of him. He ran into the mountains. Rumor has it that he is dead." The king dropped his smile.

"Rumor? Since when has the great city of Nehgrog trusted rumors?" The assassin glared.

"Your Majesty, with all due respect, if I weren't completely sure that his threat is gone, I would have destroyed him. Instead he has destroyed himself." Bôren decided he had stayed quiet too long.

"You're sure that he hasn't merely fled to a nearby town? Perhaps he is rallying support against us?"

"I'm sorry; I do not think we have met."

"I am Bôren, head of the War Council of Nehgrog. You are?"

"You may know me only by my pseudonym. It's a formality I rather enjoy. My name is Dagger." Bôren looked wholly unimpressed by the dramatic flair of the killer. The king stepped in.

"Your name is of little significance. I thank you for bringing us the information." The king withdrew a folded parchment from his cloak. "Here is the letter of our support. Take it to your master. We will win this war yet." The assassin bowed low to the king and nodded briefly to Bôren before turning and walking away. As the solid oak doors closed, Bôren turned back to the king.

"It feels wrong to trust this man. He may have executed the most difficult assassination in history, but something is wrong about him."

"Bôren, I have often told you to be wary of everyone. It is good that you do not trust him, but do not let it interfere with our plan."

"Your Majesty, you know of all people that I loathe Calarath with everything in my being. I want nothing less than their utter destruction." The king nodded and strode towards the window. He watched the silent town with a thoughtful look on his face. After a few moments pause, he spoke again.

"Do you know why we need Calarath eliminated?" Bôren seemed confused by the question. "Other than the fact that our two cities hate each other, what is the deeper reason that we want them destroyed?"

"Your Majesty has never spoken of another reason."

"Bôren, you know, as I do, that the Dark Lord will not stay silent for long. These petty attacks on the smaller towns will soon bore him. He longs for bigger game. I know that something is coming, something bigger than we've ever seen before. Calarath is too weak to withstand this new oncoming slaughter. King Mark was more concerned about 'being one with the people' than protecting and ruling the people. It was this crucial flaw that dictated that we take action." Bôren nodded. He knew this already. "With Mark out of the way and his pathetic son dead, now is the perfect time to seize the capital of the Kingdom and restore peace and order."

"But my liege, surely destroying Calarath and starting a civil war will do nothing more than weaken the Kingdom? Perhaps we should simply prepare ourselves and warn Calarath." The king looked at Bôren, irritated.

"I'm growing weary of this conversation. It's late; I will see you in the morning. Good night." Bôren nodded and followed the king out of the throne room. He exited the palace, thoughts still brooding heavily in his mind. He walked down the lane towards his house and noticed how simple it was, but he would never want anything different. Besides, what purpose would it serve to have a house bigger than his neighbors? It was more important that he fulfill his civil duty as War Council leader than to worry about competing with his neighbors.

Bôren opened the door silently and crept inside, wary of making any noise. His wife and two sons were dead asleep at this hour, and he dared not wake them. Although the hour was late, Bôren could not sleep. His mind was too awake. Something was stirring in his subconscious. As he poured himself a glass of Sno'ak, a flavorful fruit drink common to Nehgrog, Bôren remembered back to his days of training. He once had a teacher who had taught him: *The best way to prepare for the future is to look in the past. Study how things have changed. History is bound to repeat itself.* Thinking through this, Bôren seated himself in a comfortable armchair and threw a new log onto the dying fire. As he sipped his drink, his eyes glanced across the titles of books on his shelf. He knew not what he was looking for, he was merely searching for something—an answer, a solution, anything that could help in preparation for the future. His eyes raced across a myriad of books in every size and shape and color. His eyes stopped on a dusty old book wedged between two much taller volumes. Standing, he pulled the book down and dusted off the cover. *The Age of Expansion.* Judging by the cover and the age of the pages, Bôren guessed that this was an old book, one he had never seen before. He opened to the beginning pages:

The Fifth Year of Ere'thor II

I, the loyal scribe of Ere'thor II, entrusted with the duty of giving the account of the conquests of His Majesty the king, hereby record the following territorial achievements and additions to the Greater Kingdom:

Of the lands to the North, a great peninsula has been discovered as charted by the king's best explorers. The lands include various mountain ranges, plains, as well as a large Orun Oak forest in the heart of the land. A calm bay in the east opens up to the sea in which a large island, nominated "Zirikaan" is located.

Bôren reread the last line. *Zirikaan?* This meant that the land that this scribe was referring to was the same one that Bôren now lived in. Bôren continued to read.

The land is well suited for expansion, and His Majesty has set in motion plans to establish a capital city, nominated "Jedar" for the purpose of governing this newest addition to the Kingdom.

Bôren was starting to understand. This Kingdom that he lived in, from the castle of Calarath to the western shores, was all merely a part of a much larger Kingdom, called the "Greater Kingdom." What had happened to that Kingdom? Bôren flipped towards the end of the book, skipping small details. He stopped towards the end and read a few paragraphs:

With no other alternatives the new king, Ere'thor III, has given
free rule to the new lands of North and declared the land a separate
Kingdom. In addition to the vast desert and unsettled waters, the
emergence of a new enemy, the Bazrukal, has eliminated any and
all attempts at trade or travel between the two Kingdoms. This
new enemy has used flaming balls to devastate every army of the
king's men sent against them. The men were ordered to defend
Jedar and hold the Kingdom as long as possible…

Now it was clear. The Jedarac Deserts, caused by the Bazrukal, or
Flamethrowers, had isolated the northern peninsula and created a
separate Kingdom. Bôren thought through this dilemma. How was
it possible that he had never heard of this before? Wouldn't such
valuable information be recorded somewhere in the great library?
After skimming the rest of the pages, which contained more explanation on the effects of the Jedarac Desert, Bôren decided he needed
to take this to the king. In the past the Dark Lord had divided the
Greater Kingdom and then attacked the weaker parts. Surely the
same was happening now. Calarath and Nehgrog were growing farther and farther apart. Eventually one of them would be destroyed.
Bôren closed the book, threw some sand onto the fire, and retired
for the night.

Dagger, as he preferred to be called, had ridden without stopping
since he had left the palace of Nehgrog. The journey between
Nehgrog and Yambor was a long and uneventful one. Dagger had
been trained to be the best. He was a legend in his own right, the
most sought after assassin in the Kingdom. It was this reputation
that had given him the opportunity of a lifetime. However, the
glory of an assassin is personal. Only the best assassins could accept
that. Assassins were the heroes that no one could thank—or hate.
He had been trained to disappear, and that is what he would do.
The horse started to slow. The animal was simply a dumb Nehgrog

beast. If there was anything that he had learned from his years of travel and infiltration, it was that horses of speed and endurance were hard to come by. Dagger slowed the animal to a walk and looked around. Dawn would break soon, and the new day would be one exclusively of travel. Dagger accepted this as he did the stupidity and weakness of the horse he now rode on. He was a few miles away from the ends of the Plains of Goash. From there it would be a dull ride into the Orkat Forest, across the Kraan River and to Yambor. A massive sum of gold, larger than anything he had asked for awaited him there. Inspired and motivated, Dagger kicked his horse's flanks and they continued their journey.

Sir Gelaray looked around nervously. It had been that confounded dramatist that had forced him to wait under the bridge at dusk. This was no place for someone of such noble birth and intentions. Fear had gripped Sir Gelaray every time he had heard hooves on the bridge. Finally, the hooves went across the bridge and stopped. Seconds later the notorious Dagger stood before him, a dark hood pulled over his face.

"Greetings, Sir Gelaray. The darkness comes."

Sir Gelaray rolled his eyes and produced the required response. "The shadow hides us all."

Dagger stepped forward and pulled off his hood. That disgusting scar quivered again as he smiled. "Where is the gold?"

"The note first." Dagger reached into the folds of his dark tunic and handed Sir Gelaray the note from King Jonak. After carefully perusing the contents of the letter, Sir Gelaray folded the note and put it inside his cloak.

"The gold is hidden in an abandoned well half a mile outside the city. It is on the road and should be easy to find. You have my word that the amount is there in full."

With these words the two men parted company. Sir Gelaray

hated the assassin with every bone in his body, but he had lived up to his reputation. He had gained access to the most secure and heavily guarded castle in the Kingdom and after months of blending in, had finally been able to move in on the target. For this reason Sir Gelaray admired the man. The death of the king was worth more than gold to Sir Gelaray, and the sum Dagger had asked for had been inconsequential. The promissory note from King Jonak was one of many that Sir Gelaray had acquired in the last few years. Each village and city had its own requirements for joining. Most wanted money, but Nehgrog had wanted the death of the king. And so they had given it to them. The plan was surging ahead. Within days the fate of the Kingdom would be decided.

Possession

† † † † † † †

After three weeks of being in the mountains, Paul was weary from his depression. He had slept on the hard stone floor for days and days, and his back felt awful. Whenever he left the cave and scrambled to the top of the mountain, he could see the edge of Calarath. He could see the flowing river, the lush landscape, and the rolling mountains behind him. Despite this view, he saw no beauty in it. All he felt was misery. His father had died, and he had been left alone with the responsibility of the Kingdom. What did he care? His life was a pathetic waste of time. He was angry and looked for an outlet for that anger. He found some relief in solitude. He barely ate, barely slept, and barely moved all day. He was in a state of apathetic depression.

However, every now and then, he would be hunting, and for a brief moment, a sense of relief would wash over him. Then something, a deer, the sky, anything, would remind him of his father, and he would sink back into his deep pit of despair. He couldn't stand it and yet saw no point in getting out of it. There he was, alone, with not a soul in the world around him—or so he thought. For the last couple days, he had sensed something—someone—following him. Watching him. He feared that what Segan had told him nearly a month ago might be coming true, that the Flamethrower that had gripped him was hunting him down to finish the possession process. He kept up a constant guard. There were times when he thought of not resisting the Flamethrower but letting him kill or take possession of him. Anything was better than this. He slept, ate, and slept. There was no variation except for the occasional hunt to keep himself alive, and even then, he often missed that, preferring to starve than get up. His father was dead. He thought of the Oldyers and their happy little lives but cursed them in their ignorance. The world wasn't as happy as they seemed to perceive it. He couldn't even think of his mother, at least not without bursting into tears. They had probably reported him dead. He thought of making stealthy trips to the city to find news. He wanted the people to feel his loss, to be as miserable as he was. But he was sure that they had forgotten him by now. What about his mother? The loss of her husband and perhaps her son must have crushed her beyond belief—but he couldn't care. All he could think of was himself. He dwelt on his misery, feeding it like some sick monster, ever hungry and threatening to devour him. He heard the noise again and looked around. He was sure there was something there. He could feel it. He sensed a hollow feeling in the pit of his stomach.

This morning he got up and stretched. He couldn't remember a day since he had run away that he hadn't felt sore and tired. He walked to the top of the mountain and looked out. Far in the distance he could see the river that marked the edge of the Kingdom—the Kingdom that was rightfully his but of which he wanted no part. He knew by now a new king had been chosen. He burned to know who it was. No man could fill his heart's empty chasm.

Then he heard it. The sound chilled his bones. He had heard that sound before. It was the shrill shriek of a Flamethrower's black fireball. It came crashing down far in front of him, enough for him to realize that the forest around him would soon be in flames. He ran back to the cave but had to stop twenty feet in front of the opening. The Flamethrower had burnt his few belongings in his makeshift house and killed his horse. He didn't know where the Flamethrower was. Suddenly more and more shrieks could be heard—that abominable orb screaming through the thin air to deliver its evil payload. The Flamethrower was desolating the entire forest, hunting Paul down. Paul panicked. The Flamethrower was up on the mountain now, and no matter where he ran, the Flamethrower could see him. He thought of the mind-vice. He hoped that his reach weakened with distance. Then deep within himself, a sudden surge for the desire to live washed over him.

Running as fast as his sore legs could carry him, he neared the foot of the mountain and dove behind a large boulder to catch his breath. The sounds of flames and shrieks grew louder and closer. He knew that if the Flamethrower came near him, he would be killed or even worse, possessed. He wondered if the Flamethrower could sense him or reach out with his thoughts and track him down. He realized how little he knew about his enemy. He knew that there was nobody in these mountains that could help him now. The closest civilization was the castle, and that was miles away. He would never make it, even to the boundaries of the Kingdom. And even then, how much protection would that offer? His mind raced with options. He darted out into the open and began to sprint, but the Flamethrower was gaining on him. He ran faster and faster, branches cutting his hands and face as he raced through them. He felt thorns cutting into his flesh. He ran on. Suddenly he tripped on a rock and smashed face first into the ground. He looked up, fearing that a flaming orb would hit and disintegrate him. He lay dead still, listening to his own panting. Seconds dragged by as he waited for that terrible mind weapon to seize him, but he heard no shrieking ball and felt no mental grip. He cautiously looked back over his shoulder and saw the Flamethrower running away. It was a mere black dot when Paul stood, having to squint to follow it. His face was bleeding badly. Blood soaked his clothes. Paul felt dizzy and decided to sit down, but fainted before he could do so.

. . . . .

The lull of soft waves woke Paul. He looked around, wondering where he was. This was a strange place; nothing looked familiar but the vast expanse of blue water before him. He was somewhere near the coast. Looking up, Paul saw that he was lying in the shade of a palm tree. He decided to stand, but the pain in his leg stopped him short. Trying to ignore it, he balanced himself against the tree. This beach was not one he had seen before. He had been to every one of the coastal towns with his father, all except the abandoned one near the Jedarac Desert. He decided he must be in that abandoned town. A shiver ran up Paul's spine as he realized the implications. It was supposed to be crawling with Ashkah who had taken the city and renamed it Valzah, meaning "the place of outcasts." Many wounded Ashkah who were rejected after war had congregated in this small city. It was rumored that over 600,000 battle-hardened Ashkah lived in the tiny town. Paul walked towards the beach, letting the cool blue water lap against his bare feet. His face felt swollen and tight. His throat was constricted as always but thirsty and dry. He knew he could not drink the seawater but hoped there was some stream or river flowing into it. He started walking along the coast. He looked up into the darkening sky. He would have to make some sort of camp soon. But would he dare sleep? If he were indeed in the territory of the Ashkah rebels, he would be murdered as a trespasser. He walked along the sea, letting the cool water lap against his feet.

Then it struck him. How did he get to this deserted coastal town? He was in the mountains. It was a five day journey or longer to the desert. If he had been unconscious, someone must have carried him here—but who? Was it one person or many? And where were these people now? What if they were watching him? He looked around and walked faster. He was getting more and more parched. He spotted a small stream leading to the sea. He followed it back up to find a larger river. He sat down and took long refreshing drinks. He noticed the cuts on his hands looked as if someone had already cleaned them.

They still stung when he washed them, and he winced from the pain. When he was finished, he sat down under a tree and warmed himself. He sighed. His mind started to recall the last events he remembered.

What happened to the Flamethrower? Why had it fled so close to victory? Someone or something must have frightened it. But who or what was powerful enough to do that? And why would they want to help him? Did such powers exist in the Kingdom? He felt the limits of his sheltered upbringing. It would seem that not only was he ignorant of his enemies, he was also ignorant of his allies. The sun was starting to set as he looked around. His eyes felt heavy. He sighed again. His face felt raw where he had cut it on the rocks and rough branches. He sat and thought. Even if he had circled around the land by sea, it would have taken no less than four days, and that was with good wind. In four days his face would have felt differently. He leaned his head back and stared at the bluish gray sky. His eyes were closing on their own. He had to sleep. If he was near Valzah, he hoped that no Ashkah were patrolling this area. His eyes closed, and refreshing sleep washed over him.

The day was still black when Paul heard a noise and opened his eyes. Trees stood out as smudges in the dark landscape. He saw a light. Not the light of the sun but of a small camp fire. Paul slowly rose. He noticed a solitary figure standing by the fire. The figure stood still but relaxed. The pose reminded him of his father, and for a moment he thought perhaps he had died and met his father in whatever lay beyond. As he came closer, the figure doused the fire and in the same movement had his sword at Paul's neck.

"Ah! It's you. Welcome." He put his sword away.

"Wh-who are you?" Paul stammered.

"That is not important. What is important is who you are."

Paul looked sideways at this mysterious man. He was not young, but he was not old by any means and was very fit.

"So who are you?" the man asked. Paul hesitated. He didn't want to reveal himself.

"I'm Jacob."

"A pleasure to meet you, Jacob. Please, sit down." Paul sat down on a log by the stranger. The beach was beginning to take form around him as the day slowly became brighter. The strange man chuckled. Paul looked questioningly at him. "So how do you find yourself on my island, Jacob?"

Paul reeled, "Your island? Surely you don't mean…"

"Yes, I do. This is the Isle of Zirikaan, and you are here with me!"

"Then we're not at Valzah?"

"No. We are not. But I want to know how you came here with no boat or ship."

Paul looked puzzled. He didn't know the answer and told the stranger so.

"Ah, memory is the first to go they say."

"They? What are you talking about?"

The man laughed, "So will you be staying here long?" This man was mocking him. He knew that Paul had no idea how he got here.

"I am Amon. I rule this island alone. You won't survive three days alone out here." With that he stood and walked away. Paul was struck. Were his chances of survival that slim? He ran to catch up with the man.

"Sir! I need help. I can't survive on my own out here, like you said. Can you help me?"

"If you promise to give me all your effort and energy and do what I say and obey me, I will show you how to survive. But are you sure that is all you want?"

"What do you mean?" asked Paul.

"If you follow those conditions, I will teach you how to think, how to fight. I will train you."

"Train me for what?"

"I will teach you to become a man. To be self-reliant, thoughtful and competent." Something leapt in Paul's heart. In a strange way the words of the old man appealed to him. The sun peeked over the edge of the horizon and for the first time in weeks, Paul felt the warmth of the sun. It was the first clear day he had had since the battle with the Oldyers. He walked behind Amon, smiling. They walked for the better part of an hour in silence. They walked away from the bare beach and to the heart of the island. They came to the beginning of a massive jungle with trees over fifty feet tall. It was a dense lush green. As they entered, the darkness of the trees surrounded them. Paul was taking it all in with excitement. Amon moved deftly through the forest; Paul was struggling to keep up. The smell of the trees grew stronger the farther they went in. It was a foreign smell to Paul.

"These trees, what are they?" he asked amazed. Amon stopped and looked up and breathed in the fresh smell.

"They are oak…Orun Oak," he said. Paul stared incredulously. Orun Oak was extinct, and the only remaining trees were grown only for wood for the castle in Calarath. But here, on this island—such a large dense forest was worth a fortune!

"Amazing, isn't it?" They continued their march. Paul wondered where they were going. The day was getting dark within the forest. Amon stopped and looked around. They had reached an opening.

"Jacob, the day is getting late. We will have to camp out here tonight." Paul wanted to appear confident and strong for Amon. He nodded his head and looked around. They found clumps of moss and made makeshift mattresses. It was a restless night. Paul heard strange animal noises and was terrified that some hungry, malevolent predator was watching them. After hours of tossing and turning he finally drifted off into an uncomfortable sleep.

· · · · ·

The next morning Amon woke up suddenly. Something had pulled him out of his deep sleep. He looked around in the still-dark forest. Nothing moved. He looked across at Paul. He seemed very uncomfortable but asleep nonetheless. He was going to need it today. He knew he wouldn't go back to sleep. He sat on a log nearby and considered what he had committed himself to. Paul turned in his sleep. Slowly he opened his eyes and looked around. For a few moments he had no recollection of where he was or how he got there. He caught sight of Amon getting ready to make a fire. He got up and stretched. The forest around him started coming alive. Birds began to flutter; small creatures scurried around between the massive trees.

Amon

† † † † † † †

"Come on Jacob, let's get going!" Amon walked up and patted him on the back.

"Going? Where are we going?" Paul asked worried.

"For a run, of course. Every new day starts with a run. Today is the first day of your training, and we must start well! Come on, up we get."

"What about breakfast?" Paul asked, but Amon was already jogging out of the clearing. Paul looked around and felt alone, then jumped up and ran after Amon. He struggled to see Amon through the dense trees and bushes, but finally they broke out onto the beach. Amon stopped and looked behind him. Paul ran up, out of breath and panting.

"Well," gasped Paul, "that wasn't too bad."

"No, it wasn't. Now we can start running. Just try and keep up!" With that Amon took off again, and Paul forced himself to try and follow. The cuts and sores on his legs were on fire, and he was not used to running. Amon shouted back to him constantly to keep up. Paul was beginning to think that perhaps this training was a bad idea. Finally Paul couldn't take it anymore and collapsed onto the soft sand, which was still cold from the night. The sun had begun to rise while he had been running. He lay gasping for breath in the sand, the cold air burning his chest with every breath he took. Amon saw him and ran back.

"Jacob, what do you think you're doing?"

"I...I...can't run any more."

"Yes, you can, but you're too lazy to push yourself. It's so much easier to just fall on the ground and give up isn't it?"

Paul stared in anger and shock at this man. How could he not see that he was in pain? Was he really that stubborn that he wouldn't let him rest? Amon leaned in by Paul's face.

"Well, if you won't run anymore, perhaps we should try something else." Amon stood and looked down at Paul. "We will spar."

Paul looked up hopefully. He was a good fighter, and now he could beat this haughty old man and put him in his place. He got up and followed Amon. They walked back to their clearing in the forest. Paul looked around for his sword, then remembered he had left it back in the mountains when he had been attacked.

"Do you happen to have an extra sword? I...lost mine before I came here."

Amon looked up and laughed at Paul. "Who said we'd be using swords?" With that he tossed Paul a light colored stick, perfectly smooth and the length of a sword.

"We will spar with these!" In an instant he swung at an unprepared Paul who caught the blow on his arm. He cried out, more in shock than in pain. Now he was ready. He held his stick in the ready position, watching Amon to try and guess his next move. Amon faked left, then spun and struck Paul on the side. Paul fell to the ground and tried to catch his breath. He was sure that Amon had cracked a rib. Amon swung again, this time, Paul rolled out of the way. Paul stood up and ignored the pain. He was going to get this man back. He raised his stick and attacked, but before he had come close to Amon, he had been knocked off his feet, and his stick lay five feet from him. Amon spun in an elegant flurry and dealt a crushing blow on Paul's back. Paul lay on the ground, motionless and moaning. He turned over and faced Amon, whose wooden sword was at Paul's throat.

"It is a good thing that I am not your enemy." Amon turned his back on Paul and walked away. Paul pulled himself up, shaking with anger. He grabbed his stick and charged Amon to take revenge. He swung. His stick did not meet Amon but was stopped dead by Amon's stick. In split seconds Paul felt pain on his legs, the back of his neck, and his arm. He hadn't even seen Amon coming.

"Fighting in anger will get you killed. Let that be a lesson." He picked up Paul's stick and walked away. That night Amon sat by Paul at their fire. Paul sat nursing his aching ribs, arms, and legs. Amon looked over at Paul and chuckled. He leaned over and poked the fire.

"So, would you like to talk, you who call yourself Jacob?"

Paul was caught off guard. "But I am Jacob."

"Oh yes, at level one."

"What are you talking about?"

"There are different levels of communication," Amon explained. "Every time we say something, we communicate in more than one level. When you say your name is Jacob, at level one you are saying simply, 'My name is Jacob.' At level two, inferred by the tone and the quality of your body language, you say, 'I don't want to tell you my name.' At level three, we are dealing with the motive. 'What would his motive be for not telling me his name? What is he hiding?' At level four, I question, 'What kind of character must a person have to hide his true name?' At level five, we get down to your true self, your spirit, being afraid of who you really are, and although you know your name, you do not want to know who you are. So I ask you now, what is your name?"

"My name is Jacob! You are trying to be wise and clever and read into everything I say! My name is Jacob," Paul shot back defensively.

Amon smiled. "If I am to be your trainer, there must be a certain level of honesty between us."

"But how do you know that I am not telling the truth? What tells you I am lying?"

"You do. Every time you say the word, you tell me with your body language that this is not your name."

There was a long silence. Paul had run out of things to say.

"So I ask you for the last time, what is your name?"

Paul mumbled softly, "Paul."

There was a deep, long silence. Neither of them spoke. After a while Paul spoke up.

"Since we are on the subject of honesty, there is something you should know because it might affect you. I have been mind-viced by a Flamethrower."

The trainer recoiled. "I find this hard to believe. At level one I can't believe you, but on your other levels, I sense you are telling the truth. But I cannot see how."

"The Flamethrower didn't want to kill me, he wanted to possess me."

"When did this happen?"

"About a month ago."

"No, if he wanted to possess you, he would be further along by now. I would have sensed a dark taint in your spirit. I sense no such thing. However, if he wanted to kill you, which is the only other option, you would be dead."

"Unless I survived."

"Not in all my long years have I ever heard of such a thing. It is pure myth."

Paul sat confused.

"It seems that there is more to you than I thought, Paul. But we will talk more tomorrow. You will need some rest."

So ended Paul's first day of training.

Morning was Paul's least favorite time of day. Today he had to get up and run. Amon chased him mercilessly—shouting at him constantly, telling him how to run, how to breathe, how to move his legs. Paul didn't know which was worse—the running or the constant shouting. They ran for over an hour, until eventually, on the verge of Paul fainting, Amon decided that it was enough. Paul lay facing upwards on the ground, his chest heaving with every breath he took. As he walked back dripping with sweat, Amon stopped him.

"Paul, it seems that we are out of firewood. You will be chopping it for us." He proceeded to show Paul how to cut the wood, which wood was best for burning, and how large each piece should be. Then he left Paul alone.

"Ah! This is pointless!" Paul said to himself. "Why is he making me do this? He finds some sick pleasure in seeing me suffer. We probably don't need firewood." Paul felt miserable.

Amon was on the other end of the island, sorting out his thoughts. Even after all these years, even after the death of his brother, the bitterness welled up inside of Amon. The son of Mark was too much like his father. He had the same soft, lazy, spoiled attitude. Amon could tell that Paul had been coddled and over encouraged, just like Mark had been when they were growing up. At first Amon had thought it unfair, but later he saw what a detriment it had been to Mark and ultimately to Jedar. If Amon had been king, as he should have been, the city would not have fallen. Now Mark had done the same thing to his son—but no longer. Amon would beat the softness out of him.

After nearly five hours of constantly chopping wood, Amon finally returned.

"Ahh! Paul! Is this all the wood that you've cut for the last five hours? I see you chose to use the blunt axe—the one I gave you. If you had taken some initiative, you would have tested the other axe and found it recently sharpened. Instead of just assuming that the one I gave you was the right one, you would have cut enough wood, but I suppose this will have to do."

Paul grunted and stared at the axe.

"A true soldier owns his weapons. You cannot expect everything to be done for you."

"Now are we going to start training?"

"Why Paul, you've been training for the last five hours! It takes a lot of strength to cut that much wood with a blunt axe. You've also had to practice patience during this time, and patience is a key aspect of life."

Paul turned and rolled his eyes. This old man constantly thought he was better than Paul, and it was wearing him down. Paul saw that Amon had brought the light colored sticks with him. He tossed one to Paul seconds before attacking him. This time Paul pushed even harder for his revenge, but once again he was defeated. He got up time and time again, only to be knocked down. Finally he begged for a break.

"A break? You want a break, Paul? If I were your true enemy, if I were a Flamethrower, would I care if you wanted a break?"

Paul sat up and groaned from the pain.

"Why do you train me like this? Surely there are easier ways to learn to fight."

"Of course there are. That would be so like you, to want the easy way out. You want the way where you don't have to work, don't have to feel any pain, where the world is comfortable for you! Well, Paul, here's a shocking reality. Sometimes the best way to learn is to feel the pain, to do the work, to feel uncomfortable. You must push beyond your limits if you wish to learn! If the world were totally reliant on comfort, nothing would ever be accomplished! True men, real men, go beyond what they feel to do what is right."

Paul sighed and lay back down. "I understand."

"No, I don't think you do."

Amon walked over and stood over Paul.

"Get up."

"I can't."

"Get up!"

"But I…"

"*Get up!*"

Amon swung his stick down and struck Paul on the side.

"You think that once you've tired of this, once you're ready to stop, that I will? No, Paul. We will fight until I say we're done."

Paul clutched the stick and stumbled back up. They fought for nearly half an hour, and Paul was being beaten badly. Finally he had had enough.

"Why do you do this? You only fight me so you can show me how you can beat me! I know that you're better than I am, so why do you continue to fight me?"

Amon lowered his wooden weapon. "If I were your enemy, would you ask that question of me?"

"But you're not my enemy! This is training!"

"That is precisely why I am fighting with you like this. I am training you for the real world, Paul! I'm not training you so that you can say you've been trained! This is not a school; this is a preparation for life! A preparation for battle! If you go through with my training, you will be one of the most lethal fighters in the Kingdom. However, if this is too tough for you, we can always stop. Would you like to stop, Paul? It's so much easier."

Paul stood, blood running down his face from his re-opened cuts.

"No, I do not want to stop."

"Oh, but I think you do."

"No! I'm not going to give up!"

"Oh, but why not? It's so much easier. No need to go through all this; you're just going to give up later."

"Shut up, old man! I hate you!"

"Well, whether you hate me or not doesn't change the fact that you're lazy, selfish, and arrogant."

Paul screamed and charged the old man. He was stopped almost immediately and knocked down. He got up and charged again. He was bruised and bleeding all over his body, but he was not going to give up. He was going to show this old man that he was better than that.

"Paul, you're only going to wear yourself out."

Paul stood but did not attack.

"One day," he spat blood, "I will prove that you're wrong!" Paul threw his stick onto the ground and walked away. Amon smiled. This was going exactly as he had planned.

Paul was mad. He walked far away from their camp and looked out across the vast blue ocean. All he saw was sea. He looked around the island. He thought of the training sticks. The wood was light but incredibly strong. If he could find the tree that they came from, he could perhaps build a raft and get off. He decided to go look tomorrow. He walked back to the beach, but Amon was not there. He trudged back to the clearing, but Amon was not there either. Paul looked around in panic. *Where is Amon? Has he deserted me?* Paul thought perhaps the old man had been hurt and was too proud to show it. He sat down and made a small fire. He would spend the night alone.

It was near midnight when Paul heard a noise. He looked around and saw that something was moving in the bushes near him. He grabbed a branch off the forest floor. Suddenly the bushes gave way to a tall shape moving quickly through. Paul grabbed a nearby stick and swung, striking it hard on its small head. It recoiled, then turned back and retreated back to the forest.

"What was that...?"

"An Untos," came Amon's booming voice from behind him.

"Amon! Where were you?"

"I was in the trees, seeing how you would handle a situation on your own."

"What did you say that was?"

"An Untos. It's a jungle inhabitant, tall and spider-like; they are very rare. However, they are not harmful. More curious than anything else."

Paul settled down for the night. He lay awake thinking of his plans for the next morning. He thought of Amon. Perhaps running away wasn't the smartest idea.

Revelation

† † † † † † †

It was the middle of the day when Paul returned from his run. He waited on the beach letting the breeze cool him down. Amon walked with a worried look on his face. In his hand was a piece of bloodstained purple cloth.

"Do you know what this is, Paul?" Amon handed the cloth to Paul, who examined it for a moment.

"It looks likes a piece of fine cloth. Or it was, until something got hold of it."

Amon nodded, deep in thought. Paul had been on the Isle of Zirikaan for over six months. He was burning to know something of the outside world. He wanted to know something of the Kingdom, of his mother, but no one could bring him news. To the rest of the world he was a dead man. He had thought of building a raft, perhaps sailing to the Kingdom and traveling around for a few days, then coming back. He had approached Amon with this plan, but Amon told him that because of the changing currents and tides, no one, not even the most experienced sailor, could sail back to the land.

Paul had asked, "Then how do you get off this island?"

Each time Amon had replied simply, "I will show you in due time."

In the past few months Paul had grown taller, stronger, and sturdier as well as smarter and faster. Today Amon and Paul picked up the familiar sparring sticks that they had used since the first day of Paul's training. Paul was amazed that the sticks had not broken; in fact, they hadn't even chipped, dented, or cracked. The wood was a mystery to Paul. It burnt like the best wood and would burn for hours without dying. It was hard to cut and shape, and it was incredibly durable.

"Paul, remember what we said yesterday about the ready position. Keep the stick balanced and ready to move in any given direction." Amon swung and Paul parried the blow with lightning fast reactions. "Paul, after you parry you must attack or get into the ready position. Try again." Amon swung again, but Paul wasn't fast enough and only caught the tip of the stick before it slammed into his leg. He ignored it. He spun and attacked Amon twice, neither of the attacks hitting anything more than wood, and felt a sting on his left shoulder. Amon was the better fighter. He could never compete with that. Amon was lightning quick and parried every one of Paul's attacks effortlessly, no matter how complicated. Paul was getting faster and managed to parry most, but not all, of Amon's attacks. Amon leaped towards Paul, who was not fast enough to stop the blow landing on his nose. He dropped his stick in surprise as blood poured down his face. Amon smiled. Paul still had much to learn.

"That'll be enough for today; we will do some lessons now."

Paul pinched his nose to stop the bleeding as they walked quickly to the other end of the beach. The day was hot and humid. Stray clumps of bushes and palm trees dotted the empty beach. When they arrived at their little cove, Paul sat down on a log and felt his nose, to see if it was broken. Amon sat opposite him.

"Paul, do you know anything about the Jedarac War?"

"Very little, only that it was the cause of the Jedarac Desert. The massive tunnels leading to Maugrax destroyed any and all life there."

"Correct, but do you know about the outcome of the war? Do you know why the war was fought and what it meant?"

Paul shook his head slowly.

"Hmm, I thought so." *They would have avoided something like that in the castle,* thought Amon. "The Jedarian War was the greatest war the Kingdom has ever seen. There were hundreds of thousands of Ashkah as well as many of the Flamethrowers. The Dark One released every dark minion of those hellish pits to destroy what was left of the Glorious Region. Where the desert is now was once the most thriving city in the Kingdom before the war. Before it all began…" Amon's voice trailed off in thought.

"You're talking about the city of Jedar. I thought that was destroyed by fire."

"It was. Flamethrower fire. When the king saw that he was being attacked, he retreated to Calarath and rallied support. When the king attacked with his newly formed army, to take back Jedar, it was too late. Waiting for them were hordes and hordes of Ashkah. The armies of the king fought with unrivaled valor and courage, but towards the end of the battle the Dark One released the Flamethrowers, and the tide of battle turned ill. With the odds stacked so heavily against us, it was unlikely that any would be spared."

There was a brief pause as Paul took it all in. "You said…'Us— the odds stacked so heavily against *us.*' Were you there?" Paul asked excitedly.

"Indeed I was. I was among the few survivors. My brother and I were the only survivors of our family."

"Your brother survived? Where is he now?"

"He died," Amon said abruptly.

"I'm sorry."

"Now I am the only one left in my family except for one nephew."

"Who? Where is he now?"

Amon ignored the question.

Paul thought through all this—such a mysterious war, with so many unanswered questions. However, he had learned that Amon only answered questions when the time was right; there was no point pressing him for answers. *Amon had been there. And why did Amon come here afterwards? He was living alone on this island, and he was the only one left in his family.* The day was getting dark and they prepared to make camp. After they had built up a roaring fire, Paul sat by Amon and tentatively asked the question that had been burning in his mind.

"What was the city like? The city of Jedar," Paul asked.

Amon hung his head. "The city was the greatest in the Kingdom. It took over 350 years to build it all, the construction handed down from generation to generation. Everything in the city was breathtaking. From the magnificent entrance, with the large heavy doors set in the stone archway that stretched thirty feet above you, to the hundreds of small, old roads. One of the most outstanding features was the pillars. In all of the great buildings, the Library, the Lyceum, everywhere! Pillars beyond compare! They were intricately carved by hand into stone and marble and would tell a story with pictures up the entire pillar. Decades of work for one single pillar! There was the Great Library with large bookshelves of Orun Oak filled with millions of books, some dating back hundreds of years! There were large winding staircases leading to the second floor, and bookshelves and books surrounding each one. On the top floor were many more books on every topic imaginable. The Master Cognoscente, the wisest in the entire Kingdom, lived on this top floor. He had studied the books of the First Ones, and his wisdom was known everywhere. People came from all over simply to sit, read, and learn from the wealth of knowledge in that one building.

"In the heart of this great city was The Lyceum. This was probably the most important building in the city. It was built by the people and for the people. The people maintained it, the people took care of it, and the people certainly used it. Every day it was used for some purpose and often many different ones in the same day. It was used as a school, a university, a courtroom, and a gymnasium. It was used to hold contests and city meetings and every other major event. It had a large, fifty-foot ceiling and hundreds of rooms. Outside the Lyceum was a vast park. It had a lake with large, old Orun trees. The River Sluis flowed from the mountains in the northwest into the city, feeding the lake at the center. Trade with the city was busy, and every day carts and ships delivered their cargo to trade with the massive city."

Paul drifted off in thought to what he had learnt of the city. He began to get a sense of what living in Jedar must have been like. There were philosophers debating every day. The wisest and smartest of the land, as well as the curious, the simple, and the eager to learn who had come from every corner of the Kingdom to learn, study, and see the great city. Every citizen was treated equally, and even the king and his family were often around the city with the people. Jedar stood for hundreds of years and held its own through three major battles and innumerable attacks. However the final army that attacked was so massive that it could not withstand it. Amon's voice had grown sad. "All that history, all that wealth of knowledge, all those people, all the houses, all the stores, the markets, the castle, all destroyed in a matter of hours. A matter of hours, Paul! What took centuries to establish as the greatest, highest point of civilization, all destroyed—all burnt. Everything we had worked for. Those were *our* people, *our* history! We never could reclaim it. It's all gone now! This is what evil does, Paul. As good builds up and constructs, so evil tears down and destroys. When the city fell, the world panicked. It was the best-defended city in the Kingdom. When it fell, the people felt vulnerable and were sure we would lose everything. But we rallied."

"But how did you survive…against such tremendous odds?"

"There was once a great Master who devised an ingenious battle plan. He was Master Halack. He trained a small band of seven men at a time. They were the elite warriors who were trained to attack a single Flamethrower. They were called the Paladin."

"The Paladin?" Paul interrupted. He had heard rumors of this elite fighting force, but his father had told him to disregard them.

"Yes, the Paladin could distract a Flamethrower long enough to be able to decapitate him but not without severe losses. The plan was simple but brutal. They discovered that when a Flamethrower engages in a mind-grip, it consumes his full attention in that moment. The Paladin were trained to resist the mind-vice attack for up to thirty seconds, enough time for the others to attack and kill him. More often than not, the warrior who was resisting would be killed in the process. During training of one particular group, Master Halack discovered that there were two brothers who had a special gift." Amon's voice faded into that familiar story-telling mode that entranced Paul as he stared into the fire, picturing what it must have been like. "These brothers had the ability to see a movement split seconds before it happened. When they used this gift, it seemed that their opponent was moving slowly because they could see the opponent's movements split seconds before they actually moved, and this made them exceptionally lethal. The two of them alone could decapitate a Flamethrower. Master Halack promoted them as two captains of the Paladin." Amon continued his story, "However it took a long time for the band to get to each Flamethrower because they had spread out across the field."

Paul sat back and thought of that brave band of men which had saved the entire Kingdom. He would have given anything to know one of them.

Paul thought out aloud, "But you can't kill a Flamethrower can you?"

"No, but if you destroy the body it inhabits, the spirit has to find a new body and start with the possession process again, which takes months. Killing the body would take them out of the battle."

"That means that the Flamethrowers would have been terrified of these brothers! Did you know them? You were there? Did you at least see them?"

Amon was quiet for a moment. "Paul, did you ever wonder why the Flamethrower never finished you off back in the Nerek Mountains?"

Paul thought for a second. "Yes, that part of my memory is a blur." He hesitated, "But how do you know about that?" Amon looked intently at him. Paul's eyes widened with revelation, "You rescued me and brought me here."

"Yes, Paul, it was I. I found you moments before the Flamethrower seized you."

"But why would a Flamethrower leave…that means…it was afraid…but you said they were only afraid of the Paladin captains— those brothers." Amon simply smiled. "You are one of the brothers aren't you? You are a Paladin captain!" Paul exclaimed, respect rising in his voice with every word.

"Yes, that I am," said the old captain with deep longing in his voice. "Paul, now you know why you have never been able to touch me during our sparring sessions. I cannot disengage the gift—too many wars, too much training, too many Flamethrowers."

Paul stared at Amon with renewed admiration. "I have been training for six months with a Paladin captain who has killed Flamethrowers?"

Paul pulled himself up the last stretch as he reached the top of the cliff face. One of his least favorite exercises, it took incredible strength and dexterity. He sat at the top looking out over the island. It was an amazing wonder. It was divided roughly into quarters. The southeast quarter consisted of the caves, massive, huge, intricate caves that spread for miles and miles underground. The northwest side was mainly the Orun Oak Forest, a hidden treasure of immense value. The northeast side was dry desert, which amazed

Paul, considering it was so close to a lush forest and on such a tropical island. The southwest was unknown to Paul, but he aimed to explore it tomorrow on his day of rest. He wondered again how he was ever going to get off this remote island. Amon shouted up to him to climb down. He sighed and lowered himself until his feet touched the first bit of outcropped rock. Slowly, carefully, he lowered himself down to the next, his right foot stretching to find it. Getting down was always harder than going up. Amon shouted at him to come down faster, which only irritated Paul and made him lose his concentration. Paul tried to speed his descent, but felt himself slipping. Amon picked up stones and threw them at Paul. This only increased Paul's fury, and he slipped and roughly slid to an abrupt halt at Amon's feet.

"What was that about?" Paul screamed.

"You must learn to ignore distractions. Focus on your task. Discipline your emotions. Control them." Amon handed him an animal hide bag. As Paul took it, he felt how heavy it was. Inside the bag were large rocks.

"Paul, I want you to climb back up there but with this on your back. It'll help you learn to balance, and it'll build your stamina and strength faster."

Paul reluctantly grabbed the pack of rocks and started up. He found the rocks were always pulling him off balance, and he constantly had to find a different way up to keep himself from falling. After almost half an hour of climbing, he reached the top and slung the heavy bag of rocks onto the ground beside him as he sat panting. Moments later Amon was next to him. "Your physical training is an important aspect of your overall training; however, a more crucial aspect is the non-physical part of your training. Your mind is one of your most powerful weapons, but your spirit is the strongest of them all." Amon tossed Paul one of the sticks he had brought with him. "Try fighting with your spirit this time."

"But how? How do I fight with my spirit?" Paul asked.

"Do you remember the levels of communications? Try lining all of them up, focusing them on one common goal. Start with your spirit. Remember who you are. Allow this to surface into your character. From the substance of your character, drive your motives and then your purpose. Now take action. Focus on the battle, your opponent, his weapon."

Paul closed his eyes and mentally shifted his concentration. He opened his eyes slowly, and, with one purpose in mind, attacked Amon. Either Amon had been caught off guard or had purposefully moved slowly because as Paul's weapon came down and struck Amon on his shoulder, Amon dropped his sword and stared wide-eyed at Paul. Paul was overjoyed that after six months he had finally struck Amon.

"Paul? Do you see what happened?"

"I know! I hit you!"

"But how did you hit me? You know how fast I am."

"Yes, but you were moving slowly this time."

"No, Paul, I was not. I moved at the speed I always move."

"But I saw you this time. You moved slowly. I thought you were giving me a chance."

"Paul! Have I ever given you a chance or gone lightly on you?"

Then the realization struck Paul.

"Yes, Paul. You have the gift. I thought you would. It's in your blood."

"What do you mean—in my blood? How do you know? You don't even know who my father was."

"Yes, Paul, I am the older of the two brothers. A student of Master Halack," began Amon.

"But if the gift runs in my blood," interrupted Paul, "then I inherited this gift from my father, who also had the gift. He was one of the two brothers...your brother!" Paul gasped. "You're my... uncle! My...my father's brother," Paul said slowly.

"Yes, Paul. I have known who you are since I found you in the Nerek Mountains. Only now have you discovered who I am."

"My father was a Paladin captain! Why did he never tell me this or that I have an uncle?" Paul stood, picked up a rock, and threw in into the forest with a shout. "No!" He regained his composure. "Why didn't he tell me? What did he think he would accomplish by holding this from me? Why!"

"Paul, I understand why you feel this way. Sit down, we need to talk."

Paul shot an angry glare at Amon and sat down.

"Your father and I saw some brutal things while in the service of the Paladin. Things that make your blood run cold. It's not all glory, Paul. Your father never wanted you to have to experience that. He thought that if you knew who he was, you would try and follow in his footsteps. To him it was better that you didn't know."

Paul was quiet and his hands were trembling.

"Why did my father become king if you were the elder of the two?" asked Paul.

"When my father, your grandfather, was killed in the Jedarian War, in his will that he left with my mother, he said that government of the Kingdom was to be given to the younger brother! I wanted the Kingdom. It was rightfully mine! I was the older brother! So I came here, to this island. Over time I trained myself to accept it. Then when your father died, and you were in the mountains, I became the rightful successor. Instead I brought you here. Your mother knows you are here and safe with me."

"You gave up the Kingdom to train me?" Paul asked incredulously.

"Paul, I see the makings of something great in you, greatness that I will never know. I have finally found my purpose. In the long run you will far outdistance me, Paul. I have sensed it in you, and you have proven me right today. You have the gift, nephew."

Paul felt a tingling sensation down the back of his neck. How could he surpass Amon? He felt the pull of destiny on his life as Amon spoke of greatness and purpose. He had been given a gift, many gifts, and he was here to be trained to be a great warrior—but for what reason? Where was this all leading? He felt the responsibility of a great purpose. He was in the Kingdom for a very special reason.

Unveiled

† † † † † † †

Amon walked slowly through the cold desert region. He walked past a lone palm tree and looked around to make sure no one was following. He walked to a lone cave and stood high above the barren area. In the light of the moon he saw it—the narrow hole, slightly larger than the width of a man. Amon drew his cloak around him and lowered himself down. As he dropped quietly to the bottom, the musty smell of the tunnel engulfed him. He ignored it and began walking. The tunnel was crudely cut but served his purpose well. It was too dark for him to see with his eyes so he sensed the edges of the wall using his training. He traveled this way for several hours, then stopped to rest. This tunnel was a dark, narrow, cold place, but he knew it was the only way off the island. He had been through it many times before and had never had any trouble. The tunnel extended from the desert on Zirikaan to the mainland, coming out a few short miles from Calarath. He lay down to rest but kept his ears alert. He tried to get some sleep, but he could never sleep in these tunnels; they were too dark—too evil. Too much like the creatures that dug them.

Amon had captured an Ashkah captain and forced the captain and his crew to dig this tunnel to the island. Amon had been amazed at how they had navigated underground. Once they had reached the surface, he had killed them all. Amon stood up and continued walking along the wall. The only turn in a tunnel was when he would be surfacing. He would have to follow this wall until then. He walked on in silence and thought. Had he been doing a good job training Paul? Had he trained Paul the right way?

Because the tunnel was so long, it took two days to travel it. Amon could do it in less because he required little sleep, and with so much on his mind and so determined to get to Calarath, he walked quickly. Despite the gravity of the situation, he smiled. He wondered what Paul would think when he found that Amon was nowhere in sight. He knew the first thing Paul would do was look for his tracks. However, Amon had made sure that he would lose his tracks in the desert. He walked on in the quiet, empty dark.

Paul had finished his morning run and had already made breakfast. He had not seen Amon yet, but that was not uncommon. Paul often went an entire day without finding Amon. He knew he would see his uncle soon. He walked to the cliffs. The one he normally climbed looked so easy now. He decided to try one of the taller, steeper ones. He quickly mounted and started climbing. He was sure that Amon would be proud if he made it to the top. He pulled himself onto the first crevice, and he was off. There was nothing in the world that could stop him. He was going to climb this rock face. He thought of his time on the island. He thought of how he had changed. Before he began working at the Oldyers,' he never thought that he would actually be working every day. Now after being on this island, he had changed so much. He was stronger and faster, yes, but he was also a lot more confident. He was proud of what he had accomplished, but still, even though he was beginning to become more of the man his father wanted him to be, he didn't want to take the throne. He didn't want to be king because he could never live up to what his father had done. He sighed and continued climbing.

. . . . .

Amon's head shot up instantly as he heard a slight sound in the dark. He pulled out his sword silently and continued on in the dark. It was not uncommon for him to encounter a stray Ashkah or two checking out a strange tunnel, but Amon wondered why they had come out this far. He stopped. There was no more sound.

It was only a few hours journey until he would be out of this dark tunnel for good. He traveled in the dark, thinking of Paul's training, of Paul's destiny. Amon was not a thinker, he was a doer. He would rather be doing something than thinking about the best way to do it. He hadn't thought much about how he was training Paul, but he had tried to mimic what he had been taught as a Paladin captain. He continued and knew that very soon he would be above ground. Then he heard it; it came from behind him, and it lasted not more than a few split seconds. It was the scream of an Ashkah. Amon spun and in lightning quick movements struck the Ashkah through its chest. It slumped quietly to the ground, the sound echoing off the tunnel walls. Amon wiped the dark blood off his sword, sheathed it, and walked on. He hoped that the Ashkah wasn't a scout for some party. Then again, he was getting tired of inactivity, and the slight adrenaline rush it would give him would be appreciated. The darkness seemed to lighten as he drew nearer to the exit hole. It was less than a third of a mile, and already Amon was beginning to see light. He quickened his pace. He remembered driving the weak Ashkah captain with his mind and forcing them to drill the tunnel. He hadn't seen what tools they had used to construct a tunnel or how they had created it with a direct line, not going higher or lower. Suddenly he came to the opening. Unlike the one at Zirikaan, this one sloped up and was an easy ascent to the surface. As the sunlight poured onto his face, he stopped for a few minutes to give his eyes time to adjust after thirty-six hours of utter darkness. He walked stealthily away from the tunnel and toward the city of Calarath where he would meet the queen.

. . . . .

Paul was getting nervous. It had been over a day and a half since he had last seen Amon, and he had been looking all over the island. What if Amon had abandoned him? He hadn't even shown Paul the way off this island. Paul had tracked Amon's steps to the desert but had lost his trail in the wind-blown sand. Paul was annoyed but had not despaired. Amon would have to be on the island...somewhere. Then the thought struck him. What if this was an exercise to see how Paul survived on his own? What if Amon was watching to see how Paul had learnt and whether he would depend on Amon to help him survive? Paul resolved to show Amon that he was indeed capable of doing this alone. He determined to pass this test and show Amon he was worthy of his respect. He gathered some wood and started a fire. He would do the best he could to avoid panic. When Amon finally showed himself, Paul would have a few questions to ask him.

"Your Majesty, I am here, as you summoned. I am sorry that it took so long for me to come; I had to make sure that the boy was capable of surviving on his own while I was away." Amon spoke quietly to his sister-in-law and Paul's mother, the queen. He stood in the queen's conference chamber. They sat opposite each other in the large wooden chairs, drinking some of the finest wine in the Kingdom. Amon's thumb caressed the intricately designed insignia of the glass as the smell of the wine brought back memories of his greater days in Jedar.

"Yes, Amon, I am glad you are here." Amon noted that she sounded tired. "How is Paul doing?"

"Milady, you would be surprised at how well he is doing. He is stronger, fitter, runs every day, works, trains, fights, studies. I am impressed with how much he takes on in a single day."

"Paul? Paul is working?"

"Yes, milady, a lot has changed in Paul. But I am afraid of one thing. He is hesitant to be who he is born to be. Hesitant to accept how great his destiny is. He doesn't believe in himself. He has confidence, sometimes too much, but he has a very small view of his own destiny."

The queen sighed. She had lost her beloved husband six months earlier and had not seen her son since the funeral. "Do you think he is ready to take the role of king?"

Amon was quiet for a moment. He paused and looked at the pictures in the glass, images depicting a Kingdom that would never be his. "Paul is ready, milady, but I am afraid that he wouldn't take the position simply because he is afraid that he will never live up to what Mark accomplished."

The queen stood, and Amon rose with her. "I am afraid of this, Amon. Now we must meet with the War Council; that is why you are here." The queen strode out of the room, and Amon followed. When she had sent him the coded message of urgency, a purple cloth stained with blood, he knew that something was up. This was it. This was where he would find out what was going on. He followed the queen through the castle halls. They entered the War Council Hall where a long wooden table was prominently situated in the middle. Around the table stood important looking generals and officials, all standing to attention. As the queen and Amon entered, there was an audible gasp throughout the room as general after general recognized the lost Paladin captain. All of these men had been young soldiers when Amon had fought at Jedar. On the walls were large maps of Calarath and the entire Kingdom. Amon looked at one quickly and saw that the Isle of Zirikaan had been removed. That was clever of the queen. There had been reports of Sir Gelaray trying to reach the island in search of the rumored Orun Oak Forest. Amon took the place next to the queen.

The queen began, "It has long been thought that King Mark was the only Paladin remaining after the Jedarian War. An agreement between the brothers stated that Captain Amon's existence would be a closely guarded secret and that his request to be given the Isle of Zirikaan as his domain would be honored. For this reason the Isle does not show on our maps as part of the Kingdom. Today, in the face of great evil, our Captain returns." The generals broke into grand applause; then they all sat in unison. One of the leading generals looked around the room and then stood. Amon noticed that he was a highly decorated general in full formal attire, the Calarath insignia embroidered on his lapel. He decided that this general obviously had seen much combat, but he did not remember him in the Jedarian War.

The general began, "Your return is a great honor to this castle and to this city, but with all due respect, we need to know where your loyalties lie."

Amon answered, "My loyalties are to this family." The general nodded, satisfied. "Our city and our Kingdom have always been places of peace. We have always lived in harmony with one another. When we lost Jedar, we knew that something major was on its way. With the recent death of King Mark and the unknown location of the other Paladin captain, the Dark One is finally making his next move. We have been watching the desert line grow in the last thirty years. Before the war, it was a small, unnoticeable feature in the landscape. Twenty years ago, it had nearly doubled in size because of the tunnels from the Jedarac Wars. They have pushed far up the east coast and now control that peninsula. To the west, the coastal town of Faron has been attacked. Luckily it was a small army of Ashkah, and the town did not fall, but we are concerned. We must fight back."

One of the other important looking officials spoke up, "General Owra, how can you fight back a desert?" The others around the table nodded in agreement

Amon interrupted, "I can remember a time when the queen had to lead a battle. I was a young Paladin, still in training, and this queen led us to victory. I will tell you the story:

"Our army was separated from the dark army by a valley, with one or two bridges across it. The night before the battle, all the soldiers polished their shields and poured oil into the valley. When the Ashkah charged, the reflection of the morning sun on the smooth shields blinded them, and they fell into the valley or stopped at the bridges. Our archers had easy targets. When the majority of them were on the bridges, we cut the ropes, letting them fall. Then we shot flaming arrows into the oiled valley, setting the army on fire.

"With all due respect, Generals, her Majesty is probably more capable in battle than most of you. I would not hesitate to follow her into battle again." Amon looked across and caught a hint of a grateful smile on the queen's mouth.

"But who will the next king be?" said a voice.

Amon continued, slightly annoyed. "It will be none of you. It will be the true heir to the throne, Paul, son of Mark. When he is ready, he will come back and lead us!" Amon looked around the table. His eye caught that of the Master Cognoscente. Not a sound was heard. The hall was silent in shock.

Then the first general, presumably General Owra, spoke up, "You are obviously unaware that Paul is dead. He ran away and starved or was killed."

"No, General, he is with me."

The room went quiet again. He continued, "I am training him on the island. As a Paladin captain, I am passing on to him what I was taught." Amon looked around the table before sitting and again caught the curious eye of the Master Cognoscente.

It was a few moments before anyone spoke. Finally the second speaker spoke up, "Regardless of who is leading us, we still have a formidable force rising against us. All of our scouts have disappeared, and the outpost we had near Jedar has been destroyed again. We can't keep an eye on the enemy from here in Calarath. Tunnels are forming near the Plains of Goash, and we fear that all the small villages near those plains are in great danger. Our armies are weak and spread thin throughout the Kingdom. We need more men. More warriors."

Amon's calm voice contrasted with the desperate one of the previous speaker, "What we need is better trained men and better trained warriors."

One of the generals, an old looking one, who had been quiet for most of the conversation now spoke up, "Our struggle isn't against the Ashkah or the desert. Our struggle and our battle is against the ruler of the dark realm—the Dark One himself. If we destroy the head, the rest of the body will die."

"But who would be brave enough to go up against the Dark One? And even if someone was, how could you fight him? He is not in human form or even any physical form. He is a dark demonic spirit," declared General Owra.

With this being said, the idea was dismissed. Amon felt the tension between the leaders. All these years of hiding away from the darkness and small skirmishes had left them without unity. Without a king they squabbled like little children. The conversation continued to discussion of new weapons and armor as well as new placements for outposts. Amon listened to the conversation but said nothing. Finally it was time for the queen to speak again. She stood and the room went quiet. Only the soft sound of the flame in the corner hearth could be heard. Her commanding voice had an edge of weariness to it. *The responsibilities of the Kingdom are bearing down on her,* Amon thought.

"Generals, we see that there is a threat, a great terrible threat, and we must find a way to stop it. When my son returns, he will lead us." Amon noticed that the small fire in the hearth seemed larger than it had at first, as if inspired by the queen's words. They all rose, the sound of heavy boots snapping to attention on the stone floor accompanying them. Amon walked out with the queen. As they exited, the large long glass windows sent sunlight streaming into the hall. The queen turned and looked out.

"Milady, with your permission, I have other business to attend to."

"Of course, Amon. Thank you." Amon nodded and walked off. She reminded him a lot of Paul. Amon turned a corner and found the Master Cognoscente walking towards him.

"Ahh, so the great Paladin captain finally returns." A twinkle lighted in the old man's eyes. "So I hear you have the duty of training the young one."

"Indeed. Master Cognoscente, perhaps you can help me."

"Of course, Amon. Is something wrong with Paul?"

"That's just it; Paul seems hesitant to believe in himself. He has limited his own destiny."

The Master Cognoscente's deep baritone voice was calm. "The two most common problems with greatness are pride and reluctance. Either they become too full of themselves, too sure of what they can do, or they become small and fear that their destiny is less than what it is. Paul seems to be the latter."

"But how can I let him see who he really is?"

"A man cannot believe in himself until he knows himself. But a man cannot know himself if he does not know his own spirit. Let Paul see his spirit, and then he will start to understand what an important role he plays in this great struggle. Good day, Amon." The Cognoscente nodded and walked slowly away. The words still rang in Amon's mind. He felt something of his own inadequacies. He was training the next king; if he failed to conquer this problem in Paul, they would never have a king. Now Amon was wondering if he really believed in who *he* was. If he couldn't believe in himself, how could he convince Paul to believe in himself? He headed back, eager to get to Paul. Now that he saw what a great threat was at hand, he could no longer waste time in the little things. Paul needed to be ready soon. Amon sighed.

. . . . .

Paul had finished his run and was doing his daily chores. It was the second morning that he hadn't seen Amon, but he was doing everything stronger than ever because with Amon everything was a test. How he had managed to conceal himself entirely from Paul, but still watch him, puzzled Paul, but Paul nevertheless always kept his guard up and did everything he was supposed to do. He chopped wood, he climbed, and he ran. *Today*, he thought, *I will do something different, to prove myself to Amon.* He had decided to build a wooden cabin out of the special Orun Oak. He had managed to find a newly fallen tree and was thankful for not having the task of cutting down one of those massive oaks. He set to work chopping and cutting and building. At the end of the day he had almost cut half of the wood that he needed. This Orun Oak was strong but still manageable. They had fought for months with sticks made from Orun Oak, and they had not chipped. He continued his job. When he looked up, he noticed that the sun was going down, and soon it would be too dark for him to work. Amon could appear any day, and Paul wanted to have this done. However, it was impossible for him to work in the dark, and he walked back to their shelter. They stayed in the great caves, and Paul had his own cavern. He walked in and started a fire and prepared the small animal that he had killed earlier. He knew that it was a test, but he was beginning to feel very lonely on the island. He was missing Amon. He never thought he would. He chuckled. He could survive on his own, and he would have something to show for it too. He pulled his animal skin rug nearer to the fire and lay down to fall asleep. His muscles felt sore after an entire day of chopping the wood. He guessed that the wood became harder and stronger once it had been cut from the tree. While still alive, it seemed to be manageable enough, but when it was dead or separate, it was hard. He drifted to sleep thinking of plans for his new cabin.

As the sun peeked through the outer chamber and into Paul's chamber, a smell of morning rain came to Paul's nostrils. He sat up. Rain? It had never rained in the morning. Thinking of his run, he smiled and stepped out into it. It was a warm, tropical rain, not miserable and cold. He began his run with a brisk walk, and then slowly broke into a slow jog, and then into a quicker jog. Running in the rain kept him cooler than usual, and he decided to run further than normal. Amon would be proud to see that Paul didn't need him around so much. He jogged through the rain, letting it soak through his clothes. When he finally couldn't take any more, he dropped down into the sand and smiled. The rain continued to splash all around him. He got up and walked to where he had been working on his new cabin—a few small pieces of wood to show for an entire day's work. He feared he would not have it done by the time Amon showed himself again. At least he wanted the frame up. He retrieved his sharp axe from under a small rock where he had left it. He began chopping the wood, and it felt softer. The blade seemed to slice right through the wood. In a few short chops he had cut a small branch off the trunk. Amazed, he set to work. The live wood seemed to soften with rain. He would finish this and prove himself to Amon.

Amon walked back through the dreary tunnels. After spending another day in Calarath, he had finally decided he needed to head back to Paul. He had begun thinking of new ideas for Paul's training, ways to open Paul's mind to his spirit. Perhaps Paul would catch a glimpse of who he was born to be as the rightful heir to the throne and leader of the Kingdom. Amon knew that Paul had a great destiny, but he wondered how great this destiny was. Was Paul to lead the Kingdom against this present darkness that hung over the land—to fight back the evil? Amon knew that Paul was an excellent fighter, but he seemed to be a timid leader. Amon would have to change that. He walked on in silence and passed the rotting corpse of the Ashkah he had left dead on the path. The smell of a live Ashkah was sickening enough, but now that it was dead, the smell of its dark blood and rotting flesh assaulted Amon. He hurried past it.

A few days later Paul had finally constructed the basic framework of the cabin. He had even picked a strategic point for it, where it had a large open view but could not be seen. He thought Amon would be proud of that. Then he heard it, a rustle behind him and heavy footsteps. Amon. He spun around and followed the sound and found Amon looking at the ground and walking.

"Amon!"

"Hello, Paul. I am back."

"Back? Where did you go?"

"To the Kingdom. We have a lot of work to do."

"The Kingdom! I thought you were hiding, to see if I could survive on my own. Come and see what I've built." Paul rushed forward with the eagerness of a child showing his father his latest creation.

"You built this, Paul? While I was away?" He walked inside. "I see you've also picked a very strategic position for it. Well done, Paul." Amon was genuinely pleased. Paul had taken initiative and had shown strategic thinking which was crucial to a leader. Amon started to see the glimmer of hope that Paul could be the next king.

"It is a beautiful cabin, Paul, but I'm afraid it will never be finished."

"I could finish it! I know I could!" Paul said defensively.

"No, Paul, it's not that I don't think you would finish it. We must train harder...we will be leaving soon."

Heritage

† † † † † † †

In the next few days Amon pushed Paul's training harder than ever. He was determined to teach Paul to fight with his mind. The first lesson was sense deprivation. Amon blindfolded him and put wax in his ears. Paul panicked. His body trembled as he frantically tried to look around to see something. He couldn't see Amon, but he knew he was there and holding a hard stick of Orun Oak. He desperately wanted to pull the blindfold off, but he knew Amon wouldn't let him. All of a sudden the stick struck his side. Paul jumped in shock. Another blow slammed into his side, knocking the wind out of him. The next one came, and the next one, until Paul was bruised and sore. Finally Amon pulled out the wax from Paul's ears.

"What can you see, Paul?"

"Nothing," shouted Paul.

Amon plugged up his ears again and started attacking. Paul was struck time after time. Suddenly Paul caught a glimpse of a lighter shade of dark. Then he realized that this lighter shade of gray was Amon. It moved and dodged, but Paul could see no more. He couldn't see enough to know where Amon was about to attack. Thoughts raced through his mind as he tried hard to see more.

Paul coughed as a musty, dank smell choked up his lungs. Amon had decided that Paul's training was sufficient, given the situation, and had decided to leave the island. It was the middle of the day when Amon showed Paul across the island and to the small tunnel.

"Paul, it's too dark to see anything. Try closing your eyes and see if you can sense anything with your mind."

"Why should I close my eyes if it's dark?"

"To focus. To remove your senses."

Paul closed his eyes and calmed himself. Amon had told him earlier that when you are anxious and worked up, your body will try to take precedence over your mind. Instead, he had to be at peace. He tried harder to see something. He felt nothing. He sighed, and they walked on in silence. Amon was afraid that Paul had become too reliant on his senses.

They arrived on the outskirts of the city of Calarath. There were no people around, just a few lazy cows grazing in the green meadows. Paul looked around and stopped when he caught sight of the castle. It was far away, barely visible, but Paul saw it and longed to see his mother. It had been seven months since he had seen her. He followed Amon away from the disguised opening, and they started across the plains. They would not be stopping in Calarath, but continuing passed it. Along the way they passed lonely farmhouses and fields. After a few hours of walking Amon turned and stopped at one of them. He knocked three times on the door, then paused and knocked twice. A hurrying could be heard inside the house, and soon a common looking man stood before them. Amon smiled when he saw him and shook hands with the man.

"Paul, this is Hinom. He was one of the Paladin in training with me. He never finished the training, but he is still a good warrior and a great friend. He will supply horses and a place to rest for the night."

Paul looked at the man with respect. He looked younger than Amon, with a sturdy, muscular frame. They walked inside to a small cozy house. As Paul stepped in, a memory of the Oldyers' house flooded into his mind. The warm little fireplace and the wooden floors gave the house a welcoming feeling. Hinom introduced Paul and Amon to his wife, Mary, who hurried into the kitchen to make extra dinner. The men sat down in the large wooden chairs and talked. Paul was fascinated. Here was a Paladin captain, his uncle, talking with one of his old students. Paul wondered why this student had never finished the training. Perhaps with the death of Amon's father, Amon had left any and all students and headed to Zirikaan. The men talked about the wars and battles they had seen. It turned out that Hinom had been a poor farm boy who had shown some skill in fighting. Amon had seen him one day and decided to train him as a Paladin. Paul had always thought that the Paladin were only from the royal bloodline or the high nobles.

Dinner was a delicious cooked meal, better than Paul and Amon had eaten for months. They retired happily to their rooms that night. As Paul lay awake in his bed looking up at the thatched roof, he thought of the last few months. He thought back to how he had been at the Oldyers' and couldn't believe how stupid he had been to charge a Flamethrower. He knew better now. Finally he grew tired and rolled over and fell asleep. Tomorrow would be a long day.

Paul was up early and had gone for a run to settle his excitement. Today they would travel through the small forest south of Calarath and then sail across the Bay of Hope. Amon smiled proudly when he saw Paul returning from his run. He had taught the boy well. Paul had become more disciplined than when he found him in the mountains. They had a quick breakfast and said their farewell to Hinom and Mary. The horses were loaded for a journey of a few days, and Paul was eager to get going quickly. Amon and Paul rode side by side until they came across a small stream. They filled their canteens with water and prepared to embark again. Paul could see the edges of the forest ahead of them.

It was midday when the shade of the trees finally welcomed them. The afternoon sun had been beating down on them since they left the stream, and Paul was feeling hot and edgy. The cool forest air quickly changed his mood. The trees of the forest were not Orun Oak but were a mixture of regular trees. Paul had studied trees when he was growing up in the castle but had never really paid attention enough to remember which trees were which. They walked through the forest for the rest of the day and through most of the night. They stopped only for a short rest. Amon was in a hurry, and Paul sensed his eager attitude. Amon was taking Paul to the Jedarian Ruins to show Paul what he was fighting for. One of the First Ones had once said, "Before you can be a leader, you must know where you've come from, where you are, and where you are going." Amon was afraid that Paul knew too little about his heritage. He knew that Paul had studied it in the castle, but it was one thing to study something and quite another to experience it. Amon wanted Paul to experience the loss of Jedar. He had great faith in Paul and was afraid that perhaps sometimes he expected too much of the boy. He was the most capable potential captain Amon had ever seen. As the captain of the most elite fighting force in the Kingdom, the Paladin captains would search the land for the best warriors and then train them to be the level of the Paladin. All this ran through Amon's mind as they stopped to rest. Paul had drifted off to sleep. They had barely slept since their stay at Hinom's house. He turned over and tried to sleep. He knew he would need the energy when the sun arose. He lay there with a soft wind blowing across his cheek. Slowly sleep came along with disturbing dreams of the battles of the Jedarac Wars.

Paul and Amon woke within minutes of each other. Paul was going to take a run, but Amon told him they had no time. Every moment that they spent, the armies of Maugrax came closer to conquering the land. They traveled out of the forest and to the edge of the bay. The Bay of Hope was calm, and Amon was an excellent sailor. The horses they had been given were left with a friend at the port. Later the horses would be taken back to Hinom. They had arranged for a boat and quickly boarded. It was a large vessel, and Amon piloted it expertly. It took them a mere day to cross to the shore nearest Jedar. They had had an excellent wind and the seas had given them no trouble. They got off the boat as the sun was setting and made a small camp. Paul was surprised that Amon didn't want to go as far as they could, but he seemed to have slowed down now that they had crossed the Bay. They practiced the mental exercises once more.

"Paul, do you know why you are having a hard time seeing with your spirit?"

Paul was silent.

"You are too influenced by your senses and your mind. They cloud your ability to 'unlock' your mind. When you are in a battle, you *see* the blade coming at you, you use your mind to tell your body to move, and you *feel* the blade striking yours. In your mind you are not limited by the physical limitations that most people think you are."

Paul considered this for a moment. "If you are not limited by such things as gravity or anything of that nature, then you could perform superhuman feats."

Amon eyed Paul. He caught on to the idea quickly. "Indeed you could. But you would have to believe that you could. As amazing as it sounds, anyone could jump thirty feet if they believed. The problem with our minds is that they take the input from our senses and tell us that this is the absolute reality—that there are limitations. You must be able to break those limitations, for there are no real limitations, just the ones your mind creates."

Paul seemed confused. There was something about this that

rang true within him. It was true, but it sounded so far-fetched. It sounded like one of the tales he would hear in the courts of his father. They sat in silence for the rest of the night. Amon was afraid that he had come across too quickly. He remembered that this process had taken months for him when he was in training. But they didn't have months. Paul needed to learn quickly. He would have to train harder than he had. They left the fire roaring. It was a cold night, and the fire also gave them protection from any animals that happened to be lurking near them.

Amon woke up. The day was gray, and the fire was smoldering. Paul was sleeping soundly by the fire. They got up and quickly prepared to leave. Today Amon wanted to get to Jedar. He hadn't been back himself since the battle, and he didn't know what the ruins looked like. They rode for the better part of the day and finally came upon a large archway. The archway was tall and old, and the top half of the stones was missing. The large wooden doors lay shattered in pieces and off their hinges. They dismounted from the horses they had bought upon landing and walked through the opening. Paul stared open-mouthed at the scene before him. Dry stone, dusty after nearly twenty years of no use, was cracked and blackened from fire. The houses nearest to them were missing roofs and walls. Nothing moved but the two strangers. As Amon took in the scene he felt a tear come to his eye. He had known the people who had lived in these houses. Paul walked forward and felt something crunching beneath his feet. He lifted his foot and saw a human hand lying there. Then he saw them. Hundreds of skeletons lying scattered throughout the courtyard. They all held that screaming face that every skeleton seems to possess. Some had old, rusted swords in their hands; others seemed to have died with loved ones in their arms. Paul and Amon picked their way through the open graveyard and through the city. Lining the streets were statues of the great people of Jedar. Unlike most statues, these were reserved not only for royalty but also for any who had shown great service to the city or Kingdom. Now, as Paul looked at them, he saw that most had crumbled or were missing heads and showed nothing of their former glory.

With every step he took sadness swelled inside Paul. They came upon the Great Library. It was the only building that was the same height as the Lyceum and was equal in size. They walked up the flight of fifty or more stairs. The intricate pillars, covered with dust and grime and dirt, were half destroyed and lay in pieces across the roads. Inside the Great Library it was obvious that a fire had broken out. Amon's words rang in Paul's mind, "This is what evil does, Paul. It destroys." Destruction was everywhere in this city. He scanned across the bookshelves and saw the charred remains of hundreds of thousands, maybe millions, of books. The staircases were all destroyed, cutting off access to the top level. Paul stepped out of the quiet building into the quiet streets. He could picture this city when it was thriving. The stillness even got to Amon, who had been in the city when it was alive. As they walked past the old buildings and houses, Amon began to wonder what would have happened if he had been king instead of his brother. He would have prepared for the battle, made sure that the defenses were properly manned and ready. He would have evacuated the people earlier. They stopped in front of one house where a dying mother had shielded her little child in vain from the onslaught. Evidently not all the women and children had made it out in time. Amon turned away, knowing that he could have done better. There were so many corpses, so many small skeletons, that he was sickened by the thought. They walked around in silence. Eventually Paul couldn't take it anymore.

"Why did it fall? Why wasn't it better defended?" he shouted, a tear streaming down his face.

Amon looked at Paul sadly. "It would have been." Paul sensed a bitter note in Amon's voice. "The warriors were not properly trained, and the king didn't think it was necessary to build more defenses."

Paul knew that Amon was referring to his father and ignored the comment. He looked around and saw the hundreds of corpses, some with armor still on, some clutching spears and shields. Some lay without arms or legs. It was a grotesque sight, Amon knew, but he couldn't shield Paul any longer. The boy had to see everything. He had to get a complete view of what had happened at Jedar. They walked through a few houses and buildings, all of which horrified Paul. Amon had grown numb to seeing death as a Paladin captain, but seeing his city in ruins brought tears to his eyes. They marched through the city and then came to the great castle. Paul was astounded. Amon knew that Paul thought that Calarath's castle was the greatest in the land. They walked through the massive courtyard that had stone staircases leading to a myriad of different rooms. They walked through the castle's own arms room and saw swords, shields, banners, spears, and other instruments of war lying scattered across the room. It was evident that this castle had been the city's last stand. The amount of bodies lying strewn across the many rooms showed what a massive loss this day had been. Paul asked the obvious question that came to mind after seeing so many bodies.

"Why didn't they bury them? Why did they leave them to rot?"

"The dark army patrolled the city for months and months afterwards. No one dared come near here because of the myths."

"Myths? What myths?"

"It was said about the ruins that evil spirits dwelt within the buildings, that the Ashkah had built a fortress around it. But as you can see they were myths." They walked through the rest of the rooms of the palace in silence. They walked into the throne room. They saw the royal throne smashed and in pieces. The once brilliant luster of the pure gold seat was now dark and black.

Amon walked around slowly. He bent down and picked up a coin. He wiped the ash off with his finger and handed it to Paul. It was no bigger than Paul's thumb in diameter but was heavy. Paul guessed it was made of pure gold. It held an intricate picture of a city and a castle towering above it. Flags were flying from the castle and a banner stretched across the top. On the banner in large letters were words Paul didn't know or understand. He turned the coin around in his hand and marveled at it. This coin was obviously of some importance. It was not merely a coin of currency or trade; it seemed to be a royal coin, a symbol. Amon stood looking at Paul. The air was cold, and the room smelt musty.

They walked out and into the daylight, which was growing darker. Amon looked around then stated that they would have to spend the night in the ruins. The thought made Paul shudder. They found a mostly intact home and proceeded to make something of the remains of the beds and cloth. When Paul finally lay down, he could not sleep. The thoughts of death and loss and sorrow and pain made him sick. He thought of his grandparents growing up in the city and then finally losing it all. His father would have seen this city too. Sorrow swelled inside of him. He got up out of bed and walked to the window. It was dark, but the moon was bright and bathed the city in a mysterious blue veil. He knew that they still had a lot to look at as Jedar was a massive city. The world was quiet and dead. Nothing moved. It seemed that nothing had moved since they had arrived at Jedar. Every shadow stood deathly still. Every house sat deathly quiet. Paul sighed and fell back onto the bed. He knew he needed to sleep, but he had a slight fear of sleeping. Even when nothing moved, it felt too quiet. It felt too still. He was half expecting an Ashkah to pop out from under his bed and run a hard blade through his back. He kept his eyes open and his mind alert for as long as he could. Finally somehow he managed to find some rest and reassurance in his mind and drifted off to sleep.

. . . . .

He dreamed of Jedar. It was magnificent. Everywhere he looked in his dream world, he saw people smiling, children playing. He walked through the city and looked at how amazing it looked. After seeing the ruins of certain buildings, he could imagine what those buildings were like before. He was amazed. Then suddenly, like one massive arrow, the city was plunged into darkness. Flaming balls flew into the city and were spreading the Gray Slime. Fires were everywhere; people were screaming. A flashback of the Flamethrower's attack on the village of Egon came to him. This was far worse. The main gates were shut, but Paul knew that they would break through. It was as if he knew what would happen before it would. Suddenly he thought perhaps he could change the future. He ran through the city to the castle. He saw an old man hurriedly talking to a group of eight warriors. In his hand was a small gold coin. Suddenly he spun around, and Paul saw the black evil eyes of a large Ashkah. It swung its twisted blade and...

Paul sat up sweating and breathing hard. It had all been a dream. Of course it had. This felt so much more real. He looked around and saw that dawn was just breaking. He threw the torn covers off and joined Amon at the door. They continued out to the worn roads. They walked to a massive structure at the heart of the city. The Lyceum. Amon led Paul up the many stairs and to one of the large pillars. Paul could see that this one was mostly intact, and he could even see the pictures engraved. Amon showed him how to read them, starting at the highest point and reading in a clockwise spiral downwards. Paul saw in pictures the recounting of the first encounter with the Deformed Ones and the Flamethrowers and how they behaved. It told of a scouting party digging a well. The king had forbidden it, but they had gone ahead anyway. They were digging when the ground below them collapsed into a hole, a tunnel. Thus evil was released. Paul read about the first slaughters, the first Flamethrowers. At the bottom of the pillar the story ended with a word of caution about the Flamethrowers and a word of wisdom about good and evil. They walked past the pillars and through the broken doors. Inside an enormous fifty-foot high ceiling opened above them. The middle was completely destroyed, and sunlight poured through the wide opening. The room itself must have been at least 50,000 square feet. At each end were many doors that led to other rooms Amon said were classrooms, small halls, and others.

Paul was getting bored of the ruins—too much of the same destruction stories were wearing him down. Amon decided to change his plans a bit. They walked towards the castle but passed it and then turned. They were now facing the back side of the castle, which was by no means inferior to the front side. Amon took measured paces forward, then reached down and grabbed something. Paul saw that it was a rope and pulled it, opening a hatch. Amon flung it open and a cloud of dust puffed into the air. Paul walked over, excited, and peered in. It was a short drop, and Paul and Amon slipped quietly in. They walked a few feet before Amon picked up an old torch and lit it with a small flint he carried in his pocket. The flickering light cast eerie shadows onto the mysterious walls. They followed the winding tunnels and came to a small room. The clean air and walls surprised Paul. It didn't look like this room had been abandoned at all. On the wall across from Paul hung a large picture of a shield with a picture of a fiery orange bird on a blue background and two swords crossing the shield. A green banner flew across the top and simply read: "Paladin." At the bottom of the shield was a blue banner that read: "The Warriors of the Kingdom." Paul's mind reeled. This was a Paladin hideout. He looked around and noticed weapons of every kind, labeled and sorted. Books and documents referring to battles and strategies were scattered throughout the room.

In the center of the room on a stone pedestal sat a large glass case. In the case sat a sword on a cloth of red velvet. The inscription on a plaque next to the sword read: "The Sword of Jedar. May it be wielded by the greatest of warriors." Amon worked with some unseen hinge on the case and opened it. He picked up the sword. He balanced it in his hands, feeling the weight, then turned to Paul. He made Paul kneel and put out his hands to receive the sword. Paul gripped the elegant handle and took the sword. It was lighter than he expected. It was obviously one of the best swords, if not *the* best sword in the entire Kingdom. A single blue jewel sat in the center of the hand guard. There were elegant engravings near the handle and pommel in some language Paul couldn't read. Amon pulled a scabbard from under the case and handed it to Paul, simply saying, "Your new sword, Paul." They walked back up to the daylight and Paul examined his weapon.

Iniꞇiaꞇion

† † † † † † †

Amon and Paul had been talking for nearly an hour. Paul had sat gripped, fascinated with the history that Amon poured out to him. Amon could probably have written a book purely from what he had memorized. He had an amazing memory and could recount a battle with gripping details. Paul asked questions about the Paladin, the castle, the city, and everything he wanted to know about Jedar. Amon patiently answered all of his questions, and Paul was exuberant. That night was unlike any other night for Paul. Had they been on the Isle of Zirikaan, they would have built a fire and sat on their logs and talked. However, Amon warned Paul that a fire would be too suspicious and would attract attention from any wandering Ashkah. It was probably more dangerous at night than in the day because of the light. So Paul and Amon sat in the open fields behind the castle under the bright stars and the shining moon and talked for hours. After the conversation had died down Paul pulled out the leather bound book that Amon had given him earlier. Although it was dark, the moon shone brightly enough for Paul to see that the pages were blank.

"Amon, what am I supposed to do with a blank book?"

"Write in it Paul. Use it as a chronicle for you to look back and learn from." Amon lay down and closed his eyes. The night was bright enough for Paul to barely manage to see. He started his first entry:

Today, like yesterday, was a day of history. Amon and I walked through the ruins of Jedar—so much destruction. After what my teachers have told me about Jedar and now seeing the ruins, I can start to imagine what this magnificent city was like. The architecture is better than even Calarath's. We walked around silently, looking at the old buildings, Amon only saying a few words to tell me what the building used to be. I find it so fascinating but so terrible. At times I can't even bear to look at the skeletons of small children who never managed to evacuate to Calarath. Amon also showed me to a hidden Paladin hideout. He has given me a new sword and a magnificent one at that. We did some light sparring with swords today. It's a lot different from Orun Oak. The sword seems to be one of the finest made swords I have ever seen. Amon seems to hold it in high regard; this was probably the sword of one of the most famous Paladins—perhaps his father's sword? Tomorrow we will continue through the ruins, but we must leave before dusk. We are to head back to Calarath. I will finally see my dear mother again for the first time in months. It has felt like many years. I have also changed so much; I hope she will be proud. I must end now for the meager light that this night offers is dwindling. I shall write more tomorrow.

Paul closed the book and spread out the blankets they were using as beds. It was a surprisingly warm night, and Paul lay looking at the stars. Tonight felt less threatening than the previous night. Perhaps because he was no longer sleeping in a dead man's abode. He was no longer sleeping among death. He turned over and closed his eyes.

Amon's eyes flew open. Dawn was breaking. Something was moving towards them, a dark figure. As Amon watched he saw that it was three or four figures riding on horses. He was mildly relieved. These were not Ashkah. Ashkah never rode horses; they were foot soldiers. Amon woke Paul and told him to be ready for anything. Amon kept a low profile. He closed his eyes and focused his mind.

If these were malicious creatures, he would sense them. In his mind he saw three white warriors riding on white horses. These people were friendly and were great warriors at heart. He stood but drew no more attention to himself.

Within a few minutes they were close enough to see distinct features. They wore black cloaks and black tunics but had a purple sash across their tunics signifying the queen's guard—the Guardsmen. They rode up to Amon and saluted him and Paul, who stood wide-eyed. One of the riders was Master Lugaro, his sword master. There were three of them, all roughly the same build, stocky, strong and muscular. They were tall but not lanky. One of them threw back his hood to reveal a smiling face and blond hair. Paul had seen this man countless times, running messages for his mother or even accompanying her on trips.

"Greetings, Captain Amon and Master Paul. I am Ryan, Captain of the queen's guard. We bring urgent news of a large party of Ashkah moving towards the Kraan River. We expect them to emerge from the desert some time tomorrow." Amon nodded and discussed details with the Captain. It was finally decided that Amon and Paul would ride with the queen's guard and eliminate the scouting party before they reached the river. The three Guardsmen rode away to get horses for Amon and Paul. In the meantime Amon wanted to finish off Paul's experience of Jedar.

There were a few things Paul had not seen. They continued their walk through the morbid city. They walked through old houses, large and small. The soft breeze outside stirred the ashes around them. There was a house with a book left open. Paul looked through the blackened pages and found one that was not burnt. It was a grammar book. Paul choked. Some small child had been doing his studies when the devastating attack had forced him to drop everything and run. How many others had been forced to leave everything behind to guarantee their safety and that of their families? He wanted to write another entry in his journal, but the Guardsmen had returned with horses and provisions. They mounted up, and Paul turned and looked sadly back at the ruins of Jedar. This was his heritage. His ancestors had lived and died in this city.

Amon and Paul peered over the edge of the cliff. In the small valley below them, an Ashkah army was camping for the night. The moon gave little light but just enough for Amon to see how many there were. Amon estimated that there were probably around four hundred of them. He knew that it wasn't much of a threat. He had taken on armies much larger than that before. They ducked down behind the cliff and spoke in whispers.

"Four hundred strong! How will we ever defeat such an army?" cried Paul quietly.

"Paul, you forget that I am a Paladin captain, and that you and I both have the ability of speed. When we engage that, we will be much faster than any Ashkah. We also have three of the queen's Guardsmen with us. They are also trained well in combat. Suffice it to say, the Ashkah army will be dead by morning."

"Morning? We're attacking now, at night? We can hardly see anything with this light!"

"One mustn't rely entirely on one's senses to fight," Amon said with a twinkle in his eye. He crept across to where the Guardsmen were whispering and told them the battle plan. After Amon and Paul came in, the Guardsmen would circle around and attack from behind. They would all spread out to give each other killing distance. When everything was in place, Amon led Paul down the backside of the tall hill and behind a large boulder. Paul knew that Ashkah were night dwellers, and he couldn't see why Amon wouldn't attack them in the day time when they were weaker. Nevertheless, he knew Amon would have some reason, and he drew his sword. Amon told him to wait for his signal.

Silently he mouthed, "One...two...three!"

They both leapt out from behind the boulder and went into action. Paul watched stunned as Amon suddenly shot forward in a blur. Paul focused himself, and then it happened. The Ashkah slowed down. He ran forward at his usual speed and started killing easily. The Ashkah moved in slow motion, and Paul could parry every single one of their attacks. In seconds he had killed eight Ashkah without getting a scratch. He heard a commotion to his left and realized that the guards would be moving in. The Ashkah had no chance; all they could see were two blurs, blades spinning and killing their comrades effortlessly.

Paul suddenly felt a burning pain near his shoulder and spun to see an Ashkah pulling back his twisted blade to kill Paul. He rolled out of the way and thrust his sword up the Ashkah's neck. He had lost his focus and had been trying to fight with what he could see and touch. He again calmed himself and let his gift engage. Everything slowed down slightly, and Paul again had the edge. The pain from his shoulder slipped into a dull sensation. Ashkah blood flew from his sword as he struck another warrior through the heart. He looked to his left and saw a Guardsman gracefully parry two swords, push them back, and slice off two Ashkah's heads in one fluid motion. Amon, ahead of him, was surrounded by a diminishing group of Ashkah.

He turned to the Ashkah nearest to him and preformed a move Amon had shown him in training. He parried the blade, then hit it away and used the momentum to spin around and force his sword into the dull gray flesh. The sword sliced right through the Ashkah's midsection, cutting him cleanly in half. Blood spilled from both halves, and Paul moved to the next enemy. He was surprised at how sharp his new sword was, but he didn't have time to wonder long because an Ashkah captain, marked with a helmet, the only Ashkah who wore any sort of armor, charged him. He carried two swords, each spinning furiously.

Paul panicked for a second, and the captain sped up. Paul had lost focus. Frantically he tried to calm the message his mind was screaming at him—to run and panic. It wasn't working. The captain was barely within striking distance when a shaft of an arrow sunk into the neck of the captain. He let out a guttural roar and slowed for just a second. It was all Paul needed to calm himself, and he leapt toward the oncoming enemy. As they met, Paul dodged one blade and parried the other. He spun around blindingly fast and forced his sword into the chest of the stunned Ashkah captain. He saw the bloody point of his sword sticking out of the impaled Ashkah's back. Paul stared, stunned. Though the Ashkah armor might have been cheap, his blade had sliced through it as easily as butter. He slid his blade out and let the dead Ashkah fall.

He was the last one. Paul turned and saw a Guardsman, bow in hand, looking very impressed with Paul. The battle was over, and it had been a matter of minutes. Amon made his way around a heap of corpses. Paul caught something out of the corner of his eye and spun to see what it was, but he was too late. It had disappeared. Amon, Paul, and the three Guardsmen made their way to the top of the hill where their horses waited, tied to a tree. The battle was over. Paul wiped his sword on the grass and slid it into the elegant sheath. He saw Amon look away at a distant hill.

"Paul, did you see that?"

"See what?"

"There was something that disappeared over that hill. Over there." He pointed to a far hill, the same one Paul thought he had seen something on.

"I might have seen something, but I wasn't sure."

They dismissed the idea a few moments later with the prospect of food. The guards prepared it while Amon and Paul talked. First they talked about the battle, and Amon seemed unusually interested in what Paul thought of the sword.

"It was amazing, and I didn't know how sharp it was. I could slice right through the Ashkah! And it wasn't heavy and clumsy; it felt almost as light as the Orun Oak sticks we trained with!"

Amon nodded, then turned to the bloody field they had left behind. The rotten stench of death had been too strong for them, and they had moved a few hundred feet away.

"Paul, I noticed that there were times you became unsure or panicked. When you did, you slowed down and had to fight on the physical level. You were almost in trouble when the Guardsman bought you those extra few seconds."

Paul was amazed. Even though Amon had had the most enemies and had been the busiest of them all, he had noticed every moment of Paul's battle and remembered them to discus with Paul. Paul pulled out the leather-bound book and moved closer to the fire for light. He began to write.

> Today Amon, the three Guardsmen, and I tracked the Ashkah army to this tall hill. Below it was the Ashkah army which had made camp. On the way here we had to pass through a deserted town near Jedar, one that had probably been an outpost. Amon and I talked about my new sword and even my mother. He said that after this battle, we would be heading north to Calarath, and I could spend a few days with her. And now onto the battle we just had. It must have lasted no more than a few minutes, but it felt longer and more drawn out. The gift that both Amon and I have played a major role in our victory. I was able to kill many Ashkah, including the Ashkah captain. I came out of the battle with nothing more than a small wound on my left shoulder. Amon came out with not a scratch. Ashkah surrounded him constantly. They were throwing themselves at him. I wasn't as scared during this battle as when I fought with the Oldyers. It wasn't all a blur and hard to see. It was clear, and I could think straight. We are about to eat. Tomorrow will be a day of travel.

Paul looked up and saw that the Guardsmen were handing out some cooked meat. He took his share and ate voraciously. He was hungry. After dinner they all sat around the fire and told stories about past battles, adventures, waiting sweethearts, and the Kingdom. The Guardsmen proved to be fascinating; Paul viewed them as a smaller, scaled down version of what the Paladin must have been. They were well trained, knowledgeable about a myriad of subjects, and disciplined. The king would always have a group of guards consisting of roughly 200 men. They would be used for dispatching confidential messages, fighting, and of course, as guards. The queen had inherited the Guardsmen from her husband, and they were all loyal to the death. They would put their lives on the line for their queen and Kingdom. They wore the same uniform with long green capes. Two had a bow and quiver strung over their shoulders in addition to the swords they all carried. The swords were identical except for a few engravings near the hilt. They had keen eyes but had a relaxed air about them. Paul had heard much about the guards but had always thought that they were strict and stern. He soon grew tired and lay down. He kept his eyes and ears open as long as he could, but weariness overtook him, and he drifted off into a satisfied sleep.

Egon

† † † † † † †

Amon had been quiet since they had left their camp earlier that morning. There was a heavy mist hanging over them, and they chatted among themselves as they rode. Paul contributed his share of stories and discussed tactics with one of the guard. Paul found out his name was Rainier, and he was the one who had saved Paul with his perfectly timed arrow. Paul, despite much training with a sword, had never really mastered the art of the bow. Rainier proved to be an excellent marksman. They would fire a shaft ahead of them into a tree and then ride to it and retrieve it. In this way Rainier taught Paul while they rode. The leader of the Guardsmen, Ryan, was a master swordsman, and his long blond hair was now blowing in a soft breeze. Their brown horses were unusual for the guards but were being used so as not to be noticed.

The sleek black stallions from the small remote town of Melbar were bred and trained to perfection. They were more common for a guard to ride, but in situations when they wanted to remain anonymous, they would ride the brown horses. Amon and Paul's horses were brown and slightly fat but nevertheless adequate for the task of journeying up to Calarath.

The sun had just reached its peak of high noon and was still shining brightly down on them when a shadow appeared on the horizon. Rainier looked with keen eyes to determine whether it was friend or foe. They hurried their horses behind large boulders that lined the road. Rainier pulled an arrow from his quiver and drew his bow silently; Master Lugaro had his blade ready, as well as a small dagger in his left hand. Ryan, who was slightly ahead of them drew his sword and crouched low. It seemed like hours before they heard the fast gallop of horse's hooves coming near them. The men were alert but not afraid. Ryan peered out from behind his boulder. The rider must have seen him, for he paused. Paul wondered what he would do next. The rider looked around, obviously suspicious. He pulled his bow out and knocked an arrow. He paused a moment, then looked up into the sun and sent the shaft flying into the air. Ryan sighed and gave the signal for the men to stand down. This was one of the Guardsmen. The arrow to the sky was an identification method they used. It changed every month so that an impostor or spy couldn't deceive them. The rider's face was grave, and his eyes looked worn. He dismounted and walked towards Ryan. They spoke in low voices. After a few minutes Ryan turned back with a look of shock on his face to deliver the news to the others.

"Ryan, what has happened?" asked Rainier.

"It seems that while we were fighting the army in the south, Maugrax unleashed an even bigger one to destroy Egon." His eyes caught those of Amon's. "They attacked with a Flamethrower among them. This town was the closest to the Desert and a strategic victory for the dark army."

"Then what of the southern army? Where were they going?" asked the second archer.

There was a short silence. "A distraction, a decoy," said Amon calmly. "They were there to keep Paul and me, as well as the three of you, the Guardsmen, away from the battle. This is what I feared. The Dark Army knows that I am alive and also knows of the son of the king. Also, Paul, I doubt that any in Egon were left alive." Paul's heart fell to his stomach—Egon had been the city in which the Oldyers lived. Now it was destroyed. He had to know if Segan and Eston had survived.

"We will go to the city and check for any survivors," said Amon as if reading his mind, "but don't be too hopeful, Paul."

They mounted up and rode with Guardsmen towards Egon. They rode until dusk, and then stopped to make camp. Amon and Paul sat by the fire. They were in their familiar positions sitting on logs facing each other. Paul's mind was a few hundred miles away, back to the Oldyers' village and the time he had spent there. The messenger who had brought the ill news walked up to Amon and Paul, followed by the three members of the guard. The messenger spoke.

"Amon, we must leave for Calarath on urgent business. The queen gave me orders to deliver to you the message of the village and then return to Calarath with the guard. We are sorry that we must part company so soon, but we will meet again in Calarath."

Amon nodded curtly to the messenger who nodded back. Rainier, the Guardsmen who had taken a liking to Paul, walked towards Paul and handed him a bow and quiver.

"What's this for?" asked Paul.

"You will need this more than even I. Use each shaft well and take care of the bow. You are turning out to be an excellent marksman, but keep practicing. I fear that you will have need of it soon." Paul thanked his new friend, and he turned and walked away to join the others. Very soon the sound of horses' hooves galloping swiftly away was heard.

They were alone, Amon and Paul, like they had been for months before. A knowing silence settled over them. Paul turned over and closed his eyes. Amon sat awake. He couldn't sleep, not after what the messenger had told him earlier. What they had discussed at the War Council back in Calarath was beginning to take form. The desert was growing. There were rumors that a few towns were taking sides with the Lord of Maugrax. Amon shut his eyes and sighed. The darkness around them was growing deeper. For more light he would need to create a bigger fire out of the one he had begun to kindle. This fire was unlike that of the Flamethrowers. This fire would be used to kindle hope in the hearts of men and be a light for them.

They smelt the smoke and death before they even saw it. They rode up to the small wooden gates, which were standing wide open. Unlike Jedar the town had been made of wood, and therefore, it had nearly all burnt. The bodies, some with flesh still on them, lined the streets. Seeing the faces of anguish on them was too much for Paul. Amon noticed that there were hundreds and hundreds of Ashkah lying dead in the streets. The people must have put up a good fight, he thought. Suddenly they heard a noise behind them. They both spun around almost instantly and had their swords out ready for anything. They were expecting to see an Ashkah warrior, but instead, in front of them stood a young man, slightly older than Paul, looking very afraid but relieved at the same time. He spoke in a broken voice that made Paul guess that he had been crying.

"Oh thank goodness! Help has finally arrived!" he said slowly.

Amon spoke kindly to the young man, "We are here to aid you in any way we can. How many survivors are there?"

"Only six of us. Perhaps more. We haven't searched through all the wreckage yet. We are hiding in case they come back to finish the job."

"Can you take us to the survivors?" asked Paul eagerly.

The man nodded and led them away. They walked into one house that seemed destroyed. Inside there was an underground cellar where they found the wretched survivors. There were three men, besides the one that had met them earlier, and two women. One of the men was missing a leg, others had massive burn marks, but they were all wounded in some way. The cellar was dark, but Paul saw instantly that neither of the Oldyers were in the group. The air was musty and damp, and the refugees were huddled together for warmth. One of the women was trying to get an old man to eat, but to no avail. The old man just shook his head and moaned. Amon ducked his head and entered into the low room. His heart went out to these people, but he knew that he and Paul would have to leave soon. The entire Kingdom was in danger, and though Amon was not cruel, he would have to let them find their own way to the nearest town or city.

He motioned to Paul and told him the plan in a whisper. Paul was shocked. He could never leave these people like this, no matter what was going on around them. He and Amon argued in whispers.

"But how can you even consider leaving them here?"

"Paul, we don't have time."

"Of course we have time!"

Amon sighed. "We will travel with them for a while, and then they must make their own way. We must get back to Calarath. We have to leave this town before sunset."

The argument was over. Paul nodded. He wanted to help these people so much, but he knew he couldn't. Not as much as he'd like to at least. Then he remembered the Oldyers.

"Amon, I have to go to the Oldyers' house, perhaps they are alive, but if not, I would like to give them a descent burial. They were my friends."

Amon nodded, and they both stepped out into the bright sunlight. Paul blinked to adjust after the dark cellar. It took him a moment to think of where he was in the town. Nothing looked familiar with the destruction. He had been through the entire town many times during his time at the Oldyers and knew it fairly well, but now he was lost. He looked around for some landmark. He spotted the anvil from the blacksmith's shop among the wreckage. From there he knew where to go. Amon followed quietly behind Paul.

At first the sight made his eyes go wide, but Paul calmed himself.

He had prepared himself for the fact that the two might be dead, but when he actually saw them, he couldn't help but feel shocked. They were in their battle gear; Segan was clutching his sword in one hand and in the other his wife, Eston. He had obviously died protecting her. Arrows jutted out from numerous places on each body, and Segan had slash marks across his left forearm. Around them a small fire burned of Gray Slime. Helmets and shields and spears lay scattered around the area along with at least forty dead Ashkah. Amon again thought of how many dead Ashkah he had seen in the city. Something was strange about the fact that so many common farmers had managed to kill so many Ashkah. Paul set to work with Amon on preparing graves for the two. They dug the graves side by side with old shovels they found nearby. When their graves were deep enough, they pulled each arrow from the bodies and slid the bodies into the new graves. They crossed the hands of each body over the chest; Segan clasped the sword he had fought and died with. When they were finished, Amon noticed a tear fall from Paul's face onto the freshly packed dirt. They turned and walked away.

Amon wanted to talk some more with the man they had met in the streets. There was definitely something odd about so many dead Ashkah. They wound their way around the city and finally came to the house. They walked into the dark musty cellar again. The man they had met, obviously the leader of the small group, was named Alfred. They sat down by Alfred as he told the terrible tale.

"It was the middle of the night; they came from nowhere. It was so unexpected. One moment the village was asleep, the next, flaming balls came flying through the air. The next thing we knew, Ashkah were pouring in through the city, but the Flamethrower kept attacking! He continued to attack even while the Ashkah ransacked our village. The evil orbs killed man and Ashkah alike. They killed a lot of their own but almost all of ours. A few of us fought them as long as we could, but it was hopeless. They'd attacked here before but the battle took place outside of the town, and the Flamethrower disappeared after a while." Shudders ran through Paul as he remembered being mind-gripped. It felt so long ago, but it had been less than a year.

Amon sat characteristically with folded arms and said: "They have changed their tactics, Paul. Flamethrowers attacking even when their own are endangered. Their plan grows far more evil and desperate to resort to such tactics."

Alfred continued, "When we saw that we couldn't fight them, we ran for cover. They found us and slaughtered us. All of us here were unconscious, and they thought we were dead. Our entire town is destroyed. Loved ones, memories, lives, all lost. Let us come with you! There is nothing for us here."

Amon was silent as usual. He had to think of the best way to tell this man. "The road we take is too dangerous for you, friend. If you joined us you would only put yourself in great peril. We will send you on your way to Calarath. There you can start new lives in safety."

The man looked disappointed. "Calarath is nearly a week's journey. We have wounded and the elderly. We will not make it alive!"

Paul pulled Amon aside. "Amon, he's right. They would never get to Calarath. Are we not going to Calarath ourselves? Why can't they come with us?"

"Paul, we are not going to Calarath, at least not yet. I aim to find out where this army was headed. I will send them to one of the nearer towns. From there they can do as they please. They can either continue to Calarath or settle in a smaller village."

Amon turned and told Alfred their plan. They arranged that Amon and Paul would stay the night outside the city. Amon and Paul said farewell to the group of refugees and headed out of the city. They remounted the horses and rode slowly out of the northern gate and left the city behind as the sun was beginning to set. They set up a makeshift camp and lay down to sleep, Paul still furious with Amon.

Paul dreamed of Jedar. It was magnificent, amazing. The city was alive. Paul thought again of wanting to change what was going to happen—to warn someone. It all felt strangely familiar. Then he remembered why. He had dreamed this before. Once again, exactly like the first time, the Flamethrower's flaming balls came hurling through the air, and once again the Ashkah poured into the city and slaughtered the people. As Paul turned, he saw the Ashkah about to attack him, but he stabbed his sword into the creature's belly. It winced and fell back, then died. Paul turned and saw that the fighting had stopped. He stared at the ruins for a long time. Then something happened that he didn't fully understand. He saw a hole in a wall that closed itself. All around him the city began to rebuild. A voice cried out to him, "Paul...Paul..."

Amon shook Paul awake. "Paul...Paul. Wake up!"

Paul sat up lazily. It was the middle of the night, and Paul wondered why Amon had woken him at such an hour. Amon stood quiet and still, like a cat waiting to pounce on his prey. His every nerve was alert as he listened to a dull rumbling. He dropped to his knees and put his ear to the ground and closed his eyes. Yes. It was definitely an army—a large army. Moving underground. This was it.

"Amon, what's going..."

"The army. They're moving. We have to find the tunnel entrance near here. Grab your sword, prepare the horses." Amon ordered Paul quickly and efficiently. In less than a minute they were off. Amon searched for a tunnel entrance that the Flamethrowers and Ashkah would have needed to use. Paul tried to search the ground but was struggling with the need to sleep. He forced the tiredness out of his mind and pushed himself to alertness. Amon was a great tracker, but Paul knew that finding a dark tunnel at midnight with a half-moon would be near impossible. However, they scanned the ground quickly as they rode. Paul felt the wind whip through his hair as he raced along. The days were growing warmer, but the cool night air chilled him to the bone. Amon found the wind refreshing and drew on the freshness of the air to keep his mind alert. He too was exhausted, but years of training as a Paladin had taught him that he could function efficiently on little or no sleep at all. His eyes darted across the landscape before him, searching for the entrance. He halted his horse and signaled for Paul to do the same. He surveyed the landscape before him, rolling hills straight ahead of him shining mystically with the light of the moon. The Great Plains of Goash stretched almost indefinitely before him. He knew that behind him lay the deserted city and beyond that, the desert. He closed his eyes and tried to focus on the dark energy he felt around him. Then he felt it. A Flamethrower—a powerful one. Moving north. He opened his eyes and looked in the direction that the Flamethrower had come from. He dismounted and searched the area on foot. He heard Paul behind him doing the same.

"Amon! Over here," Paul whispered excitedly. Sure enough the boy had found the entrance.

Bôren

† † † † † † †

It was dark—darker than the tunnel from Zirikaan. Paul's head felt dizzy, as if from a lack of oxygen. These were the tunnels of evil, spreading out in complex networks from the dark city of Maugrax. There were myths that going near a tunnel was instant death. Thankfully for Amon and Paul, this wasn't the case. They had found the tunnel that the army had used and then had begun tracking them. Amon had told Paul that he needed to track with his mind. Paul was struggling. When he closed his eyes it was dark. When he opened his eyes it was dark. Amon had tracked them with his ears as well—the Ashkah tunneled, using some unknown method, creating a low rumbling when they dug. Being in the tunnels was oppressive. The walls were cut at sharp angles, and Paul often cut his boot by stepping on a jutting piece of rock or grazed his hands while he followed the path of the tunnel by touch. Amon had decided that they would follow the army and then attack from their rear when they finally surfaced. Risking an attack in the tunnels would stack the odds against Paul and Amon, especially since there was a Flamethrower amongst them. Paul's foot struck something soft. He bent over and recoiled when his hands met a limp body of an Ashkah. There was a thick spear penetrating from its back. Paul called Amon.

"What is it, Paul?"

"Look. One of their captains must have killed him for being out of line."

Amon frowned and ran his hand along the shaft of the spear. "No, it couldn't have been. Ashkah never carry spears. Especially not spears of this type. This is a spear made by the weapon smiths of Nehgrog."

"Nehgrog—the rebel city?" whispered Paul. "They never submitted to my father and did not care for our laws, but they are not our enemies, and any foe of the Ashkah and the dark one is a good enough friend for me." Amon laughed, something Paul had not heard him do often. They walked through the darkness in silence.

Bôren walked down the lane. His house was just like the other houses. His family lived simply. In fact, their whole city lived simply. They lived as happy rebels. They were a war people, constantly testing their strength in new and creative ways. Bôren was one of the best sword fighters in the city, but his weapon of choice would be a spear. And not just any spear, it had to be a Nehgrog Spear. They were the strongest around, partially because the wooden shaft was made of Orun Oak. Bôren smiled. The spears would have been illegal under the laws of Calarath. The Orun Oak was, after all, an endangered tree. Or so they thought in Calarath. Only the king and a few members of their government knew about their secret deal with the old hermit on Zirikaan, and his only condition for access to his vast supply was that none of it could ever be supplied to Calarath. In that there was unanimous agreement. Bôren looked back at the spear. The heads were heavy and strong but did not unbalance the weapon. The point tapered off to a razor sharp tip that could slice through Ashkah armor like butter.

Of course they pretty much left the Ashkah alone unless they were encroaching on their land. Bôren looked up and saw a rider coming through the heavily fortified gate. He walked slowly towards the stranger who had stopped to ask audience with the king. Bôren was in his early fifties, and he was one of the strongest in the town. For this reason he had been appointed Chief of Weapons and Warfare. Because of the nature of their culture, this was one of the most important appointments—*as it should be*, thought Bôren. He shook his head when he saw the Calarath insignia on the rider's shield. Too often had Calarath sent messengers. So many times they had asked allegiance from their city, but they would not give it to them. The people of Calarath were soft and put their trust and beliefs in "spiritual" things. They would rather talk to an Ashkah than kill him. It was this breed of peace-loving men that had lost them the city of Jedar. Rumor has it that their deceased king was once a Paladin captain which showed people would believe any nonsense. No Paladin captain would capitulate and abandon the great city of Jedar.

Nehgrog couldn't stand around waiting for the Ashkah to make the first move. Peace with the Ashkah was something that could never be brokered. Bôren greeted the man on the horse.

"Welcome to Nehgrog, rider. What business do you have here?"

"I am sent by the queen. I must speak with your king."

"Why should we let you? We know what your queen wants. Leave us in peace." Bôren turned his back to the man and started walking away,

"There is no peace. If you wait around thinking that the Ashkah will leave you alone, you are deluded, friend," shouted the man.

Bôren sighed. "I am no friend of yours or Calarath. If you value your life, leave my city."

Bôren walked down the dirt road away from the gathering crowd near the man. Nehgrog had eight blacksmith stores, and each produced the finest quality weapons in the land. Bôren saw a group of children fighting with sticks. He paused to watch them. There were two boys and a girl. *Not a fair fight*, Bôren thought. Suddenly the girl spun around in a lightning fast maneuver and struck the first boy across the shoulders. The second boy ducked but lost his balance. The girl smacked the stick out of his hand and held her wooden sword at his neck. Bôren chuckled. *Yes*, he thought, *not a fair fight indeed.* It was not unusual for the women to be among their best fighters.

The day was getting dark. He was supposed to be at a meeting at sundown. They planned to discuss the loss of a nearby town, Egon, and what they were to do about the dark army. The Nehgrog had no love for the Kingdom, but they realized that a loss of a neighboring town meant that an army would be coming soon. He walked up to the large stone building, one of the few in the city. It was crudely made but served the purpose of War Room. Inside two tables occupied the majority of the room. They were shaped to form a T. Around them were twelve men and women who were all in battle gear. He saluted them and took his place at the head of the table. The room was dark but still bright enough to be able to read and see faces. Torches burned around the room, offering shaky orange light. In the center of the large tables where the two met, a large map of the Kingdom had been inlaid. It was one of the most detailed in the city and one of the largest in the entire Kingdom. Small objects stuck vertically out of the map showing towns and major landmarks. The green ones showed large forests, black ones showed mountains. The blue ones showed cities that still thrived, and the red ones showed cities they had lost. He could remember a time when there were many more of the blue pegs on the map. One of the generals addressed him.

"Bôren, sir, we believe that there is more to this loss of Egon than we think. The fact that the army was not destroyed tells us that they are still a major threat."

"Indeed. We need to investigate," came a voice.

Bôren turned the idea over in his brain. "I will go, and I will go alone."

The Council looked around and nodded. "Agreed. But do not engage the enemy. There are too many of them for one man, and our scouts believe there to be a Flamethrower among them. Use caution." With that, Lonar of Stonehouse, Boren's right hand man, nodded to Bôren, who took his leave.

Outside the war room the day was still light, but the sun was beginning its descent. Bôren would leave tomorrow. He stood on the top of the steps leading to the road. As he stood and looked out upon his beloved city, Lonar approached him. Other members of the War Council filed past them. Finally it was just Bôren and Lonar. Lonar was the best second in command that Bôren had ever had. He was one of the oldest in the Council, even older that Bôren himself. He was a great fighter and a master strategist, but Bôren knew that his weakness was hesitancy. He was always too cautious about doing anything, and while he was not a weak man, this was the only hindrance that kept their places from being reversed. Bôren was an equal in combat with Lonar, and they had grown up together as friends. Lonar had lost his family while still very young in Jedar. When they had established Nehgrog, Lonar had worked off his grief by building the city's only stone house. He became known as Lonar of Stone House. Now Bôren and Lonar stood together looking at the waning sunlight. The flow of traffic throughout the city was beginning to slow. Lonar turned to Bôren, a look of eagerness on his face.

"Let me come with you, Bôren. I know you have decided to travel alone, but perhaps a companion would be better."

Bôren laughed and slapped Lonar on the back. "I'd be glad for the company. We leave tomorrow at dawn. Meet me at the stables." Bôren turned and walked quickly down the fifteen stone steps. Lonar waited a moment, then did the same, and turned right on the path towards his house. The house had become a landmark of the city itself. There were only a few stone buildings and only one stone house. As the sun was beginning to set on the war-minded city, the two friends packed weapons, clothes, and food for a journey to a dead town.

It was still very dark. They had spent the night in the tunnels. Paul had completely lost track of time, and he felt sick constantly. There were even moments when he threw up from the smell alone. They were gaining on the monstrous breed of creatures, and the smell of the army was horrendous. Not many people had ever tracked an Ashkah army before, and not even Amon had ever heard of tracking one through the tunnels, other than when he himself had forced an army to dig the one to Zirikaan. It was the very fact that people refused to go into Ashkah tunnels that had kept Amon's access to Zirikaan a secret.

Paul knew that when they finally emerged, the battle would be a vicious one. The knowledge that a Flamethrower was present sent chills down Paul's neck. Amon had discussed how they would attack it. Amon, the Paladin captain, would hold the Flamethrower with his mind while Paul decapitated him. The rest of the army was a mindless rabble of Ashkah and no problem for the two warriors. Amon had been focusing all his attention on tracking the army with his mind. It was a method not uncommon for Paladin to use when sound and sight were not enough. Paul had been strangely quiet the entire journey; Amon assumed that he was still mourning the loss of the Oldyers. Amon had known the couple briefly when he had journeyed through the city. As Amon was reflecting on the old couple, the low rumbling suddenly stopped. Amon halted and Paul did the same. The Ashkah were stopping for the night. Paul and Amon did the same. Paul could never remember being so tired, except perhaps, for some of the nights on Zirikaan when Amon had worked him to exhaustion. He lay down and fell into a dark sleep.

． ． ． ． ．

Bôren surveyed the landscape before him. The city of Egon was ruined. Lonar stood on his right, eyeing the scene as well. Suddenly a man appeared in front of them. He was ragged and looked tired. He looked like a refugee. The man motioned for them to follow him quietly. Cautiously, with their hands on the hilts of their swords, Bôren and Lonar followed the man through the empty streets. In a dark cellar of one house they heard the story of the refugees. Bôren pulled Lonar aside. "It is obvious that we must help these people. I will travel ahead and track the army. You must travel with these people to the nearest town or city. Make sure they are safe and that they are settled down, then return to Nehgrog."

Lonar nodded his agreement. They discussed the plan with the leader, whose name they found to be Alfred. Bôren helped the men and women find horses and carts, and then they left. Bôren, fierce with anger, drew the sword from its scabbard and slammed it into the ground. He looked at his sword. It would have made any king proud to wield it. It had a leather-wrapped handle, with a large round metal pommel. Inlaid into the pommel was a single turquoise stone. The hand guard was straight and was inlaid with a gold lining. Where the blade intersected the hand guard, a single blue gem had been set. The blade itself was strong and straight, tapering slowly towards the end to a sharp tip. The steel used in the blade was actually mixed steel. It was not likely to break and would not rust. Even without a polish it shone brilliantly in the sunlight. He pulled the sword out of the ground and slammed it into its leather sheath. He started walking through the rubble. He assumed that the army came from the south and was heading north. He knew he would have to find this army before they surfaced. The thought of going through the dark tunnels again made him sick at the thought, but he knew it had to be done. He had traversed the dark tunnels twice before, and each time the experience had been terrible. He walked out of the northern gate and noticed footprints that were not Ashkah. They were fresh. There were two pairs now. He saw an abandoned fire that had burned not long ago. Suddenly horse tracks appeared—running quickly. He followed them, his excitement increasing. Then they stopped. The footprints resumed again. Then he saw where they were going—the tunnel. He took a long breath of fresh air, looked into the sunlight, and ducked into the tunnel. The smell of Ashkah filled the tunnel, but seemed distant. He plunged into the darkness. The air was musty and old and made his head light. He was faster than the average man, but he thought, *Anyone who was brave enough to enter the tunnels was not an average man.* With luck he would be able to catch up with these two daring warriors.

Bôren had tracked the two men solidly for two days and passed them quietly while they had stopped for the night. He had found an Ashkah scouting around behind the rest of the army, or perhaps he had fallen behind. Bôren didn't wait to find out. He remembered the Nehgrog saying: "You don't have to fight a dead enemy twice." He had killed the Ashkah and didn't bother to remove the spear. Now he was ahead of the two. He had decided that they weren't a threat but still was worried that they would mistake him for an Ashkah. He had a suspicion that they could be trusted but wouldn't put his trust in anything that was not Nehgrog. There wasn't anything he would need from anyone else, for on this mission he could work capably on his own. He was gaining on the Ashkah, of that much he was sure. Their stench was growing stronger, and the shouting was growing louder. Bôren, like many of the other men of Nehgrog, had fine hearing and had been taught to track by sound. He had also been taught how to track with his eyes, ears, hands, and even his nose. However, in these dark tunnels there was nowhere to go except the path that the Ashkah were taking. Suddenly everything quieted. Bôren halted. If he were not mistaken, he was somewhere near the next town, Emelle. If the Ashkah army was allowed to surface, Bôren might not have a chance in changing the outcome of this battle at hand. Bôren felt a cold hand on his shoulder. He spun around silently and felt a strong arm stop his hand from drawing his sword. He realized that this must have been one of the two who had been behind him. Obviously they had traveled quicker than he had expected.

"I would think that an experienced Nehgrog warrior like yourself would have some strategy for slaying a large army of Ashkah."

Bôren faced the voice but saw nothing in the darkness. "This army is headed for Emelle." His voice sounded deep and loud in the tunnels. "I intended not to let them survive long enough to take a single life." He had been over the plan countless times in his head, but when he actually thought about voicing it, it sounded illogical and futile.

"Are you aware, my friend, that there is a Flamethrower amongst this army?"

Bôren kicked himself mentally. The War Council had mentioned a possible Flamethrower attack, but he hadn't been paying attention.

"Friend, we know that you are a ferocious warrior. We ourselves intend to destroy this army. We would be glad of your company. What is your name, friend?"

"I am not a friend of yours. My name is Bôren of Nehgrog. I will join your party, but first tell me who you are."

Amon began and told a brief description of who they were, Ketor and Belin. They were rogues who had committed themselves to kill any Ashkah that dared to venture out from the desert. Paul had not said a word since they had met the stranger. He listened with a suppressed chuckle at the story that Amon wove for Bôren. Amon continued to tell about the Ashkah they had encountered in Egon, but Paul felt something stirring within him. He decided to speak up.

"Master Ketor, we would love to entertain our guest with our tales of war, but I fear the Ashkah army is on the move." Indeed the Ashkah army had begun to stir. They were now tunneling upwards towards the surface. In a few moments the battle for Emelle would ensue. Paul felt misgivings about ever entering the tunnels in the first place. The party, now three in number, hurried down the tunnel still in total darkness. The sound of the Ashkah was growing louder when a light tore through the tunnel, yielding a roar from the Ashkah. The thundering of hundreds of battle-hungry, bloodthirsty Ashkah running across an open plain struck terror into Paul's heart. He knew now that he had to save these people with Amon and Bôren.

Bôren felt there was something very familiar about these two strangers—his new war companions. He did not believe their story, but they would have time enough for correcting that later.

Emelle

† † † † † † †

They raced up the sloping path and burst into the brilliant sunlight. Paul took in the scene before him in a split second: a large army of Ashkah surging towards a small band of men on the outskirts of Emelle. In the next split second Paul was aware that, without a doubt, the Flamethrower knew they were there. He heaved his sword out of the scabbard and felt its familiar weight in his hand. He reached the first group of Ashkah, the ones in the back of the army, at the same time as Amon. They had both begun to move as a blur. Bôren swung his blade as he pulled it from the scabbard in one fluid motion. The surging army suddenly realized what was going on and slowed its charge. Half of the army spun around to defend the rear. By the time the Ashkah at the back were ready to kill, the three men had dropped twelve of them. Paul spun, and with every downward motion another Ashkah fell beneath his sharp blade. Paul was amazed at how sharp the blade was and how light it was. Amon had become nearly a blur even to Paul. To him the Ashkah were moving slowly enough to kill easily. Bôren was a lethal fighter, but he himself was awed by the speed that Paul and Amon possessed. Bôren recognized the old hermit from Zirikaan, but immediately his attention was drawn back to three large Ashkah wielding their crude swords at him. He cut through Ashkah flesh with two strong cleaves. Then they turned. The entire army surged again, this time towards the three warriors. Arrows filled the sky as the Ashkah archers neared the commotion behind them. Then Paul caught sight of the villagers. They had caught on to what was happening and had begun to charge the Ashkah. Suddenly Amon cried out to Paul. "The Flamethrower!" In the midst of the battle Paul had forgotten the dark warrior. Balls of flaming sludge hurled into the air killing a small group of Ashkah. Bôren was stunned. He had never been so close to a Flamethrower, and now they would have to destroy it.

Amon's voice was loud but calm. "Bôren, hold back the Ashkah. We will deal with the Flamethrower." Bôren at once charged into the heap of oncoming Ashkah. Line after line, his blade sliced through the dull gray flesh. Paul and Amon cut their way through the side of the army and saw the Flamethrower on a hill. This was it, Paul thought. There was no more time for games or training. As they neared, Paul caught his first glimpse of what the Flamethrowers were really like. He wore a dark tunic with a black cloak hanging over black boots. Overall he looked dark and menacing. They were close enough to see, but the Flamethrower was too distracted by Bôren's attacking. He held out his hand, and Paul watched as Gray Slime seemed to drip into his hand from down his sleeve. The Slime hardened into a ball, and the Flamethrower pulled back his arm and hurled the orb into the air. Amon and Paul crouched for a moment against the side of the hill.

"Paul, I will hold his mind. He will be distracted, but you must move quickly. I will only be able to hold him for a short time. Be calm; don't let fear misguide your actions."

Paul nodded hurriedly. His last encounter with a Flamethrower had left him shocked and unconscious for days. This time, if he were mind-viced, he would not be as fortunate. Then they charged. Amon leapt up and charged forward. Paul's mind reeled as they neared. Amon stopped short and held his blade vertically in front of his face. He shut his eyes and focused his mind on the

Flamethrower. Paul felt his mind clear for a second, but panicked. This was a Flamethrower! He froze. Amon stood still. Paul forced his muscles to move, but they wouldn't respond. Every second he wasted he lost the window of opportunity to kill the Flamethrower. Amon suddenly let out a long shout. As he screamed, Paul saw his face darken. Then he collapsed. Paul felt the Flamethrower's mind zero in on him. Finally he leapt up and swung at the Flamethrower's head, the only part of the body he knew was vulnerable. Then almost as if the Flamethrower had given in to him, Paul felt his sword make contact with the dark body and slice through its neck. As his sword appeared on the other side of the head, a high-pitched scream could be heard. Paul reached out with his mind to try and hold the Flamethrower before its spirit fled back to Maugrax. An image flashed in his mind, and the Flamethrower was gone. The dark body collapsed on the ground.

The sounds of the battle below them quieted in Paul's mind as he raced over to the limp body of his uncle. His eyes were open and looked lifeless. Paul quickly checked for a pulse. It was there, but faint and slow. He had to get Amon to a doctor and find some treatment, but first he had to help Bôren. He looked down the hill and saw Bôren fighting valiantly through a closing ring of Ashkah. Blood poured from wounds across his arms. Paul shouted loud and clear. That seemed to work, he thought. As he charged down the hill, he used the slope to increase his speed. He raised his sword, now fueled by anger from Amon being wounded. He leapt as he neared the foot of the hill into the Ashkah. The first stroke sliced cleanly from one to the next, killing three of the monstrous creatures. Paul heard a deep roar from an Ashkah captain and saw arrows shoot into the air. Paul looked across the remaining Ashkah. Only about fifty left of the original 300 or so. Bôren fought his way through the Ashkah and joined side by side with Paul. They stood back to back, about two feet apart. Bôren's blade hacked through Ashkah upon Ashkah, while Paul fought elegantly, each blow leading into the next. Suddenly the army broke off and ran away from the two.

"They're retreating!" shouted Bôren.

Paul waited a moment, then cried, "No they're not. They're going for the town!" Sure enough, the remaining archers had begun to fire into the small band of villagers who had been fighting with Bôren but from the opposite side. Paul grabbed an Ashkah bow and found more than enough arrows lying on the ground. He remembered everything that Ranier, the Guardsmen they had fought with, had taught him. He drew back the short, crudely made bow and aimed for the nearest Ashkah. As he released the shaft, a second joined his. Bôren was firing off arrows at an astounding rate. He had his own bow, a dark wooded longbow, and was sending smooth shafts into the Ashkah. Paul was taken aback. At first he had believed that the Nehgrog warriors did not use bows. Each one of Bôren's shots dropped an Ashkah. Paul fired off six shots and hit three. Paul threw down the bow and told Bôren to draw his sword. Every moment they wasted, more of the poor townspeople were slain. They charged at the Ashkah. As they neared the small remaining army, they heard sounds from the towns- people drawing nearer. They would close in on the Ashkah from two sides. As they collided, they met little resistance from the Ashkah. These were archers, not swordsman, and were offensive units only; they wore little armor and carried no more than short knives. Screams from men on the other side told Paul that the Ashkah would not go down without a fight. Paul's arm felt heavy from wielding the sword. There were now only a few left. Paul swung his sword high above his head and brought it crashing down on one of the two remaining. The last archer had a red sash across his chest.

"Wait!" cried Paul as Bôren aimed for the lone Ashkah. Bôren halted and shot a quizzical glance across to Paul. Paul ran to the Ashkah. He knocked the bow from his hands and held his sword and the creature's neck. He wondered for a moment if they could speak his language. He would find out soon enough. The creature dropped to his knees and put his hands in the air. Bôren came up behind Paul and glared at the Ashkah. Paul glanced up at the townspeople running towards them. Many of them wore no armor and were bleeding profusely from large wounds. More than half of them had taken at least one arrow, some more.

"What's all this about?" Bôren said without turning.

"I need to find out something. Can they understand us?"

"Not in our tongue, no. But in their own, yes."

Paul glanced at Bôren, surprised. "You speak the language of the Ashkah?"

"I do indeed. I was a Nehgrog scout; it was not uncommon for us to capture Ashkah and interrogate them. In order to do so we would need to understand them."

Paul looked back at the terrified Ashkah. For a brief moment he took pity on the creature. "Ask him if he knows of a new plan of the Dark One—something new, something that a Flamethrower would be afraid of. Anything."

Paul listened as Bôren spoke in the guttural, rolling language of the Ashkah. It consisted of deep throaty sounds that cut into one another. Bôren ended, and the Ashkah hesitated. Paul pressed the sword harder into its neck. Its eyes went wide, and it looked at Bôren and muttered something.

"He says that he will tell you what he knows if you let him live, and remove the sword from his neck."

Paul considered the creature and withdrew his sword. If the Ashkah did try to escape, Paul would move too quickly for it to get far. The frightened Ashkah relaxed a bit. It began to talk to Bôren, who nodded every few sentences. Finally Bôren turned to Paul.

"He says: 'We are of the lowly order, and we do not know of the plan of the Great Dark One.'"

"Tell him he may go free."

Bôren looked from Paul to the Ashkah then swung around and sliced the creature's head off.

"What was that for?" shouted Paul. "I said he could go free!"

"I didn't."

Paul stared furiously at Bôren and stormed away to take care of Amon.

That night, over the fire, Paul glimpsed more into the mysterious culture of the Nehgrog. Apparently Bôren had been sent on a reconnaissance mission to investigate what happened at Egon and had followed Paul and Amon through the tunnels. They had carried the limp body of Amon for a few hours away from the stench of the battle before resting to make camp. Even though Bôren was strong and muscular, and Paul was fit, the weight of the captain had been enormous. Paul had decided that they would head to Calarath, and Bôren had suggested stopping at one of the nearby towns, probably Zalen's Fjord, to get a horse to carry Amon. They had agreed and Bôren had headed to the Fjord. Now as he was returning with the horse, Paul kindled the fire. There was something about Bôren that he liked. He was the type of no-nonsense person that would make an excellent general or commander.

"The people of Zalen's Fjord were more than willing to send it in thanks for saving their town. They also sent along some provisions for the road. Kind people, very simple, but very generous."

Paul nodded. It struck him as odd that Bôren would think of someone as kind or generous. He had expected the man to be very gruff and hard. Bôren sat on a log near the fire and pulled off his boots. A few small stones fell out as he turned them upside down. They sat in silence for nearly half an hour, neither feeling the need or desire to talk. Paul was too distressed about Amon to make light conversation, and Bôren simply saw no need in talking when it was not useful or productive. Finally Paul spoke up.

"It was a fierce battle today."

Bôren looked up. "Fierce? Perhaps. It was stranger than anything else. How did the old hermit over there turn into a heap?"

"I don't know. One moment we were fighting the Flamethrower, and the next, he just collapsed. I'm still trying to sort everything in my mind. Everything happened so fast."

Bôren hesitated asking a question he had been on the verge of asking all day. Paul had stopped talking, and Bôren could see he was staring into the fire. He spoke up.

"How is it that you and the old hermit happened to move so fast? You have been trained well. If I didn't know any better, I would have said you were Nehgrog."

"The hermit? The hermit, as you call him, is Amon, who was once one of the captains of the Paladin. My name is Paul."

"Him," said Bôren pointing to Amon, "a Paladin captain?"

"Yes. You know him?"

"We have met before," admitted Bôren. "Why did he lie about your identity?"

"I am sure he had his reasons," said Paul still a little annoyed. Paul turned to look at Amon, his concern growing every hour.

Bôren shook his head. "You were afraid to trust a Nehgrog? No harm done. I would be just as suspicious if I had recognized you as Calarathan," said Bôren. "And how did you two move so fast?"

He thought a moment. He himself had battled for months with the concept of the mental fighting and the gift that he and Amon both shared. The whole business was muddled, even in Paul's own mind. There were so many questions he was waiting to ask Amon, who now lay near the fire peacefully. He looked back to Bôren.

"Well, part of the reason we can move so fast is that Amon and I have a special gift."

"So tell me about this gift that you and Amon share."

Paul took a deep breath and thought of how best to describe his strange ability. "Well," he said, "when we first engaged the Ashkah, did you notice how fast we moved?" Bôren nodded his head. "This ability is not that we move fast, it's that we can slow time down—a little. To us, everyone else moves slightly slower, slow enough to parry easily. Of course I don't know why I have this gift or how I use it or what it really is. I wish I knew more."

"I have heard of such a gift. It is recorded in the ancient books, the ones of Jedar, that the great Paladin captains had this mysterious power." Bôren eyed Paul with a suspicious look.

"It is true; the Paladin had this same power. Amon was a Paladin captain in the Jedarian war. He is the brother to the murdered king of Calarath—my father."

"So that is why you have the gift. You are the heir to the throne."

Paul sighed as he was reminded yet again of the responsibility that rested upon his shoulders.

Bôren stood and walked a little away from the campfire into the woods. Paul turned and glanced around and saw that Bôren was looking out across the long plains of Goash. He turned back to Paul.

"How long do you think your friend will last like this?"

Paul had considered the question himself and had hoped that Amon would last the seven day journey to Calarath.

"I'm hoping at least seven days, until we get to Calarath, and then they can do something."

"No, we can't take the risk of seven days. In that time he might have taken a turn for the worse. We will have to ride through the night. We can make it in three or four days. The faster we get him into the care of a doctor, the better."

Paul was slightly surprised that Bôren cared enough to come with him, but he was even more surprised at how concerned he was for Amon. They decided that Amon would be tied to the horse, so that neither of them would have to hold him in place. The horse that the people of Zalen's Fjord had given them was strong, but old, and could not carry more than one person. Bôren pulled out a map of the Kingdom.

"If we ride due east, we won't encounter any towns between here and Jildath. We don't have the resources to travel that far."

"There is a Nehgrog outpost we can stop at. It is located about here." Bôren pointed to the map in the middle of the Plains of Goash.

Bôren rolled up the map and put it away. The night was very dark, and they decided that they would need to start immediately. Paul checked on Amon, and Bôren checked their provisions and helped tie Amon to a horse. Paul doused the fire with some sand and dirt, and they set off. Paul and Bôren walked on either side of Amon's horse to prevent Amon from slipping. Paul looked at Amon and hoped that they wouldn't arrive in Calarath too late.

Calarath

† † † † † † †

The city of Calarath. The long journey had been hard, and Paul could only hope that Amon's condition hadn't worsened. After leaving their camp, they had traveled for nearly a day and a half on foot. They had reached the place that Bôren had talked about with ease. There they were given horses and extra food and water for the rest of the journey. Paul had offered to pay, but the leader they had talked to had told them to just bring them back when they were nearby again. They had traveled quietly for three and a half days without rest, and they were exhausted.

Memories flooded back to Paul as they walked through the gates. Paul glanced up, shielding his eyes from the afternoon sun, and noticed how small the gates looked after seeing the splendor of Jedar. He had once thought that his city was the greatest, but now it looked so small, like a mere village compared to Jedar. He looked at his uncle's body, tied to a horse and lying motionless. He was not dead; of that much Paul was certain. They passed a crowd of women carrying large baskets. They looked at Paul and the body lying slumped against the horse's neck, then moved on and continued their chatter. The city seemed distant to Paul, and things that had once held his fascination he now passed off for more important things. He needed to get Amon to the castle to see a doctor.

Paul had convinced himself that in Calarath they would find

something that they needed, but in reality, he believed that Amon had taken a heavy blow for which there was no known cure. He had been mind-gripped, much like Paul had, but to a much larger and more severe extent. He looked across at the Paladin captain, then over him to Bôren, who had been quiet for most of the journey. To Bôren everything about Calarath disgusted him. Their people consisted of a mindless rabble of people unaware of any sense of duty or danger. They spent their time relaxing and blowing off the cares of the world while his people, the Nehgrog, spent their time training and preparing for times of trouble. *It is only a matter of time until they regret the time they spent relaxing*, thought Bôren. The buildings were built more on style than on substance. Bôren thought, *A building's styling should never compromise or be more important than its functionality*. He thought again of Paul and wondered what he thought of the city. Evidently Paul was thinking the same.

"What do you think?" The question sounded forced as if Paul were making himself talk when he didn't want to.

"The Calarathans have built their lives on pleasure and entertainment. While there is much wealth and abundance of everything, there is a lazy, laid-back attitude to the city. I wouldn't be surprised if nothing gets done here. Why their king chose this city as the capital city is beyond me. And yet, it is a symbol of the Kingdom. Frivolous architecture and self-centered people."

Paul was slightly struck by the words, partly because he knew there was some truth in them and partly because this was still his city. "I believe there is more to this city than meets the eye. There is an abounding sense of happiness in the air, and the people themselves seem cordial enough."

"Pha! These people will seem to care, but in their hearts, there is no room left for anyone or anything but themselves and their greed."

"You believe that a thriving culture is a greedy one?"

"Wealth doesn't have to change people. People can be conservative and even generous with their wealth if they want to be. The problem is the moment people get some money, the first thing they do is spend it on themselves."

Paul listened as Bôren talked about his problems with the Calarath. In fact, it seemed that Bôren's problems were not with the Calarath but more with people in general. He seemed to blame everything on Calarath. Even the death of their past king had somehow been Calarath's fault. Bôren fell silent after a while, and they walked on in silence. They neared the castle gates, and the guards on duty approached them. One of them stepped forward casually, glanced up at the body on the horse, then turned and muttered something to one of the others. He turned and faced Paul.

"What business have you in the castle?"

"I am here on a personal matter. This business is of dire importance."

The guard was taken aback that this stranger knew the passwords. He had not recognized the two walking, but he knew that the one on the horse had been here before. He nodded to the rest of the guards standing around, and they made way for the two men and the horse. Somewhere between the guardroom and the drawbridge, Paul felt the relief of being home again. He stepped onto the wooden bridge that spanned across the slow moving moat below. The hollow sound of the clomp of the horses hooves on the drawbridge followed him as he walked towards the iron gate which was being drawn up to allow them in. In the middle of the stone courtyard stood a fountain which seemed dormant and dead. Paul remembered playing in that fountain as a boy, but recently it had fallen into disrepair. A messenger met them as they walked towards the center. He had long hair, and a short, trimmed beard. He was a stocky man, and Paul recognized him as Heron, one of Paul's favorite guards. Of course Heron presumed him dead, like the rest of the Kingdom, and right now, a Nehgrog captain and a stranger, both looking worn out and messy from battle, stood before him.

Then suddenly Heron saw Paul.

"Paul!! I…is that you?!"

Paul smiled and stepped forward to embrace his friend.

"We-we thought you were dead! How…? Where…? It's good to see you!" A group of servants rushed forward and helped to lower Amon from the horse and onto a litter. Amon was then carried to a small room to be treated. At that moment Paul was led into the castle. He was greeted by stares and smiles; many shook his hand as he walked towards the throne room. As he reached the massive doors, two guards who Paul did not recognize pushed it open. Paul saw his mother and stepped forward. His mother caught sight of him and strode towards him. They embraced each other and held on for a long time. Tears streamed down his mother's face as she held her son in her arms. Finally Paul pulled back and looked at his mother. She turned back to the guards, who understood her meaning and walked away. Heron lingered for a moment. He bowed to the queen, glanced back at Bôren, shook his head, then walked through the archway.

"Paul! You've come home!" his mother said.

"I'm afraid that Amon is in danger." Paul looked back at the horse. His mother gasped.

"We shall put him into a room in the castle." She snapped her fingers and a servant appeared. She gave him orders to see to Amon's room.

"And Paul, I see you have brought a guest."

"Yes." Paul hesitated. "This is Bôren, Head of the War Council of Nehgrog."

If his mother's mood changed with this new information, Paul could not detect it. She nodded curtly to him and then turned to Paul.

"Come Paul, let us go through into the castle."

Paul walked next to his mother, and Bôren walked behind. They walked through an archway opening to a second courtyard. In this second courtyard four statues stood in each corner, the founders of Calarath. A walkway surrounded the courtyard, and a short stone stairway led to it. Wooden doors were inlaid into the stone at various places along the walkway. Above them the tallest tower soared, a Calarath flag fluttering in the wind. To Paul's left, an archway opened to another large door which led to the interior of the castle. To Bôren, the whole thing reminded him how pathetic the Kingdom had become. Jedar's castle had been much greater. They entered into a long hall with rooms lining either side of the passage. A high ceiling with a large chandelier suspended on a long iron chain rose about them. Multiple rings of flame burnt in the chandelier, casting a strange glow across the room. Normally the room would be brighter, but the shades had been closed across the wide windows. Two guards stood on either side of the large door directly ahead of them. When they saw the queen, they opened the door and bowed to her. When they caught sight of Bôren, however, they recognized him as a Nehgrog captain and moved to form a barrier. Paul stopped his mother and turned to the guards.

"Release him, he's with us."

The guards looked at Bôren, then back to Paul.

"Do you realize that this is a Nehgrog? He is a spy, a traitor. They are all traitors. We will never let any of them into the High Rooms."

The queen interjected. "Guards, I insist you release him."

"Your highness, for your own safety and the safety of everyone in this castle, we will not let this man beyond these doors."

Bôren understood the entire situation. While it only increased his dislike of the Calarathans, he decided to accept it. "I will wait here, Paul. Do what you must do."

Paul nodded and gave Bôren a sheepish look, as if to say, "They're not normally like this." He continued on with his mother. "Mother, I need to speak with the War Council. It's about Egon. And something else..." his voice faded off but only for a moment. "When is the earliest that you can arrange a meeting?"

"Tomorrow morning. Paul, is something bothering you?"

Paul slowed his walk and turned to look at his mother. "I will tell you all tomorrow. Right now I'm more worried about my uncle."

His mother looked away and walked to the window. Paul walked up beside her. "There is something still amiss between him and our family, isn't there?"

His mother straightened almost rigidly and said, "Amon chose to isolate himself from our family for reasons of his own choosing. We tried to convince him otherwise, but he wouldn't hear of it. It doesn't matter, Paul; let's not discuss it."

Paul decided not to press the issue any further. "I have to go talk with Bôren. I will see you at the Council tomorrow, Mother." He hugged her briefly, then turned and walked away.

When he had gone, his mother quietly said to herself, "My, how much he's grown. Amon has made some impact on him after all."

Bôren had grown tired of waiting near the door, and without knowing how long Paul would be with his mother, he decided to go look around the town for a blacksmith. He had asked the guards if they knew of anywhere he could find one, but they had ignored him and continued talking amongst themselves. He first went to the town center, if the tiny plot of grass and small statues counted as a center. It was more of a small park. He found a man who told him where the blacksmith was. When he followed the man's directions, he had come to a barn. The people of Calarath clearly had no intention of helping him. In fact they would even go out of their way to mislead him. He decided to find the shop on his own when Paul came running up to him. Paul was the only Calarathan that Bôren thought was decent, but from what he knew now, Paul was royalty. That probably accounted for the magnificent sword that he wielded. Bôren turned towards him and almost smiled.

"I have arranged to meet the War Council tomorrow morning. I wish you could be present, but these people do not welcome those from Nehgrog."

Bôren raised his eyebrows in mock surprise. "I never would have guessed," he said sarcastically. "I've been trying to find someone that can show me where the blacksmith is."

Paul shook his head. "Come on, I'll show you." Paul glanced up, took notice of his surroundings, then turned down a dusty road. A few moments later they entered the blacksmith's shop. Swords of every kind hung along the walls along with axes, shields, gauntlets, and other types of armor. Paul waited nearby while Bôren talked with the smith. Paul couldn't hear what they were saying, but he could see them. Boren handed over his sword to the smith and then walked back to him. They began walking together, and Paul decided that he needed someone to talk to about the meeting tomorrow, and he was almost positive that Bôren could be trusted.

"The meeting of the War Council is tomorrow. I don't know what's going to happen."

Bôren was silent, waiting for Paul to continue. They turned down a wide road lined with the typical village houses. Bôren studied the design for a moment, angled thatched roof, wooden structure, a few small windows. Simple enough much like Nehgrog. Paul continued. "When Amon and I were fighting the Flamethrower, I reached inside his mind and glimpsed something. I couldn't see what it was, but I know that the Flamethrower was genuinely afraid of it. I have a feeling that we should be too." They paused to let a group of children run in front of them, playing some made-up game with a ball. They walked on. Paul noticed that Bôren seemed confused or disgusted by the game but was trying to hide it. "I think the Dark One is planning something terrible, something that could wipe out the Kingdom. If we don't do something soon, we shall be destroyed." Bôren halted and turned to Paul.

"Have you considered that this 'thing' you saw wasn't simply the Dark One himself? Perhaps you are overreacting, Paul."

"No, it was something other than the Dark One. I can't describe it. It's…"

"It's your imagination, Paul. Right now we must concentrate on holding our borders. The desert's growth is too large to be worrying about insignificant things like…"

"It's not insignificant!" Paul interrupted. A small horse-driven cart came up behind them, and they turned into an alley to avoid it. They had to walk single file through the narrow road. It opened up to a larger road that Paul recognized as leading to the City Library. They were now heading to the more city-like, high-class area. Bôren continued.

"I understand that due to your gift, you might have power to see things that others don't, Paul. And it would make sense for the Dark One to create something more powerful if he sees that the Flamethrowers are growing ineffective. I believe you."

Paul was shocked but relieved for Bôren's sudden change of mood. He only hoped that the Council would be as positive. They headed to the library in silence. It was a small, one-story, brick building that seemed very small in comparison to Jedar's massive library. During the Jedarian War, when the people had fled, they had taken as many books as they could grab in the short time they had to evacuate. Calarath had been a small, simple, unknown town, and the king had completely renovated this section of town. The library from the original town was somewhere near where Paul and Bôren had just come from. Inside the library Bôren pulled out a book and began leafing through the pages. Paul caught sight of the title: *Calarath: Weapons and Warfare*. Paul thought that perhaps Bôren was trying to gain an insight into the minds of the Calarath warriors. Paul left Bôren and began browsing through the shelves to see if anything caught his attention. The books were sorted by subject rather than by author. He looked up and read a sign that read, *History*. Suddenly, he thought of Jedar and everything he wanted to know. He began looking through the shelves when he heard a commotion near the front of the building. Mildly interested he wandered forward to find out what was going on. He saw Bôren arguing with a man dressed in elegant clothes. It seemed that the Nehgrog's presence was causing trouble wherever they went. Bôren caught sight of Paul. Paul walked up. "What's going on here?"

The man saw Paul but did not move. Paul grabbed Bôren's arm and pulled him towards the door. They were now out in the sunlight.

"I can't stand this city. I will wait until tomorrow; then I will head to Nehgrog." Paul couldn't blame him. They walked back to the blacksmith to pick up Bôren's sword, then arranged for Bôren to stay in a local inn.

Conspiracy

† † † † † † †

As he approached the door, the guards pushed it open. This was the first time he had ever been in the Council Room. He took in everything from the long table to the intricate details of charts and maps on the walls, the pinnacle of warfare and strategy. They were all standing when he walked in. Some of them stared at him with annoyance, others with disbelief. He ignored the stares and walked to his place. He stood by his seat and waited for the approach of the queen. The doors swung open once again, and in walked his mother. As she took her place, the whole assembly sat. The queen's clear, confident voice began the proceedings.

"Thank you all for coming on such short notice, but I believe that this issue that Paul is going to address will be important."

Paul stood after a nod from his mother. He was not nervous but only slightly concerned. He pushed aside any doubts and spoke confidently.

"As you all know, I am Paul, son of Mark. It was assumed that I was dead, but in reality I was being trained. I was being trained by a Paladin captain. When he and I returned, we engaged in some skirmishes near the Plains of Goash. In the latest battle Amon was wounded, mentally, by a Flamethrower that we were fighting. He held it in with his mind, and I attacked it, a common strategy for Paladin warriors." He cleared his throat. "As I attacked it, I caught a glimpse of something in its mind—a picture, but also a feeling. I don't know exactly what the picture was, but I know that it was some creation of the Dark Lord. I sensed fear surrounding it. There is something that the Dark Lord has created that even the Flamethrowers are afraid of." He sat down, the customary signal that the time for any questions or comments from others was now open. This was the discussion part of the Council where the real decisions were made. No one stood during this time; it was filled with too much back and forth discussion. One of the older men spoke up.

"So, Paul, I presume you want us to do something about this."

"Yes, I do. I feel that we need to change style of fighting to better encounter any new foes that he throws at us."

A general across from Paul spoke calmly. "I am Kresh. Paul, you are asking us to change decades of fighting techniques in order to be prepared for something that *might* attack us? We don't even know if it exists."

"General Kresh, you don't understand. This is definitely real. I don't know how I know, but I just do!"

"Paul, it is you who does not understand. We are the military command of Calarath and the entire Kingdom. We have the best intelligence available coming from scouts all over the Kingdom, and now you stand before us and claim that *you* know more than we do, and *you* think that we should change it."

Kresh spoke up. "I agree. This is a mockery of this Council Room."

The tension was building in the room. "How many of your scouts can reach into a Flamethrower's mind and grab information?"

There was a silence in the room. Of the six generals around the table only one had an answer. It was the man farthest from Paul. "Paul, we may be old, but we are also wise. If there are any movements that we don't know about, then they don't exist."

"How can you claim to know everything that the Dark One is doing? How can you know his latest plans?"

Kresh broke in. "We can't, but now you're telling us that you can? Who are you to tell us such things?"

"I am the heir to the throne!"

"Your *Majesty*, you have hardly shown yourself to be a man capable of leading this Kingdom under any pressure at all. The fact that you ran off into the mountains to escape your own self-pity assures me that your are not able to lead, command, or rule. We will do nothing."

"Your inaction will be your undoing." Paul stood and walked to the door.

Someone behind him muttered. "Will you not even fight to win this argument?" Paul paused mid-stride and turned to the speaker. It was Kresh.

"You would do better to speak to royalty with more respect."

Kresh looked slightly taken aback. With that the meeting was finished, and they all stood and began to file out. As they left he saw Kresh walk off to the side where a man was waiting for him. When the light caught his face, Paul recognized him as Sir Gelaray, the ruler of Yambor, who had been in a meeting with Paul the day of his father's funeral. The two men talked in low voices, and Paul strained to catch what they were saying. He had misgivings about both of them, and the fact that they were working together made Paul suspicious. He decided to think more on the matter later. He walked into the outer courtyard and saw Bôren waiting by a saddled horse.

"Paul, did everything go well? Did they believe you?"

Paul looked and spoke only with the expression on his face.

"Ah. I see. But what else did you expect from Calarath? Support?"

Paul looked at the sun on its way to a mid-day peak. "I had only hoped they would believe me."

"The Calarathans won't do anything until this new enemy has already attacked them. I know they won't. They've done it before.

Now if it was the Nehgrog, we would be preparing every man old enough to fight."

Paul glanced at Bôren. "That's it, Bôren!"

"What's it? Paul, what are you talking about?" But Paul was already on the way to the stable. He returned with a beautifully groomed white stallion. "I'm coming with you."

The pieces fell into place for Bôren. Paul would rally the support of the Nehgrog. Bôren liked the idea. The Nehgrog saving the Kingdom would earn them the respect they lost when they broke away. The idea of Nehgrog's War Council being wiser than Calarath appealed to him. He laughed.

Paul called two servants and gave them orders of foods and other supplies. He himself went off to check Amon. He hated leaving his beloved mentor when he was in such need. In fact, he was more than a mentor. He was a father to Paul. While his true father hadn't neglected him or spoilt him, he had never found a way to discipline Paul enough to get him to change his shiftlessness. In a way Amon had changed Paul to the man he knew he was destined to be.

He entered the room and saw Amon. They had changed him out of the blood and mud covered battle gear and into a soft red tunic. Paul spoke to Amon, "I will save you." He stepped back from the bed and dropped the letter he had written to Amon on the bedside. If he revived before Paul returned, at least he would know where Paul was and what he was doing. He stepped out of the room and shut the door silently. He walked back to the courtyard and found the servants tying the food and extra supplies to the horses. There was a certain excitement to the whole thing, leaving on a moment's notice. Things were changing.

Paul had been quiet the entire first day of their journey. Bôren was alive at the prospect of going home, and the idea of the heir to the throne rallying the support of other Nehgrog had livened him up.

He talked about Nehgrog, war, Jedar, weapons, and every topic he could imagine. Paul listened quietly and took in the information that Bôren gave him on Nehgrog. He learnt that if the Nehgrog were to follow under him, he would have to best their leader in combat—in fact, three types of combat. They would have to fight with bare fists, then sticks, then swords. The last was a fight to the death. The idea of having to kill someone simply for a commanding position repelled Paul. He thought it would be a waste of a great general. Despite the fact that they were in a hurry, they decided to camp for the night. Bôren built a large fire and began to roast two small portions of meat. The roasting smell was pleasing to Paul's senses, and finally he began to talk.

"The Nehgrog sound like a fascinating people."

"They are indeed. They will be the best allies you'll find and the worst enemies."

"No…not the worst," Paul muttered. "Tell me more about your generals."

"Well, our king, Jonak, is one of the best warriors I've ever seen or heard about. Commander Furareo is a decent man but has a problem with being drunk when he is most needed. It is a small indulgence for his service. The War Council is probably what you would be most interested in. Being their leader, I know the limits and potential of every man under me. Lonar, my right hand man, leads like a king, but sometimes it gets to his head. A proud man is never a good leader. Scilaro, Junai, and Goarl are our most valuable assets. We send them on missions that require someone of authority but are too insignificant to be bothered by the higher ranked people. They are great men but are still learning how to wield their power."

Paul was beginning to like these Nehgrog. Their culture seemed very friendly and genuinely loyal. He hoped that he would be able to rally their support. The meat finished cooking, and Bôren lifted the rotisserie stick from the spit. Paul was starving. He hadn't eaten since a small breakfast before the Council meeting. He tore into the soft meat eagerly. The night was getting cooler, and Paul shifted closer to the fire. They ate in silence for a long time. Paul wondered if Bôren had had a chance to eat before they left. However, from the way he attacked the food, Paul presumed he hadn't. After dinner Paul and Bôren sat lazily on the ground near the fire. Bôren lay flat on his back looking at the stars, and Paul sat whittling a small stick down with his hunting knife. Piece by piece the hard bark fell to the ground revealing a smooth, light colored wood. He wondered how hard it would have been to whittle Orun Oak. The thought made him think of Amon. His mind wandered back to his training and the massive changes that had occurred since his father's death. Paul's mind was racing, and he needed an outlet. He guessed he could trust Bôren and finally turned to him.

"Bôren, there is something I need to talk to you about."

"How may I be of service?"

"I'm worried about the Kingdom. Do you believe that there is any sort of plot to overthrow me in Calarath?"

Bôren's eyes were dark, and his face was unreadable. "While I was waiting for you to finish the meeting, I walked around, and I heard things that were not meant for my ears. I believe that there is a conspiracy, or some form of it, to overthrow you. It seems as though a certain Sir Gelaray does not agree with a young man being king."

Paul sighed as realization dawned on him. That was why Kresh had been talking to him. "I think you're right, and I believe that one of the generals of our Council is with him. That accounts for his subordinate attitude towards me."

"Paul, you have to be careful. Whenever there is power, people try to take it. You left the position of king for a long time, and these men would want to take it. The fact that you want to come back now and reclaim what was yours doesn't sit well with them."

Paul was silent as he mulled over his thoughts. He lay down, and as his eyes slowly shut, he fell into a dark dream.

Voices screamed from every direction. People ran past him, but he ran against them. Curiosity drove him to find what was causing the panic. He pushed past people with terror written on their ashen faces. Then he saw it. It was nothing he had ever seen before. It looked like a Flamethrower with two heads and four arms. It was almost as if someone had pushed two of them into each other. It stared straight at him, four eyes filled with something that struck a terrifying chord within him. He wanted to run, but his feet pushed him closer. They were going towards the thing against his will. He tried to pull out his sword, but there was nothing there. Frantically he reached for a nearby block of wood, and it transformed into a sword as he touched it. When he looked up, the monster was gone, and everything felt very quiet.

Bôren watched Paul intently. The young man seemed to be having a nightmare. Bôren's mind was too busy and active to sleep. He was eager to get to Nehgrog. His Council had no idea where he was, but he knew they trusted him. He just hoped that they hadn't assumed him dead. He rolled over onto his side and let the dwindling fire warm his back. He could see a small creek in the distance and a herd of deer gathered around drinking. The fire was obviously too far away to scare them. He stood up and walked to his bag, which was tied to the saddle of his horse. He looked through its contents. A small box, he knew, contained three precious gems, a small dagger, and a leather bound book. Inside were letters from his wife. The first half were letters they had written before they had been married. He read through the letters telling of small things like events of the day, training, schooling and big things like major wars.

Some of them were long, some were short. Bôren closed the book and sighed a long heavy sigh. He lay down to get some sleep.

Four days later they rode into the boarders of Nehgrog. Paul was amazed at the fore planning that had gone into the construction of the defenses. In a twenty-mile radius outside of the actual city, scouts and their families lived scattered around. They had built a tunnel system similar to the Ashkah tunnels but reinforced with stone and lit with torches every few feet. Along the way small bunkers were dug into the ground complete with beds and necessary facilities for three soldiers to spend a few days. The tunnels were nearly ten feet in height and five feet across. Scouts could report quickly of local enemy movements without being seen. The tunnels were completed with ventilation holes that let out heat, odor, and stale air. Although the tunnels were for military use only, if worse came to worst, the entire city could be evacuated out of the sixteen tunnels radiating from the square. Each entrance to the tunnels from within the city could be concealed, and the exits lead to "safe-points." Paul and Bôren decided to take the "flat route," as Bôren called it: traversing the remaining distance on open ground.

As they approached the city, it was clear that it was made for war. A large stone wall towered above a shorter, smaller one with multiple archer towers in between them. The battlements on the top of the walls were covered with a low roof which Paul presumed hid archers and other watchmen. The whole city functioned like a military fortress. Paul suddenly thought, *If the people of Nehgrog had been given the job of defense of Jedar, would it have survived?* Paul glanced up at the gate. It was an iron grid pattern interlaced with spikes. It separated into two parts and slid off to the side as they approached. They walked across the now lowered drawbridge and to the second gate, which was now opening. Inside the first thing Paul saw was an emblem painted into the stone road with two swords meeting in the middle. Where they met, a star had been painted. Leading from this emblem were five separate roads covering the 180 degrees around Paul. The one directly to his left led to houses as did the one on his right. The left and right diagonals led to stores and shops as well as to a library and multiple dueling arenas. The road directly ahead of Paul led to a large open stone area spanning before a tall castle. This was Nehgrog. Paul looked across at Bôren who was beaming with pride. A few stable hands came out to offer to care for the horses for a small fee. Bôren paid for both of them.

"What do you think?"

"Impressive, very impressive. Definitely something to be proud of."

"Come, I'll give you the grand tour."

Paul followed Bôren down the first path to their right. The houses were similar to Calarath's upper class homes. Paul didn't see one home that was small or cheap. They were all kept in pristine order. Discipline was a core tenet in Nehgrog philosophy. They walked down a side path that Bôren knew of and went back to the main intersection which Bôren told Paul was referred to as the Five-Pointed Star. The left diagonal path led them to the large War Council building as well as four or five small villas that were dueling centers. They returned to the Five-Pointed Star and headed down the main path. Bôren told Paul that all the roads ultimately led to the city center, but they had gone back to Five-Pointed Star to let Paul better understand where they were.

Paul looked out to the large open field ahead of them. In Calarath you would have seen people reading, talking, eating picnics. In Nehgrog the field was covered in little boys wrestling, young people practicing fighting with sticks, and old men showing younger ones the finer points of martial combat. Bôren walked Paul through it, waving occasionally to a small child he recognized or one of his understudy generals. They reached the large castle which appeared more like a palace than a castle to Paul. There must have been at least fifty steps leading to its large doors. As they approached the top, Paul prepared himself to meet the leader of the fierce people.

Nehgrog

† † † † † † †

The palace of Nehgrog loomed over Paul. The massive structure was more like a fort than a palace. Inside sat King Jonak, the man Paul needed the most at this hour. He had no idea what to expect, even after hours of talking with Bôren about what he was like. He would hide the fact that he was Calarathan and the fact that he was the son of the king. The guards were more aware of everything going on around them than those of Calarath. In fact they weren't anything like Calarath. They wore completely green clothing, earning them the name The Green Guard. The cloth was dyed a dark, forest green, and they wore cloaks of the same color. They each had a bow strung across their backs, with a quiver, both dyed green. Long swords hung from their belts in dark leather scabbards. They held long spears in their hands, resting on them. In truth they were hardly resting. They were poised like cats, ready to strike within a split second of something going wrong. As Paul and Bôren stepped up onto the first step leading up to the castle, two of the guards watched them intently. Paul could feel their gaze as he confidently walked up the stairs. He tried to appear nonchalant, pretending not to notice them, but it was almost as if they looked through him to find his purpose for approaching the castle. They reached the platform on which the guards stood. One of them with long loose brown hair and deep emerald eyes stepped forward. He had strong, rugged features about his face, but not harsh. His eyes darted from Bôren to Paul. For an awkward moment Paul simply stood in front of this guard, being looked over. Finally he spoke.

"Welcome home, Bôren, son of Guthane. I see you bring our king a guest from Calarath. Nobility, I presume."

Paul was slightly taken aback that the guard had been able to pick up that he was from Calarath, but even more shocked that he guessed his royalty. He had tried to hide every sign that would have given him away. Bôren spoke clearly and confidently. "I bring this matter before our king."

"Ordinarily we would not let one like him be admitted into our courts, but I trust your judgment, Bôren." With that the guard stepped back and opened the door. Inside there was a dark marble floor and high ceiling. Windows, cut high into the walls, sent angular shafts of light into the room making this throne room seem brighter than Calarath's. Eight tall, pale white pillars lined the path to a dark green throne. Four Green Guards stood around the throne, eyes intently upon Paul. The first thing Paul noticed about the king was how young he was. The man with smiling blue eyes seemed to be only in his mid twenties. His right elbow sat on the armrest, supporting his chin. He looked relaxed but deceptively docile. They reached the throne and knelt simultaneously. The king nodded, and they stood.

"Ah, Bôren, welcome home. I trust your visit to Egon was productive? But surely that is not why you bring a guest from Calarath into our throne room."

"Thank you, Your Majesty. I present to you my friend, Paul, the son of Mark the king of Calarath."

Paul knew his cover was blown before Bôren introduced him. It was in the way he carried himself. He looked regal even in common clothes. Paul stepped forward. The king had changed his mood towards Paul but only slightly. Paul had the feeling that the king was going to react just like the Council in Calarath had. The fact that he was the heir to the throne wouldn't persuade them either. In fact it would be all the more reason why they wouldn't join forces with him. Suddenly he became unsure. What if the things he was seeing were not correct? What if he had imagined them after all? What if the Council was right? What if...

"Paul?" Bôren's questioning voice shot Paul out of his thoughts. He had to decide quickly if he was going to try to rally their support regardless. He couldn't stand before the king and say nothing however. He would take the chance. He had nothing to lose. He drew himself up and let his mind clear of the panic.

"Your Majesty. I understand that since the Great Jedarian War, our two cultures have been at odds. While we haven't been enemies or allies, a level of hate has developed between us. In a recent battle I fought a Flamethrower. I am sure you have heard of the gifts of the Paladin, the ability to reach inside a creature's mind, if only briefly. I have that gift which I inherited from my father. I caught a glimpse of something terrible—a new weapon or enemy more powerful than the Flamethrowers. I hurried to Calarath to warn them and spoke with the War Council. They were disbelieving and completely useless. They are sure that they know how to fight Flamethrowers and Ashkah, but what they don't realize is that they will not always be the only enemy we will have to fight. It makes sense now. The Dark Lord is tired of small battles here and there. A full-scale war is at hand and with an army of creatures or weapons that will be beyond anything we have had to face before. Calarath would not believe me, but surely the Nehgrog will. I ask for your support. We will not let what happened to Jedar happen all over again." He stopped and wondered if he had spoken too quickly. The king sat in the same position as when they entered, his chin in his right hand. There was something about him that made Paul think he might have an ally in the Nehgrog.

The king lifted his head from his hand and looked at Paul. "Tell me, Paul, what would you need support for?"

"I would like to engage more Flamethrowers. By engaging them

I could find out more about this enemy. We would then know what to do to prepare for or fight it."

"And you would like us to send our warriors to fight the Ashkah while you fight the Flamethrower?"

"Yes, Your Majesty."

The king was silent. Paul glanced back at Bôren who was calm, his face unreadable. The king leaned forward in his throne. "The people of Nehgrog will never fight alongside Calarathans. You said it yourself that a level of hate has come between us. You must look for support elsewhere." Paul's heart fell. "I speak for all Nehgrog when I say you are no longer welcome here." With that, two of the Green Guard standing around the throne stepped forward, and each grabbed one of Paul's arms. Paul turned at their urging and began to walk down the hall. Suddenly he had an idea. It was his last resort. "What about the challenge of leadership?" The king glanced up and motioned for the guards to stop. Paul shook himself free of their grip and walked back towards the throne. The king rested his chin in his hand while Paul approached the throne for the second time that day.

"Your Majesty, Bôren told me of a Nehgrog custom that I intend to use now. When someone desires control or leadership over the city, that man must beat the present leader in three areas of combat, the last ending in death. I invoke this custom now. If you win, I will be dead and no longer a trouble for you. But if I win, I will have leadership over the Nehgrog." Paul waited for the king's reply. It was obvious that Paul's move was unexpected as well as unusual. The king had worked his way up to a Green Guard and then became the Captain of the Green Guard. From there he himself had challenged the previous king and left his bloody remains on the town square. Now this young boy was doing the same to him. He had nothing to fear. He was the best fighter in Nehgrog and probably the best in the Kingdom. It seemed a shame to waste such a brilliant, strategic mind. However, the king had no choice. He nodded, then stood and threw off his royal cloak. He was dressed in a rather common looking tunic, other than the fact that it was dyed blue, a rare color to find for the Nehgrog. The guards escorted him down the long hall with Bôren and Paul whispering behind.

"Are you insane, Paul? Do you know what you just did?"

"I challenged him."

"You challenged the best warrior in all of Nehgrog!" Bôren was incredulous. Paul was not bold—he was foolish. His audacity would be his undoing. They walked down the long flight of stairs and saw the gathering crowds. The word had spread like wild fire. By the time Paul reached the open field, roughly 200 people had gathered in a large circle around the two. The first part would be unarmed, using only their bare hands. Paul removed his sword and other belongings that would weigh him down and handed them to Bôren. He looked across at the king. He wondered if he had had adequate training in hand-to-hand combat. He disregarded the idea and thought of his ability to slow time. Suddenly a thought struck him. What if he could push his gift even farther? What if he could slow time down even more? It was possible, surely. The king now stood tall and drew himself up to his full height. His neck rippled with muscles and a fierce frown was set upon his face. To any normal warrior he would have looked intimidating. Paul stepped forward and met the king in the middle of the circle that the crowd had formed. Then it began. The king faked a punch, then spun around and threw his elbow towards Paul. Paul saw it coming slowly, easily side stepped it, and followed through with a crushing blow to the king's face. The king stepped back, shocked.

The next move came from Paul as he ducked low and came up with a hard uppercut to the king's jaw. Paul's hand stung from the impact. Jonak was now mad. He swung three quick punches, and Paul dodged them easily. Finally he drew back a little from the king. They stared at each other for a moment. Paul concentrated on pushing his gift as far as he possibly could. As he felt the familiar sensation of things around him slowing, he leaped forward into the air. He noticed that the king was moving slower than anyone else he had fought. His leg connected with Jonak's rib cage and sent him flying. Paul landed lightly on the ground as things returned to their normal speed. Jonak lay shocked on the ground. One moment he had been staring at the young boy, and the next all he saw was a blur before being sent flying off his feet. Round one was over. Two of the Green Guard helped the king back onto his feet. He wiped a trickle of blood from his mouth. He nodded his head to Paul, who bowed to him. He approached him.

"Well fought, Paul. I must be getting slow."

"You fought excellently, Your Majesty, but it was not a fair fight."

"What do you mean? Of course it was. You proved that by winning."

Paul studied the king for a moment. "No, I mean, it wasn't fair for you. I have been trained as a Paladin. To me you were moving extremely slowly. That was why you never hit me. I could dodge and counter before you could attack me once."

The king looked at Paul as if he were slightly insane. They looked at each other for a moment. A man came running up to them with two finely made wooden sticks. Paul took one and adjusted himself to the weight. It was heavier than the Orun sticks and seemed to be slightly chipped. A small thin piece of leather had been wrapped around the bottom to give more grip. Paul noted that it was well balanced. The king stretched his arm and rolled his neck from side to side. Paul wondered if he should go lightly on the man. But no, that wouldn't prove his gift. As was the custom, the two walked eight paces from each other. Paul held the stick in one hand loosely at his side. Paul knew that the king was no match for him. An ordinary man would have been beaten in seconds during the melee combat alone. It was no wonder that Nehgrog hadn't had a new king in over nine years. One of the Green Guard held up a white flag, then brought it down, giving the signal to begin.

Both warriors raced towards the other. Paul engaged his gift and the king seemed to move slower than ever. He really was pushing his gift to its limits. As they neared each other, Paul executed a perfectly timed attack Amon had shown him. He rolled just before they reached each other and came up with a lunge. He felt the stick slam into Jonak's stomach. Had it been a sword, he would have impaled the man. He had knocked the wind out of him. The king stepped back, mouth open, gasping for breath. Paul knew that if he had gone slightly harder, he could have killed the man. However, the force he had put behind his attack had not been little. He could see clearly that his opponent was in pain. The king was a man built of endurance. He lowered his stick and held it defensively in front of him. His breath was coming in short gasps.

They circled each other a moment. Paul was confident that Jonak would lose the match. The king ran towards him and attacked with a powerful blow from above. Paul instantly blocked it. They held their two weapons crossed for a moment. Suddenly the king drove his knee into Paul's stomach. Paul stumbled back. He had been too confident and had not bothered to use his gift. Pain shot through his torso. His mind reeled. He straightened and ignored the pain. He should have never let his guard down. The king and Paul faced each other for a moment, and then suddenly Paul ran towards the king and executed a combination of four short, powerful flurries. A second later the king lay groaning on his back. The crowd was deathly silent, not risking cheering for Paul.

Again the Green Guard stepped forward to help the king up, but he refused their service and jumped up quickly. He walked towards Paul. Round two was over by mutual agreement. With a brief nod a guard stepped forward and presented two swords. Paul took the weapon from the guard and looked at the king. He examined the sword the same way as he had the stick. It was a very well made weapon but much heavier than his beautiful sword, the Sword of Jedar. They faced each other for the next duel. Paul's heart beat louder. If he fought passively, the king might kill him, but if he fought aggressively, he would have to kill the fine warrior facing him. No, he would not kill him. As he thought through his options, the king lunged at Paul. Paul saw him coming very slowly and wondered what he would do.

Suddenly he remembered what Amon had told him once: "Your mind does not have the same limitations that your body does. Too often we fight with our bodies, and our mind follows. Fight with your mind, and let your body follow." Physical limitations. That would mean gravity too. In theory he could jump twenty feet high if he chose to, couldn't he? He decided to test it. He parried the king's attack and rolled out of the way of a second attack. He backed off, putting distance between him and the king. He calmed himself and tried to remember everything Amon had taught him. The king was near him now and swung his sword from below in an uppercut. Paul parried and forced the blade to the ground. This was his chance. The king's blade was too low to cause a threat, and he was near enough to the king. He pictured himself detaching from his body and fighting with his mind. Then he jumped. What he did surprised even himself. He soared just above the king's head and landed behind him. He dropped to one knee and did a sweep with his left leg, knocking Jonak off his feet. He spun around and knocked the sword out of the bewildered man's hand and held his sword at the king's throat. It all took less than a second in real time. The king looked as if he had just seen the Dark Lord himself. An unspoken gasp ran through the crowd. Clearly the logical move for Paul would be to kill the king, but instead, he pulled his sword away from the man's neck.

"What are you doing? You must kill me to win."

"Your Majesty. I think we can all clearly see I won. Why must I waste your life? What good would it be for me to kill you when there are more important things at hand?"

"But it is not the custom! Kill me and end my humiliation!"

The air was tense as Paul stared at the king, who was now kneeling. Without taking his eyes off the man Paul threw his sword to the ground. The king trembled slightly. The crowd stared anxiously to see what would happen next. Slowly Paul walked over and offered the king his hand. With this the king saw that Paul would not kill him and allowed himself to be helped up. There was a collective sigh from the crowd, and the matter was over. As the guard brought the king his cloak, the crowd slowly dispersed leaving Paul and Bôren alone with the king and his guard.

"Excellent fighting, Paul. I swear I have never seen such amazing speed. Your gift is nothing less than incredible," Bôren said astounded.

Paul considered the statement. He had been taught that when you were given a powerful gift, you were expected to use it. He had been given this gift; now what was he to do with it? He shrugged the thought out of his mind as the king approached.

"You are an amazing fighter, Paul."

"Thank you, Your Majesty, as are you."

Paul turned to face the king. "It was not a fair fight, Your Majesty," restated Paul.

"Yes, I see that now. All the more reason why you should be our next king." Jonak let the statement hang in the air.

Paul jumped slightly. What if his purpose was to lead the Nehgrog? "I'm not sure, Your Majesty."

"Please." The king put out his hand. "Jonak."

Paul shook it firmly. They walked next to each other, and Bôren said he would have to be excused. As they discussed minor things like weaponry, horses, tactics, Paul noticed that there were Green Guard everywhere. He wondered how many of them there were. In fact he had been wondering how many Nehgrog lived in the city. He asked Jonak.

"In this city? Oh, we are not entirely sure, but I can give you a rough estimate, somewhere around 500,000, men, women and children."

Paul was shocked. That was almost as many as Calarath's 800,000. "Impressive. The city is almost as large as Calarath. How did you manage to get such a high population?"

"We here in Nehgrog see children as a joy and a necessity. The Calarath see them as financial and emotional burdens. Tell me Paul, what is the average size of a Calarath family?"

Paul thought for a second. "Four."

"Precisely, a mother and father and two children. But what good is that? To be able to increase in number, you must replicate yourself and then add to the population. If a Nehgrog family doesn't have at least three children, they are seen as disloyal."

"Disloyal?"

"Yes, disloyal to our city. We all contribute to the growing population. It is our duty. The average size of a Nehgrog family is four children and two parents."

Paul considered this for a moment. He himself was an only child. What would it have been like to have three other siblings to grow up with? They walked towards the palace and began walking up the large flight of stairs.

"Paul what are your views on Calarath? More specifically, about the splitting of our two civilizations."

"Well, Jonak, I believe that unity is the best policy. With such a large and dangerous foe at hand, I think it is pointless to argue amongst ourselves. We would prove more of a challenge if we stood together. It is all the more important if we are to face the new dark weapons of the Dark One."

"And how do you propose we stand together? Do you suggest we put decades of cultural differences behind us? My dear Paul, you obviously have much to learn about civilizations."

Paul thought for a moment. The Nehgrog were definitely rooted firmly in their own beliefs, but on the other hand, so was Calarath. He was beginning to see Nehgrog's side. They were now at the top of the stairs and walking into the palace. Paul had no idea where the king was taking him. Before they reached the throne, they turned and walked between two marble columns. On the far left wall were many doors. They reached the one closest to the throne.

"Where are we going, Your Majesty?"

Jonak smiled. "To the War Council."

The door opened, and the first thing he thought of was the Ashkah tunnel. A sloping paved path led to a dimly lit pathway underground. As they descended, Paul didn't receive the knock of stagnant air that he had expected. Looking up he saw tiny ventilation holes that kept the air moving. They walked for about five minutes before reaching another sloped path, ending in a similar brown door. The king opened it to a room of men. They were all dressed in battle gear except for Bôren, who wore a more elaborate dress. This was the War Council.

Shortchanged

† † † † † † †

Paul sat in a seat near Bôren as the Council began. It was similar to Calarath, except they had removed the need for standing when speaking. Everyone sat together. Paul noted that it was more discussion-based whereas Calarath's Councils were simply one man presenting a point to the others. Bôren led the group well and did not talk all the time. In fact he often deferred to those under him in rank if he thought they would be better qualified to answer the question. They brought up Paul. Bôren spoke first.

"It is obvious that this issue has never been encountered before. Paul rightfully should have killed our king, but instead he chose to spare his life. Paul, perhaps you can explain more?"

Paul resisted the urge to stand. "In times like these we need every good warrior we can get. The king is an excellent warrior, and what a shame it would be to waste his life simply for a new rank. He is a better leader than I as well. What would be best for Nehgrog is to let them keep their king."

A young looking man spoke. "Well said. But you must understand you are breaking centuries of traditions by doing this."

There were a couple of nods and muttered agreements from around the table. Paul spoke again. "If I were the Dark Lord, I would make every effort to turn the people in this Kingdom against each other. It's less work for him, and they prove to be less of a challenge than if they stand together. This is not the time to be worrying about petty things like tradition. Who is the better leader? The king. Let him lead."

An older man with a long gray beard that stretched to his stomach looked quizzically at Paul. "And what about you? What reasons did you have to challenge the king to the Three Duels in the first place?"

Paul sighed. This was where he would lose them. "I believe the Dark Lord might be creating a new foe. I battled a Flamethrower, and before I killed it, I reached into its mind and caught a glimpse of something."

The men passed excited looks around the table. The young man who had spoken first leaned towards Paul. "You mean you killed a Flamethrower?!"

Another man about Bôren's age looked impressed. "Only the Paladin were ever able to battle Flamethrowers—and then it was only the captains."

Paul nodded. "I was trained by Amon."

The room went quiet. The men had a new respect for him. Bôren took the silence. "So Paul, what is your plan? What would you have us do for you?"

"I request a small army, preferably of elite soldiers, to fight with me. If I can fight more Flamethrowers, I can find out more information. However, I cannot fight Ashkah and Flamethrowers at the same time. I would need someone to keep them distracted from me."

An older man who had been referred to as Orth spoke up, "You are proposing to go up against a Flamethrower? Alone? Do you realize what madness this is? Even the Paladin captains of Jedar, the best warriors this Kingdom has seen, had to fight in pairs. What makes you think you are better than they are?"

Paul was silent. "I have the same gifts as the Paladin captains. In fact I have learned to push these gifts beyond what they could. If I risk my own life to attack a Flamethrower, what concern is it to you?"

The king, who had been quiet for the most part, addressed

Paul. "You are an excellent warrior, Paul. I would be a fool not to acknowledge that. Some might consider you stupid for attempting to take on a Flamethrower, but I have a feeling you just might be able to do it." The room fell silent. Paul grinned.

Finally Bôren spoke up. "Well then, the matter is settled. We will supply you with an army of 200 Green Guard. That should be sufficient. Thank you, Paul, you are dismissed." Paul stood and shook hands with Bôren. After a nod of his head to the others and a bow to the king, he exited through the main doors. Behind him he heard the Council chatting about a food poisoning issue.

The sun was shining brightly but had begun a slow descent over the horizon. Paul would have time to explore Nehgrog and perhaps find a place to stay. He walked slowly down the steps, thinking about what was to happen next. The sound of the marketplace sounded distant in his mind. There was something bold and daring about his plan, he thought. Or was he simply stupid? Could he really take on a Flamethrower alone? If he exercised his time-slowing gift, the sword the Flamethrower wielded would not be a threat. It was the mind war aspect of a Flamethrower that he worried about. True, he had survived his first encounter with a Flamethrower at Egon, and Segan had told him that it was rare for someone to be able to resist that without any training. What if this was another gift? Anyone who had this many gifts must be destined for something great for the Kingdom.

Yes, Paul thought, *if I don't use these gifts to their full potential and for the right reasons, then what good are they?* Paul walked, passed an old looking house and stopped to consider the architecture. He had seen the splendor of Jedar and grown up with the imitation Jedar styling of Calarath, but the Nehgrog architecture truly puzzled him. The houses were simple, but nowhere he looked could he find any that were better or worse than the one he looked at now.

He shook his head. A slight headache had been growing. He needed to find somewhere to sleep. It would be his first proper bed in weeks. He saw a long building with a thatched roof and many windows. A small sign hung on the door. It said: "Henry Forest's Inn." Perfect. He walked towards the door. His thoughts were becoming muddled. The inn smelled of burning wood. A large fire burnt at the other end of the room. In Calarath Paul would have expected a smell of tobacco and smoke and would also have expected beers and other alcoholic drinks, but the Nehgrog believed in discipline. He arranged for a room and paid the owner. As he walked into his small little room, he wondered why he had paid over fifteen pieces of gold for it. The room would do for the night or two he had to stay here, but then he would be off to find a Flamethrower. He fell onto the bed and sleep came quickly.

Bôren approached the king after the Council. "Your Majesty, might I have a word?" The king stopped and turned.

"Certainly, Bôren. How may the king of Nehgrog serve his most trusted advisor?"

"Well, sir, I know we'd agreed that Paul would have 200 of our Green Guard, but I was wondering if I might have permission to accompany him."

The king clapped his arm on Bôren's shoulder. "Bôren, I can see that you and the boy have developed a friendship. However," he paused, "I think it would be better if you stayed here in Nehgrog. We need your mind and leadership skills here."

"I understand, Your Majesty, but I would also be useful on the battlefield. I could track enemy movements and…"

"He is Calarathan!" The volume of the king's voice surprised Bôren. Evidently all his good intentions towards Paul had been for show. "I intend to send 100 of the Green Guard. Let the boy die. He has sealed his own fate." With that he turned and began to walk away. Bôren knew he could do nothing against the will of the king. The king turned back.

"On second thought, Bôren, do not send Green Guard. That would be too much of a waste. Send standard infantry."

"My lord! You are sending him to his doom."

"You have concern for his life? So be it. I shall send you with them since you are so eager to save him." With that the king spun and walked away. Bôren forced himself not to attack him. He was their king, and his word was final. He thought of Paul. How was he going to explain? The door shut behind the king. Bôren slammed his fist into the table. They were to leave as soon as the army could be ready. Normally that would take no less than three hours, but Bôren decided he could delay for a day or two. He walked back to his house, still lost in thought.

Paul woke with the sound of birds chirping. He had slept until nearly noon. The sun was shining brightly. Today was the day they would leave. Excitement pushed Paul out of bed. He had slept in his tunic. He pulled on his light armor and buckled his sword to his side. He wanted to show his best to the new army that he would be commanding—200 Green Guard. Of course he had no idea how well they preformed in battle, but he assumed that any elite Nehgrog fighting force would be sufficient. After all they would only be taking out Ashkah. The real challenge would be his. He pushed the doubt from his mind. He opened his door and found a small white piece of paper lying at the entrance. He picked it up and turned it over. It had no name. Slowly he opened it and read its contents.

Paul,

You will get this in the morning. I am afraid to say our king has changed his mind and will only send 100 standard infantry. I tried to convince him otherwise. Meet me in the town square.

-Bôren

Paul slumped onto the bed. 100 *standard infantry*. Now he was definitely starting to doubt. But why would the king have changed his mind? Had a new battle arisen somewhere that required the Green Guard? He cleared his mind and walked out the door. The wood squeaked under him as he flew down the stairs. Outside he saw hundreds, possibly thousands of people. He would never find Bôren. He hurried in the direction of the looming palace. The king had changed his mind! The shock was intense. He stepped onto the wide-open plain of grass and began scanning across the crowd of people for Bôren. He saw him waving his hands. He walked briskly towards him.

"Bôren, what's going…"

"I'm sorry, Paul. The king has sent us to our deaths. All because you are Calarathan."

"Us? Our deaths? What are you talking about?"

Bôren briefly described the events of yesterday's encounter with the king. Paul closed his eyes and rubbed his temples.

"When will we meet the army?"

"They will be fully ready in under an hour."

Paul sighed. "Good. We will have to make do with what we have. The standard Nehgrog soldier is much more capable and deadly than the standard Calarath. I must remember that."

They walked together towards one of the gates. As they were about to pass through, Bôren turned sharply to his left and walked along the wall. Paul decided not to question him. Suddenly Bôren stopped and squatted down on his heels. He reached down and pulled on some unseen handle. Paul watched amazed as a hatch opened. Bôren grinned and looked at Paul, who was peering down the exposed hole.

"Where does it go?"

"To the mustering area. Come on, we don't want to be late." He stuck his hands on either side of the hold and lowered his feet in. Then he dropped out of sight. Paul did the same and wondered if he should replace the hatch. He let himself fall, and a few moments later a guard replaced the hatch. When he first landed, all he could see was a small light ahead of him, and he walked towards it. The ground beneath him changed from soft soil to paved concrete as he entered a lit tunnel. He saw Bôren waiting for him a few feet ahead.

"Wow, this is truly incredible!" said Paul. Bôren nodded, and they walked quickly down the tunnel. Paul guessed they walked for twenty minutes before coming to a turn. He noticed that the path they had been walking down was sloped downward. Before they turned, Bôren turned back.

"This is where we muster our armies. From this location, an army can take any of the dozens of tunnels to any location." Bôren led Paul around the corner. The sight took Paul's breath away. A wide cavern almost thirty feet high and over 300 feet wide opened before them. Despite its massive size it was very well lit. In a section of it, a neatly arranged army stood at attention. A few men walked around crates stacked in the corner, opening a few and perusing their contents. Bôren led Paul down a steep staircase which led to the cavern floor. As they approached, the entire army saluted and clacked their heels on the floor once in unison creating an impressive sound. Bôren stopped and nodded to Paul. Paul looked across the rigid faces—an impressively organized army, however small. He straightened and walked to the captain, who stood a little in front of the army, looking straight.

"Greetings, Captain. I am your General. Paul of Calarath." There was a slight twinge in the man's right eye. "You may not like me, but you will respect me and obey me. Do I make myself clear?"

"Yes, sir," he replied quickly. Then Paul grinned slightly. He was sure that these men would not disappoint him. He walked back to Bôren.

"Paul, which way do you propose we head?" Bôren asked quietly.

"If the enemy struck Egon, then Krisbane, I have a feeling he is proceeding up the coast. My guess is either Krisbane, since he was unsuccessful at Emelle, or south of that."

"To Arum? I doubt he would push that far in. There isn't enough support behind them to launch an attack. It would never work. They won't do it."

"Unless...unless he wants us to think that. That would be the *least* likely move, the most unexpected. It would also be the move we wouldn't be prepared for. I suggest we stay between the two."

"Good choice. Let's warn the two towns and have them prepare an army."

"Bôren, these are mere villagers, you can't expect them to muster an army of old men and young boys."

"They will muster whatever they can. If anything, they can be an early warning system." Paul nodded. He turned to the men.

"All right men, we move through the South East tunnel. We will station between Krisbane and Arum. Let's move!"

As one the army turned towards the tunnel and marched forward. Paul scratched an itch on the back of his neck. He now held the lives of a hundred men in his hands. One wrong order and he would be their end. Suddenly he felt a familiar feeling of the weight of responsibility. He wondered if he could withdraw his request. But no! What would he do then? The Kingdom needed this information. More people's lives rested on the information he might be able to find than just this small army. If their sacrifice meant saving the Kingdom ultimately, then so be it. Paul was not a cruel commander, however; Amon had trained him to view situations factually. If he didn't push hard enough with the army, he might lose hundreds of thousands of lives. He watched the army march towards the tunnel and stop before the entrance. He saddled his horse, and Bôren followed. They walked to the head of the army. Turning to his men, Paul spoke: "Today we risk our lives for the greater good of the Kingdom. Whatever happens in the battlefield will be done for Nehgrog and for this entire land. March with me today!"

Paul mentally kicked himself. It was not half the motivational speech he had heard others give. He would need to practice. However, from the looks of the men, they needed no motivation. Of course this was what they were bred for. Their lives were centered around the art of warfare. He spun his horse around and began to move forward. Bôren followed with the rest of the army behind him. There was something about leading a troop of men into battle that invigorated Paul. His nervous tension was dissipating as he guided his horse through the wide tunnel. Bôren came up beside him.

"Paul, when we exit this tunnel we will have a few options. We can either enter another tunnel that will take us nearly to the entrance to Krisbane or continue on land."

"Hmm. I think that for morale we should stay above ground. How long does this tunnel take us?"

"It will lead us to the edge of the outer perimeter defenses, thirty miles. We should reach it before this day is out." Bôren looked across at Paul. He was considering everything. While it might have been safer to take the second tunnel, Paul had realized that traveling through a tunnel for two days would make the men depressed or slow. It was a psychological thing. There was something that had changed in Paul since they left the cave. He had become more of a commander and less of a young boy. Bôren liked the young commander riding beside him. He hoped they would last the upcoming battle.

Savior

† † † † † † †

Paul walked among the tents of the men checking their swords, shields, spears, bows, arrows, and every other piece of equipment that could change the tide of battle. Every man was important to Paul. He would make sure that all of them were ready for battle, and if they weren't, he would make them ready. However, the men of Nehgrog had been trained with excellence. They had battle tactics and strategies drilled into them from the age of six years old. Paul had asked a few of them what he proposed the best plan of action would be, and most of them had suggested splitting the force up between the two towns. Some had suggested that the enemies' focus would be on Krisbane. Paul would not leave either town undefended. The enemy did not need to travel across land. They would be tunneling and able to attack from the back of either town. Fortunately the two towns were less than two hours apart. Paul had been thankful for the fact that they would be able to traverse between the two. He left the last tent of a man who had kept all of his equipment in the best condition. He wrinkled his brow, deep in thought. The Flamethrower would be after him, and if he wasn't able to stop it, his army would suffer heavy casualties. He would rely on his gift and his training. He walked back to his own tent and found Bôren waiting for him, studying a piece of paper. He glanced up and saw Paul.

"Paul, this just came in from a messenger of Arum. I think you should see it."

He handed the note to Paul, who read:

> To commander.
>
> We are the people of Arum, and we can fend for ourselves. We do not need or want any support from the Nehgrog or anyone else. We would appreciate it if Nehgrog stayed away from our battles instead of assuming we are helpless.
>
> Signed,
> General Mulas, Leader of Arum

Paul let out a sigh of annoyance. Bôren was quiet. He knew that Paul hated leaving the town alone, and he only hoped that Krisbane would be more grateful.

"We have no word from Krisbane," said Bôren, almost guessing his thoughts. Paul nodded. Bôren had proven to be an excellent second in command.

"Well, Bôren, I guess this means that we will be moving our forces?"

"Yes, technically we are on the outskirts of Arum, and Mulas would be outraged if we did not move."

"I will tell the men. We will move three miles south to Krisbane." Bôren turned to leave. "And Bôren, send a message to Arum and tell them that we will be ready to return at the first sign of danger, but we will wait for their word."

"I will see to it."

Paul sighed and ran his hand through his hair. He glanced up at the half moon that had begun to rise. As much as he hated leaving, he was relieved he did not have to separate his forces. Undoubtedly it was putting Arum at a great risk, and of course he knew the Dark Army would know of this exchange and concentrate their forces on Arum. What would he do? General Mulas had made himself clear that he wanted no assistance. Paul sighed and rubbed his temple. If the king had sent 200 Green Guard as he had promised, he might have been able to hide half of them near Arum and have a peace of mind about their safety. Standards were not trained for stealth and needed a commander. He sighed. It was time to break the news to his men. He walked up to the small fire they had built. In this part of the country a fire wouldn't attract much attention if it were small enough. While it offered little heat, it was another subtle morale booster that Amon had taught Paul. He stopped near the fire. One of the men noticed him and in a few short seconds they were all standing at attention.

"Tonight we have received word that we are not permitted near Arum. We will pack camp and head south towards Krisbane. I want every man ready to go in less than an hour. Ludar?"

"Yes sir?" answered one of the soldiers.

"I want you to personally oversee the proceedings. I have some business that requires my direct attention. My second in command, Bôren, will return soon, but until then you have charge."

"Yes sir, I will not disappoint you."

Paul nodded. Every soldier had seemed to respect Ludar. Paul had noticed that he had marched in front ahead of the men. While they were all standards and equals in rank, Paul gathered that Ludar was a sort of captain to the men. This man knew the weight of responsibility resting on him. Paul nodded one more time before spinning on his heels and heading to his tent. Men shuffled around him as he buckled his sword to his belt and untied his horse. Without a backwards glance, Paul shot off into the cold night.

Bôren had been riding for nearly an hour when he reached the first sign of civilization. Arum was a city built high. It covered very little land due to the unstable ground around them, but each building was no less than three stories tall. It was an impressive site, Bôren noticed.

Arum was a city of blockheads. No defenses, not even a gate. Just a simple archway that read: "The city of Arum, open to all."

Bôren shook his head. They were idiots and now had fought against protection. Bôren was here to make sure that they would change that. He galloped into the city, which was more like a small town with less than 100,000 people in it. The streets were narrow, and Bôren was forced to abandon his horse to be able to navigate the short streets. A few people here and there gave him strange glances and others simply smiled. He walked up to a man in a uniform.

"Excuse me, sir. Can you tell me where General Mulas is?"

The man turned to him, looked him over, then turned and walked away. Bôren was getting tired of the Aruman people already. He swung out his sword and held the tip at the man's neck and smiled at the man's pale shocked face.

"Now, tell me, good sir, where is General Mulas?"

"H-he's at the...um...in...the...er..."

Bôren pushed his sword harder into the man's neck.

"All right! I will take you to him. Please, put your sword away!"

Bôren looked around and saw that he had caused a bit of a commotion with his little stunt. He lowered his sword, and the man stumbled in front of him. Bôren followed his lead and soon they came upon a huge building. It wasn't very wide, but it stood two stories above any other structure in the city. There was something strange about the way it towered over the people. Bôren decided he didn't like the Arum city at all—and yet he was here to force them to allow Paul to save them. He shook his head at the irony. They entered the building, and Bôren was left to wait in a side room. Brightly colored tapestries were hung across the walls. Despite it being the tallest building in the city, it looked no different inside than any of the others. It was made of wood with a thatched roof and occasional windows. Bôren wondered why they hadn't put more effort into making the capitol of the city even a little more exquisite. Either there was some philosophical nonsense behind why they hadn't, or they were just plain lazy. Bôren looked around and noticed very little detail. Everything seemed to have been made quickly and in mass quantity. It was a general attitude about the city: lack of quality. Why would a craftsman or builder not take pride in his work and create something more than mediocre? Indeed the Aruman had a strange culture. A man wearing very simple clothes descended the stairs and looked at Bôren. For a moment neither said anything, each studying the other. Finally Bôren broke the silence.

"I wish to speak to the General. General Mulas."

"Then speak, sir, for I am General Mulas."

Bôren hesitated. "Of course. General, we have information of an army headed towards this region. We have centered our forces around Krisbane, but we urge you to reconsider your desire to have us move. There is a Flamethrower among them."

The General grew agitated. "We have our own ways of learning about the plans of the Dark One, and I assure you that we will be perfectly safe. We have an army greater than you think, Nehgrog." He spat the last word out as if it were an insult.

"Then you condemn yourself and your people to death or worse, slavery into Maugrax. You do realize this, don't you?"

The General's face was turning red. "You will leave now. If you refuse, I shall order my guards to kill you where you stand."

Bôren was not about to disobey his order from Paul. "I will not leave until you withdraw your request for our removal. We will not leave you unarmed."

"*Guards!* Take this man away; if he refuses, kill him."

Four men moved from unseen areas in the room towards Bôren. He decided to let the Arumans suffer their own fate. He let them take him and put up no fight. They led him directly out of the city as Arum had no walls and no gates, just archways. He found his horse where he had left it. The sun was almost up, and he needed to get back to camp. He gave his horse a short kick, and then he was

gone. The General watched through a high window as the Nehgrog
and his horse shrunk into the horizon. He turned to his aide who
sat nervously behind him.

"How did they know?"

Paul had waited as long as he could for Bôren. The enemy would not.
He had to move his forces, and he had to move them before the sun
was up. The morning was beginning, and the camp had just begun
to move. He had ridden towards Krisbane and found a messenger
that would ride and tell them if the enemy had struck. It was amazing how fast these Nehgrog worked. He had doubted that the Arum
General would change his mind but nevertheless had sent Bôren to
see. If anyone could change a man's mind, it was Bôren. Suddenly a
man came galloping towards him. At first he thought it was Bôren,
but then he realized that this man was coming from Krisbane.

"Tunnelers! They're here!"

It took a few seconds for the words to sink in for Paul. Then
the realization hit him. The dark army was faster than they had
thought. He half-expected the men to panic, but they marched on,
undeterred.

"Halt! Drop your tents and food supplies; we have to make double time. Let's move!"

Rapidly the men organized their gear in a small pile under a
rock overhang. They quickly scrambled into formation and began
to march at a brisk pace. If they were lucky, they could reach
Krisbane before the enemy did, but once tunnelers could be heard,
the entire army would be above ground any minute. Including the
Flamethrower. Suddenly an old thought jumped into Paul's mind.
Amon had once mentioned that no one knew how Flamethrowers
traveled. However, they had seen one traveling with the army that
first marched on Krisbane. Perhaps that was an unusual case. Perhaps
the Flamethrower would come from a different route. What if he

was already there? Paul knew that he was key to Krisbane's survival. The Flamethrower could take out the city alone. He turned to Ludar.

"Ludar, I'm appointing you captain. Take the men and position yourselves outside of Krisbane in a large perimeter. Pray that the army hasn't arrived when you get there. Good luck."

"Yes sir, and you." Paul nodded and kicked his horse three short times and sped ahead of the army—rocks, dirt, trees, grass, they all disappeared. He took no notice of any of it. He was focused entirely on battling the Flamethrower. He thought of everything Amon had taught him. Calm. He had to calm himself. He didn't know how far it was until he reached Krisbane, but he knew that he would get there as soon as he could. He rode for just under an hour before he saw smoke rising in the distance. His heart stopped. The city was burning. Paul raced forward pushing his horse to its limits. His cloak now billowed behind him as he reached the outskirts of the city. Still he raced through the gate that was opening for him. As he slowed, he noticed that there were people walking around calmly. He looked around wondering where the Flamethrower was. He dropped off his horse and nodded for a stable hand to take it. He ran towards the castle. Krisbane was an elegant city, a miniature Jedar. Paul had no time to notice architecture as he took the steps two at a time. Before he reached the top, the guards had opened the door and let him in. He thought of slowing down upon entering the throne room, but decided that in times of crisis, formality was less important. The old king jumped when Paul burst through the doors.

"What is the meaning of this?"

"Where is he? The Flamethrower!" Paul panted.

"Sir, I don't know who you think you are, but you have no right storming into my palace like this."

"Forgive me, I am Paul, son of Mark, heir to the throne of Calarath. I am the leader of the army that will save you. Now where is the Flamethrower?"

"There is no Flamethrower here. Not yet at least." The king stroked his long beard.

"But I saw the smoke."

"That is our traditional fire. We build it before we go into battle. Do not worry, Paul; we are safe…for now."

Paul breathed a sigh of relief.

"And where is your army?"

"They are coming. I have to be here when the Flamethrower arrives."

"Of course. Thank you, Paul. Our city will be in your debt."

Paul nodded and strode out to the walkway on top of the walls.

Bôren had reached the army literally a few short minutes after Paul had left. He had taken command and was now leading them at an impressive speed towards Krisbane. The sun had almost reached its peak, and Bôren was afraid they would arrive all too late. For him the worst would be to find Paul slain and the city in ruins—and all because of him. He would not let that happen. He pushed the men faster than he had thought possible, even for Nehgrog. They had arrived at the city an hour after mid-day and found the city unsettlingly calm. Now he stood by Paul watching for a sign of the enemy.

"I don't understand. They said that they had heard tunnelers. They should have been here hours ago. I have a bad feeling about this."

"Paul, it's possible the sound they heard was not a tunneler."

Paul looked at Bôren with unbelief. "Nothing sounds like a tunneler. The people would know what it sounds like." Paul squinted and searched the horizon. "It sounds like the Dark Lord of Maugrax is coming up with new strategies."

"Paul, you look exhausted. Try and get some rest. If we hear or see anything I'll tell you."

Paul sighed. He knew he needed to be in his best condition to fight, but his mind was too busy to be able to think of rest. "Thank you, Bôren, but I think I'll check on the perimeter defenses and sounding units." Paul nodded to Bôren and walked down the stairs towards the gate. Then he heard it. A high-pitched screeching sound that echoed throughout the city. Paul snapped into alertness and looked around. He burst through the gate and searched the hills around the city. Then he found what he was looking for. A large portion of one of the hills had begun to turn a dull gray. A huge section of the hill exploded out releasing hundreds of Ashkah. They were nearly 200 feet away from Paul and his now assembled Nehgrog army. No sign of a Flamethrower. Paul barked rough orders to his men to hold their ground and leave none alive. Then he set off towards a watchtower. The towers were scattered throughout the city. Perhaps he could see something from there, but no, too late. One of the watch towers at the opposite end of the city bust into flame. Paul stopped.

The northern side! Why would the Flamethrower come from there? Paul had no time to think. He drew his sword and raced towards the gate. It was bolted shut. In the next second three other buildings burst into flame. Archers shot arrows blindly out. Paul tried to lift the large bolt, but it wouldn't budge. He was trapped, and the city was being attacked. Angrily he kicked against the gate. A few seconds later it burst into flame. Obviously the Flamethrower was trying to get whoever was coming through. Paul climbed through the growing hole, careful not to get any of the Slime on him. A large dark figure stood out in the open. As Paul looked, an archer shot an arrow into the sky. Paul's stomach reeled at the sight, but he pressed on towards it. Suddenly everything went black. He was still conscious, but he couldn't see anything. For a moment he thought he had gone blind. Then he realized that he had. The Flamethrower had shut off his eyes. It was an exercise that he and Amon had practiced. He calmly pushed back the attack and created a mental wall around his mind. This battle would be not only between the swords; it would be between their minds.

The Flamethrower drew a sword, unusually elegant in its design. He swung three times at blinding speeds, but Paul had already slowed him enough to dodge the attacks. The Flamethrowers were hard to slow down because their attacks were faster than normal. Paul felt a barrage of attacks in his mind as he stepped forward and swung. He could see the Flamethrower's mind now. It was like a dark chasm. He parried an attack and sidestepped another. Then he dove into the chasm. Images, thoughts, feelings bombarded him as he dove through the darkness. Paul held blades with the creature, then spun out and lunged. Finally he saw it. It was like a large dark hand was spread out across the Kingdom. The Flamethrower, panicking because of what Paul was seeing, threw all its energy into blocking Paul from its mind and left itself open. Paul drew back and slashed the creature across its shoulders leaving the body cleanly cut off from the head. A familiar screech sounded, and then was gone. He had done it. The Flamethrower was dead.

He turned around as an arrow struck the ground behind him. It was the one the guard had shot before he had engaged the Flamethrower. The whole battle had lasted less than the flight of one arrow. Paul shook off a strange feeling, then sprinted along the outer walls of the city towards the Ashkah battle. He saw nearly half of his men dead and the other half fighting valiantly. There were less than ten Ashkah left. As he watched, the number dropped to zero. Everyone was silent as the quiet aftermath of battle set in. People whispered and watched Paul as he made his way back to the city. Paul overheard one of them saying: "...our savior."

Homecoming

† † † † † † †

The room was full of merriment and rejoicing as the night wore on. The people of Krisbane sang and danced and drank towards Paul and his men. Paul did not join them. He had grown worried from what he had seen in the Flamethrower's mind. He had a terrible headache, probably some attack the Flamethrower had dealt before fleeing. He retired early but could not sleep. *What did it mean? A hand stretching over the Kingdom? Was it figurative?* He needed more information. This was a step forward, but it made him realize how little he knew about his enemy. Amon had once told him that the more you knew about your enemy, the better chance you had of defeating him. Paul sighed. *Would the legendary doctors at Calarath be able to cure a Flamethrower attack? Had there ever been a case like this before?* Suddenly a thought hit him. *If the Flamethrower had used its mind to cripple Amon, perhaps* Paul *could use* his *to revive him.* The idea gave him sudden energy, and he leaped out of bed and threw his uniform over his tunic. He splashed some cold water on his face, then opened the door and flew downstairs to the inn where the people were drinking and laughing in the orange glow of the fire. Smoke drifted around him as he searched for Bôren. He found him sitting at a table quietly sipping a mug of ale and watching the proceedings before him with a sort of amusement. Paul crossed the room and sat across from Bôren.

"Bôren, how quickly do you think we could muster the men? When is the soonest we could leave?"

"It depends on the urgency. I could have the remaining men ready to go before dawn, but they wouldn't be happy. Where are you so eager to go?"

"Well, first I want to get back to your king and deliver the information as promised. Then I want to head back to Calarath and see if anything can be done about Amon."

Bôren took a sip of his ale and glanced casually around the room. He turned back to Paul. "I have studied men all my life as a General. I know how to motivate them, and I know what sort of things will slow them down. One thing I have learned is that after a battle, you must allow your men some sense of accomplishment, and to achieve that you must let them celebrate. Give them a day in Krisbane before we leave. They will march faster and be more responsive."

Paul nodded. He knew that taking advice from this experienced man would be wise, but he still felt the urgency to *do* something. "I suppose you are right. We'll give them a day. In the meantime I want to explore the strategy of the battle. Perhaps you and I could walk the fields tomorrow and discuss it?"

"I would enjoy that very much, Paul. It seems that they caught us in a pincer motion. That is a very unorthodox strategy for the armies of Maugrax to use. I think you were right, Paul. Things are changing, and we cannot expect to fight our enemies the way we did during the Jedarian War."

The next morning Paul and Bôren rode out the city gates towards the hole where the Ashkah had emerged. They came upon the hill.

"Looks like pretty standard Ashkah tactics; however, this isn't the part that confuses me," Paul said quietly. "What I don't understand is why the tunnelers waited after they reached this point. Why not simply burst through and attack?"

"Wait a moment, look here," cried Bôren, pointing inside the tunnel. "The tunnel branches! That's how they achieved the pincer. But why did no Ashkah attack from the northern side?"

Paul looked up in horror. "Arum. They must have split their forces and headed towards them. Send a rider out towards the city. See if any survived."

"Certainly."

Paul watched as Bôren quickly galloped back across the field. Paul remounted his horse and rode towards the city gates, then along the wall towards where the encounter with the Flamethrower had occurred. A single arrow protruded from the ground near a black heap. Paul nudged his horse and rode up to the body. He looked around for possible ways the Flamethrower would have used to get here. Paul rode away from the body towards a cluster of rocks. That would have concealed a small tunnel quite well and not given any sign of the Flamethrower's entry.

Dismounting he walked towards the cluster and looked between them—a crudely cut hole, even cruder than the normal Ashkah tunnels that opened into a dark void. Paul tossed a rock down the shaft to see how deep it was and was surprised when a loud hissing noise erupted from the tunnel. It wasn't the hiss of a snake or an animal. No, Paul had heard that sound before. That was the hiss of the Gray Slime eating into the rock. Paul stumbled back. So that's how the Flamethrower tunneled. They used the foul Slime to erode away the dirt and rock in front of them. They themselves would have to be impervious to the Slime. Paul closed his eyes and thought through the enemy's tactic. They had tunneled towards Krisbane and stopped when they split forces to head towards Arum. The Flamethrower had then stopped and tunneled his way through to attack the city from behind. But why separate the Flamethrower?

He would have more protection within the horde of Ashkah. Then again, he would not be targeted by anyone nearby—except Paul.

He walked to his horse and remounted, still shocked by the developments. He flew back towards the gate where he saw four men trying to repair the gate without going near the pool of dripping Slime that had eaten into the wood and stone. Flamethrowers seemed to have an array of lasting attacks that would continue to damage even if the host body was destroyed or fled. They opened the broken gate to allow him through, but the pool of Slime would prevent his horse from going further. He quickly jumped off his horse and, taking a few steps back, leaped over the small pool. Someone would get the horse later. Right now he needed to get his diminished army back to Nehgrog. He ran through the winding, stone streets wondering how long he had until the enemy regrouped and attacked again. Time was definitely running out. He found the inn where the soldiers were being housed. Fortunately Paul could count on the disciplined nature of the Nehgrog to be ready to leave when called. He only hoped that most of them were sober enough to march.

The sun was beginning to crest, and Paul knew they would not reach Nehgrog before nightfall, especially if they had to stop to collect the supplies they had dropped. Time seemed to be slipping out of Paul's hands. He walked into the inn and looked around. The men were up and eating breakfast. The clatter of forks and knives and the low chatter of talk around the table buzzed around Paul as he made his way to the burly innkeeper. Paul liked Krisbane. The people were laid back and relaxed but not lazy. He wondered when the messenger would return with news about Arum. Something felt very wrong about the situation with the city. Why had they not wanted help? Surely they were not that senseless.

"Ahh…Paul. Can I help you?" the innkeeper's gruff voice trying to sound respectful cut Paul from his thoughts.

"Oh yes, Alan, have you seen Bôren anywhere?"

"Sure, came in here 'bout…I'd say, ten minutes ago and took one of them boys with him." He pointed to the tables of soldiers. "A fine lot of infantry you got there, General."

"Thank you. Will you tell me when he gets in?"

"Yes sir." Alan, being an innkeeper, was generally a dirty and greasy man with rough stubble constantly on his chin. He had a tendency to scratch his chin frequently when he talked, oftentimes irritating those he was speaking to. Paul turned and walked towards the table where Ludar sat talking animatedly with a few men. He was using his arms expressively, flailing about and making all sorts of weird motions to animate his story. He stopped mid-sentence when he saw Paul.

"Good morning, Ludar. Might I have a word with you?"

"Certainly, sir." Ludar stood up and wiped a piece of food off the corner of his mouth with a napkin. He followed Paul to a corner of the room.

"Ludar, we must set off for Nehgrog this afternoon. We must leave before mid-day if we are to reach Nehgrog during daylight. Prepare your men, and don't forget the supplies we left near Arum."

"Sir, with all due respect, retrieving the supplies would be a waste of time. I'm sure we could do without them."

"Nevertheless, Ludar, I do not want to waste them. Gather the tents and weapons. Let the Krisbanes or Arumans take the food."

"Yes sir," said Ludar with a brisk nod. He was a strong, well built man, showing no signs of old age despite being nearly forty. He was from a middle-class family and was trained like most Nehgrog for the army. Paul turned and looked around the room. Most had finished eating and had pushed their empty plates away. It was time to leave.

They were back in the tunnels. The old stone and strange light cast by the torches had begun to get very monotonous. Paul was growing impatient. Bôren had advised Paul not to take any of the Krisbane horses through the tunnels, so he and Bôren now walked on foot in front of the men. He hurried his men. So what if they were a little tired? They would have ample time to rest at Nehgrog; however, these men wouldn't need rest like the normal Calarath soldier. Paul felt as if he was wasting time going through the tunnels. He knew that the tunnel would open before they would head into the direct tunnel that led under Nehgrog to the mustering area. He watched the men.

Despite their happy celebrating the night before and the energy that came with victory, Paul was surprised to find them neither talking nor sulking. They celebrated when it was time to celebrate, and they marched when it was time to march. He liked the complete discipline of the Nehgrog. Perhaps they should teach some of the children in Calarath. Paul noted that throughout the long tunnel, he never came across a single torch that was not lit or a stone that was missing or a breathing hole that had caved in. Everything was kept immaculate. Paul wondered if anyone knew that these tunnels spread under their cities, towns, and farms. The marching grew tedious as the day wore on. Still Paul heard no grumbling or complaining from the men. They seemed perfectly content with marching until they dropped dead. He turned to Bôren.

"How much longer does this tunnel stretch?"

"Well, from the last marker it should only be about another two miles."

"Marker? What marker? I didn't see anything."

"In our tunnels we mark how long the tunnel is with colors—a yellow stone in the center of the wall to our right means that you are marching towards Nehgrog. A reddish colored stone on our left means that you are walking away from Nehgrog. The stones have numbers engraved into them. The last one said 15/18."

"Wow. That's brilliant. I really admire the Nehgrog." Paul glanced over at Bôren who was trying to hide a beaming smile. He would be smiling too if the heir to the throne admired his city. They marched on in silence. Paul kept an eye out for the colored stones Bôren had mentioned but saw nothing. They came to a smooth, gentle slope that led to a large wooden trapdoor. Bôren expertly unlocked it and threw it open. He did a brief scan of the surrounding area, and then, content that everything was safe, stepped out. Paul had barely noticed the scenery during the journey towards Krisbane, but now he saw that they had come up near a large green forest. A small pond sat off in the distance surrounded by cliffs that reflected the setting sun into Paul's eyes. Although the tunnels were well ventilated, they could not mimic the freshness of pure air and the warmth of the light of the sun. The last of the men made their way out of the tunnel and closed and locked the door behind him. Paul knew that in one of those cliffs lay the door to the last tunnel.

"All right men, take a breather," he shouted to the small army.

"Paul, are we heading into the next tunnel or staying above ground?"

"I think it would be safer to travel in the tunnel, but we do need to keep the men fresh and ready. What do you suggest?"

Bôren noted that Paul was not stubborn like most commanders. Paul was interested in Bôren's advice, and he knew that sometimes his plans were not always the best. "Paul, I know these men. They will march regardless of whether their morale is up. They are Nehgrog."

"Then we go through the tunnel. Let's go. We only have three more hours, probably less until sundown." Bôren clapped twice, and the men stood and fell into formation. Paul once again walked to the front of the line next to Bôren and led the way. They reached the cliff face, and Bôren stopped. He slid his hand across the rock face searching for a seam. Finally he found it and took out a small knife. He stabbed the knife into the rock and pried it open. A small chunk of rock no bigger than Paul's fist fell out revealing a large wooden handle. Bôren sheathed the knife and, pulling on the handle, opened a large square door. He quickly placed the chunk of rock back in the hole before following Paul in. Once again Paul was greeted by the monotonous sight of hard stone floors and walls and hundreds of torches stretching miles ahead of them.

He thought back on the last few days. He had beaten the king of Nehgrog and earned an army. He had taken that army into battle and lost less than half his men. True, it was an extremely high casualty rate, but it was not entirely his fault. The king had promised 200 Green Guard but delivered only 100 standard infantry. The odds had been stacked against them, too. He had also defeated a Flamethrower entirely on his own. It was a historical moment, one that Paul would not soon forget. He had learned new information about his enemy's weapons. The tunnel seemed to stretch to infinity to Paul, and every moment felt as though they were running out of time. He didn't know exactly what had caused this sudden feeling of rushing, but he knew he needed to get to Nehgrog a lot faster than he was going now. Something in him screamed to just get the men to run. Then Paul caught sight of a single stone in the wall that seemed discolored. The first mistake he had seen of the Nehgrog tunnels. However, as he came closer, the numbers 16/30 engraved into it reminded Paul of what Bôren had said. At least Paul knew they were over halfway.

Emerging out of the tunnel into the large open underground chamber flooded Paul with relief. They were back in Nehgrog. Strangely it felt like returning home to Paul. He shook hands and thanked each of his men before Bôren led him through another tunnel to the surface. The night was dark around them as they walked quietly through the city, occasionally getting a nod or glance from a watchman. Bôren turned to Paul.

"Where are you staying tonight, Paul?"

"I was thinking of going to the inn that I stayed at a few days ago."

"Well, why don't you stay at my house? We have an extra room, and my family will gladly accept a guest."

"Thank you, Bôren, I'd much prefer a real house than that inn."

So together Paul and Bôren walked towards a large neighborhood. They passed three houses, all looking exactly like the other. The fourth house was Bôren's and identical to the others. Bôren walked up to the door and produced a key from his belt with which he proceeded to unlock the door. They entered into a well-kept, clean house. The rooms were dark, and the house felt empty. Bôren smiled and walked further into the house into a small study. Open archways led to other rooms of the house, one into a dining room and another into the kitchen and one up to the stairs. One more door lay off to the side and sat closed. Bôren lit a fire and the room grew brighter.

"Come, Paul, sit. I don't want my guest to be standing while he is in my house."

"Thank you," said Paul, taking a seat, "but shouldn't we keep our voices down so that we don't wake the others?"

"Paul, in Nehgrog culture when a man marries a woman, the man will build his house near his father's. This way all the members of a family are in the same area. A clan, you might say. You saw how reliant we are on our tunnel network. Well, between all the houses are tunnels leading to the other houses in that clan. This way when the men are at war or away, the women of the clan move in with the other members and help with the chores. It helps with the loneliness and gives the women more security. Right now my wife, Aris, will probably be at my brother and his wife's house."

Paul shook his head. "Unbelievable. Nehgrog is truly underestimated by the outside world. I used to think Nehgrog was a city of barbarians with little shacks. Now I see that they are practical, hardworking, disciplined, and smart. The people of Calarath would do well to learn from you."

Bôren poured a strange smelling clear liquid for them both before sitting down again. "We tried to teach them, Paul. Do you know some history about Jedar?"

"A little but not much."

"The Nehgrog were a sub-culture of Jedar—we were the warrior caste. All the greatest cities have their subcultures. Jedar had many. We were the biggest and most disciplined. Almost all of us were trained to one day join the ranks of soldiers that defended Jedar. But when Jedar fell, our leader, Mura, led us away through a secret tunnel system he had ordered built. Over 200,000 men, women, and children traveled those tunnels before arriving here where Mura had already begun construction."

"He knew Jedar would fall? Or at least expected it to?"

"No, I don't think so. He was just very practically minded; he realized that every city had its weakness, and he knew the Jedar would probably one day fall. Despite everyone around him telling him that its walls were impregnable, he built the tunnel system that saved our lives. The enemy never knew of our retreat—the entrance to the tunnel was in Mura's home which he set fire to as the last person entered."

Paul sat back, feeling as though he was back with Amon, trading stories and histories over a fire. He picked up the glass Bôren had poured for him.

"It's Sno'ak. It's a common drink in Nehgrog. Try it."

Paul sipped the drink and was barraged with a mixture of flavors. It tasted like a mix of apple cider, grapes, and something else. It was a wonderful blend, soothing to the tongue.

"Paul, why are you here?"

Paul swallowed a mouthful of his drink. "I came to Nehgrog seeking support for a campaign to find out more about this new threat."

"No, I know that. I mean why are you here in this Kingdom? What is your purpose? Your destiny?"

Paul was surprised by the question. He had never really given it much thought. He had presumed he would find out when he was a man, but the line between adult and child had blurred.

"I don't know. I realize the gifts I have been given must be put to their fullest use and that there must be something great on the horizon, but for right now, I don't know."

"I see. My father asked me the same question when I was younger. I had never really thought about it. What was my purpose? As I grew older, I realized I had a strategic mind, and one day someone noticed and told the Council. Slowly through many battles, I worked my way up to where I am. But do you know what, Paul? This isn't my purpose. I can sense that there is more to my life than being a great general. Everyone has a great purpose, and while it may seem small to them or even to others, when you look at the large picture, every part counts."

Paul stared into the fire, caught by Bôren's words. He had never thought the Nehgrog were thinkers either. Perhaps Bôren was different. Yes, Bôren did seem different. He was kinder, softer than other Nehgrog he had seen around. And he was a good leader as well as a good follower. He knew his place well.

"I've never really thought about it like that before. I suppose..." Paul was interrupted by a door opening behind him and a woman with two boys coming through. Bôren leaped up and hugged the woman, giving her a brief kiss before turning to each of the boys and hugging them. He turned around and beamed proudly at Paul.

"Paul, I would like you to meet my lovely wife, Aris." Paul bowed courteously to her. "And my two sons, Jerael...," he ruffled the younger child's blond hair, "...and Serak," he said, putting his arm around the older child with brown hair. Paul smiled at them both before Bôren continued. "Aris, this is Paul. He will be staying the night with us and possibly a few days in Nehgrog. He is the commander I was telling you about."

Aris hurriedly prepared the room for Paul and welcomed him into their home. It was now long past midnight, and the children were slowly walking to their rooms. Bôren and Paul retired to their separate rooms.

Deposition

† † † † † † †

Paul spent the next few days at Bôren's house. He helped around the house as much as he could, serving when necessary and even sparring with the two children. Serak, the older of the two, was shy and preferred to study and be left alone than to spend time with other children. Jerael preferred to laugh and play with the other children. Paul found them both to be extraordinary fighters for their age, and often he underestimated them when they practiced. On his first day in Nehgrog, Paul had decided to report back to the king. However, the king had seemed nonchalant about the news, and although Paul stressed the point that it was definitely a major threat, the king's prejudice had led him to disregard anything Paul said. On the second day he again went before the king to desperately try to raise his awareness, but the king would not hear of it.

"This is a typical Calarathan ploy. They are obsessed about this crazy idea of mental wars. The only real war that goes on is the one you can fight with steel. A good mind and a strong hand will go farther than any mental weapon. I saw how you fought Paul when we dueled, but that does not convince me any more than your words."

Paul had left the throne room angry and talked to Bôren that night. Now he stood before the king for the third time in the three days.

"It's you again? What do you want?" the king asked angrily.

"Your Majesty, I am taking my rightful control of Nehgrog. I am to be the new king." Paul waited to see the older man's reaction. Instead of appearing shocked, he simply rested his chin on his hand and scratched at the stubble that was growing there. Paul continued, "I have the rightful documents, signed by both of your Councils that give me full permission to take control of this city. Please step aside." With the mention of the documents the king's face grew dark. He knew that there was nothing he could do to change the Councils' decision. If the War Council and the Government Council decided on something, they could overrule the king. Now he was stuck.

"How can my Councils give a Calarathan the permission to rule the great Nehgrog? It is lunacy. No, worse, it is treason! I don't know what games you've played with them, but I assure you that I will never hand over leadership of this glorious Kingdom!"

Paul's eyes grew intense. "You will hand over Nehgrog whether you do it willingly or not." With that the doors behind him burst open and nearly fifteen Green Guard stepped forward to escort the dethroned king out. Paul now ruled the city. True, it was his right to rule an entire Kingdom, but now this was his by Nehgrog standards. As the screams of the struggling king grew quieter, Bôren stepped forward.

"Well done, Paul. I never thought he would go so easily. Now we are rid of him. You have complete control over Nehgrog, Paul."

Paul looked back at the throne and then to Bôren. "Bôren. You know that I am young, and I know nothing about running an entire city. Would you take my place as king?"

"Me? Paul! How can you hand over control of an entire city so easily! We spent the whole night getting those documents! I really can't accept."

"Bôren, you have led the War Council for years now. You have proved that you are capable of leadership. Take the throne, Bôren. Please."

Bôren looked at the throne and furrowed his brow. It was apparent that it was a major decision for Bôren. Paul pushed his advantage. "Remember when you spoke to me about purpose? Perhaps this is the next step for you. I want you to be king."

Bôren looked directly at Paul. "I will do it, Paul. I'll take the throne. But you must realize this feels like treason for me. I helped in dethroning the king so that you could rise to the place you earned from the Duel. I didn't aide you for personal gain or power." He looked to the door that Paul knew was a tunnel to the War Council Room. A cloud passed over the sun, and the room grew darker for a moment. Paul now saw the hundreds of torches burning for what must have been 100 meters behind the throne. Bôren smiled. "I am king of Nehgrog. It's unbelievable. After all these years of hoping for a new king, I rise to take the place. Incredible." Just then a messenger ran in.

"Paul, I have a message for you. It's from Calarath." Paul walked towards the man confused. Why would his mother send him a message? He opened the letter and read.

Dearest Paul,

Your uncle's condition is worsening by the day. The doctors say they have never seen a case like his before. Please come home soon.

There was no signature, but Paul knew who it was from. He looked at Bôren. "I have to go back, Bôren. I have to go back to Calarath. I will return shortly. Thank you for everything, Bôren." Through the last few days a new, strong bond had begun forming between the two. With a last look he tore down the stairs and toward Bôren's house. He had not bothered to unpack his small bags, luckily, and grabbed them before dashing out the door. The stables were on the other side of the neighborhood. He set off with the pack over his shoulder at a brisk walk so as to not attract attention. When he reached the stables, he found the horse that Bôren had given him a few days ago. He opened the pen and looked for the supply of food. The Nehgrog kept this small bundle of food for journeys that needed immediate attention and could not wait to find a pack of food. Paul saw it in the corner, safely away from the horses. He only hoped that the Nehgrog tastes were not different from his own. His horse was soon saddled and ready to go. With one last look at the city he galloped through the open gates. Knowing that the first thirty miles would be protected by Nehgrog defenses, he pushed his horse as fast as it could go. It took them just over an hour to reach the small bunkers Paul recognized as the entry point to the tunnels. It was a glorious city.

Bôren stood in the empty throne room. It was so strange. Surreal. Something had happened he never would have dreamed of. And yet, something that Paul had said had awoken something in Bôren. Perhaps this really was his destiny. He and few others had really noticed the decreasing condition of Nehgrog. Sure, the city was still alive and growing, but nothing was being made to improve it. That had always been the philosophy before Jonak had risen to the throne. He had been a two-sided king. To the public he was courteous and kind, but in reality he was greedy and hardhearted. He had done that very thing to Paul. Jonak had promised 200 Green Guard and delivered 100 standards. Bôren laughed. Paul had succeeded in the face of insurmountable odds.

He took to the door to discuss the matter with the War Council. He knew that they would accept him as king. They had even collaborated in saying that he should challenge the king in the Great Duel, but Bôren was content with where he was, and that was before he became aware of the cruelty of the king. This was the beginning of a new age for Nehgrog. Their chance to get on track and maybe even ally with Calarath and join back into the Kingdom. These were things the previous king would have scoffed at and perhaps even imprisoned Bôren for suggesting. He opened the door leading to the Council Room and saw that the room was empty except for two of the older members having a heated discussion over the map.

"...But that's absurd. Surely they would have realized the stupidity of the location?" said one pointing to the map.

"Apparently not. Who knows, maybe when they chose it, it was different?"

Bôren decided to interrupt. "Excuse me, gentlemen, has anyone seen Lonar? I presumed he would be here."

The man who was pointing to the map spoke. "He is in the armory inspecting those new Hren spears."

"Thank you," said Bôren with a nod and walked towards the door in the back of the room. As he opened it, the two men's conversation started up again. He found his old friend walking amidst hundreds of boxes. Some were open displaying a new prototype spear that had been in development. A few lay scattered across the floor; others had been thrown into targets. The room was a large rectangle with the targets on the far side of the room from Bôren. Swords, spears, bows, axes, knives, maces, and other Nehgrog weaponry were neatly arranged along the walls. Lonar looked up and saw Bôren.

"Ahh! My old friend! How are you doing? Any news?"

"Lots, my friend, lots. But first, what do you think of the spears?"

"Well, I must say I am very impressed. These are Class 6 spears. I believe they may even be more powerful than the 5G spear, but I have yet to test that." The weapons of Nehgrog were all organized into classes. Only certain warriors had the access and capability to wield certain classes. Everyone could use Class 1 weapons; they were available to the public. These were generally blunter, cheaper weapons for practice. Class 2 was standard infantry issue. Classes 3–5 were the higher classes, reserved for advanced soldiers and commanders. Class 5 weapons were potent and often required extra training to learn how to use them. The Green Guard's weapons were classed in the same way; however, they would tag a G to the end of the number. Green Guards oversaw the production of their weapons, and somehow they always were more effective than the originals. Before the Hren spears the highest class had been a 5G. Hren spears were the first Nehgrog weapons to be made elsewhere. A small town off the coast, so small most maps didn't even include its location, Hren was a branch of Nehgrog culture mixed with Jedarian-Calarath influences. The whole town was less than 2000 people, but they had access to their secret minerals, making weapons at exorbitant prices and excellent quality.

"Interesting. Perhaps they should make more of our weapons."

"Perhaps. We still don't know how they hold up in battle. But come, what is your news?"

"This may be hard to believe, but…" Bôren paused, pondering how to phrase it. *How would one announce becoming king?* "I…have succeeded Jonak as king. I have approval from the War Council and Government Council. I will be inaugurated tomorrow." Lonar clapped his friend on the back.

"Well done, my friend. I always said that you would make a fine king. Don't disappoint me—but tell me one thing. You say you have approval of the War Council, but I was not present when this meeting took place. It was an incomplete Council, and for tradition's sake we should recall a Council. Who knows, perhaps you would have been accused of unauthentic documents and beheaded." Lonar smiled. "I will call a Council tonight shortly before sun-down. Congratulations again, Bôren." They shook hands, and Lonar of Stone-House returned to the spears.

We will need these spears. Sooner than we think, Bôren thought sadly. The time of war seemed to have been forced upon them again. He left the room deep in thought.

. . . . .

Paul had traveled all day and most of the night. He had found a small cave and camped the few hours until morning inside. It was relatively small, probably no more than ten feet high, and tapering to less than two in the back. Overall the whole length would have measured about fifteen feet. It was small but gave him enough protection to build a small fire and sleep without worry of being seen. He was alert and constantly looked around the site for possible escape routes. When he was content that he was safe, he drifted off into a light sleep.

Paul opened his eyes and looked around. A large clear blue lake stretched infinitely to his left—to his right, the same. The small strip of land he stood on was less than his shoulder width. Slowly as he watched, a ship sailed from the horizon to his right. It was a large ship, the largest he had ever seen. It was painted white and blue and gold. It shimmered as it sailed towards Paul. The large, tall masts held in place massive sails that billowed softly in the wind. Paul, still amazed, turned to his left and saw a similar ship, but it was painted pure gold. The second ship reflected the sunlight towards Paul's eyes. Then both ships seemed to pause, both equal distances from Paul. The captain of the second, gold ship seemed to appear on deck dressed in fine purple and blue robes with a large crown on his head. He spoke to Paul.

"Paul. Follow me. You were born and destined to be with me. Come, join me," He spoke in a soft, soothing, compelling voice. Paul turned and looked to his right. A simpler looking man stood with his arms outstretched to Paul.

"Paul. You are one of mine. Do not be deceived by him!" He thrust a finger towards the other ship.

Paul realized his situation. He was caught between two captains of two great ships, each wanting him to follow them. He turned to the first.

"What will I gain by following you?"

The man smiled softly and spoke quietly but still clearly audible. "You will become what you were destined to be. You will become the leader of many. You will become the hope of the Kingdom."

Paul turned to the captain of the other ship. "What will I gain by following you?"

"I can promise you that in my ship you will find anything your heart desires. I can grant you wealth beyond your wildest imagination. You will even be able to see your father again."

Paul's eyes widened. His decision was made. He leaped from the shore and swam towards the shimmering gold boat. The captain lowered a rope and pulled Paul up. Suddenly the deck turned a sickly gray, covered in filth, dirt and Slime. The ship was now black, and the finely dressed captain now stood wearing dark robes. He spoke harshly, jarringly.

"I am the Dark Lord. You are now mine…" he hissed the last words. Paul spun towards the other ship where the captain stood weeping over the edge. Paul suddenly realized his mistake. He felt cold hard fingers press against his back…

Paul's eyes flew open. For a moment he had no idea where he was and what had happened. He looked around and recognized the cave. Slowly he realized that he had been dreaming. But it had not been a normal dream. He rubbed his eyes and saw that dawn was breaking. The fire had burnt low, and Paul threw some sand to put out the small flame. He spent a few minutes clearing the cave of evidence, then mounted his horse and set off towards the sun. His mind still raced from the aftermath of the dream. What if it wasn't merely a dream? Realizations struck him as the sun began to slowly rise higher and higher. He rode for a few hours, his mind racing through the dream's reality. He noticed that his water was only half full. In this area, although green and lush, it was often hard to find a good spring. He had seen a reflection to his right and rode towards it. While his horse drank and he refilled his water, the biggest realization hit him. The captain of the black ship was the Dark Lord. The Dark Lord was a real, physical threat in Paul's world. If the captain of one ship existed, wouldn't the captain of the first ship exist as well? He remembered when he was younger he would spend hours in the library. Many books had asked a simple question he had never given any thought: Did the legend of Ara'tel exist? Was there a supernatural being that was on the side of justice? Did he have a being equivalent to the Dark Lord on his side?

According to ancient Nehgrog customs, it was not unusual for the two Councils that had kept Nehgrog running to meet with the king in a ceremony referred to as the Twin Councils. A large hall in the lower part of the palace had been established when the people had fled Jedar. Now Bôren sat at the seat of honor in front of the two Councils. The room was a large circular hall with a long table shaped in a U following the curve of the room for the Councils. A small silver line at the base of the U separated the War Council from the Government Council. Bôren's seat sat adjacent to the U so that he faced inwardly towards the long table. Many generations of kings had sat in the seat he sat in now, awaiting final decisions on whether they would be granted control of the greatest military city known to mankind. Bôren calmly placed the stack of documents on the table and returned to his seat. One of the women on the Government Council eyed him with suspicion. Her name was Luille, and she had a reputation for being hard and suspicious. Most members of the Councils were male, but a reformist king in the past had opened the Government Council to women also. It had been a wise move; Luille had saved their city countless times in times of crisis. She had a quick mind but was never entirely trusting of anyone. Then again, every Nehgrog man, woman, and child was trained to have a healthy suspicion. However, Bôren suspected that something in her past had made Luille so stone-faced. She simply stared. To most it would have been unnerving, but Bôren had developed a stare of his own. They had gone over every document and had adjourned for over an hour to discuss amongst themselves. Finally they had called Bôren back into the room where he sat now.

"Bôren, son of Guthane. We have decided as a joint Council that your role as king is now legal," said an old man with a long flowing white beard and small glasses. "The inauguration ceremony will commence tomorrow. Congratulations." The Council stood as one and bowed to Bôren, who bowed in return. Servants of the palace came forward and began to extinguish the torches as the company filed out. Bôren smiled.

Paul walked into Amon's room and was shocked by the sight he saw. Amon had begun turning a ghastly white, his mother had told him, and had begun to lose hair. Paul pulled a chair next to the unconscious form as the door opened and a doctor walked in.

"Greetings, Paul. I'm afraid that there is something we must discuss." The young, black-haired man pulled a chair up opposite Paul. "Firstly, where were you two when he collapsed?"

"We were..." Paul cleared his throat. "We were battling a Flamethrower. Somewhere near Emelle. Within view of the city." The doctor began writing on a piece of paper when he paused.

"You say you were battling a Flamethrower? As in, hand to hand combat?"

"Yes...using the ancient Paladin techniques."

The doctor studied Paul with surprised eyes before returning to his paper.

"And how do you say he collapsed? Was it random?"

"No sir, I believe it had to do with holding the attention of the Flamethrower with his mind. The Flamethrower attacked him with some mental weapon. He collapsed instantly."

The doctor was scribbling down frantically. "I have one question though. You say you were using the Paladin technique; I know it well, and I studied the Paladin writings. However, I have never heard of anything of this nature before. Do you think it was a new attack? Surely the Flamethrower would have used this before?"

Paul swallowed. "I, um...hesitated. The Flamethrowers would have used this before, but the Paladin were trained not to hold longer than thirty seconds. Amon held it longer so that I could attack. I waited." He looked again at his uncle. *This was all my fault*, Paul thought morbidly.

The doctor finished his notes and nodded to Paul before leaving. Paul thought back to his dream. *If there is a dark, there must be a light. If there is a lock...there must be a key.*

Ԅren

† † † † † † †

The city of Nehgrog had grown in value in Bôren's eyes. Although he had always loved the city, he now viewed it as his own responsibility instead of simply his home. Within the first week of becoming king he had realized what a major responsibility the city was. Every day he had hundreds of people waiting in lines to bring him their requests and problems. He had two tunnels that had collapsed and a roof that needed repair. True, the Nehgrog were not a people dependent on others to fix their problems. For that he was grateful as most of the time.

Bôren thought of Jonak and his corruption. It was amazing how well Jonak had started reforming the Kingdom and improving everything he could, but slowly, over time, the power that he wielded possessed him, and he abused it. Bôren considered himself. Would he too fall prey to the pull of greed? Or would he be a noble king, worthy to be buried among the greatest of the kings of the past?

Bôren walked to the window and looked down. An archery lesson was being held near the palace grounds, and Bôren watched them. Most were between the ages of twelve and fifteen, both girls and boys. A half-dozen instructors walked between the young archers correcting posture and explaining what they were doing wrong. Bôren heard the whistle and thump of arrows flying through the air and striking their targets. It was a shocking realization. These young boys would be the soldiers he commanded someday. He would have to make the decisions that would affect whether they lived or died. There it was again, responsibility. Bôren, however, was made, perhaps even destined, for this weight. He had been tutored by some of the finest instructors in the city as well as having had the chance to study at the feet of some of the finest swordsmen and warriors. He remembered his first position as a squire to a Green Guard, Jarac. As was the custom, the Green Guard were referred to as Sirs by other people. The Councils and the king, those higher than them, called them by their first names only. Bôren had been perusing the thick pile of documents he had been given upon inauguration. He picked up a few and browsed their contents:

> Major losses and desert growth information: With major losses of cities to the south, the desert seems to be growing larger and faster than ever before. Strong reinforcement of Egon and Krisbane needed. Egon must not fall.

Bôren tossed the paper onto a table and wondered why Jonak had not responded earlier.

> Dorodish tribe raids on northern cities: Scouts report that the nomadic tribes of the Dorodish people have begun raids on the smaller cities to the north. The king's reinforcement was inadequate. More guards are needed to continue...

Bôren put the paper down next to the other one on the table. Finally there was one that really caught his attention.

> Hidden Green Guard: To prevent the people feeling like they were overly controlled by the Green Guard and to stop spies from reporting on exact numbers, a small village near the west coast has been selected as a Green Guard training and housing city. Estimated number of Green Guard in the Third Year of Jonak

is 560,000. Those who complete the training may be sent back to Nehgrog for blending in with the people. Harsh conditions and a diverse selection of terrain make the area good for grueling training. Approved solely by King Jonak. Approval of War Council never granted. Operation codename: Hren Project. City name: Hren.

Bôren lowered the paper. Hren. That's where the new spears had come from. He would locate the city and see if the program was still running. 560,000 Green Guard? It was unbelievable. And the fact that Jonak had acted without grants from the War Council disturbed him. *What else are you hiding, Jonak?* Bôren thought. He ran down the stairs to the lower room of the palace. He found the large map on the wall and searched the coastline near Nehgrog. Nothing. Bôren stopped. Obviously if Jonak had hidden this project, it would be on no maps. He walked to the back room and found three Green Guards he had met before and told them to ready five horses. He then walked through the short tunnel to the War Council building. He went into the armory and saw that it was empty. The boxes of spears had been stacked off to the side with a piece of paper reading:

Inspection Complete, field-testing required.

Bôren walked out the main doors and towards the tall Stone House at the top of the hill. He knocked three times on the door before Lonar appeared with a book in his hand.

"Ah, Lonar. I need your help."

"I'd be honored to help Bor...err...Your Majesty, come inside." He showed Bôren into the large study filled with books. A large oak desk sat in the center in front of a large leather chair. Two oil paintings hung behind the chair, each by the famous Nehgrog artist, Hesari.

"Sire, what can I do for you?"

"Well, firstly, I need to know what you know about the Hren weapons."

"Hmm. By my standards they seem to be excellent, very well made and designed. There is some mystery about that however. A simple town producing better weapons than a large city puzzles me. Why do you ask, Sire?"

"You know that when I became king, I was given all the reports of Jonak's doing. Well, I found that he had begun a secret Green Guard training program…in a coastal town named Hren."

"Ahh…so what we really have are guard spears? Fascinating. But this program must have taken place without the Council's decision. It surely must have been shut down?"

"Well, that is what I aim to find out today. I would gladly appreciate your presence."

"I would like to come, Sire. I'll get my horse ready…"

"No need, I already have them saddled and ready to go. Bring a map, although I know it won't have the location of this hidden city." Bôren noticed how quickly Lonar fell into calling him Sire. *Nehgrog discipline.* Bôren smiled.

Within an hour Bôren, Lonar, and three Green Guard were galloping out of the Northern Gate. It was a unanimous decision that the town must be north because the Arumans or Krisbanians would never allow a town in their territories. The terrain was rocky and barren for most of the way. Bôren and Lonar talked in low voices about Jonak. The king had obviously acted more than once without permission from appropriate Councils. The Green Guard rode together in silence. Then they saw it.

As they came around a large boulder, they caught sight of hundreds of men standing in formation. In the distance Lonar saw archery and jousting training. To Bôren's left an entire platoon was running with gear. Large, tall buildings that Bôren recognized as barracks stretched towards the distant coastline. From somewhere to their left a trainer could be heard shouting his orders to the men.

They all took in the hive of activity before they saw a scout planted on the boulder holding a loaded bow, drawn and aimed at Bôren. Behind a tree were two others, both aiming for Lonar. They halted the horses.

"Password?" the guard on the boulder called.

"Nuira." Bôren turned to look at the Green Guard behind him that had answered. He bowed his head towards Bôren. The scouts put away their weapons and shrunk back out of view. As they entered the large field containing hundreds upon hundreds of troops, Lonar felt shivers creep down his spine. An army of this size and of this caliber would be close to unstoppable. *What had the king planned on using it for?* They approached a small building and dismounted, and a Guard took the five horses away. Inside they saw three men: General Mulas, General Kale, and Nehgrog's own General Grek. The three men looked up as Bôren walked in. The room was messy, disorganized, and hot. It was cramped, and the large desk layered with maps and papers in the center of the room blocked all accessibility.

"Generals, I am Nehgrog's king. Who is in charge here?"

General Grek, a man that seemed to be made of rock and muscle, spoke in a deep gruff voice. "We have orders from Nehgrog's real king, Jonak. Any orders you bring must have a warrant by him."

Bôren slapped the document proving his ascension to the throne on the desk. "Is that good enough? Now who here is in charge?"

The three men peered at the document and then back at Bôren. Finally the Aruman General, Mulas, spoke. "We were told that this program was ratified by all members of the Twin Councils. Surely you, Bôren, as former leader of the War Council, know who is in charge?"

"General, I must inform you that Jonak acted outside of the Councils' knowledge." All except Grek looked at each other surprised. "I need to speak with someone who is in charge."

General Grek spoke again. "Jonak has put me in charge of most of the activities, but we three run this program intermittently. No one must know about this program. We will trust you though. What do you need?"

"How many Green Guard train here?"

"We currently have over 400,000 troops in training with well over 600,000 troops ready for battle."

"That's over a million soldiers!" Lonar said.

"Indeed, Lonar of Stone-House. But these are not normal soldiers. These are all Green Guard." Grek smiled.

"What possible reason could Jonak have had for creating such a massive guard force?" Lonar asked. "Surely the Guards we have in Nehgrog are enough for security?"

"Jonak said, 'It was preparation that saved the people of Nehgrog in Jedar. There will always be war. Wars will always need soldiers.' There would be nothing wrong with having the most powerful army in the world now would there?"

Lonar shifted uncomfortably. "Do you think Jonak was planning to control the Kingdom with an elite fighting force? Perhaps the man was greedier than we thought." Bôren looked across at the reaction from Grek. He furrowed his brow, then looked at the only person who hadn't spoken during the whole conversation, General Kale. The old man from Krisbane was Grek's cousin, and Lonar could see a definite resemblance.

Kale's voice was similar to his cousin's. "In the beginning years of Jonak's reign Jonak set up a secret alliance, an alliance between the towns of the north. The towns agreed to send young men ready to be trained if we would give them protection from the upcoming war with the Dark Lord or with the city of Calarath. This army would be used for that purpose. "

With that the men nodded before exiting. The shouts of trainers and officers could be heard throughout the camp. Why had no one found this place before? Why had no one reported on it? It was a strange thing indeed.

Paul had spent the entire night searching through the "Protected" section of the library. This is where the oldest, confidential writings were kept, and only a signed permit from the king could allow one to enter its forbidden halls. Paul had found the information on the Paladin and their mind capabilities. It was believed by some that they were gifted with the ability to read minds and even tell the future. Paul doubted it, but it led to a very interesting idea. What if the mind could be pushed beyond what the Paladin had accomplished? How far did its power reach? Paul wrote down a few notes from Paladin trainers and even found information that Amon had written along with the other Paladin captain…his father. He made his way silently into Amon's room and sat down again by his bed. Closing his eyes, he reached into a realm he had very little experience in—the realm of the mind. Then he detected it.

Much like fighting the Flamethrower, he found a deep well of black in Amon's mind. As he tried to dive in, he felt as if he hit a wall. He searched along it looking for a crack or break. He finally found a weak spot. The sun began to rise through the window. Still, eyes closed, he pushed the weak spot but felt a lock. It was as if it had been chained closed. He opened his eyes and looked around. It was beginning to grow brighter. How did one break a lock? With the right key. Paul closed his eyes and re-focused. He found the wall and lock and quickly calmed himself. Mentally he reached inside the mind lock and began twisting and turning the workings of it. Suddenly it broke free. He felt as though he had fallen through deeper into Amon's mind.

He opened his eyes and wiped the sweat from his forehead. He jumped when he saw that Amon's eyes were open. Slowly, Paul understood this complex attack. The Flamethrower shut down each individual part of Amon's body by locking up that area of his mind. Amon could move his eyes but could not speak or move. Paul closed his eyes and surged forward to the next obstacle. This one was harder. He noticed the longer he spent on a lock, with time the solution would come—even if he simply pushed without trying to break the lock. His mental presence was weakening the power of the Flamethrower's mental cage. Within an hour Amon could move his eyes and mumble with his mouth. Paul had a headache, but the progress was helping him push past the pain. There was something encouraging about Amon's unintelligible muttering. The strain on Paul was growing with each lock, but after a few more hours, the biggest lock broke through.

"Paul!" Paul jumped at the sound of Amon's voice.

"Amon! You're...I did it!"

"Well done, Paul. You're saving me. I can't move, but I can speak. What happened?"

"I hesitated, and it gave the Flamethrower enough time to lock up your mind. Each part of your body will be locked until I can break it. I have to take a break; it's like swimming in Gray Slime, mentally."

Amon laughed heartily. "Thank you, Paul...don't worry about it...it wasn't your fault." Amon's eyes widened. "Then...did you kill the Flamethrower?"

"Yes...I actually killed another one near Krisbane. They attacked again."

Amon's jaw dropped open. "You...killed a Flamethrower on your own? How did you hold its mind vice?"

"I concentrated. It was easy to keep up with his blade. The gift is growing. It gets faster, Amon..."

"How fast...?"

"Blindingly fast...think of a Flamethrower going this slowly." Paul moved his arm is slow motion. Amon's eyes were enormous.

"Paul...not even a Paladin captain would be able to move *that* fast...and you haven't finished your training."

"Amon...I defeated the king of Nehgrog...I handed over the role to our friend Bôren."

"I wouldn't trust the Nehgrog farther than I could throw them—but it does give us access to resources."

"Oh, and Amon, there is more…" Paul recounted everything he knew about the new enemy. Amon didn't react.

"Paul, you are confirming my suspicions. The enemy has been too quiet…also you have taken out two of the Flamethrowers. In order for the Flamethrower to come back, he must possess some-one. That process takes months, sometimes as long as a year."

Ambush

† † † † † † †

Nearly two weeks later, after intense struggling, Paul had managed to unlock most of Amon's mind. Even with his uttermost concentration, Paul had not managed to get Amon able to walk. He could sit up on his own, and his mind and intellect were both completely restored, but Paul guessed he would never walk again. Almost every day, Amon would be carried out to the training rooms and there he would sit on a chair and train Paul. Paul would be facing an opponent, while Amon would teach him how to use his mind. Today Paul was fighting three of the queen's guard, one of which was Ryan, another, Master Lugaro, his old sword trainer. He had agreed not to use his gift of speed. Instead Amon insisted that he try to fight using his mind.

"Paul, stop concentrating. You are trying to fight too much with your body. Let your mind fight the battle; the other will follow." Paul raised his sword again and thought of how he was not supposed to use his body while fighting. Paul had not practiced using his mind since the Isle of Zirikaan. The three guards attacked at the same time. Paul parried one of their staffs and spun it back towards the other two. The second guard caught the stick on the side of his head, but the third came down with a crashing strike on Paul's collarbone. Paul winced but jumped back and swung aimlessly at the guard. He missed all three times. Amon held up his hand to halt the battle. The guards lowered their defense, and Paul did the same. He walked over to the chair where Amon sat. Amon had an expression on his face that Paul had seen a hundred times. It was the face that said, "You're doing something wrong." Paul put his stick down and stopped in front of Amon.

"Well, Paul, it seems we have more training to do." He looked to the guards. "Thank you, that will be all for today." The guards bowed to Amon then turned and walked out the doors of the training room.

"Amon, how do you fight with your spirit? Why do I need to fight with my spirit if I can defeat anyone with my gift?"

"Paul...the battle of the spirit is much greater and far more dangerous than the physical battle. Also fighting with your mind offers you advantages. You are not bound by the limits of the physical realm. You can sense enemies even when you can't see them. In time you will see that you will need more than physical strength. I fear that this new enemy you have told me about will be too powerful for one man to attack."

Just then a man walked into the training room. He wore a simple brown tunic and had disheveled brown hair. He walked up to Amon and Paul.

"Excuse me, but the queen has summoned Paul to a meeting of the Council."

Amon wiped his forehead. "Send a message and find two servants to take me." Paul knew Amon hated being reliant on anyone. He nodded to his uncle and walked quickly out of the room. Stopping briefly to change into fresh clothing, Paul headed up to the Council Room, still nursing his collar bone.

It had been almost a week since Amon's recovery when Paul decided he couldn't wait around much longer. He knew that every day he spent in Calarath with Amon cost him precious time. He packed his belongings and said his farewells to his mother and uncle. He set off alone towards Nehgrog. Within the first day he reached the outskirts of Calarath, leaving the more rural, farmland inhabitants behind shortly before nightfall. Summer was nearing and the night was still warm after the sun set. Paul continued riding as the sound of birds faded and was replaced by the chirping of crickets. Paul was alert, partly because of general habit when leaving Calarath but mostly out of a growing fear of this new weapon the enemy was forming. So many scholars had taught the value in the expression "Know your enemy" and now Paul wished that he did. It was unnerving not knowing what the enemy would throw at him next.

He rode past a small forest with glowing yellow eyes peering quizzically at him from the shelter of the trees. Paul looked for a cave or outcropping to sleep under, but this part of the country was mostly flat. Paul was content with sleeping out in the open. He didn't bother making a fire but instead pulled out his mat and laid it down. Normally on a journey of this length Paul would have taken a tent to sleep under, but the extra weight would have slowed him down. Paul could not sleep even though he told himself he needed the energy. He started thinking about himself. It had been the hardest few months of his life, beginning with the loss of his father and the terrible few weeks of depression that had followed. Then there was Zirikaan, the crucial turning point. Although it had been hard, the training with Amon had been exactly what he needed to force him to pick up and face himself. Paul was growing tired and closed his eyes, pushing the thoughts aside.

Paul stood on the battlements of an old, long, stone wall. He looked out across the long field before him at the large mass moving towards him. The wall stretched as far as the eye could see between two large mountains. By the V-shaped crest of the one mountain Paul recognized it as Mount Baerst, one of the tallest and oldest mountains in the world. Suddenly Paul heard his name being called from behind him. In the small valley behind the wall an army had mustered. They were well armed and organized perfectly. Paul caught a glimpse of their shields. He had seen that crest before—the orange bird on the royal blue background. These were Paladin. The wall shook as trebuchets hurled hundreds of huge rocks at it. Paul steadied himself and then flew down the stairs to where the army stood.

"General! Your horse and sword await you. Lead us to victory!"

Paul spun and leaped onto his horse while a servant handed him his sword. The gate crashed down, and Paul surged forward with an army of Paladin behind him…

Paul was dimly aware that he had been dreaming and slowly opened his eyes and thought. Within a few minutes the dream had faded and Paul looked around. He had no idea where he was, but he knew he had better be moving. He quickly rolled up the light mat and untied his horse from the nearby tree. The sun had risen a few minutes before Paul awoke, and now he rode away from it. The day was calm as it had been before, but Paul sensed that something big was coming. He had a strange premonition that today would hold something terrible. He pushed the thought away determined to not let it hinder his thinking. Paul rode his steed hard and pushed the animal to its limits. Whereas the day before had been a slow ride, today Paul felt wary and alert.

By the afternoon he passed the abandoned fortress known as Arcoth. It was Paul's third-way mark for the journey to Nehgrog. He was making excellent time, but within a few hours his horse began to slow, and Paul was forced to slow his pace and give the animal time to rest. It was near a lake when he heard it—the increasing wail of one of the Bazrukal's deadly orbs. It came crashing down a few short feet from where Paul sat on his horse. He leaped off his horse as the second came crashing down near it. The Gray Slime ignited and within seconds the horse was dead and burning. Paul drew his sword instantly and searched for the Flamethrower. The terrain was much like before, flat and green, and Paul saw nowhere to hide. A third orb crashed a good distance behind him, and he suspected that the Flamethrower was guessing where he was. Another crashed down in front of him and then two more simultaneously on his left and right. Paul was surprised to see how far off the Flamethrower was. Then in one motion the Gray Slime all ignited and began burning. Suddenly the idea struck Paul and he ran. The flames were forming a ring around him and he sprinted towards the closing gap ahead of him. Then as he neared it, the flames completed the circle, and he was trapped. Paul looked around and panicked.

Suddenly behind him the earth exploded and there stood the Flamethrower. Paul raised his sword as the Flamethrower drew its own. The flames surged around them as they circled each other waiting for the first move. The Flamethrower leaped forward and swung a crushing blow at Paul. The force knocked Paul down, but he held onto his sword. The Flamethrower stabbed downwards at Paul on the ground who rolled out of the way of the blade as it stuck into the earth. He stood up and spun to face the Flamethrower—then the mental battle began. This was the second Flamethrower Paul had taken on by himself, and he knew the way the Flamethrower would fight.

At first Paul had the advantage and pushed the Flamethrower back, but the Flamethrower surged, and Paul began to hesitate. He frantically warded off the blindingly fast blade of the Flamethrower before finally he slipped and caught the tip of the blade on his arm. The steel sliced into his skin drawing a vast amount of blood from the wound. It was then Paul realized he had been trying to fight with his physical self. He let his mind take over and suddenly everything slowed. Paul engaged the mind war with the Flamethrower. He used light, quick stabs with his sword. The Flamethrower was pressing its mental advantage, and Paul began to feel overcome. Then he saw the opportunity. He spun and struck the Flamethrower's sword and twisted his wrist in a classic maneuver that Amon had taught him. Now the Flamethrower's sword lay on the ground nearly six feet away.

Paul kicked the Flamethrower onto the ground and held his sword at the creature's neck. He focused all of his will power into disarming the Flamethrower's mind. Now he had it where he wanted it. He held the Flamethrower at bay while he searched through the mind. It took focus and concentration to sort what was useful and what was not. Then he saw it. It was a cloud raining down the Gray Slime. But it was no ordinary cloud. It was a presence, a being. Suddenly the Flamethrower collapsed, but Paul sensed that it was not dead. It had fainted. Paul released his grasp and looked up. The flames were closing in! With a push of his blade Paul sliced the Flamethrower's neck in half.

Running, Paul quickly searched for the Flamethrower's tunnel. An area of loose dirt quickly showed Paul what he was looking for. He slipped into the tunnel and fell into darkness. He ran a few feet before the Slime fell through into the hole and burnt for a few minutes before extinguishing itself. Paul was now stuck in complete darkness. Paul felt his way along the crudely shaped tunnel with his hands. Apparently after a short period of time, the Gray Slime would lose its flammability and also its acidic properties. Paul knew if he followed the tunnel, he would come out where the Flamethrower had originally attacked. Paul once again felt the oppression that came from traveling in the dark tunnels.

Elizabeth

† † † † † † †

Paul had made his way through the tunnels and finally found the entrance the Flamethrower had used. As he climbed out, he looked back at the ring of fire which was slowly burning down. He was now without a horse and had no means of knowing where to find one, so now on foot Paul began to walk towards the west where the city of Nehgrog lay. He had lost most of his provisions and all of his water when the horse had been killed and had no idea how he would survive the rest of the journey. At dusk Paul saw a deer but lost any hope of catching it when he realized that his bow had been destroyed in the fire. Then an idea came to him. He drew his sword and focused and calmed his mind. The world slowed, and he charged up to the deer and severed its neck before it had time to react. He wiped the blood off the sword and sheathed it. Now at least he had a food source and a means of hunting. The night wore on slowly, and Paul finished cooking his prize. He enjoyed the good flavor of the meat and complimented himself on the perfection of cooking. Nehgrog was only a two or three-day journey by horse, but on foot it could be more than a week. Unless he found a nearby village or town, he would waste much time traveling. Paul wished he had more knowledge of the lands around him. A map would have been useful too, but he had none. All he had was a rough sense of direction and a few landmarks from previous trips. Paul felt lost and lonely. Perhaps if he had taken Bôren with him, none of this would have happened. Paul ate the last bit of the meal that he could force down and went to sleep. He hoped the fire wouldn't draw any attention, but at the moment he was too tired to consider putting it out. He had walked half a day on foot and knew that he had many more to go.

The queen of Calarath, Paul's mother, had watched her son ride out of the castle gates in an attempt to stop this new force. She feared for her son but knew that she could not hold him back because of her own concerns. She had to let him do everything he could do against the enemies of the Kingdom. For nearly three days straight kings, generals, and other leaders of outlying lands had visited her demanding more security against the growing Ashkah raids. Those nearer to the desert, in the west, had formed together and presented a request for at least 2000 soldiers per city as a means of defense. The queen had listened to their request but had not been able to grant it. They barely had enough soldiers to defend the capital of the Kingdom, Calarath itself. The towns had been disappointed, upset, angry, and a variety of other emotions.

The queen had been stressed with news that the cities in the north near the Shathasor mountain range were preparing to break away from the Kingdom. They feared nothing from the Ashkah or Flamethrowers because the mountains could not be tunneled under. The queen had politely requested that they delay until negotiations could take place, but the cities would not hear of it. The agricultural department had presented multiple requests to extend the borders of Calarath to allow more farming. Food was running low, and most people who owned farms were too busy to work them. A despondent father had presented a case before the court to sue a man for trying to hire his son into the blacksmith shop. Sir Gelaray had formed a group of "Loyalists" and was threatening to take over control of the Kingdom. The citizens of Calarath were all edgy towards each other, and hostility was growing, especially between the higher and lower classes. The queen stood in her study perusing documents and trying to sort through the masses of petty issues to something that actually demanded her attention. She had a new appreciation for what her husband had done. A few documents spoke about the lower class threat to burn the library if they were not treated equally. The queen filed these in a pile of petty issues then saw something that caught her eye:

CONFIDENTIAL

This documentation is to be presented to Queen Elizabeth of Calarath. The information provided here is for her eyes explicitly. The facts in this document are accurate and have been independently confirmed.

Your Majesty, I am King Bôren of Nehgrog. Recently the former king Jonak was dethroned due to violation of terms set in place for governing. While reading through the history of his reign, I came across a project that had been started without permission from either of our Councils. This was a Green Guard training program. In case you are not aware of what Green Guard are, they are our Elite guard, trained very similarly to the Paladin. They are, of course, lower caliber than Paladin warriors, but they are lethal, effective and rare. I went to the site and discovered we have over 600,000 troops plus another 400,000 currently in training. This army is lethal and gives us an extremely high advantage in combat, as well as diplomacy. As you know, the Calarath and Nehgrog are not allies, and we will not share our troops cheaply. If you wish to discuss this, come to our courts.

Signed, King Bôren

The queen stared in amazement. Here was the solution she had been looking for. The Nehgrog were a stingy, greedy lot, and she knew that Paul was on their side and even a friend of their king.

That gave her a slight advantage, she thought, but what sort of price would they demand for their troops? They were absolutely correct; a city with an army of a million soldiers would be a military super power and could even threaten Calarath. If they wished it, Calarath could be in flames within a week. Negotiations would be advisable.

"Jaelen!" she called.

A well-dressed man appeared at the door. "Yes, Your Majesty?"

"Ready my horse and a bodyguard. I am going on a diplomatic trip. I will be back within a few weeks."

"It will be done quickly, milady." The man disappeared down the stairs to complete his task. The queen read through the paper again and called a maidservant to pack her things. Within the hour four of the queen's Guardsmen stood by their horses with everything packed. The queen mounted her own white stallion and gave a few last minute instructions to the man she had left in charge, the head of the Council, Commander Kerak. Then they were off. The queen rode in front with the four guards behind her.

Paul collapsed under the tree and panted. He had gone without food or water for almost an entire day. The landscape had changed to hills and trees everywhere, and Paul was grateful for the shade; however, he had not found a single animal or water supply. He knew there had to be one around because of the fertile lands and many trees, but none could be seen. It was almost as hard as some of the exercises he had practiced with Amon. He lay back against the tree and fell into a restless sleep. He faded in and out of consciousness as the day wore on. He lost track of whether he was dreaming or awake. Twice he woke up and thought he had seen a horse walking up, but instead he had been dreaming. Finally he woke up and forced himself to get moving. He had to find a water source soon. He hoped that when he found this elusive water source, he would find many animals searching for the same thing. Paul had no recollection of where he was and started to panic. Perhaps he had wandered off the path and was drifting towards the desert. Perhaps he had traveled all this time only to find out he had navigated incorrectly. He stopped and waited for sundown. The sun rose in the east and set in the west; therefore, Paul should be traveling into the sunset if he were heading towards the city of Nehgrog. When the sun began to drop significantly, Paul noted that it was almost directly to his right. He set off to travel the remaining daylight hours in the right direction.

The guards set up the campsite with practiced precision. They set up separate tents for each traveler and posted a guard on sentry duty. A small fire roasted the day's provisions slowly. The queen sat in her tent with all the intelligence that Calarath had on Nehgrog. She had read through their culture, diplomatic proceedings, their structure of thinking and was now reading a document on how they trained their children. It seemed rather cruel to force children to fight from a young age. However, these children were not only fighters, they were disciplined. They were respectful, considerate, courteous, and seemed to be extremely well behaved.

Elizabeth put the document on the side and picked up another. This one was referring to the defenses. It seemed to be a vastly under-defended, vulnerable city. An army could march right up the gates before the city knew about it. No watchtowers had been reported, and although the walls were unexplainably stronger than other walls, the city seemed to be geared towards withstanding a siege rather than repelling attackers. The next paper had various facts about the location of Nehgrog. The city sat in the plains of Goash. The Nehgrog weapons were apparently of extremely high value and were in high demand from the other cities. Many scholars of both Calarath and Nehgrog believed the Poison of Maugrax to be the cause of the unsettled seas. The Poison was not a proven weapon of the enemy but had the power to kill trees, plants, animals and supposedly upset great bodies of water. Many people claimed to have seen the poison, similar to the Gray Slime, but thinner and darker in color. Some even believed the myth that it was the blood of the Dark Lord himself. The queen was not one to be swayed by popular myths. She tossed the paper onto the pile of the others and lay down to go to sleep.

Paul opened his eyes. He was lying face down on the ground. He breathed deeply and sat up. He swallowed and suddenly realized how thirsty he was. Then he remembered. He had not had water in nearly a day and a half. It was nearly dusk. If he did not find water soon, he was finished. He glanced around him. He was passing through a small forest. He stood up. He glanced at the trees and suddenly realized that something was different about them. He couldn't exactly put his finger on it, but he knew he had seen something like that before. Regardless he drew his dagger from his belt. He quickly carved three horizontal lines in the tree nearest him. Then he shaped the ends into arrows pointing west out of the forest. In the event a traveler crossed this forest, they would see the lines and hopefully be able to help him. He began to walk towards the dimming light ahead of him. He would have to travel quickly before night set in. Paul knew by the lushness of the trees that there had to be a water source nearby. He continued walking until he reached the end of the forest. Night had come and around him small creatures scurried. Using his gift Paul caught and killed four small rodents. Using a small tinderbox he was able to make a small fire and cook his dinner. After eating he felt immensely better. He lay down flat on the grass and looked up at the sky. Suddenly he sat up. The sky was not clear. A thunderstorm seemed to be brewing. With any luck he would be able to catch it.

. . . . .

They had packed up camp quickly and had set off first thing in the morning. The sun rose slowly a few hours later. It was an unusually cold morning. The queen pulled her cloak tighter around herself. One of the guards had been appointed navigator, Araun. He frequented the compass and checked their course every half-hour. The other guards stayed on high alert. The queen rode in silence, lost in her thoughts. She thought of her husband and how he had handled the pressures of the Kingdom with such ease and that she had taken his service for granted. However, the queen was strong-willed and courageous and was a master at organization. She could rule for at least two years, she thought. One of the guards rode towards her, stirring her from her thoughts.

"My lady. I think there is something you should see…" he said. He kicked his horse, and it sped forward. The queen did the same. The sight made the queen catch her breath. A huge fire burnt ahead of them.

"I rode forward to scout the area. I smelt burning and followed it to here. And look," he dismounted and knelt down near the edge of the flames, "this is the Gray Slime. This was the work of a Flamethrower."

The queen looked from the guard to the flames. She too dismounted and walked along the edge of the flames. Suddenly she stopped and turned back.

"What is it, milady?" the guard asked.

"This flame burns in a circle. It was purposefully ignited to trap something or someone." The queen looked around at the surrounding trees.

"Ryan, I need you to climb one of these trees. See if you can see anything in the center of this ring of fire."

"Yes, milady." The guard nodded and scurried towards the tree nearest him. He unbuckled his belt and let his sword fall, and then he unstrung the bow off his shoulders along with his quiver. He reached up and grabbed the first branch. He quickly pulled himself up and climbed the tree. As he neared the top, he stopped and looked out. The queen saw him searching and peering into the mass of flames. He climbed higher and looked out again. Shortly he began his descent. He dropped the last few feet and landed lightly. He gathered his weapons and walked towards the queen.

"There certainly is something inside there." he hesitated.

"Well…?"

"Your Majesty, I believe it's the Flamethrower itself trapped in there. He looks dead."

The queen furrowed her brow. How? Why would the Flamethrower be trapped within his own snare? Unless…

"Captain, was the Flamethrower's sword drawn?"

"I believe so, Your Majesty. Why?"

"The Flamethrower obviously set this trap for someone, then battled him in hand to hand combat. Who do you know has ever defeated a Flamethrower?"

"Why, only Master Paul." The captain's eyes widened as he realized what she meant. "So you mean Master Paul came this way?"

"I believe so. If we hurry we just might catch up with him."

Paul looked up and heard the rolling thunder. At last. Water. The rain started lightly at first, then turned into a torrential downpour. Paul lay on his back soaking in the rain. He let the cool water wash over him. The rain fell generously into his open mouth as he drank of the fresh water. Within ten minutes Paul was soaked through and decided to get off the ground. The grass was wet and clung to his boots. Refreshed and motivated he set off in the direction of the setting sun. He guessed he had at least an hour of daylight in which to travel. Paul had never learned how to navigate using the stars and would have to wait until sunrise to set off again. He noted to himself that the first thing he should do upon arriving in Nehgrog would be to ask Bôren to teach him nighttime navigation.

Paul had never focused in his studies when he was growing up. He never saw the need. Never had he thought his father would die so soon, never had he thought he would need this training. He had never thought that this was the course his life would take. How had all of this happened? Was it really less than a year ago that he had been serving the frail old Oldyers? Paul remembered with a slight pain that they were now dead, killed by the very enemy he was now sworn to destroy.

Suddenly, Paul understood something. Someone somehow would have to be the hope and savior of the Kingdom. One man would have to lead the people. Was he that man? How could he be appointed with such a great destiny? It was other men, greater men that always became people's heroes. He was simply Paul, the son of the king, true, but that was only his birthright. As a person he was set-aside because of his gifts, but there were greater men than he. Surely others had gifts too. He was thinking too highly of himself. He chided himself for thinking that he alone was the only gifted man in the Kingdom. He looked ahead at the sunset and decided to start looking for a place to sleep. A new day would come tomorrow.

Unity

† † † † † † †

They caught up with Paul at dawn. He had just risen and was traveling slowly when the scout stopped him. The three other guards and the queen caught up soon. Paul filled them in on what had happened with the Flamethrower and how he had lost his horse. One of the Guardsmen gave up his horse to Paul and walked. They set off at a quick pace. The captain, Ryan, rode in front as the scout; the other two guards took the rear, and Paul and his mother rode between them. They whispered amongst themselves about the new army of Nehgrog. It was obvious that an agreement would have to be made; Calarath could never hold its own with what limited men they had. Around noon Ryan stopped and checked the direction with the other guards. If they traveled quickly, they would make the outskirts of Nehgrog by nightfall. Paul recognized one of the guards as Ranier, the Guardsman who had first taught him to use a bow. Ranier rode in absolute silence until Paul rode near him. Once they began talking, Ranier came alive. They talked mostly about archery and different woods used in bows, different arrows, tips, and more. The queen talked with Ryan about accommodations once they reached Nehgrog. The sun was beginning to set, and the outposts were in sight. Paul kicked his horse slightly and passed Ryan. He dismounted and walked up to the guard on duty.

"We would like to enter the tunnels."

"Password?"

"Nuira," said Paul, remembering when he and Bôren had traveled through these very tunnels. The guard nodded and stepped aside. The horses were reluctant at first, but the Guards soon calmed then and led them in. The tunnels were as immaculate as ever, and there was not a single burnt-out torch. They passed the halfway station and did so with obvious contempt from the guards on duty. The Nehgrog hated Calarath, and he was bringing their leader right to the city. When they finally surfaced, the night was gone, and morning had broken. The streets were not yet busy, and Paul hurried them onwards. They reached the palace and dismounted. Everyone was stiff and exhausted. As they ascended the steps, the Green Guard recognized Paul and opened the gates. Inside they were led up the stairs after leaving the queen's guard below. The throne room was exactly the same as when Paul had last seen it. Bôren sat in a corner at a desk looking between an arrow and a large book. As the door closed, Bôren looked up at his guests.

"Paul! And Your Majesty!" Bôren stood and walked around the desk. "Welcome to my court. I have been expecting you, Paul, and also you, Your Majesty. I hope we can work out something with this army."

"Thank you for your welcome, King Bôren, but I must retire."

"Of course, Your Majesty. But I must warn you; you will not be as welcomed in the city. Stay in the palace; we have plenty of rooms. We can house you and your guard as well as Paul and any other guests you might have brought along."

"Thank you, your generosity is most appreciated."

Bôren bowed to the queen who returned the honor and walked gracefully away. When she had left the room, Paul turned to Bôren.

"Good to see you, friend."

Bôren shook Paul's hand. "How are you, Paul?"

"I could be better. I encountered another Flamethrower on the way here."

"You killed it?"

"Yes. It trapped me in a ring of fire. They're getting smarter Bôren. But something...something is different. They seem fearful."

Bôren grinned. "If I were a Flamethrower, I would be scared of you too."

Paul laughed. "No, I believe that there has been a shift of power amongst the armies of darkness."

"Paul. Are you suggesting that the Flamethrowers are losing their power?"

"I don't know." Paul paused and walked to the window. He looked out at the large city below him. "Nehgrog is the Kingdom's last hope. You do know that, don't you?"

Bôren sighed. "Yes. At least we have the Green Guard." Bôren paused. "Paul? Have you ever seen Flamethrower archers?"

"No...Flamethrowers don't use bows. They rely on the orbs."

"That's what I thought. Take a look at this." He led Paul over to the desk with the arrow on it. "This arrow was shot into a tree. Its target was a trader, but it hit the tree instead. When it struck the tree, the whole tree seemed to die. The trader plucked it out of the tree and brought it here. I examined the tree myself; it was completely dead."

Paul picked up the arrow and looked it over. "It's poisoned with the Gray Slime. This is an Ashkah arrow." Paul placed the arrow on the desk.

"Are you sure?"

"A Flamethrower would have no need of a bow; only an Ashkah would use a bow. How deep was the head of the arrow?"

"Three, maybe four inches."

"That sounds about the right power for an Ashkah bow..." Paul stopped. "Do many of your traders or travelers get attacked while on the road?"

"Normally, no. But these last few days we've had at least a dozen people report Ashkah groups camping on the road. I sent two squads of Green Guard to clear them out, and this was the last report."

"How did they get so far inland? Surely the tunnels were noticed?"

"No, I had my men check everywhere for tunnels. Nothing."

Paul furrowed his brow. "This probably means a new method of transportation."

"I was afraid of that."

Paul stretched and yawned.

"You look tired, Paul. Get some rest. We will talk more tomorrow."

Paul was too tired to protest. He nodded and walked out of the room.

"How many men do you need?"

"Well, Your Majesty, the men are not all for us. The other towns and cities are beginning to demand protection."

They had begun the meeting after a large breakfast. Paul had gone to the weapon masters for a new bow. He was trying to get some archery practice in before he would need it. Bôren had seemed reluctant to sign over any men to Calarath. The queen had offered huge sums of money, but it seemed that Bôren's men would not be bought.

"Your Majesty, I am a king and you are a queen. Let us simply refer to each other by our first names. I am Bôren, and you are?"

"Elizabeth."

"Good. Now, Elizabeth, you must see my point. A million-man army is worth more than any sum of money."

"But is it worth more than the Kingdom? At least a million lives could be lost if we are not adequately prepared for the major attack."

Bôren stood and walked over to his map. They had chosen the War Council Room but had decided against having the Council there. Once Bôren's decision was made, he would consult the Council.

"I am not fighting you, Elizabeth. I know that in order to survive our two great nations must work together. You and I must be allies. A rift between us will only make it easier for the enemy to destroy us."

The queen inwardly gave a sigh of relief. "Well said. But something must be done about these Green Guard."

Bôren walked back and sat across from the queen. "I'll make you a deal. I will sell you half of the Green Guard, 500,000 men on two conditions. Paul stays here and commands my army, and secondly, the men will be used for defending the towns of the north." The queen looked puzzled.

"Since when has Nehgrog cared about the northern towns?"

"There is a treaty signed by King Jonak in which the towns of the north enlist their young men in turn for our protection." The words hung in the air, undecided. The queen thought it over.

"I would accept, but it is not my decision to make. I must ask Paul. If he agrees, we have a deal."

Bôren grinned. He knew Paul would stay. There was nothing in Calarath for him. "Now, let's discuss where exactly these Green Guard are going."

The bow was truly a work of art. It was the finest bow Paul had ever seen. The seller had agreed to lend Paul a few arrows to shoot it in the archery range he had set up behind his store. Paul had never been a good shot, but the bow seemed to work well for him. He nearly hit the bull's-eye on three occasions. It turned out that the bow was over a hundred pieces of gold, but the store owner would throw in nearly 500 arrows free simply because he liked Paul, and he knew that he was a friend of the king. Paul paid the man and took the bow. He also bought a quiver and headed out to the target range. The arrows at the range were free, and Paul took at least 300. He spent the whole day shooting at different length targets, improving his skill. Towards noon he took a break and found Ranier coming to the range.

"Ranier! Over here!"

Ranier looked up and spotted Paul. He walked over to where Paul sat in the grass. He glanced at Paul's bow.

"Where did you get that?"

"Just bought it from an archery store."

"Incredible. May I?"

"Of course."

Ranier picked up the bow and walked towards the shooting line. He knocked an arrow and drew the bow. He aimed for all of three seconds and then let the shaft fly. It struck dead center with a quick thud. Ranier turned back grinning.

"This bow is even better than mine. How much did you get it for?"

"One hundred gold. And the clerk threw in 500 arrows free."

Ranier's eyes opened wide. "What type of arrows?"

"These," said Paul indicating the silver arrows lying by his feet.

"Paul...do you know what these are?"

"No. What are they?"

"In archery circles they are referred to as Crystals. The silver shaft is made from Orun Oak, and the point is a rare metal known as Jyak, found in only one specific mountain in the Shathasor range. The feathers of a pure white bird are used for the fletching. Each one of these arrows is worth at least eight or ten pieces of gold."

"Wow. What a gift. Ranier?"

"Yes, sir?"

"Do you think you could teach me how to shoot well?"

"Of course. I came here to shoot anyway." He grinned.

They both stepped out of the Council Room happy. They had divided the entire 500,000 man army amongst the cities and towns that needed them. The only thing left to decide was whether or not Paul would come or stay. Bôren was sure he would gladly accept, but the queen had her doubts. Actually she wished privately that he would come back home with her in order to take control and lead the people, but she knew it was not something he would be willing to do, not something he was prepared for yet. Besides the situation was getting out of hand. Without proper defenses there would be no one to govern anyway. If Paul would not stay, they would have to convince him otherwise.

"Well, Elizabeth, I must be getting back to the palace. I'll send a guard to find Paul and bring him back. In the meantime is there anything you would like to see or do while you are in Nehgrog? I'm afraid most of our activities are not fit for a lady like yourself."

"Pardon me, but what would you mean by that?"

"Oh, you know, things like sword fighting, jousting, archery. Things I'm sure you are not in the habit of doing."

Queen Elizabeth was not a proud woman, nor was she overly sensitive, but there was a hint of contempt and almost mockery in the man's voice that edged her to show him that he was wrong.

"Bôren, would you please show me to the nearest dueling arena?"

"I beg your pardon?"

"I would like to get some dueling in before we leave. Which way is it?"

Bôren was almost too stunned to answer, but he never let it show. "Follow me, milady."

They walked onwards to the dueling area. The beginners were forced to start with wooden swords, the intermediates were one-on-one with blunt swords, and the experts were one-on-one with sharpened swords. Nehgrog men knew the risks of entering the dueling arena on the expert level, and it was only used by the brave few. The queen walked past the first two arenas straight to the expert. The crowd parted for her. Everyone was too stunned to argue or protest. The administrator directed her to changing rooms where she could change out of her dress into armor. When she returned, she found Bôren on the field, also armored up. A large crowd had gathered around. As Elizabeth stepped onto the field, she heard whispers behind her.

"…The queen of Calarath…"

"…easy on her because she's a lady."

"I agree. Not a place for a Calarath woman at all. Puts the men in a tough position."

"…can't very well go all out against her…"

The supervisor stepped onto the field, and the crowd went silent.

"The rules for this engagement will be standard. By requests of Her Majesty of Calarath, there will be no unfair bias or changing of rules. The rules are as follows…"

As the man in the center of the field talked about the rules, the queen took in her surroundings. It was a circular, grass field, roughly thirty or forty feet in diameter surrounded by a small fence. The grass was not slippery, fortunately, but was hard and gave good traction. When the supervisor was finished, the two saluted each other and donned their helmets. Elizabeth smelt the stench of sweat in hers. She looked down at her armor. It was well made. It would protect against a sword, and despite the weight she was glad to have it.

Bôren made the first move. It was all she needed. He tried to strike a controlled lunge at her head, but she ducked, rolled, and came up with a stab. Bôren saw the attack and used his momentum to twist away. The queen's blade glanced off the corner of his shoulder plate as he rolled and stood. He swung his blade sideways, but the queen was too fast. She parried the blade and pushed it back. She tried a diagonal vertical attack, but he met it halfway.

They stood there with their blades crossed for nearly five seconds. Elizabeth felt her grip on the sword slip, and Bôren forced her blade down. He lunged forward catching her right arm hard with his sword. The blade did not penetrate, but the force pushed her arm back to a sickening angle with a loud crack. Elizabeth flinched but changed hands quickly. Bôren was obviously feeling slightly guilty for hurting her, but she would not take his pity. In a flurry of four fast attacks she had him confused and overwhelmed. She ducked a horizontal sweep then summoned all her strength and slammed it into his blade. The weapon clattered out of his hand and flew a few feet to his right. Elizabeth landed a kick on Bôren's chest and had him on the ground. She held her blade between his helmet and neck guard.

"I win," she muttered through the helmet.

The supervisor ran out onto the field and called Elizabeth as the winner. She removed her helmet and helped Bôren up. They walked off the field to applause. A doctor came to the arenas to inspect the queen's arm. After removing her arm plates, he told them she had broken her elbow, and there wasn't much he could do. Bôren thanked the doctor and apologized again to the queen.

"Bôren, it was not your fault. I willingly walked onto that field knowing the risks. If I had not wanted to get hurt, I would have stayed away."

"It wasn't as if you were soft on me either," said Bôren, indicating his chest. "You knocked the wind out of me." The queen grinned. Bôren noticed that she had appeared to be so young while on the field, but once she was off and out of the armor, he realized how much older she really was. The stress of losing her husband and governing the Kingdom was showing its signs.

"Come milady, let's go back to the palace, shall we?" And with that they headed back.

. . . . .

Paul had been about to launch an arrow when Ranier stopped him.

"Paul, there's someone here with a message for you. Green Guard. Probably from King Bôren." Paul turned and the Green Guard bowed.

"His majesty requests your presence at once."

Paul sighed. "Thank you. I will come." He unstrung his bow and shouldered the quiver. He had to take a bag for the many extra arrows he had and thanked Ranier for the time. He had hit a bull's-eye multiple times and had never missed the target except once. Paul carried his bow back to the palace where he handed it with the arrows to a servant to take to his room. He found Bôren in the throne room waiting for him.

Clouds

† † † † † † †

"It can't be possible. They would never strike something so large."
Captain Lonar, now the head of the War Council, was furious.
"There have been many attacks in the last few weeks, but this could
not have been one of them!" The room was quiet. Not one of the
generals spoke. A runner from the Green Guard camp had brought
in the news of the event he referred to.

"Captain Lonar, I do not believe that this was a Flamethrower
attack."

"Paul…er…General Paul, what else do you know has the capability of hitting something that big so precisely?"

Paul thought for a moment. "Where is the runner?"

"Waiting outside. Shall I call him in sir?"

"Yes, please." A few minutes later a simply dressed young man
walked into the room. He looked to be about eighteen or nineteen,
around Paul's own age. "Sir, I have a few questions for you."

"Of course, sir."

"What was the total extent of the damage done?"

"We lost exactly 654,098 men with at least 85,000 wounded."

Bôren had been quiet up until now. "That's over seven hundred
thousand! That means we only have three hundred thousand men."
Bôren's voice was consistent and calm, showing no signs of stress.
Paul, however, had spoken to him privately once the news arrived.

Whoever had given the runner his message had been thorough and detailed. Paul had read the note aloud:

> To His Majesty, King Bôren, a catastrophic event has just taken place. The training facility has come under a major attack. It was completely unexpected. It was slightly after noon, and we had every man not on duty or training form up for drills. The bulk of our army was in the main field when the sky grew very dark. Ordinarily this would not have bothered us, as we continue our training regardless of weather. But then the rain started to fall. Although this may be hard to believe, the rain was not water, but rather the Gray Slime. It ate into our army like a knife into butter. Most of the men were killed instantly. A few were able to take shelter quickly, and even those were wounded badly. The rain ate through our buildings, fields, horses, everything. We are devastated. The remaining survivors and I took as much as we could and left. We are currently somewhere between Nehgrog and the coast. Please send help.

The message was not signed in any way. Paul had guessed it must have been for security purposes. They had called an immediate War Council session shortly thereafter. Paul had re-read the letter to the Council, and they now sat deciding on what to do next. Nehgrog's new hope and power had been this Green Guard army, but now they had only a third of their original power.

"One thing is for certain, we cannot give out any of our troops. Especially not to Calarath. The Northern alliance is broken; the troops sent down from the towns means nothing," sneered one of the men at the table. Paul ignored his angry stare.

"One thing is for certain. The enemy has a new weapon."

"Or a new soldier," ventured one of the older men.

Paul remembered the last encounter he had with a Flamethrower. He remembered the picture he saw in its mind—a torrent of Gray Slime. Suddenly everything clicked. Paul's mind raced as the members of the Council debated courses of action. The Flamethrowers were afraid of something—a rainfall of Gray Slime. Perhaps there had been a change of power within the Dark Army or maybe a new soldier. Something or someone had been created, something greater than the Flamethrowers. But how did they get in? Through the clouds? In that case some dark power must keep them up there. Paul tuned back into the conversation.

Bôren had just asked one of the Captains if he thought it would be fair to withhold the men they had promised from Calarath. Paul spoke up in the silence that followed. "My friends, I believe I might know what caused this attack." That got their attention. "I have been in the minds of three Flamethrowers, and I have found things I didn't understand until now. I believe that the Dark Lord has created a being or warrior more powerful than the Bazrukal. This being rides the clouds and uses this Slime rain as his weapon. I have seen this all fit together in the minds of three different Bazrukal. What to do about them is the next question. Regardless of how many men we give Calarath, the enemy will still exist if we do nothing about it." The room was quiet. General Kresh spoke next.

"Hmm. A strange concept. This warrior would be practically invincible. Nothing could strike him, and even if it did, where would you strike? All you would see is a large dark cloud. The being himself could be anywhere in it. We would need to know more about this... *Cloudrider.*"

The new name fit well and sent a chill down Paul's neck. "I believe I might be able to get more information from the remaining three Bazrukal. But I can guarantee nothing."

"How will you find them?" Bôren asked.

"I shall lure them in. I'll travel alone south towards the desert. That will certainly provoke them."

"But what stops the Cloudrider from attacking you? If he were the new, most powerful enemy, wouldn't the Dark Lord send him against you? He knows you are more powerful than any of his Flamethrowers."

"That's a risk I'm willing to take. I think the Dark Lord has other plans for his new servant." No one said anything more after that, and the meeting was adjourned. Once outside Paul gave instructions to Bôren to alert him if any more cities were attacked. Bôren wished Paul luck on his mission, and they parted.

Three days later Paul received word that Chiron, one of the smaller towns to the north, had been utterly destroyed. Now the whole Kingdom knew that something was wrong. At first the Nehgrog could keep the matter to themselves, as it was an internal affair. Now that Chiron had been destroyed, the people would be demanding an explanation. Paul had told his mother not to say a word to anyone about the Cloudrider. It would only create panic.

A squad of scouts had gone to the Green Guard training site and had reported that the Gray Slime had spread and was still burning. It seemed to have changed, become more powerful. It had eaten away at the ground itself. The main training field had been eroded down a full eight feet in some places.

Paul continued his journey down south and reached the remains of Egon and camped there. The city was even worse than when he had last been there. Ashkah hordes had rampaged through a second time burning houses and fields. Clear signs of a vast tunnel network were everywhere. Paul walked slowly through the village. The city stood no chance against the attack. It was exactly what would happen to Nehgrog and Calarath and every other town, city, and village in the entire Kingdom and beyond. Paul had brought nothing to sleep on but managed to find an old mattress that was in reasonable condition. He knew he would never sleep. He was in an enemy-held city with death all around him. He dragged the mattress out of the town slightly east and lay down.

. . . . .

Paul woke up and looked around. He could not see, and for a moment he thought he might be blind. It must have been the middle of the night, but it was difficult to tell with no moon. He took a few unsure steps forward and suddenly fell. He picked himself up again and put his hands out in front of him to guide himself. He heard whispers, voices around him. He tried to find their source, but nothing helped. He felt something strike his arm. An arrow. He stifled a cry of pain. He knew he could not speak. Someone was out there trying to kill him. Suddenly a face appeared and whispered, "It all ends here, Paul son of Mark. It all ends here, young Paladin." Paul drew his sword and swung into the darkness. He heard the familiar sound of a blade being drawn from a scabbard. Then slowly, all around him, a light grew, and he could see the face of his enemies. There were two of them, identical. They both held jagged swords. Then as one they lunged out at him.

Paul woke up and looked around. The day was just dawning. He had been dreaming again. These dreams were becoming more intense. Perhaps there was something more to these dreams; maybe they weren't dreams at all but rather a new gift. Slowly the effect of the dream wore off, but he still felt as though something was gnawing at him. It had felt so real. He dragged the mattress into the town and left it there. He remounted his horse and began riding. These parts of the lands were unmapped. So many villages had been destroyed that the map makers hadn't bothered putting them in. Paul looked up and saw a sight he had never seen before. Ahead of him stretched a vast desert. Nothing in sight moved. Everything was still and dead. The desert wasn't like the normal deserts Paul had heard of. This one was dry, gray, dark, and empty. It was completely flat too, which gave it an endless feeling. Paul stopped his horse. The desert began somewhere far on the horizon, but Paul knew he would be near it soon. This was the Jedarac Desert. Paul guessed that he must be somewhere near Jedar if he headed east for a few days—but that journey would be long and wasted. The best way to find a Flamethrower was to draw attention to himself and seem vulnerable. He dismounted his horse and lay in the grass. It would be the last time for a while. He had checked his provisions this morning and found that he had enough food and water to last him a few more days, but then he would have to head back. Paul rolled over and drifted into sleep.

The queen had been overjoyed when Paul had accepted the trade. He had become the first Calarathan general of Nehgrog. He had seemed happy that the men needed for Calarathan defenses would come because of this choice. The queen was about to leave when the news of the strike reached her. Bôren had come before her himself and apologized. The queen was surprised at his fair deal of splitting the remaining three hundred thousand men equally between their two cities. Bôren told her of Paul's decision and his comments on this new "Cloudrider." She had agreed with him based on what they knew. She stayed another day to discuss more plans about the remaining Green Guard and then set off with her own Guardsmen. They made good time and within a few days reached the halfway mark. The Guardsmen were silent on the whole, and Ryan was the only one who spoke, and even then only when necessary. The queen felt the tension that hung in the air. The news of the Cloudrider had left them silent and thoughtful. The queen didn't even venture to create a conversation. The men wanted to be left to their own thoughts, and she would let them. They rode on until night and set up camp. The queen wrote down the recent events and went to bed. She lay in her tent and heard the men finally begin to talk.

"Things are about to change. For the worse." It was Ranier.

"I believe you're right. The attacks are unstoppable." The queen guessed it was Lugaro, the third in the group.

"At least we have those Green Guard, that's a help," said Orion, the last guard. Ryan hadn't said a word.

"What help? The fact that we have to go to Nehgrog to get help is insulting. It disgusts me," Ranier spat.

"Do not let your prejudice get in the way of your better judgment. I've seen these Green Guard in action, and they are noble warriors. We need all the help we can get." The queen sighed. Ryan spoke true words. The queen wondered what they would think if they knew that they were really facing the devastating power of the Cloudriders. They were running out of time and resources.

The sun rose, and Paul was still asleep. He wearily opened his eyes and looked out. He sat up. His horse was nowhere in sight. *Great. Just perfect. Stuck at the edge of a desert, and my horse decides to run off.* Paul stood and walked around. He knew the horse would go nowhere near the Jederac Desert. Then Paul remembered. He had tied the horse to that tree. How had it managed to get free? He walked over to the tree and, confirming Paul's suspicions, the rope had been cut. He suspected thieves but dismissed the idea. There were no towns nearby, and anyone who had seen him wouldn't have followed him all this way simply for a horse. The only logical explanation was...

Three arrows whizzed by Paul's head. The Ashkah archers had spotted Paul as soon as he reached the tree. Luckily they were inaccurate. Paul pulled out his own bow and knocked an arrow. He had his back to the tree. In one fluid motion he drew the bow and spun around the tree. The three archers were in three separate trees about thirty yards from Paul. He aimed quickly and let the first arrow fly. He was using his "Crystals" and was surprised at how fast and straight they flew. The arrow struck the first archer in the chest, the force knocking him out of the tree. The Ashkah lay still. The other two archers reacted by shooting at Paul. He ducked back behind the tree. He knocked a second arrow and spun to shoot, but there was no one in sight. Paul turned slowly and searched the nearby trees. Empty. Strange. He returned the arrow to his quiver and put the bow over one shoulder across his chest. He had brought about fifty of his Crystals and couldn't bear to lose one of the precious arrows. With the arrow returned he walked over cautiously to where the dead Ashkah lay. He plucked the arrow from its chest and wiped it clean. *Not a perfect shot*, he thought, *but it got the job done.* He returned it to the quiver on his back. The Ashkah attack left him weary. Rarely did Ashkah travel in packs as small as three, and rarely did they retreat. Then again, rarely did anyone come this far south. Paul guessed they were scouts and were regrouping; this kept him on high alert. He was still horseless. "Hmm…Seems I have a knack for losing horses," he said to himself. He decided he would get nowhere if he waited around for the Ashkah raiding party to return his horse. The fastest way would be to track them. It was easy enough. The Ashkah footprints were faded, but the horse left a clear trail. The tracks led east. Paul had nothing better to do; in fact facing more enemies would give him a higher chance of being attacked. *I can't believe I'm doing this,* he thought.

The Council had been furious. The queen had been given permission by Bôren to discuss the matter with them once she returned home. The fact that she had bargained with their hated neighbors had infuriated them. She told them of the Green Guard reinforcements, but this only made them more frustrated. It seemed that they, too, had let their prejudice get in the way of their better judgment. She had told them that her decision was final, and any insubordination would be punished. Times were too stressful to be bickering with each other. Now she sat in the Council Room with only

Ryan. He had seemed wiser than any of the decorated generals and officials who had sat in that room earlier that day.

"Milady, I understand your distress. Even amongst the guard there have been complaints and tempers toward this new decision. However, I believe it is not that they are angry at the Nehgrog; it is because they are afraid of them. They know that that city has the power to control the whole Kingdom. They are also overly proud of Calarath and believe that we are self-sufficient. Personally I don't mind as long as we come out of this alive." He paused and took a deep long breath. "Your son is our only hope. If anyone has the power to save us now, it will be General Paul." The queen smiled. She knew it was true. Unfortunately this meant that the lives of millions rested upon the shoulders of her seventeen-year-old son. Ryan was a smart man and utterly devoted to serving the queen. He had lost his wife and fourteen-year-old son in an Ashkah raid on his hometown of Faron, the town south of Egon. He had single handedly defeated the entire army of nearly a hundred, or so people said. He had wandered to Calarath in need of a job. His quick reflexes and unbreakable loyalty had attracted the attention of the court who were in need of a new Guardsman. He had taken to the role instantly. He was promoted to his current position within a few short months. Now the queen needed him more than ever.

"Ryan," she said softly, "I have a mission for you."

Evacuation

† † † † † † †

Bôren was the ruler of an unsettled city. Lonar, his trusted adviser and friend, had come to him with a proposition. "Evacuate the city. A Cloudrider attack would be devastating, especially since it could not be stopped," he had said.

"I see your point, Lonar, but where would they go?"

"The Great Cave. It is true the old tunnels were sealed off, but if we begin digging now, we will be able to evacuate before the end of the week."

"Lonar, there is no way we can evacuate in four days. We will need at least two weeks."

Lonar sighed impatiently. "We may not have two weeks. For all we know, the Cloudrider will attack us tomorrow."

"You are right, my friend." Bôren looked across at the gold ceremonial sword hanging on the far wall. "It will be like Jedar, all over again. A city with no hope, no choice but to run and hide."

"And like Jedar, we must make preparations before we are attacked."

"How long do you think we can stay in the Cave?"

"The Ancient Army camped in there for several months, my lord. It was not easy from most accounts, but it was doable. And it will be safe. That is our primary concern."

Bôren sighed. "All right. I'm putting you in charge. Find as many men as you need that you can trust. Clear only the northwest and west tunnels. The more concealed we are the better. You will also be in charge of acquiring provisions. The storehouses will hold more than you can find. Get to it." Lonar bowed quickly and left the room.

Bôren was due to head out to the Green Guard refugees today. He would take more of his doctors along to help the wounded. The bulk of the medical resources had been dispatched as soon as the news arrived, but Bôren knew that more help would be appreciated. It was just before midday when they set off with nine Green Guard and five doctors. The procession went out of the city through the king's personal hidden entrance through a tunnel beneath the palace. The entrance to the tunnel was in the palace cellar, hidden behind a huge rack of old wine. They spent the entire day at the camp. Bôren left with the leader and told him of his orders to divide the men for the deal with Calarath. The other half of the men would be sent towards the Plains of Goash, and from there they would enter the Northwest tunnels. They would depart in two days. It was after dusk when Bôren left to make the three-hour journey alone. He arrived back in Nehgrog around midnight and went to bed with thoughts racing through his mind about his people and the upcoming evacuation.

Paul tracked the two Ashkah for nearly a day before finding a tunnel. This one varied slightly from the few he had seen before. It was wider and more smoothly cut and ended with a decorative rock formation as opposed to a clump of loose dirt. Paul guessed it was carved by men as no Ashkah horde would create something this precise. Paul followed it for the first few feet but stopped when he came to a solid rock wall. Apparently the Ashkah had covered their tracks. The wall would not break through. Paul resurfaced and pulled out his compass, something he had remembered to get before leaving Nehgrog. He faced north. The desert would be behind him. Calarath lay to the northeast and Nehgrog to the northwest. If he traveled directly east, he would reach Jedar. But he had no time. He knelt down and pulled the map from his belt. His best guess would be that the enemy would attack the towns of the Kraan River. It was only a matter of time before the entire southern half of the map he looked at now would be covered in this gray desolate desert. The thought made him miserable. He decided the best way to be attacked was to go where the enemy would be. That meant he had to head east, then slightly south. He got up and began to walk. As he stood, his vision blurred. Instead of seeing the landscape like he saw now, he was back in his dream. It was dark as before; he tripped and stood up again. The arrow pierced his arm, and that hideous voice sounded. It was deeper than before and seemed garbled. "It all ends here, Paul, son of Mark. It all ends here, young Paladin." Paul reached for his sword and drew it. Suddenly Paul saw that his sword had no blade. The light grew around him, brighter this time, and he saw the faces of the two creatures before him. They were hideous. Paul felt like vomiting. He saw them together, hands reaching out at him. They grew twice their size. Paul collapsed.

Lonar's men had finished clearing the tunnels. The Great Cave was a massive underground cave fifty miles outside Nehgrog. It was manmade, but judging by the architecture and remaining tools, it was definitely Pre-Jedarian. The "Ancient Army" was the name of an 800,000-man army that had camped in the caves during a previous war before the Kingdom had been united and settled. A simple scribe had recorded everything but had left his journal behind, becoming a treasure for the first Nehgrog tunnelers. Originally there was a magnificent entrance built with stone archways, but they had degraded into ruins, and the Nehgrog had simply cleared them away. They had tunneled eight tunnels from each major and minor directions—north, northeast, east, southeast, south, southwest, west, and northwest. The Cave had been used only once before; during the transition from Jedar, the tunnels that were not in use had been sealed off.

Now Lonar was riding back to tell his king that his task had been accomplished. Unfortunately one of the workers had returned home in the night and told his wife of what was going on. Undoubtedly she told her neighbors and friends, and word spread that the city was evacuating. This helped in some ways as most people began to pack and prepare. Others, however, had begun to revolt. Bôren controlled them by coming forward and giving the evacuation notice himself. He called the city to an open meeting and addressed them saying, "The reason for our departure is because a new threat has dawned on the horizon, one that could challenge even the greatness of Nehgrog. A new enemy, one that rides the clouds and rains the Maugrax Slime—a Cloudrider. Even the elite Nehgrog forces cannot withstand such a foe. If we evacuate we will save our lives. Those who do not wish to move will not be forced, but they put their own lives at risk." Afterwards Lonar had reported that the Arumans and the Krisbanians had requested to send their people into the Cave. Nehgrog's 520,000 plus the two towns together would only be about 770,000. The Cave could take another 30,000. Bôren planned to fill the remaining space with as many Green Guard as possible. In the case that the enemy did find them, he wanted to give them at least some protection. His doctors had returned from the Green Guard camp and given him the numbers of men they had saved. It seemed they had a total of 356,870 men. Bôren sighed.

Dawn broke on Calarath. The queen had been up all night and had finally found a solution to the new Cloudrider menace. Large steel canopies were to be built over the key structures. The obvious problem would be that the Slime would eat through the steel and fall on the buildings anyways. In order to stop this a second canopy would be built four feet under the first and filled with stone. Although the Slime would eat into the stone somewhat, it would not go through four feet. The queen had brought in an engineer to look at ways to make this possible and determine whether he thought it would work. He approved of the plan, and they set to work on final design. They could be built fairly quickly, roughly a week for each canopy, but they could be built simultaneously. Tomorrow they would begin construction on the first ones over the castle, library, war facilities, and the troop houses. The city would hire ordinary civilians to do the work. It was the only way to get enough manpower to complete the job quickly.

The queen knew that Calarath would be one of the enemy's first targets. After Calarath, Nehgrog would be attacked. Once those two cities were destroyed, it was only a matter of pouring out Ashkah to sweep through the Kingdom. The queen shuddered to think that this one Cloudrider could decide the fate of an entire Kingdom. The queen knew it was impractical to try and build protection for every house throughout the city. Word had reached her through a messenger that Nehgrog was evacuating to a large underground cavern along with two other nearby towns. The agreed Green Guard would be sent to Calarath when Paul returned. He was due to be back tomorrow. Suddenly the queen had an idea. She got up from her desk and walked towards the rooms. The third door on the right stood open. As she walked in, she saw her brother-in-law sitting in a chair reading. He glanced up from his book when he heard her walk in.

"Elizabeth! What a surprise! It feels like I haven't seen you in ages. What brings you to my room?"

"Amon. I need your help. There is a new enemy." The queen described the Cloudrider incident along with the Green Guard training facility. She also told him about the new canopies they were busy building. He listening quietly, nodding every now and then. "I believe that the next target will be Calarath. I don't know how we're going to save everyone. We will have to evacuate, but where to? There is no place big enough to hide 800,000 people."

Amon smiled. "I have an idea. How many citizens do you have? 800,000? Very well. There is a vast cave under the Goash Plains that has been abandoned for centuries. It will easily hold your population…"

"Amon…Nehgrog has already sent their people there along with two other towns. There will be no room. We need somewhere else."

"Ah. Hmm."

"I thought of the island, Zirikaan, but because the enemy is airborne it will make no difference."

Amon's eyes widened. "That's it! Zirikaan. On the island are vast caverns. I have explored most of them. You would probably fit a million people in them, if not more."

"Are you sure?"

"Certainly. Now to get across you must travel through the tunnel. It will be difficult and slow as the tunnel will only be wide enough for five or six people. It should take a few days to get everyone through, but in the meantime, keep building these canopies."

"Thank you, Amon. I don't know if I ever would have found a solution without you." Amon nodded and rubbed his head.

"I'm glad I could be of service."

"Of course." The queen stood and Amon dipped his head. Evacuate the city. It was a hard chore and would take some coordination and planning. The queen walked back to her study and began to think of how they would evacuate. They would have to go by district starting with the closest to the castle, then to the furthest away. Each district had about a thousand houses, but the total of districts was somewhere around 320. Those districts were divided into groups of forty totaling eight groups. The groups were named, but they were decided per group, and the queen knew them only as numbers. The order would be one through eight. They would set off group one, then let them travel for a day, then set off group two, and so on. By the time the eighth group entered the tunnel, the first group should be getting out. She would have to make the announcement today, so the people could pack and be ready to go early in the morning. She would use her Guardsmen to facilitate the move and help with any problems that arose.

Paul rubbed his eyes. It was nearly dark. He had passed out. Why? He had seen something. What was it? A vision? A dream? Perhaps it was a hallucination. Either way he had to start heading back to Nehgrog before they evacuated. Once he arrived, the Green Guard would set off for Calarath. He pulled out his compass and found north. He began to walk, angry and disappointed in not finding a Bazrukal. Perhaps there were other ways of finding information. His mind wandered back to his dream and the hallucination. Why had they been the same thing? Why had Paul been able to see more clearly in the second one? Unless...Paul's eyes widened. What if this was another gift? What if he could not only slow time down but also see into the future...or different points in time? Almost like the ancient Jedarian prophets he had heard about. Another gift. But how did he use this one? Was it chance? Random? What if others had this gift? They would be able to construct a picture of future events and plans before they happened. Just when things were beginning to seem hopeless, a new answer and solution slowly presented itself.

The tunnels were wide and spacious, and the people were coopera-tive. They had moved half the city in less than two days. Impressive. The Nehgrog people knew when they had to do something and did it well. It was evident that although the tunnels could hold them all, it would be rather tight and close. Bôren would give a speech to the people once they had all arrived. He knew the Nehgrog well enough for there not to be much trouble, but he knew not how long they would be in there. Patience and consideration would make this easier. On the other hand, they had over 150,000 Green Guard in the tunnels with them, and discipline would be strict. General Grek would be among them, and Bôren knew him well enough to know that he would take charge regardless of whether they were Green Guard or not. If he saw an act of disrespect or an argument, he would step beyond his area of jurisdiction and deal with the matter. It was early dawn and the endless caravan of people and horses and carts passed beneath Bôren. He stood on a rock overlooking the road. A few Green Guard were scattered along the road to keep order. Lonar stood beside him marking down the groups that had traveled. They had given every 100th family a red flag. There were 300 red flags in total. This way they could keep track of where they were. Lonar marked down the 167th flag as it passed him.

"How long do you think it will be, Lonar?"

"Sorry, Sire…how long will what be?"

"How long do you think it will be until Nehgrog is destroyed?"

Lonar lowered his paper. "My lord, you know as well as I that Nehgrog is the second largest city in the whole Kingdom. However, we are the strongest military power and the greatest threat. I believe we have no more than a week. Calarath will be attacked shortly after."

"Lonar…I've been wondering. How did the enemy know about the Green Guard camp?"

"My lord, it's a cloud. It can go wherever it wants without being noticed." Lonar's eyes opened wide. They both instinctively looked up. There was not a cloud in the sky yet, but it was dawn, and clouds would be passing by soon enough.

"Post a guard to watch the skies. Any unusual dark clouds he sees will be reported straight to me."

"Yes, my lord, I'll get to it." Lonar walked down the slope towards the road. He quickly crossed and spoke to the guard on duty who looked slightly puzzled but nodded his agreement. Lonar looked up at Bôren and nodded. Bôren nodded back and pointed towards the city. Bôren mounted his horse and kicked his heels. The horse shot off towards the city. A group of civilians had decided to stay in their homes, confident that nothing could attack the power of Nehgrog. Bôren had warned them, and when he came back and found their flesh burnt and singed, he would know it was their own choice. They had bought a variety of spears, bows, swords, knives, shields, armor, and horses from the various stores and were prepared to defend themselves. Perhaps if the new foe had been something similar to a higher form of Ashkah, Bôren would have seen their efforts as brave and noble. However, because the threat was in the clouds, he saw them as foolish and stubborn. He would go back to these people and tell them exactly what they were facing. If they chose to stay after that, Bôren would know that he had done everything possible to save them. The city of Nehgrog lay towards the western end of the Plains of Goash while the Cave lay somewhere towards the middle. It was a two-hour horse ride into the city from the Cave. Bôren was going at a fast pace and managed to cut that time in half. He arrived and turned his horse towards the northeast part of the city. It lay lower than the rest of the city, and the pathway towards that area of town sloped down quite steeply. He saw a small fire cooking outside the house of the man he knew to be the leader of the resistance. As Bôren dismounted, the man dropped to one knee.

"My lord."

"Oberon. I need to meet with you. Privately." They went inside his small house and into his study. There were two chairs similar in style to what Bôren had in his palace.

"What can I do for you, your Highness?"

"I want to warn you again about the danger you will be facing. This foe you fight is not something you can stab or throw a spear at or shoot an arrow at. This enemy of ours rides in the clouds and uses a torrent of acid rain as his weapon. You've heard of the Gray Slime of the Flamethrowers? It's the same stuff but more lethal. I beg you, Oberon, don't be foolish. Come to the Cave. There is enough room for all of you."

"The glory of Nehgrog shall never fall."

"The glory of Nehgrog can be rebuilt. Lives cannot! If you stay here, you sacrifice yourself and all who stay with you. Warn the others first and let them make their own decisions. I have too much to do to spend time arguing with you. Good day."

With that Bôren left. He knew that soon these people would join him.

Vision

† † † † † † †

It is often said that people are united more in times of hardship. It is when an entire culture is threatened that people will drop their differences and stand together. In one area of the Kingdom a group of around 800,000 people from three separate cities were living in a cave underground and another 800,000 people were traveling through a dark narrow tunnel under the sea. Calarath and Nehgrog were both in extreme danger. The people knew that something terrible was coming—something that would destroy their entire city. The people were calm on the whole and managed to make the transitions without much difficulty. Paul had returned to Nehgrog to find only the palace inhabited, and even then it was merely a skeleton staff helping move the more valuable items to the Cave. Bôren was in the Cave, he was told, and he set off to find the king. When Paul arrived, the murmur of voices could be heard echoing around. Bôren sat at a table with the War Council. He was on the far side of the large cavern. The sloping entrance into the cave turned around past the stables which already stank with the smell of livestock. He walked across to where the king sat. Paul passed hundreds of silent faces trembling with fear. Paul wondered how wise it was to let the people's imaginations run wild. People would assume the worst, and rumors would get around. It was inevitable. People were just like that. Paul walked up to the Council.

"…head south towards Egon. From there we could watch the approach of the Cloudrider."

"He could still be in the north."

"What about placing sentries in the north, east, south, and west?"

Paul walked up to the table.

"Ah, General. Good to have you back." Bôren stood and shook his hand. "Any new information?"

"Unfortunately, no." Paul took an empty seat. "I wasn't able to find a Bazrukal, and my horse was stolen by Ashkah scouts. I had no supplies and was forced to return."

"Ah, most unfortunate indeed. I suppose we will find out about our new enemy soon enough. Good thing there is only one though," General Grek said.

"We don't know that," replied Lonar.

Paul spoke again, "I believe Lonar is right. If one discovered a powerful weapon, it would be foolish only to produce one."

"Unless it's impossible for the Dark Lord to make more than one," said Bôren. No one spoke for a while. Finally Paul broke the silence.

"Gentlemen, the people need to be assured of their safety."

"I think he's right though; people have strange imaginations," declared Grek.

The men around the table nodded, and the decision was made. Two hours later Paul stood watching Bôren deliver a well-worded speech describing the strategy in terms the people understood. Paul guessed that the Calarathans wouldn't take it so easily. The Nehgrog people were stronger and seemed to be better at handling that sort of thing. While he spoke, Paul took in the Cave.

It must have been at least sixty feet high, and Paul guessed that it was roughly a half square mile. The Cave was bustling with people who all started to move once Bôren finished his speech. The hard floor could barely be seen. Already people had begun to unpack.

The neatest area was the northeast corner where the Green Guard had taken up occupancy. It was a square-shaped, dim Cave, but the air was clear enough and the only smell was of the horses and sweat. Paul guessed that they would be here for a while. If Nehgrog was attacked, the rebuilding would keep them here; if it wasn't, the fear of being attacked would. Paul sighed. The only way to make sure it was safe would be to destroy the enemy and know that he had no chance of coming back. Paul walked up the slope towards the surface. Only the king and the Council members were allowed out of the Cave and even then not all at once. Every two hours sixteen Green Guard would ride in through the northeast entrance and trade places with the next sixteen for sentry duty. There were enough of them to make the time between duties long and restful.

The night was dark around Paul as spring was breaking into summer. The days were sometimes hot, sometimes cool. Tonight Paul saw a Green Guard leaning on his spear looking around his area. Paul knew that it would be pointless to try and engage in conversation with him. The Cave was situated directly in the middle of the Plains of Goash, which were fortunately lush and had plenty of water and animals. It wouldn't be long before they would have to have hunting parties sent out to catch food. Life in the Cave would be hard, but it would be better than death. Half of the resistance in Nehgrog who had refused to leave had already joined with them in the Cave, but the other half had stayed. They would take up residence in the abandoned palace, no doubt. Paul stretched and yawned. He had been traveling for many days and was tired. He went back down into the cave. The bustle of activity had increased when Paul walked in. A man was arguing with General Grek about the Green Guard encroaching on his allotted area of the cave. Both Bôren and Lonar stood by trying to calm the man down. Already they were starting. Paul headed down towards the argument.

"My whole family has to live on this space and your Slime-spittin' soldiers have to steal the land for their comfort and pleasure. By all the poisons in Maugrax I'll never allow it to happen! And yet this king sits by and lets you push me around!" Paul stepped up and grabbed the man's hand as he was about to strike the General.

"And who are you, some keeper of the peace? Let me go!"

"Sir, is something the matter?" The man seemed to calm slightly.

"This soldier has moved his tent onto my land. I only have half the space I had before, and my family of four needs more room than this!"

"I'm sure we can come to some agreement that doesn't involve violence or disruption." Paul spoke calmly and gently to the man, and it seemed to calm him down. He thought about it and nodded slowly. Paul addressed the General. "Is there inadequate room for your soldiers, General?"

"Yes, sir. You see, with the wounded and all, we had to move out a bit."

"I see. Is there any way your men could bunch up closer together?"

"It would be a tight fit."

"General, everyone in here is a tight fit. There's no one here who has as much room as he needs. Now if you could bunch your men up closer, this will all be resolved." Paul's voice held a strong tone of command. The General nodded and walked off to tell his men. The situation was resolved. Paul dreaded facing more of them in the coming days.

It had been a full week since the construction of the canopies had begun. That had also been the day the queen had to evacuate slowly and carefully. So far everything had gone better than planned. The tunnel had proved incredibly small and dark. The first group had volunteered to carry torches and set them every ten feet to provide light for those behind. The first few groups had already surfaced and followed Amon's instructions to the Caves. The spacious caverns were divided into thirteen sections equaling out to roughly 62,000 people per section. There was approximately a three-quarter square mile of space throughout the whole cavern system.

Amon watched the proceedings and the way the people organized themselves. Half of the people bickered quietly, and the other half simply followed orders from the others. It felt strange to have so many people on Amon's own island where only one other person had ever set foot, but he knew that there was no other option for the city. Amon felt weakened and useless lying on a mat and not being able to walk around. He knew that he would never walk again, but he was grateful that he at least had his mind. He had told Paul that the most important thing to protect was your mind and your spirit. Amon had both in safe condition and was content. The queen knew his capacity for control and organization so she had put him in charge of everything on the island end. A few people had come to Amon to ask why the groups hadn't gone by boat. He told them because the boats would never get across the dangerous waters and because they simply didn't have enough to get across in time.

The queen's guard arrived at last signaling that everyone had come through. They didn't bother closing up the tunnel; it was too well disguised to be able to find on the other end. The people were told to elect a group of leaders, one from each separate section. The thirteen leaders would be in charge. The people were not permitted outside the caves. If they were seen from above, the caves would be attacked, and inevitably they would all die. The leaders were to appoint a group of fifteen people to collect food and water for that day. They were to keep watch in the skies every second. Each section had enough food to last them a week, but Amon suggested that the leaders start getting food before they began to run out. Amon told the leaders of a certain bird known as the Mork that was easy to catch, easy to find, and easy to cook. They bred like rabbits and there were plenty for each group to have enough. Water was not hard to find as the lake on the island was not far away.

One day Amon had asked to be carried around the island. During this short trip he found the structure of an Orun Oak house. He slowly remembered when Paul had begun to build it. He smiled. This island had been the best school the boy had ever attended. The attack in the mountain had left Paul desperate. Amon was glad he had found him when he did.

Meanwhile, back at Calarath, the queen's builders were finally finished. The canopies could not be tested as there was no Slime available. The queen had each of the people left on the mainland to ready a horse in case the canopies failed. The books from the library had been packed into extra thick boxes and buried twenty feet underground. The builders had discovered an abandoned tunnel and had used the length of the tunnel as storage. The city was eerily quiet, slowly awaiting its own destruction. The queen sat reading, something she had not had the chance to do since the death of her husband. All the reading she had been doing lately had been documents and paperwork. It was good to finally relax and read a good story. This one was a romance novel about a rich knight who loved a poor beggar. The queen smiled. Her husband had never been able to understand her love for romance books. He himself had been a romantic man, but he was more interested in stories of war and conquest. A tear ran down her face. She ignored the thoughts and continued reading. The day slowly faded into night. The queen retired and went to bed relaxed.

That night the queen had a dream. She saw the Cloudrider like a dark outline of a horse in the sky. It galloped towards Calarath. Suddenly the horse multiplied, and the second horse turned west and set off towards Nehgrog. Each of these split in two and headed for separate cities. The four dark horses doubled yet again totaling eight. Now all eight raced out at once. Then Elizabeth saw something different. All the horses had a long string attached to them almost like a marionette. One horse reached Calarath and suddenly...

The queen sat up breathing quickly. She knew that she had a gift for seeing things before they happened, and often they appeared as visions in her dreams. Sometimes they were metaphorical, sometimes they were simply literal. This dream must mean something. The eight horses, could they be Cloudriders? Perhaps. But what was the string for? Control. They were not separate beings. They were controlled by something—a master puppeteer. Nehgrog and Calarath were about to be attacked. It was near midnight, and the queen knew that in her dream it had been night. She knew she had better warn the remaining Council members and Guardsmen. She quickly got up and dressed. The Council members had taken the guest rooms on the lower floor of the castle. The queen walked quickly down the stone steps. She summoned a servant to go tell the men to meet her in the Council Room. The moon shone brightly through the floor-to-ceiling windows outside the Council Room. One by one the men arrived dressed and trying to look alert before their queen. They went inside.

"You may all be wondering why I brought you all here in the middle of the night. I have seen a vision of something that frightens me. I can tell you today without a shadow of a doubt that there is more than one Cloudrider. In fact there are eight of them." Murmurs rolled around the table. "I know that at least two of these Cloudriders are going to attack Calarath and Nehgrog simultaneously. We don't have much time. They are also not each individual beings. They are simply...fingers of a hand. The attack might come at night, and I thought it best to warn you as soon as possible. You may all go if there are no questions."

"Just one, milady."

"Go ahead, General."

"We all here know of your gift of prophecy, and we know that you have never been wrong. But what purpose did you have in telling us?"

"It's easier to take a punch in the stomach if you are ready for it. Any other questions?" Silence. "Good. Council adjourned. Good night." They all filed out of the hall and headed back to their rooms. The whole meeting was less than five minutes. Elizabeth lay down and tried to sleep.

"King Bôren, come quickly. Something has happened. We have more news on the Cloudriders."

"Cloudriders? More than one?"

"Yes, come quickly." General Grek had found Bôren outside breathing in the fresh morning air. A messenger had been dispatched to Nehgrog on the instruction to look for Green Guard sentries and ask for King Bôren. The messenger had given the message to Paul, who had sent Grek to call him in. Bôren rushed down and saw Paul pacing. The makeshift Council table had been moved closer to the entrance. Bôren reached it quickly.

"Bôren…we have news. You had better sit down." Paul did likewise. "We were wrong about the Cloudriders. There are eight of them, not one. But they are not each separate. They seem to be one being." Bôren glanced at Paul who nodded his confirmation. "The queen has a gift of prophesy I'm sure you have heard about. She knows that two Cloudriders have been sent out to attack Nehgrog and Calarath at the same time. We believe the attack could come soon." Commander Kreld finished and looked at Paul, then at Bôren.

"What are we going to do?" Grek looked at Bôren questioningly.

Bôren rose to his feet and seemed taller and stronger, "We will wait it out. It will attack the city, not here. Pull back all the Green Guard sentries; make sure there is no sign of occupancy here. The enemy probably doesn't even know about this Cave, and even if he does, he doesn't know that we are here. Have the people keep quiet. If this…thing has a way of hearing, we don't want it to suspect this place. Questions? Good. Get to it."

The people set about to prepare for the attack of the most powerful enemy that any civilization had ever faced. It had wiped out 70% of the strongest army in the Kingdom, and now it was about to attack two of the most powerful cities ever, second only to Jedar.

Paul had been as shocked about the news as Bôren but for a different reason. He now knew that he had two gifts and that he had inherited the gift of these "visions" from his mother. He had dreamed about this before, an octopus—eight arms and one mastermind. It was so obvious now; all he needed to learn was how to interpret it. He watched as Bôren quickly calmed and figured out ways to hide. Every one in the War Council was busy doing something, and Paul, being Nehgrog's new General, felt obligated to help.

"Paul, I want you to command the Green Guard. If the Cloudrider attacks with a group of Ashkah I want you to deploy them through the northeast tunnel. But do not take the first exit out of the tunnel; take the second one, further away. Avoid detection by any costs."

"What if they use a tunneler…what if they break into this place by mistake? It'll be easy slaughter."

"Split your force in two…send them south and dig trenches. Deep ones. If they do pass you, they should run into your trenches. Good luck."

Paul glanced at the huge mass of people and frowned. "We need more than luck, skill or military power. It is now the enormous force of darkness and the force of light." For the first time in his life Paul felt he was starting to see the world as it really existed. *If ever the Kingdom needed the power of the Creator, now is the time for Ara'tel to come to our aid.*

Destruction

† † † † † † †

Bôren had to visit the place himself. From just the accounts of the scouts it had been too hard to picture. The first thing that entered Bôren's mind was Jedar. He had seen the ruins of the place a few years later. Now he was reminded of it. This time, however, at least they had been able to evacuate. Bôren knew they had to wait at least a week for the power of the Slime to deteriorate.

After the endless wait they made the trip back to their beloved city. The palace roof had collapsed, and only two walls remained standing. The floor of the palace had been destroyed, and the ground beneath had obvious signs of utter destruction. Every single one of the houses had been completely flattened. The roads were gone, and every Nehgrog monument and landmark were nowhere to be seen. It was devastation and destruction at its apex. It was heart wrenching for Bôren to see. Something stirred deep within him while feeling sick in the pit of his stomach. He could taste it in his mouth—the bitterness of the destruction.

A group of them, Bôren, Paul, Grek, and Kreld, had headed out to inspect the damage. Oberon and his men were nowhere to be seen. The town square was no longer green and lush; instead it was simply dirt. An entire seven feet of the ground had been removed in some places. Small parts of city still burned seven days later. There had been a large band of Ashkah, but the Green Guard had dispatched of them before they reached the city. They seemed to have a new confidence in the Cloudriders and seemed to have abandoned their tunneling methods. They had traveled above ground during the night. The Green Guard archers and spear throwers had taken out half the army, and then swords were drawn. There had been close to a thousand Ashkah versus a few hundred brave Nehgrog. Bôren insisted the remains of the dead be buried before leaving.

They rode back to the Cave in silence. Bôren knew that he would have to tell the people something. One simply did not just walk up and say, "I'm sorry, your homes have been destroyed. Sorry." He would have to think of a tactful way, however, to say just that. No one would react calmly. They would have uproar. Unless of course the people took it like the men he traveled with now. Absolute silence. Bôren noticed that even Paul, who was not even Nehgrog, had felt a deep pang of sorrow at the sight. Paul was more Nehgrog than most citizens he knew. Even though he was Calarathan. Then he remembered. The queen had said that the two cities would be attacked in the same night, at the same time. He wondered if they had been able to evacuate in time. They were only now arriving at the entrance to the Cave. Green Guard kept watch as the men rode quickly through the entrance. Then they disappeared into it and pulled the huge grass-covered hatch behind them. As they dismounted and headed towards the table, Bôren pulled Paul aside.

"Paul, we have had no word from Calarath. The queen...your mother...said that they would be attacked on the same night. I would send a rider to see, but I have a feeling you might want to see for yourself. You have family and history there." Paul nodded. "I would go with you, friend, but I have responsibilities here. Someone has to tell these people something."

"I understand, Bôren. Thank you for everything. I shall return as soon as possible."

"Oh, Grek said he's sending a few Green Guard to Calarath...for some reason he didn't say. Perhaps you should travel with them."

"Thank you. I'd better get going." The two men shook hands. Paul packed only things that were necessary—weapons, map, compass, and rations. The Green Guard to be delivered was ready to go, and they set off.

Paul arrived to see his home city, everything he knew, destroyed. It was a different sort of destruction to Nehgrog. Here everything had been destroyed but the palace and library. Paul saw that a huge thick covering stretched over both places. The fires around the city burnt heavily, and it was impossible to get within twenty feet of the palace. The Green Guard had met the man they were supposed to meet at Arcoth, and Paul went the rest of the way by himself. As Paul sat on the grass far outside the city, his sorrow turned bitter. He was now infuriated. He knew not how or why, but he had to stop this. The whole Kingdom would be destroyed within the next few days if no one did anything.

By now Paul was used to having to initiate action. He remounted his horse. The people looked as if they had abandoned their houses. Paul knew they were probably safe. Right now he had a mission. He felt a strange sensation as he galloped back. Paul thought. If one wanted to kill an octopus, you wouldn't worry about the tentacles. You would dodge them and go straight for the head. Once you kill the head, the tentacles were useless. It was up to Paul to kill that head. It was the only thing he could do now. To spend their lives in fear of the Cloudriders would be pointless. If he could save the Kingdom, even if it meant sacrificing his life, he was prepared to do it or die trying.

He rode until he reached the Cave and didn't stop once. He made the journey in two days. His horse was exhausted as was he. He said no word to the Green Guard on duty. It was time to do something. He found the Cave unnaturally quiet. Night was falling, and the people were either shocked or tired or both. Paul didn't mind, as long as they were safe and peaceful. The biggest challenge would be convincing Bôren. Not that he needed him convinced. If Bôren held him under his oath to serve as the General, he would rebel anyway. His allegiance lay more to the Kingdom and the people in it than one king of one city. He was sworn to protect them. He knew he had to. Bôren was sitting on a blanket reading some papers. Paul approached him.

"Bôren. I need you to hear me out."

"Paul…what's the matter? Did you go to Calarath?"

"Yes. Bôren, have you ever tried to kill an octopus?"

"Yes. Back in Jedar I took a trip and I had to…"

"Never mind. Did you try and attack the tentacles or the head?"

Bôren paused then his eyes widened. "No, Paul. You're tired. The stress is affecting your thinking. You *cannot* try and attack the power of Maugrax!"

"I aim not to attack Maugrax. Just the controlling mind of the Cloudriders."

"That would be the Dark Lord! You would have to go through tens of thousands of Ashkah to get to him."

"True, but I'm not going for the Dark Lord. I believe there are two beings that the Dark Lord created solely for the purpose of controlling the Cloudriders. If I kill them…then we have a chance of surviving."

"Paul…"

"Trust me Bôren. I know that I know this, but I cannot tell you exactly how."

Bôren saw that there was no way to convince Paul not to go. "And how will you deal with the Ashkah?"

Paul breathed deeply. "That's where I need you—and Calarath. If we combine our forces with every soldier we have across the whole Kingdom, we might be able to withstand the Ashkah hordes. They will come, as will the last three Bazrukal, but if you can hold them off for a while, I can have a chance at saving our people."

"Paul, only you can deal with the Flamethrowers. What if we fail? What if we all die?"

"Bôren, we are all going to die anyway. Whether it's in here by Ashkah and Cloudriders or out there makes no difference. At least this way we have a chance! A very small chance but the only one I can see" Paul was desperate, and Bôren could tell.

"Paul, I know we have little choice. You know we can only survive a short while against a Flamethrower. If all three arrive, our chances drop dramatically. Add to that a Cloudrider, and it will be the end of our civilization."

Paul looked deeply into Bôren's eyes for several minutes. "I understand" was all he could muster in response. *It has all come down to this,* he thought.

"Paul, I see no other way. As you said, we die here or we die trying."

"Good. Send out Green Guard riders to tell the towns to send all their fighting men to this field. I have to leave soon. The entrance to Maugrax is a place no man has ever found."

The next few days were a chaotic rush. The leaders of every major city and every minor town were contacted about Paul's plan. Many wrote back saying that men were on the way; some wrote back saying that the plan was foolish and that they didn't trust the Nehgrog. Then Calarath responded. Their new Green Guard reinforcements were summoned. Their normal army of over 200,000 strong was grouped together. Once Calarath had sent its army, the nearby towns seemed to have a change of heart. Bôren's men tallied up the total fighting men who had arrived. They would need to move quickly so as not to draw unnecessary attention before they were ready. Finally the string of incoming men seemed to wane, then stop altogether. The total tally was well over 1 million. It was an amazing sight. Tents stretched across the plains in every direction. Bôren was surprised to see a good spirit among the troops. "Unity" was the one word that came to his mind as he looked at them. Bôren decided he would talk to Paul. It was no use to try and convince him, but perhaps if he talked to him, Paul might think more clearly about his plan. He found his friend packing a small bag of food and water. He had his armor on and his sword and bow ready to go. A quiver holding fifty white arrows Bôren recognized as Crystals was strung across his back. Paul's plan was a foolish one, and Bôren knew that Paul would probably die along with the rest of the Kingdom army. Paul drew his sword and checked the blade and wiped a small piece of dirt off. Neither of them had said a word. Paul glanced up at Bôren then down at his blade. Finally he sheathed the weapon.

"I already told you, Bôren, there is no other way."

"I'm not trying to stop you. I want to know what your plan is."

"I don't have one." Paul shouldered his bag and nodded to Bôren. Bôren would have to trust that Paul knew what he was doing even though Paul just admitted he didn't. Suddenly a Green Guard ran up to him.

"My lord, the queen has arrived." Bôren followed the man outside and saw the queen riding on a white horse while all around the people bowed. Bôren noticed that none of the Nehgrog warriors bowed, but all of the Green Guard were on one knee. The queen nodded every now and again until she reached Bôren. One of her Guardsmen helped her down from the saddle.

"Bôren."

"Elizabeth."

"I would like to talk to Paul."

"Of course, but you must know he won't be swayed."

"I know. One of the scouts saw him riding away from Calarath. He said he looked angry." Bôren led the queen down to where Paul was talking with a Green Guard. He looked up when he heard his name.

"Paul! Thank goodness you're all right!" Paul hugged his mother and then gave her a look that said, "There is no other way mother; you see that don't you?" Paul turned and saw that Amon was being carried in through the doorway. It had been a long time since Paul had last seen his uncle. If anyone had the power to stop Paul from his mission, it would be Amon. He was like Paul's father. He walked up to his old trainer and shook his hand.

"Good to see you, Paul," was all that Amon said. He seemed tired and frail. The rest of the day was spent talking about strategies. Paul did not participate. He spent the evening in silence, preparing himself for the battle ahead.

Alliance

† † † † † † †

Paul headed out of the Cave at dawn. Most of the soldiers were awake writing notes to loved ones to be delivered in case of death, sharpening weapons, talking, and relaxing in any way they could before the battle. The Nehgrog soldiers saluted him as he passed slowly and quietly on his horse. This was the last chance. He might never see a single human again. It took nearly an hour to pass the entire campground of the army. *Bôren better move his men soon before the Cloudriders attacked them.* Paul felt no fear or anxiety about whether or not he would return. He was calm. If he died, then at least he would try taking those…*things* with him. The scenery around him began to change indicating that he was leaving the fields of Goash. Soon he would be coming to the edge of the Egon borders. Direction was easy enough. Luckily he had found an old map in the Nehgrog library archives. The map marked where the Desert had been only a year after the Jedarian War. This way he had a better indication of where it began.

Somehow time flew by as Paul was lost in his thoughts. He checked every now and then with his compass to make sure he wasn't drifting. Twice he drew his sword and looked at the blade. This was the legendary Sword of Jedar. Paul himself had never heard of it until he had spent time in the Nehgrog library. The Sword had been wielded by the founder of the Paladin centuries ago. The last time it had been used was by his grandfather at the battle for Jedar. Nehgrog storytellers said that it was enchanted, but Paul knew that it was the Paladin training that made the sword seem special. Indeed. It was a special sword. Its blade had never dulled while in Paul's service, and the weight was light. The length of the sword was longer than Paul would have preferred, but that was understandable as it had been made for people twice his age. The inscription on the blade must have been some ancient language or code that Paul could not read. The writing began at the base of the blade and continued for about half a foot. It gave a sort of mystery to the sword.

By noon he stopped at a small river to refill his canteen and let his horse drink. He had been in this area less than a week ago. He guessed he was somewhere slightly south of Egon and to the east. From the map and his own instincts he guessed the entrance to Maugrax would be almost in line with Jedar. He would keep heading southeast. Suddenly he was aware of something, someone—a presence nearby. He spun and searched the horizon. There, to the southwest. Paul guessed it was an Ashkah horde, dispatched to kill him or perhaps on patrol. Regardless he pulled his horse behind a tree and knocked an arrow. The Crystal arrows he carried were both deadly and efficient. Paul pulled out from behind the tree only enough to be able to see. He let the arrow fly. It was hard to miss with so many targets. He struck an Ashkah in the chest. Instantly it collapsed causing the others to trip behind him. The group stopped at a shout from the Ashkah captain. Paul heard some growling and muttering. It was not usual for Ashkah to talk among themselves. Paul saw them pluck the arrow from the dead Ashkah and examine it. The Captain threw it on the ground and spat. He drew his sword and the others did likewise. With a guttural bark they charged towards Paul. In a few moments they were within fifteen feet of Paul and his horse. Paul spun around the tree, sword in hand, and leaped towards them with a shout. He could never be able to explain how he engaged his gift or how it felt to be using it. All he could compare it to was turning the enemy Ashkah into statues while he danced among them slicing heads and stomachs. The Ashkah captain was no harder than any of his men, and within less than two seconds the place reeked with the stench of Ashkah blood. Paul's horse began to grow uneasy, and they left the bank of the river. Paul noticed only later how fast the fight had really gone. His gift was definitely growing. Soon it would be needed for the greatest challenge any man had ever faced in history.

Bôren and the queen had begun to work together. The armies were getting along by following their example. The plan was to leave at dusk, traveling through the night and through most of the next day. Bôren had posed a brilliant suggestion. Take back Jedar. The enemy had known Jedar as the Kingdom's strongest city and biggest threat. To retake the city would be a bold and arrogant step, sure to draw attention. It was also the harmony point for Nehgrog and Calarath; the last time they had been together as one was in that place. The queen admired the courage of Bôren. He knew the limits of his men, of course, but he was prepared to take steps and make moves that most people wouldn't even dream of doing. It would be befitting for the final struggle for the Kingdom to be fought in the old capital. Over a million men had been able to keep to themselves and without quarrel for the last few days. It was time to get them on the move.

The queen took half of the army regardless now of whether they were Nehgrog, Calarath, the Northern Alliance, or a village. The army marched under the name of the Kingdom Army. Their first and last quest would be to defend Jedar. If they died in the battle ahead, at least they gave Paul a chance, but if they won, then they gained back the jewel of the Kingdom. Bôren would take his men thirty miles out of the city and form a semicircle perimeter. The queen's men would be within the city walls setting up defenses. Rumors had begun among the men about the extraordinary battle skill of the queen. His reputation grew with each passing minute.

They set off on the long march. None of the men had horses. The people of the Cave had been given time to say their good-byes, and now the men marched somberly. Every now and then someone dropped something or tripped or coughed, but on the whole it was a very monotonous and boring march. The queen and Bôren rode among the men.

They marched for three days straight like this only stopping for short breaks of about an hour. The men were complaining but only among themselves. They reached Jedar at dawn on the fifth day. The plan had changed slightly; all the men would build defenses first, then they would set out. With a million men they could get the work done quickly. They erected catapults, trebuchets, onagers, ballistas, and more. The holes in the walls were filled, and the doors were remounted. Wooden boards were nailed over smaller holes in the wall. The southern wall was easily the strongest, but it had been under the most attack. It was still sturdy, however. While the men busied themselves with work, Bôren and the queen met in a separate room.

"I have an idea, Bôren, that might prove effective. How big is the field to the south?"

"Well, there is no field left, Elizabeth. There is only desert."

"Of course. Well, how hard do you think it will be to tunnel under the desert?"

"It would be a simple task. What do you have in mind?"

"If we can tunnel under the Ashkah army, when they arrive, we can come up behind them and close in on them. We would need several wide tunnels to move men quickly and a way to get out without too much attention. But there is one problem. The Ashkah will probably use tunnels themselves. If we go too far, they will tunnel straight into our tunnels. A battle within could be hard and dangerous."

Bôren nodded. Suddenly a runner appeared at the door. "Your Majesties. There's been a collapse of a roof in the northern district.

Three men were killed, and some have been injured." Bôren stood and nodded to the queen. He hurried out with the messenger and came to the site. A doctor was there already treating a man who had been cut by a sharp piece of stone. The doctor informed Bôren that the biggest section of the roof had crushed the three men, and they were still under there. To get them out they would have to move the roof. Bôren got an account of what happened from a man sitting clutching his arm.

"The three of them," he pointed to the broken piece of roof, "were up on the top checking for holes and seeing if the structure was sound. We tied ropes to them in case they fell, but the rope broke. They got to the center of the roof, and suddenly it collapsed. They fell, and as they were getting up, that piece of roof crushed them. They are definitely dead."

Bôren nodded and thanked the man. If Jedar was ever going to be lived in, it would need to be completely rebuilt. Bôren wondered how secure anything in Jedar was. He walked slowly through the city inspecting what needed to be repaired. Among other things there was a broken statue blocking the southeast path and an enormous hole in the Great Castle wall, a thousand cracks in the pathway and a dried up river. The lake in the center was empty and dry, as was the city. The soldiers spent the rest of the day burying the bones of bodies. After the city had been cleared, the solders were assigned residences according to their area of defense. The night wore on, and the men were quiet as usual. A few talked, some practiced fighting and archery, but most were silent from exhaustion. Bôren was walking alone, thinking, when a soldier approached him.

"Your Majesty, we have a situation."

Paul stood on the rough line between the desert and the grass. One more step would make him the first willing traveler in the desert. From here on out there would be no water or food. He hoped he would find the entrance to Maugrax. No, he knew he would find the entrance. He hoped he would be able to defeat his enemy. He breathed deeply once, and then took the step. The ground was hard and rough. He remounted his horse and began to ride quickly. There was no scenery other than the dead trees every now and then that sprouted up from the earth like claws reaching for the sky. Hundreds of miles of this desert lay before him. He wondered how far south of Maugrax it stretched. What about the other Kingdoms? Paul had never been outside his own Kingdom; in fact it was impossible that anyone had. The only other Kingdoms in the land all lay to the south far beyond the desert. They had been isolated when the wars had begun a long, long time ago, and when the seas had become too wild to navigate, they had been isolated and forced to become a self-reliant Kingdom. Now he rode through the desert, the only moving thing for miles. The air was musty and smelled like sulfur.

Suddenly his horse stopped and bucked back and forth, throwing Paul off. Paul jumped to his feet and calmed the startled horse. He looked around to see what might have scared the animal. Nothing moved. Paul pressed his ear to the earth. He heard a faint rumbling. He stood dead still, and eventually it passed him. Paul wandered if it was the first wave sent to attack Bôren. He wondered how they were doing but knew they would manage. The day was growing old and night was beginning to set in. Nothing moved. The air was still. He walked around to stretch his legs. He would have to sleep soon. Tying the horse to the nearest remains of a tree, he lay down and tried to sleep. The ground was hard and rough. If he moved, it scratched his skin. Paul decided he would not sleep but at least rest. He sat with his back to the tree. He looked at his armor. It was the finest Nehgrog armor ever made, crafted by Arlan Gagney, the best blacksmith in the Kingdom. It was gold plated but not so much as to make the armor heavy or too soft. It allowed room for maneuverability and allowed the wearer to move any part of the body freely. It had been customized to fit Paul perfectly. It consisted of a light leather inner armor surrounded by the gold plate body. A thin layer of a secret material had been spread over the gold that made it impervious to rust and denting. The armor would hold up against a powerful sword strike from even a Flamethrower. The leather gloves and boots he wore were his own; he had inherited them from his father. Paul pulled out his journal and began to write:

> Just as the seasons change from winter to spring, so have I. There is no doubt that a dramatic change has occurred in these last few months. I have seen two great cities destroyed in the last few weeks. I know that if I do nothing, I shall see many more until I myself am destroyed. That is why I am here in the foreboding Jedarac Desert on a mission that is as daring as it is foolish. I doubt I will come back alive, but I'm not worried, if it means saving the Kingdom, because in the end that's all that really matters. A life not lived for others is a life wasted.

Paul paused and looked up. That sentence had profound truth in it. Perhaps one day someone would find his journal and note it as a memorable quote. Paul put the pen inside the journal and put it in his bag. It was getting cold—very cold. Paul tried to sleep again, but it was no use. At first it had been the hard ground that had prevented him from falling asleep, but now the cold, icy wind that chilled him to the bone was the problem. Paul looked up. The dark sky was clear. *At least it won't rain*, thought Paul.

It was early morning when Paul sat up. He must have been sleeping. He felt tired and sore. His horse was neighing. He stood up and removed his armor. He pulled out some Mork meat from his pouch on the horse. The meat of the bird never seemed to decay or become unhealthy, and Paul had packed a lot of it for his journey. He fed some to his horse and untied him from the tree. He put the rope away and put on his armor. He then mounted, and they rode off leaving their campsite.

It was early morning, and Paul planned to ride as long as he could. They had traveled over fifty miles yesterday; Paul wanted to do at least eighty today. His horse had rested well despite the conditions, and Paul could feel that he was ready to do a good day's work today. Paul had to check the compass and map to chart where he was. When he found the entrance to Maugrax, he would plot its position and send his horse back towards Nehgrog. For the first time since the beginning of the desert, Paul noticed the scenery changing. It was about noon when he started seeing large boulders and what looked like dried up riverbeds. They rode on past these. They continued for at least thirty miles. When they stopped for dinner, Paul guessed they had traveled at least seventy miles. The horse was tired and so was he. Only ten more miles and they would stop to sleep. Paul sat patiently gnawing at his food when suddenly something stirred.

A group of at least two-dozen Ashkah appeared growling and snarling at one another. The captain walked along in front of them and kept sniffing the air. Obviously Paul was attracting attention. He pulled out his bow and knocked an arrow. It slipped off the string, and Paul placed it back on. He drew it to its full length and held it there for almost a minute while the Ashkah grew nearer. The party was a few hundred yards away, and Paul knew he would never hit them from this distance. He waited patiently until they were within a hundred feet. He let the arrow fly. It missed his target, the captain, but struck an Ashkah to his right in the eye. This caused commotion, and Paul let two arrows fly before they began to run at him. The first arrow struck the captain on his leg causing him to limp. The second caught another Ashkah in the neck. Paul drew his sword. The odds were unfair—-for them. They were all dead within a few seconds. Paul walked over to the three Ashkah and plucked out his arrows. He wiped them clean before returning them to his quiver. As he pulled the arrow out of the captain's leg, he noticed that the captain had a piece of paper on his belt. He removed it and tried to read. The sketchy handwriting and the fact that it was in the Ashkah tongue prevented it. Paul guessed it was some order. Strange that he had never seen another with one. He tossed the paper in the bag on the side of his horse and remounted. They rode the last ten miles and stopped. Paul slept soundly that night and dreamed.

It was dark as it always was. Paul walked forward and tripped. He walked a while knowing that he would be struck soon by an arrow. The shaft flew by and struck his arm as it always did in this vision. The voice cried out, "It all ends here, Paul of Calarath, it all ends here, young Paladin." Then they appeared. They were definitely twins. They grew in size and attacked him. They seemed to coordinate their attacks but did not communicate. Paul reached for his sword, but there was nothing there. The sword was gone. He tried dodging the blades, but they trapped him. Suddenly both blades came down simultaneously. Paul used his last weapon, his mind. He sensed only one being. He looked for the other. It was nowhere. He spun and suddenly he saw a sword. It gleamed and shone, but there was no light. Paul reached for the sword and grabbed it. He swung it and parried the blade coming at him...

Paul opened his eyes slowly. It was not one of the shocking dreams where he woke up panting. This one had been different. Stranger. He knew for sure that this was a "gift dream." It was something he should know and remember for when he fought those "Twins."

"Fire when ready! Give them everything you've got!"
    "Groups one through twenty-three to the upper defenses!"
    "Secure the courtyard!"
    The shouts of the battle had just begun. They had come in the night, the whole army. Bôren had no idea that so many Ashkah even existed. It was as though he was seeing double. The whole

plain in front of Jedar was covered in them. They had brought their war machines and war beasts. Siege towers crawling with Ashkah rolled forward. The huge catlike creatures were over seven feet tall and more than double that in length and shook the ground around them with a thunderous roar. The army had never seen these massive beasts before. Then they appeared. They walked calmly through the ranks of Ashkah towards the very front of the massive army—three Flamethrowers in full black armor. They wore no helmets, and Bôren could get a good look at one up close. The only visible skin was their heads, and it seemed charred and diseased. The battle began.

Jedar

† † † † † † †

The trebuchets were launched on both sides almost simultaneously. The large rocks flew into the sky and came hurtling down
like comets from above. Orders were barked everywhere. The great
siege towers slowly made their way towards the wall. The archers on
the walls rained down arrow after arrow onto the Ashkah hordes.
They began to march towards the wall. Bôren caught sight of ladders. This would not be easy. Their army was trapped behind a wall
and had to fight on the battlements. Suddenly Bôren shouted out,
"Groups one through fifty into the courtyard with me. All other
groups to the battlements!" Bôren raced towards the massive courtyard with over half a million men. He stood in front of them knowing that they now hung on every word he uttered,

"That we may die seems certain. That we may live is yet unwrit-
ten," he began. "If we die, we die for the glory of the Kingdom. But
if we live, oh, if we live, what a grand and glorious victory that will
be. Never before in the history of the Kingdom have so few stood
to gain so much. And never before has such a great evil been on
the verge of utterly annihilating everything we hold to be good and
true." Bôren paused and let the words sink in.

"Let eternity take root in your spirits, strengthen your bones,
and power your weapons. The great Ara'tel has destined each of
you for such a time as this, to bring down and crush this powerful

Dark Army, and this victory will ring for centuries to come. Stories will be written about you; songs about your great feats in battle and your names and deeds will be forever celebrated. Stand together for our unity is our strength. Think not of your abilities nor of the overwhelming abilities of the Ashkah horde and their Dark Lord behind them. Think only of this. Let the power of Ara'tel surge through you now." The men had grown dead silent even while the dark army advanced.

"This might be your last hour, men. It may be your last chance to live, but also let it be your last chance to prove yourselves as men! Men of the Kingdom!" Bôren shouted the last word, and it was emphasized by the silence

"Put aside your race. Put aside your grudges. Put aside anything and everything." Bôren was interrupted by the large gate clattering. "Focus only on one thing. To bring glory to our Kingdom!" The men were eerily quiet. A strange new peace had settled over the army. It was as if the battle around them had drifted away. Then they cheered. As one mighty voice the sound surged around them and rose to a great height, like an eagle soaring into the sky. The cheers rose even further as the gate was pulled open, and the men charged out behind Bôren, their courage infallible. Four of the cat-like creatures snapped down at men as they raced into the Ashkah.

There was nothing but the roar of the two armies vying for power and control. The sounds of blades, arrows, screams, and roars could be heard. Bôren looked up to see that the first siege tower was nearing the wall. It stood tall enough to breach it. An arrow glanced off his armor as he turned the army along the wall. They raced by, swords slicing Ashkah as they went. The growls and howls of death were heard everywhere. And yet they kept coming. Wave after wave they poured onto the wall like water on stone, like an endless dark waterfall onto a magnificent rock. Bôren's horse was speared, and he leapt off the horse and used the momentum and his shield to block the attacks. Men around him charged onwards to the tower. As they reached it, they saw that the men on the wall were using flaming arrows, setting the wooden structures on fire. The men below began killing anything they could reach. The internal ladder system collapsed sending a hundred Ashkah to their deaths. Bôren kept his blade moving constantly, fed by his adrenaline. The earth began to shake as the giant cats began to turn on the small band of men. They used a combination of claws and their teeth to tear through the army. Bôren drew his only spear quickly. The great beast neared him, and he took aim. He thrust the spear with every ounce he had in him. It flew straight and struck the creature between the eyes. It swayed a moment and then collapsed. Bôren, distracted, spun to see a torrent of arrows raining down on him. He covered himself with his shield while slashing beneath it with his sword. He looked back. His men had gained for themselves at least twenty feet since they had raced from the courtyard, and yet the Ashkah storm was relentless.

Paul stood there, the final plunge. It was a massive hole at least a hundred feet in diameter. It stood like a gaping mouth ready to swallow him up. He had plotted its position and set the horse free. He knew it was smart enough to get back to the land beyond the desert by itself. All he had now was his training, his weapons, and his armor. This was it. This could possibly be the last time he would see daylight. He took one last breath and stepped in. Almost immediately he vomited. The smell overwhelmed over him, and he felt like dying. He desperately wanted to run out back to the fresh air, but he knew once he was out, he would never go back in. He forced himself to adjust to the smell. He wiped his mouth and swallowed. He could see only what the light behind him illuminated. The tunnel stretched straight as far as Paul could see. Slowly the light faded, and the mouth of the tunnel grew smaller.

It was in this moment that Paul heard the first sounds that sent chills down his spine. It sounded like a giant choking but at the same time trying to speak. A maniacal laughter was heard in the distance. Then silence. Paul stopped. Nothing. He moved on. The darkness around him grew complete, and he could no longer see. He looked for a source of illumination but found none. He was on his own. He traveled for what he guessed was at least a few hours before he felt a steep drop in the tunnel and a turn. Slowly and carefully Paul descended, step by dark step. It was depressing, but Paul knew that if he gave in to it, he would be weakened, and that would be exactly what they wanted. They were after him. He began to hear growls, voices around him. He reached out to the walls and found none. He must be in a large cavern. He tried to make his moving as still as possible. He knew that the Ashkah army was gone and that if he had not asked Bôren to help, he would be dead already. He walked on.

Suddenly he felt a wall in front of him. He turned and found that he had come to a dead end. He felt up and down all three walls. On the second wall he found an opening. It was only tall enough for him to fit in on his stomach. He lay down and found that his bow restricted him from continuing. He took it off along with the quiver and dropped it. He doubted he would need it. He lay down again and pulled himself with his arms. He could feel the closeness of the passage all around him. It felt as though the hundreds of feet of earth above him were suddenly going to collapse. He crawled on. The sounds of creatures moving in the darkness made him stop. He looked around. He saw nothing. The sounds seemed to come from his left. He turned and found that the passage continued in that direction. For two straight hours Paul dragged himself under the rock. It was dark, and the smell still made Paul feel sick. The air around him felt thick and musty. Suddenly the roof opened above him. After hours of crawling he had made it to another cave. The air was cold here, and a slow icy breeze drifted by. The draft carried sounds of hammering and forging.

Paul was completely disorientated and had no idea where he was. If he had been able to see, he would feel better about what he was doing. Shadows of doubt and despair had begun to creep into his mind. Paul summoned everything he had learned about doubt hindering performance and pushed the feeling away. Then he remembered. Amon had taught him to see when there was no light. He knew that the power that the Twins held would be translated as a massive dark space. He could focus on that and perhaps see where he was going. He had never been good at this "mental tracking," but now he needed it more than ever. He closed his eyes and concentrated. Slowly in the darkness in front of his eyes, he saw a shape. It was white and stood still. Paul moved forward and the shape did the same. It was himself! He was seeing himself somehow. He looked around, and the cave around him slowly illuminated. The longer he stood there focusing on it, the brighter it grew. Paul looked around and saw an Ashkah perched on a ledge about twenty feet up. He resisted the urge to kill it. Slowly its glowing eyes saw him, and it drew its bow. Paul saw the arrow flying before it even left the bow. He quickly sidestepped, and the arrow clattered to the ground beneath him.

Blades and shields were everywhere. The mass of colliding bodies was a dizzying experience. After almost an hour of the battle raging on, Bôren's men had forced the Ashkah hordes at least forty-five feet back. The trebuchets were now shooting faster than ever. The onagers and ballistas had been wheeled out of the main gate and sat launching projectiles into the mass of gray bodies. Then Bôren saw them. They had been quiet and inactive for most of the battle letting the Ashkah deal with the men; but now they saw that they were wasting time. The Flamethrowers stood on a huge mound of dirt that Bôren knew had not been there before. They calmly launched the first of those hideous black orbs which burst into flames above the men's head. Now they were at an enormous disadvantage. Bôren knew they would not survive against even one of the Flamethrowers, let alone three!

"Pull back! Pull back!" he shouted. He heard the order relayed along the wall, and they began to race towards the gate. It opened for them, and they filed in. Fifty men stood at the gate protecting the others running in. As they were inside, Bôren split them up. They were going to use the queen's tunnel idea. However, they had underestimated the amount of Ashkah, and the tunnels would come up almost in the middle of the black army. The eight tunnels were roughly thirty feet wide, and the men raced through them. Bôren let them run and he ran to where the queen stood. Her arm was in a sling in an attempt to heal the broken elbow. She was in her own full battle armor, sword raised, shouting orders for the archers and those who manned the trebuchets. Bôren pulled her aside.

"We're sending the men through the tunnels now. Focus everything on the front so you don't hit our own."

"Yes, but Bôren, watch out. The tunnels won't reach behind them."

"No, but we can cause confusion. And I'm actually hoping the Flamethrowers will attack us there. At least there the flames will eat into the army. I must go."

Bôren raced down the stairs and towards the huge opening for the tunnels. He chose the third entrance where men were still running in. They had lit the tunnels using torches, and Bôren saw that the beginning of the army inside the tunnel was not far ahead. He pressed through the crowd to the front. He raced on with them behind him. The rumbling of the battle above continued. Each time the great cats leaped or charged against the wall the whole tunnel shook. Bôren had a feeling that it might collapse. They reached the massive opening where they would go directly up. The cavern had a long wide slope up to the roof of the cave. Bôren walked up a little and turned around.

"You all know what to do. Watch out for the Flamethrowers and take as many of these cursed Ashkah down as is humanly possible. For *Jedar!*"

The men were invigorated and charged forward. The men with the drills began to break the dirt. As soon as it loosed, the men around began using their shields to dig. They broke into the sunlight and poured out. This time they had nearly a full minute of confusion. The Ashkah, being individually unintelligent, relied on the orders from the captains who had not yet realized what was going on behind them. Suddenly one of the Flamethrowers screamed a high-pitched wail. The Ashkah turned on the men while still being massacred from the front. It was a clever design. A man to Bôren's left shouted, "Orb!"

A second later at least fifty Ashkah had been killed by their own commanders' attacks. The orbs kept flying. Inevitably they were killing off Bôren's men, but for every one man they lost, at least twenty Ashkah were killed. It was easy killing; every time Bôren swung his sword he killed. However, their sheer numbers made them dangerous. While two or three attacked, another five lunged at Bôren from behind. Had he not had his armor, he would be dead. He saw a man he knew well. Lonar Stone-House. He was wielding two blades at once, killing Ashkah at a frightening pace. Lonar had trained in the ancient art of Umbar, which was the style of using two swords and no shield. The speed of the blades alone acted as a shield repelling any attacks that were made at him. Bôren cut his way towards his friend.

Paul walked slowly, eyes closed, watching the light grow in front of him. The pathway was easily visible now, and he saw that it sloped downwards even further. Suddenly he tripped. He looked down and jumped back. It was a human skeleton. It still had its armor on. Then Paul caught sight of something that made his bones chill. On the back of his helm where the name of the soldier is always engraved, Paul saw only "Jedar the Great."

This was Jedar, the man who had founded the great city all those centuries ago. Now Paul understood. This man was the founder of Jedar, the great warrior whose sword Paul now carried. Paul felt a strange sense as he stood in the presence of such ancient history. Paul saw a pendant around what would have been the man's neck. It had an engraving of a massive soldier wielding a sword, but the sword was not in his hands, it floated somewhere above his head. Paul pulled the pendant off and put it in a pocket of his leather armor. Paul stopped. This man had been in these tunnels. Why had he been here? What had been his purpose? Was he doing what Paul himself was doing? Had he driven himself to attack the Dark Lord and failed? Paul stood straight. He would continue the legacy of Jedar. He would do anything he could. This man had given the Kingdom glory, honor, and a home. Now he would return the favor. He stepped over the remains and continued. Paul raced forward, eyes still closed, watching the path unfold in front of him. Paul's mind raced as he suddenly saw something that made his heart stop.

It was their final hour. If they died now, they would have at least done well against the dark army. The queen raced back and forth telling the archers where to focus their attacks. They had begun using flaming arrows as the day slowly smudged into night. The arrows would strike into the Ashkah, and he would begin to burn. He would run straight into the Ashkah around him catching them on fire. It was a simple but effective plan, and without fail the Ashkah would end up killing more of his comrades than the archers had planned. The queen could not see Bôren, but the effects of his attack were evident. The groups nearest the tunnel had turned on the new attackers, but the groups in the front had continued to run forward. They were trying to get their ladders to the wall, but each time the archers killed the Ashkah before they erected the ladder or kicked the ladders off before the creatures had a chance to scale them. The queen had her archers rotate with two at every post. One would keep the other with a fresh supply of arrows, and the other would shoot. Then they would rotate. Fifteen men ran back and forth between the posts delivering arrows. The archer would have to be careful, as his assistant would hand him the arrow already ignited. It was a brilliant and majestic sight—for the second time the flaming arrows streamed from the walls of the great city of Jedar. The queen had remembered. She had been almost twenty when the attack came. A few years later, after the death of the king, the heir had chosen her. She remembered watching the wars from the caravan leaving the city. She remembered the sounds, smells, and sights. The air had been thick with blood and the sounds of men and Ashkah screaming. That was when the Flamethrowers had been their greatest fear. She sighed and looked up. A ladder was erected on the fifteenth section.

"Group fifteen, ladder!" The ladder was kicked by a strong looking archer. They had divided the wall up into long segments. Each group was with the segment. A number had been painted behind the wall at each section. Sections two, nine, and four suddenly clanged as the iron ladders struck the stone. The queen was standing near two and raced forward. The ladder fell before she reached it, and she saw at least ten Ashkah fall from the ladder. It was a brutal fight, and the queen felt so helpless. It was true that she was a great warrior, but both Paul and Bôren had insisted that she command the battle from within. Suddenly the queen heard a great screech. She looked up in time to see the massive missile from an onager, the great siege weapon, slam into a Flamethrower. Panic erupted from the Ashkah, and a cheer arose from the men. Six trebuchets turned their attention on the last two Flamethrowers. The Flamethrowers dodged the massive rocks easily letting them fall on the crowd of nearby Ashkah instead. Then the Flamethrower on the right did something the queen had never seen before. It drew a long black sword and began to fight. The second Flamethrower followed shortly, and they began hacking into the men. They were brutal. The queen could see the men struggling against the lightning fast attacks.

. . . . .

Bôren was stunned to see men in front of him being slaughtered like animals. They stood no chance against the Flamethrowers. Their only chance would be to distract them and run.

"To the wall!" Bôren shouted. Again the order relayed quickly, and the men began cutting into the Ashkah army with ferocity that surprised even them. Then again they had a Flamethrower on their heels ready to slice each of them apart. They reached the wall only after nearly thirty minutes of hard struggle. The men looked ready to collapse. Bôren looked up at the queen.

"All trebuchets against the Flamethrowers! *Now!*" Almost at once nearly a hundred massive rocks flew down. With astounding speed one of the Flamethrowers began to demolish them in midair with his powerful orbs. However, because of the sheer numbers he was eventually overwhelmed. A large shout rang up among the men as nothing moved from under the rocks. It was a great victory of a battle for a war they knew they could not win.

Aspiration

Now that Paul had a way of seeing through the darkness, he felt as thought he was stronger, more confident, and more ready to do the deed. Of course he had realized that the battle would not be easy. He would need every part of his gift to be able to match them. Paul remembered his second gift. What if it had not been a metaphorical dream? What if his sword really was useless? Would he find another during the battle? No, the sword had been above him. Paul froze with a sudden wave of realization that made his skin quiver. The sword had been above him. He glanced down at the pendant. It had a picture of a sword above a man's head. It was a clue. His sword was not the one he would need. There was another sword—a physical sword? No, that didn't seem right. Paul again raced forward. He had been feeling the dark spirit of the Twins before he had even seen or heard them. He came to a massive room. It must have been a hundred feet high and five hundred feet wide. It was lined with a spiraling passageway along the edges leading into what Paul guessed were homes or housing for the Ashkah. In the center of the room a massive black pool swirled. Paul couldn't resist the urge to peer in. Suddenly a voice called to him from the pool: "It all ends here, Paul of Calarath. It all ends here, young Paladin."

It was in that moment that Paul knew he had to dive into the pool. The way to the Twins was through this black pool. Paul held his breath and leaped in. He fell into a thick milky substance that seemed to stick to him; slowly it began to pull him down further and further. He felt something grab his feet and force him under. The hand pulled his leg and in a few moments he reached the bottom. By now he had almost no air left in his lungs. *What a cheap trick…to drown me*, thought Paul. *Doesn't even have the courage to stand up to a small challenge.* Suddenly the pool around him was still, and the hand released his foot. The substance seemed to be draining. It pulled him down through a wide hole, and he splashed down against the floor. He sucked air into his lungs as the strange substance dripped off him. He found that it was trickling off somewhere. His spirit sensed that the room was not empty. A profound sense of evil commanded his attention.

Bôren stood by the queen. It was relatively calm except for the enemy's relentless trebuchet strikes. They had pulled all the men back. Had they been two normal, human armies, a temporary truce could have been made for the armies to rest, but as these were Ashkah, they wanted no rest until they had victory. There was no doubt about it; the defenders of the great city were losing, badly. It was only a matter of time before they were completely obliterated. They had the majority of the men waiting and resting within the tunnels while a skeleton crew checked for ladders and rams. The great beasts, which Bôren had named the Irien, meaning "tall feline," had continued their pounding across the fields. They had stopped for a short while. The Ashkah had continued shooting arrows for the last few hours while the remaining Flamethrower inflicted incredible damage on their walls and the evil Slime was killing men at an alarming rate. Every now and then they would surge up, roar, and shout, then charge the walls and pick up their dead comrades' ladders only to have them knocked down.

Jedar was under siege, no argument there, but the army within was under the command of two master strategists, and they had enough food and water and sources to last months. The Ashkah had nothing and needed nothing but destruction and victory. It was now early morning. Some of the men had fallen asleep. Bôren walked over and woke the men. They counted each man as he walked out of the tunnel—only 452,984 men. That meant they had lost over 550,000 men in the battle so far. At this rate they would not last another day. There seemed to be no dent in the Ashkah armies. A strong wind blew that morning as some of the men were served a meager breakfast. There was no chatter now. No joking, talking, or arguing. Just silence. Bôren watched them from the doorway. Occasionally someone would drop a fork, but no one even bothered to look. Bôren knew what they were thinking. It was suicide to go out there. There was no hope of winning even if they summoned every ounce of strength and courage. There were roughly fifty Ashkah to every one man. One of the men stood up slowly and walked over to Bôren.

"I've been asked on behalf of the men to speak. We will not go out and fight." Bôren noticed it was a Calarath soldier, marked by his blond hair and small crest on his forearm. "We will not throw our lives out to that endless sea. We want no part in this." Bôren looked sternly at the man, breaking him inside. He said nothing, just stared. The man shifted uncomfortably and averted his eyes. Bôren looked up.

"Is this true?" he shouted. A few nervous nods told him all he needed to know. "All right. I shall go out there with any who will fight. If need be, I will go alone."

"I will go, too." Bôren glanced behind him and saw the queen in full gear, sword drawn, ready to go. She threw a "don't even think about it" glance at him before he said anything. They waited for someone to join them, but no one spoke. No one moved. Bôren turned and walked away with only the queen behind him. They stood in the empty courtyard. Suddenly Bôren gave the signal to one of the men on the walls, and the doors swung open, enough to let them both pass, then closed again. As soon as they stepped out from the gates, a large sleeping Irien blocked their path.

"Shh, follow me." Bôren leaped up onto the creatures back and gripped its fur tightly. The creature awoke as the queen gripped the hair and began to pull fiercely. Bôren rode loosely to let his body move with the beast instead of trying to stay still. He twisted the hair to the left and the creature turned. It raced forward, driven by pain and confusion, crushing Ashkah in its path. The two of them were doing some damage. The Ashkah were either too stupid to attack the beast or too afraid for they simply jumped out of the way when possible. Bôren glanced to his left where he heard a commotion. It was Lonar, riding an Irien with as much skill as Bôren. Bôren knew that he could trust his old friend. Lonar was not alone either. The men must have either talked among themselves or been moved by the way their two commanders faced the army alone. Either way, the gates were flung open, and the men charged into the army—archers on the sides shot arrows with new vigor. The warriors swung their blades with a new dexterity and strength. All around the screams of the Ashkah could be heard. It was a valiant effort, and yet they still had no hope of winning.

It was dark in the room. It felt even darker because of the being Paul could see. Paul's physical eyes could not see the being, or rather beings; instead he saw them with his mind. They were massive evil giants. Paul became aware that he himself was nearly as tall as they were and that they shone a brilliant white while the two Twins were translated as dark silhouettes. The room around them was large and circular. Suddenly the Twins broke the silence. They spoke in a dark, guttural growl and shook the room. Their voices were one, perfectly pitched and timed together, "You have come here, Paul, son of Mark, to challenge us, the Vorok. You come here in vain. We know you. Your weak power and misguided ambition will be your downfall. You have confidence that is ill based. Your life ends here. Now. It all ends here, Paul of Calarath. It all ends here."

Now it was Paul's turn. He drew his sword slowly and looked at it. "I come here today to rid the Kingdom of this great menace. I stand for everything that is true and noble. I stand for everything that is worth living for and everything that is worth dying for. I stand for those I love. I stand for the Kingdom and the great Ara'tel. You aim to destroy, and that is why I am here. The good and true will always prevail. If I die today, another will come, and another, and they will keep coming until you are destroyed. There is no hope for you now. I have come here today to rid the Kingdom of you!

"I may just be Paul, son of Mark, but it is not who I am that matters; it's who I represent!" With the last word Paul, filled with power, shot forward, blade swinging. He met the first Vorok's blade in midair and spun to avoid the second. The battle was intensely well coordinated on the side of these hideous Twins. Paul had guessed they were telepathically linked, and his suspicions were realized when they began to fight. They fought like one being with two bodies. Paul could not see a thing in the physical. He had switched over his entire body to battling the creatures in his mind while drawing power from his spirit. He was using every ounce of his training; every part of his gift he pushed to its extreme limits. He pushed the delay to almost a half minute. The Twins were not affected at all by this trick.

Paul was fighting defensively, and he knew he could not keep it up. He only had enough time to parry and dodge besides trying to guard himself enough for an attack. He knew that if he fought like this, he would eventually lose. He locked blades with one of the Vorok and pushed back. The creature pushed back against him with a roar. Their strengths were equal and the blades sat in the middle, undecided. The second Vorok swung at Paul's head. When Paul ducked, he lost the hold on the creature's blade and fell down. He rolled out of the way of a downward stab and righted himself. They were relentless. A blade swung by his foot, and he leaped to jump over it. The second blade swung at his neck while he was in midair. Paul saw the blade and turned his jump into a high flip over the Vorok's head. He landed lightly, spun, and lunged towards the moving Vorok. He caught it on the arm, and it yielded a scream of rage. The second creature attacked, meeting Paul's blade, then shooting out a fist catching Paul in the face. Paul staggered backwards and tried to think. He could not see. The Vorok onslaught was a blur of blades and venomous power.

The army was completely surrounded. The enemy had formed a massive circle around the army and began to close in. The army had countered by forming a massive ring facing their enemy. Each man attacked only the Ashkah in front of him. They were temporarily holding their ground. They barely lost a single man during this stage of the fight, and when they did, they closed the gap quickly. The men used every available weapon whether it was a dropped Ashkah sword, their shields, or at times only their bare hands. And yet there was no way for them to win. Everyone knew this, and yet they continued to fight. It was truly a brave and valiant moment. The great beasts had been neutralized and tied down and could not escape. The queen had killed nearly eighty Ashkah on her own with a broken arm, more than most had killed with both arms. The day was growing dark when the order for retreat was given. The ring moved as it was towards the gate, those in front cutting the path and those behind and on the sides protecting. They made it inside the gate. Suddenly Bôren saw something—or rather someone. It was an archer standing at the wall, but Bôren knew he was not one of their men. His tall longbow released arrow after arrow into the masses, and each time a terrible cry was heard. Bôren ran up the stairs.

"Who are you?"

"I am Aidron. I am the leader of the Rangers of Valzah."

"Valzah? The Ashkah rebel outpost?"

Aidron laughed heartily. "Clever story, don't you think? There is no Ashkah rebel outpost."

"Why are you here?"

Aidron glanced over at the mass of Ashkah behind the wall. "My people are much like yours, King Bôren. The Nehgrog and the Rangers have much in common. We, too, do not want to be associated with Calarath or the Kingdom."

"So why have you come now?"

"The battle is not only for the Kingdom; it is for the land and the lives of all who dwell in it. We are secluded, but we are not fools. We know when we are threatened. I have brought my archers, over 100,000 of them. It isn't much against that the enemy, but they are well-trained. We have secrets that most men would die for. We will aid you in your fight."

"Will you serve under me?"

"Yes. We first went to Nehgrog and saw it. I am sorry for your great loss. We followed your tracks here." Aidron was a tall, well-built muscular man. He had no beard and had long brown hair that rested on his shoulders. He wore a dark green leather body suit with matching leggings and gloves. He had a dark red cape with a crest of an archer under a tree. He had keen, mysterious eyes. Something within Bôren told him not to trust the man, but they needed all the help they could get. Bôren showed him to the room where he and the queen normally sat to discuss the battle. The queen stood to welcome their guests. Bôren introduced him and told the queen the story. The archers had taken residence in the northern parts of the city and were fresh and ready to fight.

"This conquest is not for ourselves…Aidron. This battle is for those who will come after us. We do not fight for ourselves."

"My reasons for being here are my own. I will fight as will my men—regardless of why or how. If we win, that's all that matters."

Bôren spoke up. "And what if we don't win? What will you do?"

"My men will not run. We will fight to the death if that's what you mean."

The queen sighed. "While we may not agree with your motives, we are glad you are here, Aidron. Our men are tired and few in number. Welcome to Jedar."

Within two hours the battle died down. Both armies withdrew to rest. The night grew quieter. Even the Flamethrower ceased. Bôren went to meet the new archers. They were all well dressed and well armored. They each carried a longbow with two quivers full of arrows. A sword rested on their backs. Aidron drew his to show Bôren. It was a long, slightly curved blade. A thin line ran down the length of the blade. There was no hand guard, just an ivory handle.

"We use this only for emergencies," Aidron told Bôren. There was something strange about the quivers that bothered Bôren. It was like looking at a fine piece of jewelry that you knew was stolen. Bôren decided not to ask Aidron about it. Bôren was given the enormous honor of shooting Aidron's bow with one of his arrows. Bôren was not a particularly good archer, but when he struck a target nearly 200 yards away, he knew that there was something strange about the bows. The men looked suspicious of the Nehgrog king, and Bôren knew he would have to live with it. He needed the help, and regardless of what they thought, Aidron was right; his motives were his own as long as they won. Bôren noticed that there were many women among the Rangers. That night it rained—a torrential downpour that soaked everything. Luckily most men were sleeping throughout the tunnels and were dry. The Rangers, sleeping in the broken houses, were almost all completely wet and miserable by morning. When Bôren walked out to wake the men, he saw that a massive crowd had gathered by the wall. He walked over and looked out. The ground was clear. The only Ashkah left on the field were those that were dead.

Paul's arms were quickly growing tired. Even when he pushed his gift to his limits, he felt overpowered by the Vorok. Then suddenly the Twins roared and their swords burst into flame. They swung them at incredible speeds and lunged at Paul. Even in his mind's eye they blurred, too fast for Paul to keep track. He furiously tried to parry the fiery blades coming at him from both directions. He slipped. He tripped on an outjutting rock and fell. One of the blades screeched down his back cutting open the flesh. Paul screamed in agony as the wound began to catch fire and burn. He writhed on the ground, and he felt his blood boil. He looked up. The Twins circled him in slow motion. He felt his life ebb away slowly. *So I was wrong. This is really the end...*thought Paul. Then slowly, as if a light were being turned on, the room grew brighter around Paul.

"Paul. Do not fear, for I am with you. This is not the end. Your story does not end here." Paul looked up and saw a shining figure standing above him. "Yes, I am Ara'tel. I have always been with you, Paul." Suddenly the pain across his back disappeared. "Take your sword and conquer your foes." Paul looked down at the blade of his sword which had snapped. Paul turned his gaze upwards to see the man handing him a shining golden sword. The true Sword of Jedar, not its physical reflection he had used so far.

After waiting the entire day for the Ashkah, for some surprise attack, the men had decided that they had won. The Rangers checked the tracks and confirmed that the Ashkah army had headed into the desert. They buried the bodies of the Ashkah in a mass grave a few hundred yards out. The day was spent celebrating and talking. Bôren, along with the Rangers, refrained, still suspicious. There was no reason for them to leave. *It's an ambush to get us unprepared while they attack.* He positioned sentries around the city and in the towers to watch for a surprise attack. A whole day passed, and still the sentries had seen nothing. Bôren had sent Rangers into the tunnel to check that the army hadn't hidden in there, but it was clear. He even sent out a group of riders at least thirty miles in each direction and still nothing. But this did not ease the Nehgrog's heart. He sensed something deeper was at hand—a master attack. What reason would the Dark Lord have in pulling them back? To save them? From what? Even he must have seen that there was no chance for the Jedarians. Unless. Bôren's eyes went wide with shock—unless he was sending in something that could threaten the Ashkah by mistake. Something like a Cloudrider. Bôren guessed that all of the Cloudriders would be heading towards Jedar soon if they were not already there. It made perfect sense! Why hadn't he seen it before? He pulled every man back and into the tunnels. They grumbled about not finishing their victory feasts. He found Aidron and the queen. He pulled them aside.

"I fear something terrible has happened. Why would the enemy pull out the Ashkah?" His question went unanswered. "To save them but not from us—from something else. The Cloudriders!" The queen's eyes went wide. Aidron cast a questioning glance and Bôren.

"We have heard of these Cloudriders and seen their power. Are you sure they are headed here?"

Bôren was frustrated at the question. "Of course I'm sure! By the blades of my fathers I'm sure!"

The queen tried to diffuse the situation. "Why would he have waited this long to attack us? Why not send them instead of the Ashkah?"

Aidron answered, "To force us into a false security." Bôren nodded his agreement. "Although we knew we would not win, the sudden withdrawal made us feel victorious. We fell into the trap." Aidron had a quick mind. Bôren noted that he would make an excellent general with the proper training.

"What we need to know is what we can do to help. Jedar will be destroyed, no doubt about that. The men will hide in the tunnels, but they are not very deep, and the Slime will eat into the earth and kill them. We are truly trapped."

"Bôren," said Aidron, "You told me of your friend, Paul. What did he say about the Cloudriders? That they were connected to something?"

"Yes. There is a mind behind them. They are not individual beings; they are linked by one mind," spoke the queen.

"He also said that if we cut off the mind, the rest will follow," added Bôren.

"Is he not there fighting it now?"

"Yes," answered the queen distantly. "He is our last hope if he still lives."

Axis

† † † † † † †

If one had seen Paul in the physical realm, he would have seen him bare handed, moving only to dodge the attacks of the Twins, with eyes closed. What Paul saw however, was himself, armed with a lethal sword. Paul, armed with his new sword, was unstoppable. In a few moments he had struck both of the Vorok at least twelve times. The last time he had severed the left hand of one of them. It had been enraged, and they had increased their attacks. Paul fought on, almost amused. He knew that he would win, and it was almost as if the fear inspired by the Twins had been broken. With the Sword of Jedar he was unstoppable. Suddenly he met blades with the Vorok. Its fiery blade, which before had seemed powerful, now began to weaken with the contact of his blade. His strength had doubled. The Vorok on his left executed a well-placed, fast maneuver. Paul ducked, and the blade missed him by a good margin. Paul was gaining the upper hand. He surged with confidence and strength and, unexpectedly, the blade of the Vorok broke. It screamed and jumped away. Paul drew back and threw the sword at the Vorok. It was weightless, but it struck the creature with enough force to knock it over. It lay still. The second Vorok screamed too and felt equally as weakened. Paul saw the still silhouette disappear and fade into light.

. . . . .

The Gray Slime poured over the field in one massive long torrent. Slowly it began to increase and draw nearer to Jedar. The flames began to lick the wall reaching out like claws. Then the clouds drew above the wall. Destruction began. The men within the tunnels had been forced out the moment the rain started. It had seemed to grow in power and had eaten through the thirty feet of earth quickly. The first few thousand men had been killed instantly. Jedar was being destroyed, not only the city, but also the men who stood for it. Screams of suffering filled the tunnel as the men raced out. In vain the archers tried to strike the clouds with poisoned arrows but to no avail. A scout ran to Bôren telling him that the Ashkah army had begun to turn north and was closing in their rear. They were being trapped and slaughtered like cows. Bôren felt utterly helpless. Never before had he been forced to watch his people suffer and die and not be able to do anything.

Aidron had pulled his Rangers back outside the city to the North. He assured Bôren that he held his promise—he was not running away. They set up defenses for the oncoming army while Bôren ordered his men to follow Aidron's lead. The roar of the falling Slime nearly deafened Bôren as he followed to the North. He watched from a hill as Jedar was overrun by flames. The great stone wall had crumbled easily, and the buildings went up in flames like parchment. The great library was the northernmost part of the inner city. But alas, the Cloudriders rode onward, destruction following in their wake. Aidron's men were efficient. They had set themselves up in order to attack the oncoming Ashkah. They were now barely visible in the distance. The flames rampaged through the city. The crashing of falling roofs and the crackle of burning wood mixed with the sounds of the Gray Slime falling and eating into the earth produced a sound that made Bôren feel sick. This had been his home over thirty years ago, and now he watched it being destroyed for the second time—-this time, completely. A tear ran down his face. He turned to the queen who was transfixed by the sight. She caught his eye and nodded. They walked down to where Aidron stood, his cape billowing in the wind.

"My lord and lady, I want you to know that whatever befalls us here, I will die with honor. I will put aside my pride and do my best to defend what was once ours. Though the city may be destroyed, its memory and glory shall reign in our hearts."

"Well said, friend." The queen noticed the way Bôren had said "friend" carried a ring of sincerity that she had grown to admire. The Ashkah charging towards the meager defenders created a low rumbling in the earth like an executioner's drum. It was today that the Kingdom would know its end unless their only hope, Paul, could destroy the Dark Lord and bring peace. Bôren had faith in his friend, but he knew the power of the Dark Lord would be unmatched. Pictures from Bôren's life flashed before his eyes. Stray thoughts wandered here and there, "What have I accomplished?" "What was the point?" and on it went. The queen was calm and collected, sword resting at her side in her right hand. In her left she fingered a locket with a picture of the dead king in it. Aidron busied himself with his men and allowed his mind not to dwell on the fact that his life was over. Aidron was not one to worry, but when he did, he knew it only weakened him, something he had learned at an early age from his father. His father had been a Paladin, a master warrior. He too had been killed at this very city. It was only fitting that he should go the same way. After all it was an honorable death. It wasn't like dying of sickness or age. It had a ring of valor and nobility to it that Aidron had always longed for. He took his bow off his back and pulled an arrow from his left quiver.

"My men," he began calmly. "We have seen many battles and wars together, side by side. Each time we came out the victors, though we lost brothers. This time we will not. It is inevitable. Stand now, stand firm." The men joined him, "*stand strong.*" As one, each of the men released an arrow into the sky. At least 10,000 arrows soared high into the sky and reached their peak. When they began to descend, Bôren saw that they would hit the Ashkah army. There was something strange about these Rangers.

The spirit of one had been broken. The second Vorok, startled and angry, had begun to falter. It was impossible for Paul not to win. His blade hacked away at the armor. The Vorok avoided crossing blades with Paul. He would parry, then draw back. Paul had him where he wanted him. After hundreds of mock fights with Amon, he knew when one had the upper hand. The creature was fighting defensively and was not even trying to attack. Paul spun and slashed at the Vorok. In one single blow he shattered the fiery blade. He reached out and gripped the Vorok's neck and pulled the monster towards him.

"This day...the glory of the Kingdom shall be restored." Paul released his grip and slashed the Vorok across its neck. Its head rolled onto the ground near its Twin. Paul sighed. Suddenly the ground began to shake. The room compressed. Paul closed his eyes and focused. He saw nothing but the darkness. Then he saw a tiny light. He realized that the Dark Lord's presence was around him. It hovered for a few seconds; then in a loud, earth-shattering roar, it vanished. The roof above Paul shot open as if a giant arrow had been driven through it. Paul could see the sky above him. He paused. What about his friends? What about the battle? The ground was too high above him to climb out, so he looked around for a second way to go. He looked at the roof and saw the hole through which he came. He scurried out and retraced his steps. When he passed the corpse of Jedar, he picked up the sword and sheathed it where his old sword had gone. He ran to try and help his friends.

It had been entirely unexpected. Instantly the clouds had parted. The power of the Cloudriders had been broken. The only hints that they had ever existed were the flames and remaining Slime. The city of Jedar had been half destroyed, but thanks to Paul, it had survived. The Ashkah horde had paused in the middle of their charge. Confusion and panic broke out among them. Their source of organization and control had vanished. The Dark Lord had gone. The Flamethrower collapsed in a heap with an eerie shriek. The evil spirit left the possessed corpse. The Ashkah captains barked orders to an army that no longer listened. Then as one, they broke into a run and began to run towards Jedar. The archers knocked arrows as Aidron counted "ONE!" The Ashkah ran a few hundred meters. On "TWO!" they drew their bows. They had incredible strength and bow mastery as they held the taut strings in that position for at least a minute. On "THREE!" the torrent of arrows shot forward, each passing through an Ashkah and the one behind it. In one motion the Rangers had killed 20,000 Ashkah if not more. Suddenly the ground flew up behind the Ashkah. Rock shot into the air at least twenty feet. The sounds of blades swinging and Ashkah dying could be heard. The warriors of Jedar surged forward on Bôren's command. If one had been able to observe the battle from above, they would have seen a massive Ashkah army being slaughtered by a warrior with no sword. They were being trapped by hundreds of soldiers, while thousands upon thousands of arrows rained on their heads. Paul had discovered the power of the Sword. Paul almost laughed as he cut through the Ashkah. Suddenly he had an idea. He pulled back from the Ashkah and ran, using his gift towards Bôren and the army. The Jedarian army saw a blur shoot towards them. In the next moment it was by Bôren's side.

"Tell the army to stop attacking. Just do it." The order was shouted out and the men pulled back, the Ashkah trailing after them. Paul closed his eyes and sensed each Ashkah. Then in one powerful move he sent a mental message to all of them:

"Put down your weapons. See that you are outnumbered. Join us. Help us rebuild Jedar!"

Paul sensed a change throughout the army. All across the battle field every Ashkah put down his shield, sword, spear, and other weapons. They had surrendered.

Paul had recounted every detail of his battle to the queen, Aidron, and Bôren. He had shown them the Sword of Jedar and told them about his encounter as well as the new weapon and armor. They talked for hours until the early hours of the morning drew upon them. Paul told them his ideas.

"I don't believe I was given the sword because of anything special about me. These weapons are available to anyone and everyone. All they have to do is believe. Don't you see? The true 'Sword of Jedar' was not the sword itself. It was this other sword. This sword that has more power than any sword. I am not the first to know this, but now that I think about it, there were signs of it everywhere."

"So what's this new plan of yours, Paul?" asked Bôren.

"I want to teach this ability to everyone. Imagine if every soldier in the Kingdom had the power that I wielded today. Just imagine!" Paul's voice bubbled with enthusiasm. They spent the following days ordering the Ashkah to help rebuild the wall. Messengers were sent to the Cave in the Plains of Goash as well as the Island of Zirikaan to tell them the war was over. They had won.

Progression

† † † † † † †

The next few weeks and months were dedicated entirely to rebuilding Jedar. The first thing the people did was clear out the old houses and all the buildings other than the library, the monuments, and the great Lyceum. Bôren was put in charge of building a tunnel network even greater than Nehgrog. The Ashkah army was invaluable for the tasks such as acquiring stone, cement, rocks, tools, etc. They worked cooperatively with the promise that they would be given a land to themselves. There was no hatred or instinctive malice towards the humans as it had been before. Paul had broken all of that in one single strike. Bôren worked hard with a team of both Nehgrog and Calarath engineers to create a massive tunnel system. Paul declared that once the city was running, a new law would be made that every house legally had to have a tunnel leading out. This way the Jedar situation would not be repeated. The Ashkah proved to be phenomenal tunnelers, and their sheer numbers built the entire tunnel network in a few weeks. The main buildings—the Lyceum, the library, and the castle—were left where they were, and the queen was put in charge of monitoring the repair and restoration of the buildings.

As for Paul, he and Amon sat down and designed the structure for something Paul had been planning. The project that captured his imagination. Amon, though crippled, had become swifter with his mind. He had realized it was his only tool now, and he had studied and read even more than before. His mind was overflowing with information. Aidron was made captain of all construction of houses and civilian buildings: markets, stores, etc. Once Bôren had completed his task, he began the job of taking back the desert. They began by planting hundreds of grass seeds. The desert, no longer fueled by a dark energy, did not resist. The Ashkah were sent in rows to march, stop, plant, march. A second group would water behind them. Bôren then took command of a group of men and volunteer women to help revitalize all the flowers, shrubs, trees, and herbs that once grew in Jedar. They imported seeds from all over the Kingdom, a new sign of unity in diversity. Aidron and his Rangers had created magnificent houses. They had worked on a base model with about a hundred variations. No house was better or greater than any others; this idea was taken from the Nehgrog. Aidron had a wild imagination while also utilizing all practical space. The houses were all made of stone and were two stories high. A clay-shingled roof was angled on top, all gray. Paul, after talking with Amon about his secret plan, took the job of the road restoration. To preserve the old roads but still wanting to create an efficient and smooth roadway, they came to the conclusion that they would simply repair and not replace the roads.

Paul rode on a horse between the different groups coordinating efforts. The queen finished her tasks within the first few months. The library had been completely redone in Orun Oak. Amon had told them of the massive forest on Zirikaan and woodcutters had been dispatched. It had taken weeks to cut and transport enough wood. The older citizens, those who had lived their whole lives in Jedar, had been brought in to give the place an Ancient Jedar feel and style. The books from Nehgrog, Calarath, and Jedar as well as from all the minor towns and villages were combined into one massive library escalating the number into the millions. The Lyceum, the center for all schooling, training, arts, city gatherings and so forth had been designed in a modern Calarath style. The Nehgrog discipline was used in the schooling rooms inside. A Pre-Jedarian War picture that stood thirty feet high had been found on the main wall. The rooms had not yet been painted; Paul had planned for all painting throughout the city to be done in one effort.

The castle was the most magnificent of the buildings. The stone battlements were redone completely and seemed to shine. The massive courtyard had been expanded as well as walkways added about it. The inner rooms were basically the same, but the throne room had been moved to the highest room. The castle was filled with hundreds of quarters for servants or guests and the massive kitchen was adequate for the 100-seat table. The table had been hand crafted out of Orun Oak. It had intricate flower designs engraved lightly on the top covered by a transparent veneer. The legs were thick and heavy with a matching flower pattern. In the throne room the crest from the pendant Paul had found of Jedar himself had been recreated using colored tiles. The ornate golden throne from Jedar had been re-forged and covered with ornate purple cloth. Thousands of jewels lined the armrests and headrest. The windows faced every direction, some towards Jedar, some towards the fields below, and some towards the main courtyard. The massive portcullis would most likely not be used ever but was built to the same standards as the rest of the castle. The moat and bridge had been eliminated. Outside the castle were nine huge fields still within the city walls that could be used for food in a siege. From the fields one could see the walkways of the castle. Traditionally most of the walkways would be indoors, but a Nehgrog had suggested that some of them be open with marble pillars. It was a stunning effect.

In the center of the city the great field and massive lake were almost complete. Aidron's Rangers, being skilled in the subject of wildlife and poisons, had dealt delicately with the Slime-infested waterways and the lake. After months of hard work they had managed to restart the water flowing from the mountains to the north. The once small stream had been widened to a larger one nearly twenty feet in width. Bridges had been built at intervals, but generally the water was open for all to enjoy. The lake in the center, surrounded by the once green field, was expanded. It was now around 800 feet in diameter. The fields, however, had not been shortchanged. Those had expanded along with the lake. Once the water began flowing in Jedar, significant progress on the grass and trees began to be seen.

It was time to begin painting. First, they would bring in the painters. For the next two months the entire city was repainted—outsides of buildings, insides of houses, tables, trim, bridges, etc. There was a mixture of color that contrasted highly with the dull grays and whites.

The city seemed alive. The markets were stocked and within a month people began to move in. They organized the initial citizens in no order but simply assigned houses. The cities to the North around the Shathasor Mountains had sent word that they were happy for Paul but wanted to stay in their homes. Paul sent the Ashkah builders along with instructions for them to build a massive capitol building. Paul had added a long circular stone tower that began at the bottom of the great lake and stretched higher than anything else in the city. This, he said, was a monument to the true king under whom they all served as equals. Paul and his mother went over the curriculum in the schools with Amon and began hiring teachers. They handed over the revised curriculum after months of work. The teachers were due to start schooling in less than two months.

It was now almost fall. It had been a little more than a year and a half since Paul began his startling journey into manhood. The next week Paul would be crowned king. He had also announced that he was planning on revealing his surprise. The preparations were made. The War Council of Nehgrog and the War Council of Calarath combined into the War Council of Jedar. The Governors from the villages and the Governing Councils from Nehgrog and Calarath were combined likewise.

Coronation Day finally came. The massive courtyard was packed with people, all dressed in their best clothes. Paul sat regally on the throne as the oldest member of the Council placed the royal crown upon his head. Paul smiled. If only his father could see him now, how he had changed, what he had done. The ceremony was rather traditional ending with thunderous applause. The next day Paul announced his plan. He stood on a platform, projecting his voice across the large crowd.

"As many of you know, Jedar was once the home of our most valiant and trusted warriors, the Paladin. This order was exterminated slowly after the Jedarian War. Today I stand before you, however, with news. All of those that fought beside me at the Battle of the Wall will know that I have a gift. A great mentor once told me that gifts are meant for others, not for yourself." He glanced briefly at Amon and smiled. "To that end I have spent months considering how others may be served with this gift." The crowd was quiet, and curiosity buzzed silently between them. "I present to you today, Aidron and Bôren, the first two captains of the New Paladin!" Paul stepped aside and the two Captains stepped forward and bowed to each other. Suddenly Bôren shot forward and flipped over Aidron's head. A clash of steel was heard while he was in mid air. The fight between Aidron and Bôren was blindingly fast, both of them a blur. Amon watched as Paul beamed with pride. The audience began to murmur as Aidron ducked and spun into a blur only to meet Bôren's blade at his neck. They both grinned, and the applause erupted. The cheers went on for nearly three full minutes. Amon smiled. Paul finished the ceremony by stating that he had begun training twelve teachers, and these teachers would soon begin teaching more and more soldiers the ways of the Paladin.

The sun set on Jedar. It was a brilliant, picturesque, bright red sunset. Amon, Paul, Bôren, Aidron, and Elizabeth, now the Queen Mother, stood on the balcony. They spoke for a while, and Elizabeth announced that she was going to retire for the evening. Aidron left a few minutes later leaving Paul, Bôren, and Amon alone.

"Well, Paul, you finally did it. You surpassed me in a way I could not have imagined. You have regained the city of Jedar, rebuilt it in a matter of months, and reinstated the noble order of the Paladin."

"It was only by your wisdom and teaching that I managed, Amon. If you had not found me in the mountains over a year and a half ago, I would have been killed by the Bazrukal. Also, if not, I never would have learned the skills that I would need. This Kingdom owes much to you, Uncle. You have played a key role in my life, shaping me into who I am and who I was meant to be. There were times I was frustrated with you, times I was furious at you." They both grinned. "But through it all, I knew that you were doing it for some great purpose. I had never dreamed I would be the one to take back Jedar. Never in a thousand years. I owe it all to you." Paul looked down at his mentor. He thought he saw a glint of a tear on the old man's cheek as he looked out on the blazing sun. Bôren realized the impact of the moment and started to leave.

"Bôren. Wait," said Paul. "I have not forgotten your kindness. This city is in your debt. You held it with your life even against tremendous odds. You believed in me when no one around me would. You supported the union of Calarath and Nehgrog. We would not be standing here today if it were not for your great leadership."

"You have a great destiny, Paul. I would be a fool if I did not see that. I am honored by your words." They shook hands, and Bôren walked briskly down the stairs. The sun was nearly completely set. Below the two friends the lake sat peacefully, interrupted only by the flow of the river. People mulled about buying and selling. It was just like his dream, the one he had when he and Amon had visited Jedar. Amon broke the silence.

"A wise man once said, 'A city is only as great as those people that live in it.' Jedar is a great city because it has people that aspire for greatness. You have taught them that, Paul. You have shown that every one of them has a great destiny and each of them has an important role to play. You have shown them that nobility, truth, and justice can prevail over evil against astounding odds. You have shown them what it means to be a servant and what it means to lay down your life in self-sacrifice. You have discovered the power of Ara'tel and let him use you in his great plan. You have not gloated about your feats or your gifts but instead found a way to make others equals with you. You have established and put into place what Jedar is truly about." Amon ended his speech, still focusing on the red sun and orange sky. Paul looked back at his life. It was strange. When he had sought to lose his life, he had found new life. When he had sought to give his life for others, he had become praised as a hero. When he had handed over himself completely to the glory of Ara'tel, he found this had been the most effective. His thoughts drifted to the Dark Lord.

"What of the Dark Lord, Amon? Where has he gone?"

"My guess is that he has fled across the sea to an unknown place."

"Will he return?"

"That I cannot say for certain. What is for certain, Paul, is that there will always be enemies of the Kingdom, and there will always be enemies of justice. The power is in the courage to face them and fight them as you did. You have saved countless lives by your self-sacrifice, and for that, Jedar and the entire Kingdom owe you."

Paul turned around and looked at Amon. Suddenly the shocking reality dawned on him. Neither of them had said a word in the last hour of conversation. Amon smiled knowingly. Paul realized he was still the mentor, still investing in him, still training him. The truth of it all suddenly seemed so clear. There is no end to your gift if you will use it for the service of others.